# Doves Cry Two

# Doves Cry Too

K. McCoy

Published by be a muse productions, LLC, 2024.

# Table of Contents

# DOVES CRY TOO

Written by K. McCoy

---

1.  http://www.authorkmccoy.com

## Acknowledgements

MY SINCEREST THANKS to fellow authors (and good friends) Mo Flames, E.A. Noble, and A.K. Hughey, for not only supporting, but keeping me grounded and focused these last three years. Your encouragement along this author journey has meant the world to me, and without it, I truly would be lost. Thank you.

# Dedication

I wish to dedicate **Doves Cry Too** to all of those still on their journey toward finding happiness and love. Please know that you are entitled to both and don't let anyone ever tell you otherwise as you discover them for yourself - on your own terms.

# Playlist

FOR THE READER THAT appreciates a more immersive experience, here is a sweetly curated playlist for *Doves Cry Too*. While writing this story, I came across songs that really "locked in" on a moment, or the character that was in my head while penning a scene. With this happening time and time again, I decided to combine all of my favorite repeat tracks into one fly ass playlist to vibe to while reading.

Enjoy!

- "Gone" by Alex Isley & Jack Dine

- "Same Space?" Tiana Major9

- "Exclusively" by Tiana Major9 (featuring Jvck James)

- "ILWY" by Olivia Escuyos

- "Should've Been You" by Kenyon Dixon

- "Love Again" by Alex Isley

- "No Tomorrow" by Brandy

- "Unconditional Oceans" by Brandy

- "How Does It Make You Feel" by Victoria Monet

- "Only One" by Jon B.

- "All That I Am" by Joe

- "Exclusively" (Acoustic Sessions) by Tiana Major9

# Chapter One

## Finding Peace

### Jerome

After finishing up his latest tour, Jerome was glad to wind down for the next six months. Sending a head nod to the bodyguard on duty as he passed through the metal detectors inside *Bottom's Up*, Jerome made his way to the VIP section in the back of the gentlemen's club. His crew wasted no time grabbing girls from the floor to entertain them while they waited for the bottle service to get to their table.

"Your usual, JPK?" a petite hostess asked sweetly, batting her eyes in his direction. Jerome nodded as he settled into the soft leather seat. "Be right back." She purred, swaying in time to the beat of the music as she made her way toward the main bar.

Each of the guys now had two girls sitting on their laps. The girls' delicate hands could be seen even under the dim light, grazing across each other's skin, stopping ever so slightly at their hips and breasts. One girl in particular, with a tawny complexion and shiny red lips, brought her arms closer together when she was touched by her lap mate, a bronzed beauty whose jet black hair spilled down to her backside. This made the tawny girl's already large chest burst through the thin straps of her floss, giving the entourage even more of a show.

Jerome continued to watch as the dancers in their VIP section giggled while rolling their hips and sinking further into the front of the guys' midsections. Any other time he would have looked away, but tonight he found himself almost welcoming the distraction. It was better than the thoughts he had about the latest tracks he received from the new producers that the record label paired him with for his next album. Considering that Jerome hadn't released any new music in over a year, he was in no position to put up a fight.

*The beats are good, but I ain't feeling them.*

The VIP hostess had returned with his drink, a double whiskey with a cola, cold and still in the can. He handed her a fifty-dollar bill, and the woman winked as she sat his drink down. His soda sat unopened as Jerome picked up the glass of whiskey and took two quick sips.

He looked out into the crowd and watched the men surround the closest stage, tossing bills onto the floor in front of the nearly naked women dancing in front of them. Jerome released a heavy sigh as he sank deeper into his seat before shutting his eyes.

*None of this is for me. Lord, what am I supposed to do?*

**Tasha**

Hearing the news about the woman who birthed her being dead was one thing, but as Tasha stared down at the simple tombstone, her heart was a drift.

She stared at the engraving, which was basic to say the least in comparison to the more elaborate and grand tombstones that surrounded it. For a second, Tasha briefly wondered why her little sister chose to add the simple sentence following Kitty's name at all.

*Tabitha 'Kitty' Daye*
*Beloved daughter and mother*.

It'd been four years since she'd been home, and longer than that since she had a kind word to say about her mother. Maybe that was why Tasha's mind still needed a tangible confirmation of Kitty being six feet underground. It was something she had wanted to see for well over a decade, and only having Trisha's word and her eyes to serve as confirmation of Kitty's departure was not enough. Taking out her film camera, Tasha kneeled in front of the tombstone until she was at the level of contrast she wanted. Holding her breath, her hands remained steady, even as her eyes wavered before snapping the picture.

*I hope her soul is at peace. That's more than I thought I would ever hope for her.*

To calm her rapidly beating heart, Tasha decided to take a walk around the cemetery. With it being the middle of the day, only a handful of people could be seen sitting or making their loved ones' tombstones prettier with flowers and balloons around the quiet grounds. Several large clouds shielded her from the bright sun, which encouraged her to stay longer. Soon she was back in front of the gravesite entrance, just as a steady gust of wind swirled around and added to the sting around her eyes. She allowed herself one last glance behind her to where Kitty's final resting place was and clenched her jaw.

Her feet stomped along the patches of grass and dirt road gravel as she went to her motorcycle. Since she only came to town to see the tombstone in person, Tasha decided not to get a standard rental. Now that she had done what she had come to do, she longed to hop on the bike and sail out of town as fast as she could. Turning the key into the ignition, Tasha's thoughts went from seeing Kitty's final resting place to her therapists' advice on how to begin forgiving her mother for what her illness cost them.

Having to say goodbye to someone you never really got to know was a strange thing. But in order to find peace for the little girl in her heart to heal, Tasha was willing to try.

*I need more time.*

Hearing a familiar voice, one Tasha didn't think she'd get to hear again, she turned around. A little boy could be seen running her way, and Tasha's heart leaped into her throat. "Devin?"

He nodded excitedly as she squatted down to look at him closer. He was the spitting image of Trisha. Devin asked with wide eyes. "Titi, why you wasn't at the goodbye thing for granny?"

Before she could answer, Tasha noticed Trisha, with a very swollen belly, and her youngest nephew, Darnell, wobbling toward them.

"I told you to wait, De-" Her sister stopped and stared as Tasha stood back up. "It really is you." Trisha said while rubbing her lower belly.

"Darnell, this Titi. 'member?"

Darnell tilted his head as he looked up at Tasha before walking behind his mama.

*He doesn't recognize me. I've been gone that long?*

"TiTi, can you come to my school next next Friday?"

Completely caught by surprise, Tasha managed to ask, "W-why do you want me at your school D?"

The boy beamed, hearing her call him by his nickname.

"It's professions week! All the other kids have their mama's and daddy's coming to talk about their jobs, but mama ain't working so she can't come."

Tasha stared at her sister's stomach and offered a weak smile.

"Well, she needs to rest, D." Tasha walked over to Devin and patted the top of his head.

"You ain't gotta come, Tash." Trisha finally said, as someone called out to them.

Tasha watched as a guy, about six feet tall and with bleached blonde hair in a set of cornrows, marched over to join them.

"Didn't we tell ya to wait for us?! Why that boy just up and leave like that?" he barked.

Tasha watched as Trisha looked between the man and Devin.

"Baby, he ain't mean to. Just - he saw his auntie and wanted to say hi, is all." Trisha explained.

The guy frowned down at Tasha and she didn't like him on site.

As he slowly glanced at her from top to bottom, he drawled out, "Well, shiiit, my bad. I thought Tina was your only sister." Tasha willed her stank face away as Devin stood closer to her. "You ain't gonna speak, sista-in-law?"

Tasha's eyes narrowed. "I'm not a dog."

Turning back to Trisha, she asked, "What is he talking about? Sister-in-law?"

Trisha giggled as she waved her left hand in Tasha's face. "I'm finally married! Lloyd, this my sister Tasha, Tasha, this my husband, Lloyd Wrice."

At hearing that news, Tasha took a step back as she looked between Trisha and the man now looming over her.

"Congrats." was all Tasha could manage to say before she kneeled down to talk with Devin again. "What school you go to now, D?"

"Woods Edge Elementary," he told her.

Tasha smiled as she cupped his cheek. "Okay, I'll call the school and sign up for your event, okay?"

He flashed her a big grin and nodded. "Okay Titi!"

Not sure if Devin was still a hugger like when he was younger, Tasha made a fist with her right hand and held it out in front of him. When the little boy did the same with his hand, the two leaned in and tapped their knuckles together. Tasha looked up at her sister and Lloyd. He was standing close to Trisha, whipping his head back and forth between them. It had been years since Tasha had to endure anyone doing a blatant double take when it came to her or one of her more 'presentable' sisters. With their tan brown complexions, light brown eyes, and slim thick figures being the exact opposite of hers, many folks didn't believe they were really related until they learned her last name.

"Why wasn't you at the funeral?" Lloyd questioned.

Tasha's stank face was now on full display as she ignored him and turned to face Trisha.

"Tina thought you wouldn't come, but I still thought you should know, you know?" Trisha said.

Tasha offered her little sister a smile. "Thank you. I just left her gravesite."

She saw her sister's eyes get a little glassy and decided it was time to go.

"Well, I have to go check into my hotel, so... take care, Trish." Tasha said gently.

Her sister held her stare for a beat before she wobbled over and wrapped Tasha in a hug.

Trish sniffled and laughed. "These babies got me all emotional these days."

Tasha blinked several times. "Babies?"

"Yeah girl, twins this time."

Tasha grinned. "I'm happy for you."

She truly was happy for her baby sister. All Trisha wanted was a big family to love and care for, Tasha knew that. She just hoped her gut was wrong about her new husband.

"TERROR! GET DOWN!"

Tasha tried not to laugh at the sight of Alexa stepping over the doggie gate to open the door to let her in. She took off her helmet and shook her twists loose, enjoying the feel of them swaying softly near her backside as the tiny French bulldog's barks echoed from inside the house.

While Tasha was away, Rachel and Alexa bought a new home, just on the outskirts of town. The two-story house was one of the few on the new street, and from the sense of quiet that Tasha felt after riding to their place, she understood why the lovebirds chose to live so far away.

Seeing Alexa open the door, Tasha grinned as she strolled closer to her friend and hugged her. "It is so good to see you!"

"You too! Rachel should be home soon, and I ordered us some takeout."

Nodding as Alexa let her go, Tasha looked around at the open layout of the house. She noticed a few of the photos displayed in the foyer area. Seeing Alexa and Rachel in their college days, spending holidays with their families, and dressed to the nines for an event. Tasha couldn't have been happier to see her two friends' journey in life together. Until she spotted a photo in the far back of the stand. It was their last New Year's celebration together, and the image tugged at her heart, causing Tasha to look away.

"How long have you two been living in the boonies?" she asked, as the tiny dog made its way to her feet.

"You got jokes." Alexa said before answering Tasha, "Two years. As soon as I got my promotion, we found this place."

Taking off her shoes, Tasha made her way to the living room to sit on the large suede couch. She looked out at the patio area and noticed the bright tea lights that were strung up outside, surrounding a small sitting area and what looked like a fire pit.

"I'm happy for y'all." Tasha told Alexa sincerely.

She hadn't seen them since their surprise visit three years ago, when she was shooting for a new concierge company in Portugal. Although she loved her work, Tasha couldn't help but feel separated from everyone that she knew and loved before going abroad to pursue her dreams of seeing the world as a photographer. Thinking back to her run in with Trisha and the kids, Tasha felt a hollowness begin to grow within her chest. Until the dog jumped onto her lap, wagging their tail in Tasha's face.

"Terror, no!" Alexa shouted as Tasha laughed.

"It's alright." She said, reaching out to scratch behind the puppy's ears.

Alexa joined her on the couch and looked on as Tasha continued doting on the little dog before clearing her throat.

"We heard about your mama. You okay?" Alexa asked softly.

Tasha nodded. "I went to her burial site before coming here."

The two sat in silence until they heard the sound of keys jingling at the door.

"That's my baby." Seeing Alexa's eyes light up as she jumped off the couch to greet Rachel made Tasha smile.

MUFFLED VOICES MINGLED with the sweet sounds of smooches reached Tasha while she stood and took her time walking back toward the foyer area. She didn't get halfway around the large couch before Rachel sprinted toward her, throwing her whole petite self into Tasha's arms.

"Hey Rachel!" Tasha squealed as she lifted the shorter woman into her embrace.

"Aye, I'mma need you to unhand my woman, Tash." Alexa called out.

Teasingly, Tasha bumped her hip into Alexa's before releasing Rachel, making sure to bring her in for another quick hug.

"It's good to see you Tash!"

While swaying back and forth in Rachel's arms, Tasha fought back more tears. *I didn't know I needed this until now. Thank you Lord.*

As Tasha started to let her go, she reached out for Rachel's left hand and quickly gasped, "Well, okay now! Y'all finally going to stop living in sin, uh?"

Alexa and Rachel looked at one another again as they realized Tasha had noticed the vintage platinum ring on Rachel's left hand.

"It's about time." Tasha said, as she smiled at Rachel.

The couple shared a quick glance with one another, and Tasha tried to shake the feeling that they weren't telling her something. *It's not like I'm always forthcoming right away with them. Just enjoy this time with your girls, Tash.*

Taking her hand away, Rachel reached out for Alexa's and made their way to sit on the wide, dark brown couch. When the two sat down, Tasha joined them.

"Umm...yeah. I popped the question a week ago." Alexa tried to explain. "Before we heard about your mama."

Seeing Alexa struggle to say more, Tasha looked on as Rachel rubbed the top of Alexa's hand with her own. "Yeah, um, we wanted to wait until you arrived to tell you in person. But then Trisha reached out and told us the news."

Tasha slightly brought her head back, taking in everything that they were telling her. *Is that what's bothering them? Right now? Why?*

"Is that why y'all invited me over today? To tell me in person?'"

Not wanting to be the reason they feel awkward sharing their good news, Tasha made sure to add extra merriment to her voice as the corners of her lips turned upward again, "Awww! Y'all are too cute!" The confusion at her behavior was written all over their faces, so she tried again, "What? Did y'all have something else on your mind?"

Rachel started to speak, but Alexa cut her off. "Tash, it's us. You ain't gotta front like everything is okay."

Frowning, Tasha asked, "What you mean, Alexa? Why would I put on a front with y'all?"

After a few seconds passed, Alexa scooted closer to Tasha, as Rachel let go of Alexa's hand and took Tasha's in its place before speaking, "You haven't been home in four years, Tash. And to come back after hearing that your mother passed away? No matter how strained y'all's relationship was, that would be hard for anyone to process."

"We worried about you sis, that's all." Alexa added gently.

Thinking back to when she first read Kitty's tombstone and how she couldn't put into words what she was feeling, Tasha's eyes welled up with tears, which she quickly blinked away. "I love y'all for worrying about me, but I am okay. Really."

Tasha then took their enclosed hands into her own before releasing a shaky sigh.

"My relationship with Kitty has been strained since I was a kid. By the time I finally left, to say that we were well past estranged would have been kind."

Alexa leaned in closer to Tasha, resting her head on Tasha's shoulder.

"And I can work through my feelings about her AND still be happy for y'all! So, what else you two want to talk about tonight? How y'all got the smallest dog ever and had the nerve to name it 'Terror'?" Tasha joked.

Rachel rolled her eyes. "His name is Tyrone Banks-Shaw. Alexa only started calling him 'Terror' after he chewed on a pair of her sneakers."

Seeing Alexa pout, Tasha burst into giggles, and Rachel joined her. Though seeing Alexa's pout deepened before she sucked in her teeth and glanced the other way made Tasha throw her head back in laughter.

"Now see, here I was all ready to ask you to be our maid of honor for the wedding in five months, but I don't think I want to anymore."

Tasha stopped laughing as what Alexa said registered in her head. "Wait, what?" She whipped her head between her two friends. "Y'all want me to what?"

Rachel beamed at Alexa as she confirmed. "Yes, we would like you to be our maid of honor for the wedding."

Tasha launched herself at the two of them, wrapping her arm on either side of her and Alexa before pulling back to look at them both. "Oh my God! Seriously? I would be honored!"

# Chapter Two

## New Intel

### Tasha

After saying goodbye to Alexa and Rachel for the night, Tasha called up her freelance partner in Spain, Ximena. When her internship in Argentina ended the first year she left the States, Tasha took a six week second photographer assignment in Spain and fell fast in love with the country. It soon became her home away from home. She met Ximena in the Fall of the same year at an expat networking event. There she learned that Ximena was also an up-and-coming photographer, who used her English fluency skills to assist English-speaking foreigners in her home country. Though for the last three years, Ximena now worked almost exclusively with Tasha.

"I'm glad to hear from you, Tasha. A source told me that Pablo Coslado's Gala is set for fourteen weeks from now."

That got her attention.

While in Murica, Spain for a lifestyle magazine assignment, Tasha had a brief exchange with the reserved, yet globally known photographer on a flight. Though they said no more than a few pleasantries to one another as they went to their business class seats that day, something about him captivated her. When she returned from her trip, Tasha reached out to Ximena to schedule a meeting with him. They learned that he preferred to work alone and even his team had trouble getting him to commit to a schedule. Tasha couldn't shake the need to at least try, so she and Ximena put in the work to find out all they could about the private photographer.

With more failed attempts to secure a meeting with Pablo than Tasha cared to count, they were able to establish a strong business relationship with his people. That kept them up to date on his schedule, which included a yearly gala that the photographer held in a different location. This was the first time in over a decade that the event would be held in his home country, and everyone in the industry wanted a ticket.

Now that they had a timeline, Tasha needed to see about getting an invitation to the highly anticipated gala. "Do you think anyone can secure us tickets?"

"You want *me* to go with you to this event? Why?" Ximena questioned.

Hearing her friend's question, Tasha chuckled, "Why not?" When Ximena remained quiet on the line, Tasha used the time to remind Ximena of just how instrumental she had been in her getting to someday work alongside Pablo Costado. "You have put in as much work as I have to get in the same room as this man - no way I'm leaving you out of the party."

Tasha could hear the excitement in Ximena's voice, "Oh Tasha! That would be incredible! Thank you. "

"Don't thank me yet. I'll get to work on his socials and see if I can find someone who can help us." Tasha told her. "Can you call his team and see if they may be willing to provide us with two tickets, please?"

"Of course Tash!"

Hearing the joyfulness in Ximena's voice when she used her nickname made Tasha fight the corners of her lips from turning upward. Before ending the call, Ximena asked, "So, when will you be returning? Do you have work elsewhere?"

Tasha took out the key to her bike as she looked back at Alexa and Rachel's house. "I just lined up two personal projects. First one is in two weeks, and the next one is a wedding that'll be taking place in four months, which would be right before the gala."

"A wedding? That's quite the surprise. I assume that you still had a preference for not shooting union ceremonies." Ximena stated.

"That's still true, but this happy union is between my two closest friends. And they've asked me to be the Maid of Honor." Tasha explained brightly.

"I see. Congratulations are in order for your friends," Ximena quickly reminded her. "Just please keep me posted, and be sure to rest while away, love!"

Tasha laughed, "You too! I'll be in touch."

FINALLY MAKING IT TO Creek's Cove Hotel, Tasha settled into her suite and logged onto her computer.

She managed to make it on time for her last appointment of the night, and it was one that she definitely needed after today.

"Hello Tasha."

Looking at the woman who smiled softly back at her on the screen, Tasha offered a small smile of her own. "Good morning, Doctor Richardson."

The woman laughed, "Doctor? You haven't addressed me that way since our first session together a year ago. Is everything alright?"

Tasha stared at the screen as she let the weight of her feelings come forward. "I think so. Just hoping you can help me make sense of why I feel the way I do."

"Well, let's start at the beginning. How are you feeling?"

This was always the hardest part for Tasha when it came to her therapy sessions. She'd learned to keep her feelings to herself. Either to avoid Kitty's hands when she was coming down from a high, or from adults at school who made her feel uneasy whenever they asked about how things were for her at home. It was just safer for her to not tell anyone what was going on in her mind. But now that she was grown, and had found a few people in her life that she felt okay with sharing some things about herself with, Tasha wanted to really explore her thoughts in a safe space. That's when she started looking for a therapist online, and a month later, she found one.

She slouched in her chair and stared at the corner of her screen before answering. "I feel a lot of things. But really, I feel lost. Is that even possible?"

Her therapist scribbled down notes on a notepad and then met her stare. "Yeah, it is. Remember what we talked about Tasha, all feelings are valid, even those that you think aren't possible."

"Right, yeah." Tasha tried to lift the corners of her lips up, but the stinging sensation from earlier returned with a vengeance. She hated crying, especially when talking about something like her feelings. Dabbing her eyes with the helm of her shirt, Tasha went on, "So, my sister Trisha was telling the truth. Kitty died."

"I'm sorry for your loss."

"That's just it. I don't feel a loss. At least not for her." Tasha explained, "I feel bad for my nephews, they really loved their granny. And I'm glad that Trisha wasn't lying just to get money from me."

"You still worry that your sister only reaches out when in financial trouble?" Dr. Richardson asked gently.

"Well, after what happened with Tina, can you blame me?" Tasha snapped.

A few seconds passed before Tasha cleared her throat and spoke again. "Sorry. I just can't help but doubt that either of them want to talk to me about anything else. And Tina still hasn't apologized for what she and Kitty did."

"Do you want an apology from her? Your older sister?"

Picking at the helm of her shirt, Tasha thought the question over. "It would be nice, but so much time has passed... And I'm never gonna get one from Kitty, with her up and gone now."

"You haven't answered the question, Tasha. Is an apology from your sister something you want?"

"I don't know what I want. Which is part of the problem, I guess."

"What do you mean?"

Tasha rolled her neck and took a big inhale. "Well, after seeing Kitty's tombstone, I met Trisha's husband. Then she tells me that she's having twins–how could she tell me about Kitty, but not that she got married? And speaking of getting married, my two closest friends told me tonight that they're finally jumping the broom!"

"You learned all this in one day? That is definitely a lot to take in."

"Right?! Like, yeah, I left home, but seriously! No one thought to call and tell me anything?" The more Tasha thought about the news she got today, the hotter her face felt. "When someone needs my help or my money, they know how the phone works, but when there's good news, I'm the last on their need to know list?"

"It can feel that way, to you."

Sitting up straight, Tasha sent a side eye glance to her therapist. "What's that supposed to mean?"

"Have you ever reached out to your loved ones when things are going well in your life? Just to say hi, or ask about their day?"

Tasha stared at the screen as her left foot bounced against her right leg. She honestly couldn't remember the last time she'd reached out to just randomly call anyone, much less her little sister. "I... I don't - no. I haven't done that." She admitted. "I just figured Trisha was busy with the boys."

She tried not to let her therapist's rapidly moving hand bother her as the woman jotted down more notes.

"It can be difficult at first, but I want you to try to be the one to initiate contact." Dr. Richardson instructed. "Start small, with a simple call to say hello. And see what happens."

"Okay, I'll try." Tasha mumbled.

"So, you received news that your mother passed, your sister is expecting twins with a new husband, and your best friends are finally getting married. Anything else?"

"No, that's about it."

"You said you felt a lot of things, mainly lost."

When Tasha looked down at the keyboards, her therapist continued, "There is another feeling associated with how you're feeling now. And it is common to feel when one is away from their family and friends for long periods of time. You see that their lives are going on, and you are happy for them. But a part of you feels left behind."

"Well, I wouldn't say I feel left behind. Maybe left out of things." Tasha tried again. "I am happy for them, really. I just can't help feeling a little, um, out of the loop."

"What you are feeling, Tasha, is disconnected from those you love. And that's okay." Dr. Richardson quickly wrote down something else on a notepad before sending another small smile to her through the screen. "So to help you reconnect, I have a small exercise that I want you to try sometime this week before our next session."

Remembering the promise she made to herself to really commit and give this therapy journey all she had, Tasha squared her shoulders back. "Okay, doctor. What is it you want me to do?"

"I want you to disconnect. Spend some time away from your work, your planner, and especially your phone." Dr. Richardson explained, "You've just received a lot of heavy news, and when this normally happens, you retreat from those you are interacting with.

So, before your mind begins to go into sensory overload, I want you to spend some time alone with only your thoughts."

Tasha narrowed her eyes at the computer screen as she fought the urge to roll her eyes. "Are you really telling me to shut down? Like I'm a laptop or something?" She chuckled as Dr. Richardson continued, "Well, yes. This is a coping mechanism you've developed as a child. When you feel threatened, or in this case, overwhelmed, you tend to distance yourself from others, for fear of losing your cool or being miss understood in a conversation."

*Well, she ain't wrong. Still hard to hear though.*

"Take that time to be honest about how you feel and journal those thoughts." Dr. Richardson finished.

Taking a deep breath in, Tasha let her eyelids close as she parted her lips and slowly released the air from her lungs.

"I'm glad to see you're still using the breathing techniques from our earlier sessions."

Tasha stared at the screen and seeing her therapist smiling back at her, Tasha sighed, "They've been helpful."

"And so will disconnecting. Just give it some time, Tasha."

"Well, you haven't let me down yet. So I'll give it a try."

THE NEXT DAY, TASHA went strolling through the new town plaza next to the hotel. She was hungry and the welcoming smell of fried chicken had her walking toward a small mom and pop restaurant out front. Though before she stepped inside, Tasha saw another building next to it that caught her eye. Curious, she walked closer and stared at the rich, red wooden panels that had several large windows attached to them. Rows of newspapers were used to cover them from the inside, but a few pages were starting to fall down, exposing what looked like empty bookcases and a winding staircase that matched the panels outside. Stepping up to the windows, Tasha brought a hand to her forehead to get a better look.

Nothing was on the grayish concrete walls, but she noticed several large wooden ladders still leaning against the walls in the far back, and half of a large banner that had the word 'Corner' printed on it laying on the floor. Just as Tasha began to leave, a man made his presence known, "You looking to buy this building, ma'am?"

Tasha turned around toward the voice. He was dressed in a pair of jeans and a light blue collar polo that complimented his deep sandy complexion. Seeing no reason to be rude just yet, Tasha answered him. "Umm, no. It just caught my eye."

The young man stared at Tasha for a minute before grinning. He took a few steps toward her and Tasha quickly took two steps back. Watching his eyes for any sign of his next move, Tasha blinked as the man in front of her laughed.

"You really don't remember me, Ms. Tasha?"

Confused, she began studying the young man in front of her, relaying his last words in her head. *Wait, he called me Ms. Tasha. Only students I tutored called me that.* "Did I tutor you?"

A grin slowly spread across his face before shouting, "It's me, James! Jay Jay - from Christ Corner."

Recognizing the name, Tasha stuttered out. "W-wait, seriously? Little Jay Jay?"

She heard him laugh again, and now a little embarrassed, Tasha joined him. "I see you finally got that growth spurt you prayed for." She teased.

Watching him bow his head a little and rub the back of his neck, Tasha waited for him to speak.

"Yeah, I did. How you doing Ms. Tasha?"

She waved her hand at the young man. "You grown now, call me Tasha."

Jay Jay flashed her another grin and Tasha couldn't help but notice the crescent moon shape his eyes made when his cheeks lifted, showing her all his teeth.

"I'm doing alright." Tasha told him.

Remembering the property behind her, Tasha asked, "So, you the owner of this building?"

Jay Jay shook his head. "Nah, I just work for the real estate company that does."

"How long has it been vacant?"

"Oh, about two years now. I just come out from time to time to make sure the kids haven't tagged it."

While Tasha was observing the abandoned building, Jay Jay reached into his pocket and pulled out a business card. Handing it to Tasha, he spoke. "Well, it seems like you might be thinking of buying, so here is my card."

"Thank you. It was good to see you."

"Good to see you too, Tasha."

AS TASHA WAITED IN line to pay for her pre-made combo meal from The Pub Grocers deli, she noticed an older woman with their salt and pepper hair in an updo standing a few people in front. *Is that who I think it is?*

Not wanting to embarrass herself or disturbed the woman, Tasha quietly took two small steps to the side as she stole a longer glance at the front of the checkout line. The woman wore a plain pair of slightly loose fitting jeans and an old white t-shirt that had the Christ Corner logo in its center along with the words 'First Lady' written in a fancy script on the left sleeve, which confirmed who she thought the woman was. Tasha's lips instantly turned upward as she stepped out of the line and walked to Jerome's mama. "Mrs. Evelyn?" she called out gently.

When Evelyn turned and faced her, Tasha's heart soared at seeing her return with a smile. "Tasha? Is that you, baby?"

Closing the distance between them, she nodded.

"It's so good to see you!" Evelyn exclaimed, reaching out her arms to embrace Tasha. The two held one another for a minute before Evelyn pulled back to get another look at her.

"You look good, baby girl!"

Tasha's cheeks grew warm from the compliment, and she quickly covered her hand with her mouth.

"You look good too, Mrs. Evelyn."

"Oh, chile hush!"

They shared a laugh before silence fell over them. When Evelyn's grip on her hand tightened, Tasha met her stare. "I heard about your mama, baby girl."

She should've known that Evelyn would have known about Kitty's passing, but it didn't stop Tasha from focusing on the ringing chime sounds of the registers around them as she reminded herself to breathe. Glancing down at the floor, Tasha forced herself to look up and wished she was back inside her hotel room. "Thank you. I just hope she's at peace now."

Evelyn then stepped to the side, gently guiding Tasha along with her. "I know you might be busy, but you want to have lunch together sometime?"

"I'm never too busy to have lunch with you." Tasha said. "How about we both get a meal to go now?"

Evelyn reached out to hug Tasha again. "I'd like that."

The weather was gorgeous, clear skies and a steady breeze welcomed Tasha as she brought her motorcycle to a crawl and stopped in a parking space next to Evelyn's four-door car. Hopping off the bike, she took off her helmet and made her way toward Evelyn, who held their lunches in a plastic bag.

"There's a few empty benches under the pavillon. You want to eat there, baby girl?" Evelyn asked.

"Yes ma'am. Eating there is fine with me."

As she sat everything out, Tasha went to the nearby vending machine to get them something to drink. Coming back to two bottled sweet teas, Tasha handed one to Evelyn, and they sat down together as Evelyn blessed their food.

"So, Tasha, how are your sisters doing?"

Tasha put down her fork and answered, "They doing alright. My younger sister is married now, with twins on the way."

Evelyn's eyes widened. "Twins?!"

"Yes ma'am, twins?" Tasha confirmed, letting out a small chuckle.

Evelyn quickly asked, "You thinking of doing the same someday? Settling down and having some babies?"

She should've known that question was going to come up. And it took considerable effort, but Tasha managed to keep her voice light as she answered, "I think my sister is having enough kids for the both of us. Besides, my work keeps me busy."

"That it do, baby girl." Looking over at Evelyn, who seemed to be miles away. Evelyn's face turned downward and Tasha called out gently, "Is everything okay, Mrs. Evelyn?"

Soon she saw unshed tears fill Evelyn's eyes and Tasha quickly spoke, "I'm sorry, I didn't mean to make you cry."

"I'm fine baby, it's just good to see you, is all."

Tasha took a napkin out of the plastic wrapping from her meal and handed it to Evelyn, who chuckled, "I'm sorry to get like this in front of you."

"It's okay."

More tears fell from Evelyn's eyes as the two stared at one another. Seeing the woman who had always been kind to her, who treated her better than Kitty did while alive, tearing up started to tear at Tasha's inside. So much so that she couldn't ignore the gnawing ache in her chest.

"Please, tell me what it is, Mrs. Evelyn." Tasha gently asked.

Evelyn glanced up at her and wiped the corners of her eyes. Sniffling, she finally answered. "I'm just worried about Jerome. I-I ain't seen or heard from him in weeks! And I don't know what he's been doing these days, or the people he's with. It's just too much sometimes... All I can do is pray he is okay."

Clearing her throat, Tasha pushed aside the many questions she had, questions Evelyn clearly didn't have, as she placed what was hopefully a comforting hand on top of Evelyn's. "I'm sorry Mrs. Evelyn." The older woman grabbed ahold of Tasha's hands and she blinked back her own tears. The need to make Evelyn feel better, to give her even a small amount of peace in that moment is what led her to say, "I promise you, before I leave, I'll find out what Jerome has been up to for you, okay?

The hopefulness that shone back to her from Evelyn's tear stained face was all Tasha needed to fight the small voice in her mind that told her to not make promises she couldn't keep.

*I can do this, find him and let Mrs. Evelyn know he's alright. I can do this - for her.*

"Thank you, baby girl."

AFTER HAVING LUNCH with Evelyn yesterday, Trisha and the kids were on her mind. Along with thoughts of her last therapy session urging her on, she picked up the phone and scrolled down until she spotted her little sister's name.

*Why am I so nervous to call Trish? Has it really been that long since we talked?*

After two rings, Tasha sighed in relief to the sound of Trisha's voice.

"Hey Trish! It's Tasha." she said, letting out a nervous chuckle.

"Oh, hey! What's up?"

Hearing Trisha's casual reply helped calm her nerves a little as Tasha paced back and forth inside her hotel room. "I forgot to ask the other day if you had a baby registry?"

"I do, but don't worry about that." Trisha said

Tasha thought that's what she'd say, so she was already prepared with a response. "Now how can I call myself a good auntie if I don't help out a little from time to time?"

The line was silent for a beat until Trisha spoke again. "Oh, okay. I'm sure by now most of my old co-workers ordered most of the things already. The registry is under 'Wrice for Two' at Loveable Ones Baby Shop."

Tasha wrote the information down. "Okay. I'll see what I can get from the list soon."

Hearing the boys in the background, Tasha remembered the second reason she called, "Oh! I was also wondering if you and the boys had plans today? I would love to see y'all again."

Tasha heard a muffled voice in the background, followed by laughter, before Trisha answered. "We ain't got no plans today, since the kids don't have school. Wanna meet up at Sunshine Park?"

A smile started to spread across Tasha's lips as she remembered spending time with Trisha at the same park, back in the day. "Yeah, I can meet y'all there in an hour."

Quickly getting dressed in a pair of acid washed jeans and a purple tank top, Tasha grabbed her messenger bag and helmet as she walked out of her suite.

# Chapter Three

## Take Care

### Alexa

Wayward Waffle's was packed, but Alexa spotted Tasha quickly as they walked inside. Waving her over, Tasha grinned at her and Rachel before joining them at the table, putting her helmet on the empty seat.

"So, why did you offer to treat us to breakfast today?" Alexa asked.

"I was in the area yesterday, visiting Trisha and the kids. So I thought I'd see y'all too." Tasha said cheerfully before adding, "Plus, as your maid of honor, I gotta make sure I know the itinerary so I can help y'all jump the broom in style!".

Rachel grinned. "That's what I'm talking about!"

Alexa watched as Rachel pulled out her planner and Tasha took out her phone. "So here are the dates for the outfit fittings and cake tasting with SweeThangs..."

Seeing the two of them syncing their schedules brought a smile to Alexa's face. And as much as she wanted to believe that Tasha inviting them out for breakfast was only about their upcoming nuptials, Alexa couldn't shake the feeling that there was more to it.

*Time will tell soon enough.*

Minutes later, a server came by to take their orders and Tasha waited for them to leave before asking Rachel, "How's work been? You like officially running things?"

Alexa looked over at Rachel as she and Tasha started talking about her new position at work. "Yeah! I finally feel like my job is worthwhile again. And being able to pay off my student loans faster with that raise don't hurt none either."

They were all smiles when their server returned with their drinks.

*Maybe this really was just a surprise social visit.*

Twenty minutes flew by, as the trio chatted about all the things that had changed since Tasha was last home. Everything was going pretty good, until her fiance gasped, "That's right! You missed the last Jamboree! It was pretty good, even though Jerome -"

Rachel cut her eyes over to Alexis and picked up her drink, taking two deep swigs.

*Dang. She would drop his name just when the vibe was so chill.*

Tasha seemed unfazed by hearing the preacher's kid's name. She looked at the two of them and sighed. "Y'all can talk about him around me. The man does still live here."

Rachel looked over at Alexa as Tasha continued, "Besides, I already met with his mama the other day. It was... a little awkward at first, but good."

*Tasha back in the day wouldn't have told us that. Maybe she really is cool with everything.*

"You might be good and all now, but PK ain't." Rachel said. "He's changed over the years and it ain't for the best."

*This woman here! Ain't she the one that told me not to say nothing before we got here?*

Both Alexa and Tasha look at Rachel incredulously.

"What? I said what I said!"

Watching her fiance double down on her thoughts about Jerome didn't surprise Alexa. Ever since she reached out to him three years ago on behalf of her company to ask him about possibly mentoring the kids at her center as part of a workshop event, and he all but ignored her, choosing to mail out some autographed CDs and t-shirts instead of calling Creative Chords back. Alexa knew when Rachel tossed the fan mail into the trash that her baby was too through with Jerome 'JPK' Grant.

"Whoa, okay. He must really be something for you to be so vocal about it."

Before Rachel could go in anymore about Jerome's antics over the years, Alexa took out her phone and logged into her social media feed. She handed the phone to Tasha. "I guess you don't follow him online, uh?" she said as Tasha looked at the phone's screen.

She studied Tasha's face as her friend scrolled down the social feed. When she saw Tasha's free hand curl up slightly, Alexa slowly brought her eyes to the ground. Sure enough, Tasha's left foot was bouncing like a hot rabbit's tail.

*Gotta give it to you, Tasha, you almost had me fooled.*

"They're just behind-the-scenes pictures of him on stage while touring." Tasha tried to joke, but Alexa wasn't having it.

"He was quiet at first, the year that you left." Alexa looked on as Rachel explained. "Then he started touring more and got real bougie on his socials."

"Rachel, I hear you. But what has he done that is so bad? He looks like every other rapper online these days."

"That's just it Tash. He ain't supposed to be like every other rapper!" Alexa hissed. "He said he's rapping about God to reach the kids, but how that gonna work? With him saying one thing on stage and then going out and partying like the other rappers at Trap Sons?"

The trio got quiet as their server brought out their food. Though the longer she stared at Tasha, who grinned like a little kid as the server placed her plate in front of her, the hotter Alexa's face grew. They watched on as Tasha cut into her fried chicken and waffles, closing her eyes when she brought the food to her opened mouth.

"Dang Tash - you wanna be alone?" Rachel snidely asked.

Rolling her eyes at her fiancé, Alexa looked on as Tasha took another bite of her meal. "What? It's been a minute since I've had fried chicken." Looking down at her plate and bringing her lips together once more, Tasha added, "I love mixed paella as much as the next girl, but it don't hit the spot like this plate right here."

"Everything okay here?" Their server asked.

Tasha looked up at them and grinned. "We good. Can you bring us the check, please?"

Their server nodded and walked away.

"So that's it? You ain't got nothing to say about your boy?" Alexa asked Tasha directly as she added, "And he's married now - with a son. You still don't wanna say nothing?"

Taking a swig of her orange juice, Tasha answered. "What should I say?"

Alexa watched Tasha as she tilted her head. A small, tight smile appeared on her face before she continued on. "We wished each other well, and it looks like he's doing just that."

Rachel stared at her plate as Alexa glared at Tasha. "No, actually, he isn't. Not really." She said evenly.

Tasha continued eating her food, seemingly done with their current conversation.

"And I'mma need you to stop frontin' about this Tash!" Alexa finally snapped. "One of our associates at the firm is a member at Christ Corner. They say that folks been whispering about Jerome for years now. How he been missing from service for months, and when he does show up, him and his wife don't even sit together. Some of the kids that he's given autographs and take pictures with say he smelled like a skunk!" Alexa harshly whispered, "Now you tell me - is that behavior normal for a Christian rapper?"

"I wouldn't know. I don't work with entertainers." Tasha replied as their server handed her the check.

"You ain't fooling me Tash with this attitude of yours. Back in the day you and Jerome - *Rome* - y'all had something. You mean to tell us that you don't care what he's been up to now that you're back in town?"

Both Alexa and Rachel stared at Tasha. She finally put down her knife and fork before softening her gaze. "Yeah, years ago, Jerome and I were *almost* more than friends. But I chose different and left. He went on with his life, and I sincerely wished him well. The end."

Hearing Alexa scoff, Tasha went on. "From what y'all have told me, he's done that. Jerome is a successful rapper, husband, and father. Even if I did still have feelings, it wouldn't matter. And if I did have worries about him, it's not like I have the man on speed dial. I don't even know how to get in touch with him these days."

"I bet you'd find him at BU. Last I heard, that's where him and his crew like to go these days."

Alexa was going to have a strong talk with her fiance later about oversharing. Tasha could pretend all she wanted, but Alexa wasn't fooled.

*If she cool with seeing Jerome's mama - it's only a matter of time before they see each other. I just hope it doesn't send her running away for another four years.*

"I've got no problem with going to Bottom's Up. It's been a minute since I've been there. Too bad y'all sold The Fast Fix. I could've put in a shift, you know, for old time's sake."

Tasha took another sip of her juice before slowly standing up. "I'm gonna go take care of the bill right quick."

Rachel and Alexa watched their friend walk to the front counter, and Alexa sighed.

"You believe her, babe?"

Alexa slowly shook her head. "I want to, but she trying too hard to convince us that she don't care about him anymore."

"She always did keep her feelings to herself, but babe, I'm really worried for her."

Rachel took Alexa's hand and kissed her knuckles gently. She knew her girl was thinking back to the day Tasha came home after being out with Jerome for the weekend. She and Rachel had spent the weekend indoors, watching reality TV and sipping wine on their couch. Both were tipsy and giggling when Tasha entered the house. They didn't even realize anything was wrong as they started to tease Tasha about getting the preacher's kid to 'sin for the weekend' until Tasha dropped her overnight bag and fell to the floor.

Alexa sobered up real quick at seeing her usually together friend bawling and shaking like a leaf in front of them. That night, she and Rachel took turns passing by Tasha's bedroom door, listening to any hint that she was okay. They'd fallen asleep on the couch and were woken up by the smell of bacon and eggs, along with an apology from Tasha. She told them about the internship she was accepted for, completely avoiding any further talk about her time with Jerome.

And just like that, after one night with Jerome, her best friend of over a decade was gone from her life. All because she fell for the preacher's son and got hurt. *I'm not about to let that happen again, not if I can help it.*

"I just don't want her to get hurt again." Alexa spoke softly as Tasha made her way back to the table.

"Me too babe, me too." Rachel whispered, taking Alexa's hand in hers and kissing it gently.

### Sofie

"That boy is getting so big!"

Hearing mama comment on little Ro for the second time that day, Sofie rolled her eyes. "Ain't that's what he supposed to do? Can't stay a baby forever."

Lillie Ward tsked at her youngest child before going over to pick up her now sleeping grandson. She grinned as she walked down the hall to put him in bed. While her mama was fawning over her son, Sofie took a glance in a nearby mirror and frowned as she looked down at her stomach. The thin jagged lines that went around her torso were light, only a shade darker than her overall complexion, but she still detested the sight of them.

*Those stretch marks won't go away for nothing!*

"I wish you paid as much attention to your baby as you did your body." Lillie Ward shook her head as she marched past Sofie. "Where is my son-in-law these days?" she asked.

Sofie honestly didn't care where her husband was, as long as he kept paying the bills. In fact, the less she saw of him, the better. "He'll be home soon. Which reminds me, do you think you can look after Ro for a little bit? My girl Regine just got back from Miami and I wanna see the new ride her man got her."

Lillie Ward sucked her teeth, "Everybody in town knows that that boy ain't her man."

Not in the mood to hear another one of her mama's lectures, Sofie tried being sweet instead. "I'm just trying to be supportive of my friend. Is that bad?"

Lillie cut her eyes at Sofie. "Fine. Go and see about your little friend."

She quickly threw her arms around Lillie, making sure to give her a peck on the cheek as well.

"Thanks mama! I'll be back soon."

The drive out to visit Regine didn't take as long as Sofie thought it would. Pulling her ride into the guest parking area, she gawked around at the manicured hedges and freshly cut grass that expanded up about a mile, leading to a mansion that was at least half the size of a football field. She knew that Buckem signed with the label a month ago, but now she wondered how much of an advance he got for his first album. Besides her car, three others were parked in the driveway as Regine grabbed her hand and squealed.

"Look at us Sofie! Finally a bunch of married ladies!"

Sofie's arched brow raised as she turned to her friend. "Did you and Bentley get married while y'all were in Miami?"

"Nah, girl. He still tripping about that. But he made sure to ice me up real nice while we was away."

Regine's voice was light, but Sofie didn't miss the pout that came after her friend spoke.

*I bet he did 'ice' you up.*

Sofie snorted as Regine kept talking. "When we got back, the label told him they was throwing him an album release party! They having the party at BU and invited a whole bunch of artists."

Regine smirked as she lightly touched the sparkling necklace around her neck. "They even invited JPK. I saw the guest list this morning."

Sofie kept her smile in place while looking at Regine, but inside she was ready to go off. She made it clear to her husband once he got back from touring that she wanted to be kept in the loop about where he was at all times. That way, they could continue to live their separate lives and not worry about being in each other's way. But if he got an invitation to this release party—she was going—no matter what their living arrangement was like these days.

*I'll find out what happened when I get back home.*

"He said that with the mixtape doing so good, they want him in the studio recording. That's why he ain't here now."

That suited Sofie just fine. Bentley 'Buckem' Robson was well known in town, but only recently for rapping. Growing up in the projects, he first showed promise as an aspiring writer. He was featured in a few spoken word events too, until his mama up and died from cancer when Bentley was fifthteen years old. Soon after that, he dropped out of school and was in and out of juvie until he caught an assault and armed robbery charge on his seventeenth birthday. The courts tried him as an adult and he did seven of his twenty five year sentence before being released on good behavior.

Sofie wondered exactly what the system deemed as 'good' behavior, because any time she was within two meters of Bentley, she felt uneasy. She knew of dudes who pretended to be the baddest in their crew, but Sofie knew at first glance that Bentley never had to fake it - he was nothing but bad. The further she was from him, the better. Though once her girl saw Bentley gaining attention as a new rapper on the scene, Sofie knew it was only a matter of time before Regine would try to lock him down.

"That's good." Sofie said absently.

Regine jerked her hand even closer toward her. "Good? That's better than good!"

Using her free hand, Sofie unlocked their tangled hands and tried to rub the feeling back into her arm. "You right. The sooner he gets in the studio, the sooner he can start paying all this stuff off."

Regine cut her eyes at Sofie. "Don't be like that, Sofie. Just cause you bagged a lame -"

"At least *my* rapper put a ring on it. You really think Bentley's gonna do the same?"

Seeing the crestfallen look on her friend's face, Sofie softened her tone before speaking again. "I ain't mean to say all that. I'm just trying to look out for you sis, that's all."

Regine rolled her eyes as she bumped hips with Sofie. "Girl, look 'round you! Someone IS looking out for me - I'm in this big ass house, with three whips to choose from when I wanna roll through town! I'mma be alright."

Sofie looked back at the parked cars and sighed.

*I should stop being petty. Regine's my girl.*

"You right. So, what you got to eat in this big ass house?"

The two laughed as they began walking toward the front door of the house.

**TASHA**

After breakfast with her besties, Tasha decided to spend her afternoon editing photos from her last photoshoot in Mexico. Time always did get away from her when she got in the zone of perfecting her photos, and when she looked out the window to her suite, Tasha wasn't surprised at all to see that the sun had set. While submitting the batch of photographs to her client, Tasha's computer rang. She quickly pressed the green receiver button on the screen.

"Hello Ms. Daye. This is Dr. Richardson's office calling. We would like to know when to schedule your next appointment."

Tasha completely forgot to schedule her next therapy session. "Yes, hi. Can I see Dr. Richardson in two days, please?"

Confirming her appointment, Tasha noticed the time and started putting away her things.

*Bottom's Up should be in full swing now.*

She made her way to the door, grabbing her helmet and keys.

With all the work traffic gone for the day, Tasha was able to pull into the strip club's parking lot within thirty minutes. Like everything else in town, *Bottom's Up* had gone through its own renovations. There were now two separate check points, each with someone from security standing by once patrons stepped inside the building. Tasha paid the entrance fee and waited her turn to be patted down for contraband before being scanned by the metal wand the female security guard held in their hands. One of the guards, a fair skinned, short woman with blondish red hair pulled back into a low ponytail, eyed her a little too long before Tasha finally went through the detectors.

"Empty your pockets," the female guard demanded.

Doing as asked, Tasha eyed her wallet and keys as she went through the detectors again.

Once she was cleared through, Tasha took in more updates of the club. There now were three mini stages, instead of one long stage for the dancers. The only seats available on the floor were directly next to the stages, as the others were elevated up, similar to stands at a colosseum or a football stadium. There were also mini bar stations in opposite corners, giving those walking inside more space to ogle and mingle with the dancers. The lights were still their vibrant neon purple, but glow lights had also been installed, making everyone in white stand out more.

Even the VIP section got an upgrade. Now there was a velvet entrance and two guards that stood in front. Tasha pitied the fool that would try to start something in there, with those menacing gladiators guarding the area. Several hostesses fluttered around in uniformed mesh black dresses. Tasha closed her eyes and tried to re-familiarize herself with the smell of smoke and cheap cologne before she went to talk to the girls. When she opened her eyes, Tasha was greeted by a familiar face.

"Hey Tash. It's been awhile."

Velvet didn't hide her smirk as Tasha took her in. She was only slightly more dressed than the hostesses, yet the nude dress she wore made the woman appear naked when the light hit her just right. Her signature braids were on full display, though now she wore them with beads on the ends. Even over the bass line in the club, Tasha could hear the faint clicking sound they created as Velvet turned to survey the activity around them.

"Velvet. It's good to see you." Tasha finally said.

"The guard out front told me you were here, and I had to see for myself. What brings you by?" she asked.

Knowing that information inside BU came with a price, Tasha made sure to stop by the ATM on her way to the club.

"I'm in town for a few weeks and wanted to swing by. For a friend."

As she removed several bills from her wallet, Velvet grinned. "I always did like that about you, Tash. How you got straight to the point and came prepared."

"One thing I learned from working with y'all is that time is money."

Velvet turned and Tasha followed her to one of the mini bar stations. When she sat down, Tasha joined her and placed two twenties on the counter. Velvet turned her attention to the bartender running the station, and they grabbed a glass and a bottle of what looked like brandy.

"You want anything?" Velvet asked.

"Nah, I'm good, thanks."

Feeling Velvet look her over, the woman tilted her head toward Tasha. "That's right, the other girls used to talk about how you never drink while working. Smart."

The bartender brought Velvet's drink, and Tasha was about to ask how much it was until they said, "Here you go boss."

Tasha waited for them to leave before asking, "Boss?"

Velvet grinned, letting the vivid purple and blue neon lights shine wickedly against her white gold iced out grillz. "For the last two years, I've been managing this place."

"Congratulations." Tasha said as she watched Velvet sip her drink.

"So, what is it that your friend needs from BU, Tash?"

"Just some information, that's all. But it's about a customer. At least I think they may be." Tasha answered as best as she could. "Goes by the stage name 'JPK.'"

Velvet gazed out at the crowd passing by as she took another sip of her drink.

"Who wants to know about JPK?" Velvet asked.

Taking out two more twenties, Tasha placed them with the others. "His mama. She says she ain't seen him in some time, and a friend told me that he might come here."

Velvet nodded, putting her drink down on the counter and eyeing Tasha, who finally had a seat next to her. "He mostly comes in and has some drinks. Buys his boys a few dances in VIP before leaving."

Tasha tried not to let the shock of hearing that Jerome drinks show on her face as she slipped Velvet another twenty.

"Has he been in recently? His mama hasn't seen him in a minute and she's worried." Tasha asked as a new song began to play. Three dancers went to each mini stage at once and they must have been a fave among the horny herd, as all the seats near the dancers quickly filled up. She watched as bills sailed into the air and the girls flirted with the masses, one after the other, taking their turn to show off their pole skills to the cheers of the crowd.

Velvet signaled for the bartender to come over again as she picked up her drink and knocked it back in one gulp. "Yeah, he's been in recently."

Tasha could feel Velvet's eyes on her again and returned her stare as she took out another twenty. "Thanks. It was good to see you again."

She hopped off the stool and surveyed the crowd a bit more.

*Just what happened to you Jerome?*

Before she could walk back to the entrance, Tasha felt a soft tug on her elbow. Pausing to look at Velvet, the woman casually spoke. "A year ago, we had a girl working here, went by the name Cream. She was the only girl he ever bought a dance for himself from."

Tasha kept her face neutral before tilting her head at Velvet. "I only wanted to know where he is now, not who he got a dance from in the past. But thanks."

Velvet reached into her cleavage and pulled out a small black case. Removing a cigarette, she turned to the bar counter and picked up a pack of matches as she spoke again. "You and Cream favor."

Tasha froze.

"You say his mama looking for him? Why ain't I talking to her instead of you, then?"

Slowly turning to face Velvet, Tasha tried her best to keep her voice neutral. Locking eyes with Velvet, she answered evenly. "His mama's the First Lady at Christ Corner." Sighing, Tasha rolled her shoulders back. "I really don't want to be the one to tell his mama that her only son has been skipping church services to drink at BU. Trust - the minute I find him and give him her message, I'm on the first thing smoking out of here."

Velvet nodded slowly and took a drag of her cigarette. Seeing her completely calm and in her element, Tasha reached into her back pocket.

"I know you run things now, but if you ever want some photos done, I would love to collaborate with you." Tasha said sincerely as she handed Velvet a business card.

She watched Velvet take her card and look it over. The woman then grinned as she slipped the card inside the black case.

"Thanks again for the info."

"You welcome Tash."

# Chapter Four

## These are Our Confessions

### Tasha

After their last meetup, Tasha and Trisha decided to have lunch with the kids the following week at Roger's Playground, a kid-friendly arcade style restaurant. Tasha arrived before they did and saw Devin and Darnell barreling toward her.

"Hey Titi!"

Bending down to swoop them both in her arms, Tasha listened to their giggles and Trisha tsking.

"Stop picking them up like that girl! You gonna put your back out."

Putting the boys down, Tasha reached into her pocket and took out her wallet. Their eyes lit up as she gave each of them ten dollars. "Y'all can get change inside to play the games. Come back when we call y'all to eat, okay?"

"Okay Titi!"

Tasha laughed as they made a beeline for the change machine.

"You spoiling them, girl." Trisha told her as she sat at the table.

She knew Trisha was right, but Tasha couldn't help it. "I already missed so much time with them. I can't help but be a little extra while I'm here." Tasha explained. "Also, did you get my email? About your registry?"

Trisha squirmed a bit in her seat as she looked at Tasha. "Yeah, I did. Lloyd and I looked at it twice to be sure what we saw was right."

Tasha smiled, "Good. So, how you feeling? What else you need?"

As her baby sister narrowed her eyes at her, Tasha started to brace for a pushback to come. She knew getting everything that was left on Trisha's registry was a bit much, but Tasha remembered when Devin was first born. Trisha worked throughout her pregnancy and still came up short when it came time to get all the things the hospital told her she needed. Hearing her sister cry at night as her newborn slept in the bed beside her, Tasha silently promised that if she could ease Trisha's worries with anything related to taking care of her kid that she would do so without hesitation. And the number of things still left on their registry, with just a few months left, didn't sit right with her, so Tasha bought everything and made sure to schedule it all for delivery by the end of the week.

"It's a lot, Tash, that's all. But thank you." Trisha said. "Lloyd's job has started to cut back on everyone's hours, so things have been a little tight."

"I'm glad I could help, Trish."

And she was. Her little sister seemed to be happy with the family she created, and Tasha couldn't help but be joyful for Trisha.

A server finally showed up and took their order before Tasha spoke again. "I won't be able to see y'all again for a minute. That's the other reason why I wanted to meet y'all today." Tasha continued, "I'll still be here, but Alexa and Rachel are finally tying the knot and asked me to be their maid of honor."

Trisha shook her head as she let out a nervous giggle. "Oh, girl! You had me worried for a minute! All Devin's been talking about is you going to his professional's day at school on Friday."

They shared a laugh as Tasha explained, "That's why I wanted to squeeze in a bit more time with y'all, to let you know that I'm still gonna be at his school."

"That's what's up!"

Tasha looked on behind Trisha, and her eyes narrowed a little. Turning to look in the same direction as her sister, she saw her older sister Tina walking toward them. She wore a pair of form fitting khaki pants and a bright yellow polo shirt that made her fair brown skin pop while showing off her petite frame. With her signature cornrows highlighting her high cheekbones, Tina briefly paused while staring at them.

Tasha hadn't seen her since their fight at Christ Corner four years ago, and it was clear from Tina's dismissive stare that she wasn't here to apologize for helping Kitty steal her scholarship money back in high school. Cutting her eyes over to her baby sister, Tasha watched as she quietly lowered her head.

"Did you invite her?" Tasha asked Trisha directly.

"Not really. I did hope that she had a shift at The Lunch Grill when I messaged her though..."

Tasha rolled her eyes as Tina leaned over the railing of the patio area, completely ignoring her. "Hey Trisha. Where the boys at?"

"They inside on the games until the food gets here."

Tasha looked on as Trisha and Tina shared a glance at one another. She didn't know what it was about, and she didn't care. All of Tasha's instincts told her to get up and leave. But with Doctor Richardson's words about giving people a chance to prove her wrong ringing loudly in her head, Tasha steadied her breathing. *Just try Tash. Not for Tina's sake, but for Trish and the boys. Try.*

"You ain't gonna say hey to Tash?" she heard Trisha say to Tina.

Relaxing her shoulders, Tasha struggled to keep her resting bitch face away as Tina finally looked her way.

"She got eyes too." Tina scoffed before adding, "What, she too good to speak to me?"

"Hey Tina." Tasha mumbled.

When her big sister cackled, it charged up all the horrible memories she had from hearing Tina laugh at her as a kid. Every bone in Tasha's body screamed for her to leave. To be anywhere but here. Tasha glanced behind her and relaxed her jaw at the sight of Devin and Darnell being well out of earshot.

"You don't sound happy to see me, uh biggie smalls?" Tina questioned, pulling out one of her favorite nicknames for Tasha from back in the day. Tasha focused on her breathing as she watched Tina tilted her head before sucking in her teeth. "Food must be real good where you been - you just as big as I remembered."

Trisha frowned. "Really Tina?"

"What? She still can't take a joke? At her BIG age?" Tina countered.

Memories of Tina first picking on Tasha for being fatter than her and Trisha back in the eighth grade came flooding her mind. How the harder she cried from the teasing jabs only made Tina go harder in on her - from her weight to her non relaxed hair - everything about Tasha became one big comedy show. Until Tasha started to use her weight to her advantage and fought back with her fists.

"Forget I bothered." Tasha finally said, "I see you still ain't worth talking to."

Tina rolled her neck before cackling again and looking at Trisha. "See, she don't want to talk to me no way. I guess all that bougie ass traveling ain't changed her for the better."

Tasha turned to face Tina, and Trisha snatched up the silverware near Tasha, causing Tina to laugh.

"Maybe if I had started traveling earlier, like when I was supposed to after high school, I would be more willing to change. Guess that plan, along with yours back then, went up in smoke."

"I see you still think you better than everybody else."

"I see you still broke. By the way, how is that even possible?"

Tasha leveled her eyes at Tina and spoke as evenly as possible. "I did the math. You and Kitty had at least twenty thousand dollars transferred to your bank account. You didn't think to save some of the money you stole for a rainy day?"

Tina narrowed her eyes at Tasha before leaning in closer to her face and spitting out, "You always think you got all the sense! If you really was as smart as you act, you would've been knew what happened."

When her hands balled into fists, Tasha heard Trisha harshly whisper, "Y'all, please don't do this here! Tina, just say you sorry so we can all get along again."

Tina whipped her head toward Trisha. "When did we ever get along? Is that why you chose to drag Saint Tasha down here for lunch by my job?"

With both Tina and Tasha glaring at her, Trisha tightly shut her eyes and took a deep breath. "Yeah, okay! With Kitty gone, I thought y'all would be ready to try and make peace with each other." Trisha looked between her two sisters before crying out, "We all we got!"

Tasha looked at Trisha, "Trish, I know you meant well–"

"You don't know shit!" Tina barked out. "When granny died, Kitty would leave me alone at home with y'all for days. I was only 12 years old, alone in a house with no food, sometimes no water or lights, looking after y'all!"

Tasha opened her mouth to speak but Tina stopped her, "Strange folks knocking on the door, all hours of the night, you two crying from either being hungry or scared of the dark... I finally started working under the table at that dank ass laundromat, cleaning up behind folks in the bathroom and outside, just to make sure y'all had somewhere to go after school."

Tina looked down at Tasha and rolled her eyes, "And here you is, crying about that little bit of change? I earned every bit of that money - looking after yo ass!"

The tremble in Trisha's voice was unmistakable, and Tasha knew she was on the verge of crying as she spoke. "What Kitty did messed us all up Tina, but what y'all did.."

"What WE did?!" Tina said incredulously. Leaning in toward Trisha, Tina's bitter laugh rippled throughout the tiny space between the three of them. "Is that how you wanna remember what happened?"

Trisha's eyes widened as she looked between Tina and Tasha. She said nothing as Tina went on. "After getting caught up on the bills and fixing what I could around the house, I had to fight Kitty for the rest of that change. So I treated myself and I don't regret nothing!"

Tasha gripped the sides of the table as she stood. Though before she left, something about what Tina said had to be addressed. Because the one thing Tasha could say she learned from Kitty's death was that tomorrow wasn't promised to any of them. And that alone was enough cause for her to lock eyes with Tina. If this was possibly the last time she would ever speak to her big sister, Tasha had to make sure Tina knew the whole story. No matter how much it was going to hurt them both in the process. Remembering the therapy session that she had with Doctor Richardson that unlocked the painful truth, Tasha blinked back the oncoming tears as she held Tina's glare.

"You think we don't remember what it was like then? How you looked after us?"

A stray tear escaped and Tasha brushed it away as she continued. "Do you even know why I chose to major in English in the first place?"

More tears fell as Tasha pushed her chair back while looking at Trisha and Tina.

"You two never read any of my scholarship essays, did you? They were all about my big and bright sister, 'Super T' and how she protected me from the big, bad world when I was too little to understand why it was so scary. How that led me to writing stories and my love of learning how to write better. So much so that all I wanted to do was to use my talents in storytelling with a pen to hopefully help others someday that found themselves lost in the darkness back to the light."

Feeling the heat of both of them staring up at her, Tasha pushed down the large lump in her throat. "You and Kitty taking the money ain't what hurts, Tina. It's the fact that as much as I wanted to leave town, if you had asked me then to give you the money, my dumb ass would have. All because of how much I worship you for taking care of me when Kitty couldn't."

The table was silent as her sisters processed what she had shared, and even though Tina's eyes no longer met her, Tasha knew she heard every word. Just as Tina was about to say something, Darnell and Devin rushed to the table.

"Mama, Titi! We need more money!"

Tina used that moment to step away from the railing, wiping her eyes.

"Not right now, y'all. Go sit inside for a minute." Trisha told them quickly.

When the boys started to walk over to the empty table, away from them, Tina laughed. Hearing the sound made Tasha's heart ache even more than it already did.

"Nah Trisha, go ahead and finish spoiling them with Tasha's cash. Ain't no telling how long she's gonna be here, gotta make sure to get all you can."

Not bothering to wipe away the hot angry tears that trailed down her cheeks, Tasha stared hard at Tina. *I tried. Lord knows I really tried this time.*

Standing up and reaching into her pocket, Tasha took out a few more bills and placed them on the table. "Enjoy lunch."

"Tash, please stay." Trisha pleaded.

Tasha ignored her as she turned to face their older sister instead. "Go to hell."

Trisha and Tina looked on as she picked up her helmet. Before turning to face Devin and Darnell, Tasha grabbed a napkin from the table and dabbed at her wet cheeks. Walking over to the boys, she gave each of them a kiss on the crown of their heads. "Titi's gotta go. See y'all again soon, okay?"

"Why you gotta go?" Devin asked softly.

Her heart ached seeing the confusion in his warm brown irises. Rarely was Tasha loss for words, but she was at that moment. *How do you tell a kid that you're all messed up because the person who was supposed to raise you failed?*

"I have to help Auntie Alexa and Rachel with something."

It wasn't a lie, but it wasn't the truth either. Tasha leaned down again and kissed Devin's forehead.

"Love you."

### Sofie

Two weeks after hearing about Trap Sons album party from Regine, Sofie got out of bed when her alarm began going off, reminding her that she did have something to do that day. Now that they had potty trained Ro, she could enroll him in Pre-Kindergarten at Woods Edge Elementary.

She loved her little boy, but it was time for Sofie to get back to having her own life. And the sooner Sofie got Ro signed up for school, the sooner she could get back to getting the figure eight body she had before she was pregnant.

Quickly getting dressed and hopping into the SUV, Sofie drove Ro to her mama's house and dropped him off before heading to the school with all of his paperwork. As she was walking to the entrance, some idiot on a motorcycle came flying through the parking lot, causing her to drop a few of the documents.

*Who rides a damn motorcycle to a kids' school anyway?*

Rolling her eyes, Sofie bent down to pick up the paperwork. Once she did, she noticed the person hopping off of the bike and taking off their helmet. Curious, Sofie continued to stare at the woman as she reached into the backseat of the motorcycle and took out a medium-sized messenger bag. The woman placed the bag over her shoulder and put the helmet inside the seat, locking it with a key before turning to walk toward the building.

Sofie had never seen Tasha Daye in person, but she knew it was her. After hearing one too many of them uppity negroes at Christ Corner talk about Tasha inside the ladies' restroom during her first visit, Sofie looked her up online.

*What's this bitch doing here?!*

Soon Tasha walked past her, offering a small head nod, which Sofie didn't return. Instead of frowning as Sofie hoped she would, Tasha smiled at her, causing Sofie to deepen the crease on her forehead.

She waited until Tasha opened the main entrance door and followed behind her, listening in as she took her ID out of her bag and spoke to the front desk clerk, a short woman, with salt and pepper hair and a pair of reading glasses on the top of her head.

"Morning! My name's Tasha. Tasha Daye. I'm here for Mrs. Wallace's Professional Day. Here is my business card and my ID, as the school requested."

Sofie watched as Tasha smiled at the clerk.

"I'm not too late, am I?" Tasha asked.

The older woman placed the business card into a small envelope before handing back the ID. She was all smiles when she answered, "You right on time, baby girl. Mrs. Wallace's class is down this here hall. You'll see a sign for today's class, so just gone right in."

"Thank you." Tasha said, as she walked straight ahead.

*She just takes pics of half naked hoes. Why would she be here for a 'Professional' anything?*

Lost in thought, Sofie didn't hear the older woman call out to her until she did so for a second time.

"You lost girl?" The woman asked, raising her voice.

Hearing the woman call her 'girl' pulled Sofie out of her thoughts, as she whipped her head toward the older woman.

"Nah, I ain't lost. And I'm a grown ass woman, don't be calling me 'girl'!" she snapped.

The woman looked at her for a second before closing her eyes and sighing. "How may I help you, Miss?"

Sofie didn't miss the monotone voice the woman addressed her in, but she wanted to get this over with. Shoving the paperwork along with her ID at the woman, Sofie straightened her stance as she eyed the older woman. "I'm *Mrs.* Jerome Grant. Here to enroll my son into Pre-K as soon as possible."

## TASHA

The sign for Professionals' Day was down the hall, as the woman at the front desk stated. Tasha took a peek inside the class before walking in. When Devin spotted her, Tasha's heart grew heavy from the sight of him jumping up and waving at her. Putting a finger in front of her lips, Tasha used her other hand to remind Devin to sit down.

While the adult in front of the class talked about what they did for a living, Tasha used that time to set up her equipment. Though as soon as she had her laptop up and turned on her portable projector, clapping could be heard around her before Mrs. Wallace spoke, "Thank you Mr. Aalegra for that wonderful lecture on working in architectural design! Up next, we have Devin's guest. Devin, please come to the front and introduce them."

Tasha watched as her nephew made his way to the front of the class and grinned as Devin spoke, "My titi -"

"Aunt." Mrs. Wallace corrected.

"My AUNT," Devin said loudly, causing the other children to laugh, "is here today. She takes pictures all over the world."

Tasha walked over to Devin, and she placed her laptop down on the empty desk and her messenger bag in the chair behind her. Balling her fist, Tasha reached down to Devin as he brought his tiny fist to connect with hers. "Thanks D."

When he returned to his seat, Tasha double checked her laptop and aimed the projector at the whiteboard, before smiling at the students. "My name is Tasha Daye. But those closest to me know me as Titi, or Titi Tasha."

The kids laughed again and the slide show that she created days ago began playing on the screen, causing a few quick whispers to fall over the group. "For four years, I've been lucky enough to work as an international photographer."

As more pictures showed up on the screen, Tasha briefly told them about when and where each photo was taken. The woman that Tasha saw earlier on her way to the class was also in attendance. She kept staring at her, but Tasha brushed it off as she went on, making sure to slowly explain to the kids the basics of being a photographer. When the slide show ended, Tasha asked the audience, "What questions do you all have?"

A little girl, almost half of Tasha's five feet nine frame, stood up before blurting out, "Are you married?"

Blinking several times, Tasha answered, "No, I'm not married."

"Why not?" A boy with cornrows asked.

"Well, I don't want to be married, I guess."

Tasha managed to squeak out before another boy with a pair of thick blue glasses suddenly spoke, "You can't really be a photographer. I ain't never seen a girl photographer before."

Tasha tried to keep her 'teacher face' on display as she looked directly at the young boy, "Firstly, anyone can be a photographer, and second, just because you've never met a woman photographer before doesn't mean that we don't exist."

Mrs. Wallace could be seen opening and closing her hand at Tasha, which she took to mean that she had five minutes left. Movement from her left hand side caught her attention, and as she looked over in that direction, Tasha saw the woman that was staring at her earlier quietly slip back out of the classroom.

"That is all the time we have for questions, but I do have a small gift for you all before I go. Devin, could you help me pass these out, please?"

Devin hopped out of his seat and sprinted toward Tasha, who handed him several small silver keychains. Each one was engraved with her matra *Inspiration is always a click away. Don't be afraid to capture it.*, as well as her initials.

When Mrs. Wallace stood, Tasha handed the last student their keychain before making her way back to the front of the class. "Thank you all so much for welcoming me into your classroom today."

Picking up her bag, Tasha quickly scooped up her projector and laptop as she went to sit in the back of the classroom to listen as someone else talked about what they did for a living. Once they wrapped up their presentation, a low bell rang throughout the building.

"Guest, please stand. That's the lunch bell, signaling the end of our time today. Thank you all for attending Professionals' Day and have a great day. Wave goodbye class." Mrs. Wallace said, turning to lead the children out of the room.

On her way out, Tasha stopped by the front desk and thanked the older woman for their help.

"Oh, I am happy to do it, baby."

As Tasha began to head out, the woman called out to her. Turning around to look at the older woman, she smiled. "I'm sorry. Do I need to sign out?"

"Oh, no, not that. The school is trying to raise money to get more netbooks for the kids with a fundraiser, and I wanted to ask if you would be willing to donate your time for the event."

*As long as it's before the gala, it should be fine.*

"I would love to help. What would you like me to do at this event, ma'am?"

The older woman brought her glasses down from the top of her head as she chuckled, "You can cut out all that "ma'am" business, for one thing. My name's Willie Mae."

"Yes, Ms. Willie Mae. How can I help?" Tasha asked again.

"Well, you say you a photographer, right?" Wilie Mae confirmed.

"Yes, ma- Ms. Willie Mae." Tasha corrected herself as Willie Mae chuckled again.

"Good, good. Then leave me another business card and I'll let the committee for the event know. They'll be in touch."

Tasha reached into her messenger bag and took out two business cards. Seeing that she still had a few extra keychains as well, Tasha grabbed one to give the older woman.

"I look forward to hearing from the event committee soon then."

**Sofie**

She spent the entire night side-eyeing her husband after seeing Tasha at Woods Edge elementary that morning. Every move he made, from giving her son a bath to the way he ate was under heavy scrutiny. He was usually easy to read, which helped Sofie when it came to getting more money for the month or knowing when to play nice where Evelyn was concerned. But if Jerome knew about his ex being back in time, he was doing a damn good job of hiding it. *He's acting like his regular degular boring self. So why am I wishing he was hiding something?*

Lost in her thoughts, Sofie didn't see Jerome as he made his way toward her on his way to his bedroom. "Is something wrong?"

Hearing his voice snapped her back to the present, and she quickly countered, "Why would you think something's wrong?"

"I can feel you watching me." Jerome bluntly replied before adding, "Do you need money again?"

Sofie narrowed her eyes as she jerked her head backward. "No, I don't need money." Not liking being on the defensive, she blurted out the first thing that came to mind, "Just trying to figure out when you gonna tell me about Buckem's album release party."

She watched as Jerome's shoulders dropped. *Maybe he really doesn't know about ole girl being back in town.*

"The invites just went out. And I ain't tell you because I'm not going."

He walked past her and opened the door along the opposite wall to his room, but Sofie wasn't done.

"Why? Regine says it's supposed to be a big event and that everyone from your label is going. It would be nice if you took me out for a change."

When he turned to look at her, Sofie felt like she was seeing him for the first time in years. He let out a heavy sigh and her eyes went to his chest. Soon she was checking out the rest of her husband's well toned frame. He may be lame, but Jerome was always easy on the eyes, even if he wasn't six feet tall or had a mouth full of grillz, like the dudes she was used to. *Looks like he's been hitting the gym hard lately.*

Her thoughts briefly turned to how she might be able to persuade Jerome into taking her to the album party. While she was remembering the few things he liked when they were sweating out her hair together, Jerome spoke. "Sofie, I'm not going. So what would it look like for you to be there without me?"

Before she could get out another word out, he walked into his bedroom and shut the door.

The next day, Sofie got the call that her son's paperwork was verified and Ro could start Pre-K as early as that afternoon. She made sure to wake up early to get him ready for his first day of school. Her little man didn't seem to mind the change in their schedule, as he walked beside her into the colorful classroom. The Pre-K teachers introduced themselves to him, and just in case he got uncomfortable or scared, she stayed behind at a desk a few feet away while they included him in their normal class session. After almost an hour and not so much as a wail or backward glance to her, Sofie snuck out of the classroom to leave. She almost did the electric slide as she thought about how she would spend her weekdays now that Ro was officially in school.

*Time to get my body right at the gym with my girl Regine! Thank you Jesus!*

Though as she was walking down the hall to leave, the woman at the front desk called out to her. "Mrs. Grant?"

*I see she learned to address me correctly.*

Sofie grinned as she turned around slowly to answer. "Yeah. What else y'all need?"

The older woman sighed. "Well, the school is holding a fundraiser -"

"I ain't got no money."

She watched as the woman blinked several times before continuing, "You misunderstand. We are looking for volunteers to help us the day of the event. And I remembered that you were married to a local celebrity..."

Sofie rolled her eyes. "So you want my husband to write a check? Okay."

The older woman then pushed a flyer toward her. "Our scheduled entertainment had a last minute emergency, and I was hoping that your husband would be willing to join the lineup."

A bell then chimed throughout the building, and the classroom doors opened. Dozens of kids sprinted past her, screaming and crowding the hallway.

*Ugh! Where all these damn kids came from?*

Thinking quickly, Sofie took the flyer from the woman. "I'll tell him about it later."

Turning on her heel, she made a beeline to the exit before more kids came near her.

# Chapter Five

## Faded Pictures

### Tasha

A week later, Tasha found herself standing outside at the 'locally famous' Seafood Shack. She was twenty minutes early, but Tasha didn't mind. Using that time to process what she was feeling, like she had learned with her therapist, Tasha realized that when she first left home, it wasn't just Jerome she didn't say goodbye to, but to Evelyn too.

Seeing her again and having time to reconnect was a gift, one that Tasha would continue to be thankful for. And after her visit to Bottom's Up, Tasha had called Evelyn the following morning and shared as much as she could about Jerome's whereabouts like she promised she would. Once she was finished, Evelyn asked to see her, thanking her for keeping her promise. To know that she enjoyed spending time with her as much as she did warmed Tasha's heart. So, of course she had no problem making time to see the older woman as soon as possible.

After a few minutes, she saw Evelyn's car pull into the small parking area. Rushing to the driver's side of the car, Tasha opened the door and waited for Evelyn to get out. The older woman's laugh was light as she greeted Tasha, "Well, hello to you too!"

"Hey again Mrs. Evelyn." Tasha said with a smile.

The older woman glanced between Tasha and the motorcycle before shaking her head. "Baby, you ain't scared to ride around on that thing?"

Tasha laughed, "Not at all! I like living in the fast lane."

"You have to, I guess, to be riding around on that there bike." Evelyn narrowed her eyes down as she noticed Tasha's helmet. "At least you're being smart about it."

After the two stepped inside the restaurant, they were escorted to a table and seated.

"So, I want to hear about what you've been up to since you left - don't leave out nothing!" Evelyn finally said to Tasha.

Tasha told Mrs. Evelyn all about her travels, including her slowly learning Spanish and taking photos of all the places she dreamed of visiting back in high school.

She watched as Evelyn listened to her before the older woman asked, "Do you have any photos that I can look at?" Beaming, Tasha took her tablet from her bag and turned it on. "I always keep my portfolio ready - that's part of the job." She replied before entering her password.

Tasha handed Evelyn the tablet after she selected the General folder and let her browse through the pictures. Wordlessly, Evelyn stared at the pictures and Tasha worried that she may have clicked on the wrong folder. "Is everything alright Mrs. Evelyn?" She asked as gently as she could.

The woman put down the tablet and placed Tasha's hands into hers.

"I'm happy for you baby, that's all. I know leaving wasn't easy, but you had to follow your heart."

Tasha squeezed their hands together as she looked at Evelyn.

"Now that I've had time to look back, I shouldn't have been surprised when Eva left for New York," Evelyn said.

Curious, Tasha looked on patiently as Evelyn continued. "When she was little, I would show her pictures of the city all the time. Ever since I was in high school and learned that that's where all the great performers lived. But when I graduated from high school, my daddy introduced me to Jerome and that was that."

Tasha felt a wave of sadness wash over her as she saw Evelyn blink away tears.

"You did get to visit New York eventually, right? I remember-"

Thinking back to her time with Jerome wasn't the problem, it was having to talk about it with someone else. Especially his mama. Evelyn smiled sweetly at Tasha and answered her question.

"Yes, I finally did make it to New York to see my daughter and grandbaby. That was one of the best weeks of my life. But New York wasn't as I had pictured it."

Tasha had to ask, "How was it? Compared to what you thought it'd be like?"

Evelyn chuckled as she replied, "It was busy and alive with all sorts of folks, but none of that compared to meeting Marcus and my grandbaby."

Tasha's hands started to get sweaty, so she went to pull them away, only to have the older woman hold them tighter in to her own.

"I know you loved my boy, but I was hoping to call you my daughter someday."

Tasha's chest tightened as Evelyn continued, "Seeing you today, I wanted to be sure to tell you that. I'm happy that you went out and saw the world, I truly am, but I can't help but wish things had been different."

"Me too." Tasha whispered.

### Jerome

Driving home to see his son after leaving the studio, Jerome took his time. With all the windows in his SUV open, he inhaled the crisp scent of clean air and enjoyed the little rays of sunshine that landed on his wrist as he waited at the red light. Driving past the plaza, Jerome thought he saw Evelyn's car parked outside The Seafood Shack.

*Should I surprise her by coming in and paying for her and her friends' lunch?*

Making a U-turn at the next light, Jerome pulled into the restaurant's parking lot and got out of his ride. Luckily, it was still early and not a lot of people were out, so he was able to step inside without being seen. Though once the doors closed behind him, Jerome wished there was a mob of fans waiting for him outside instead of the sight in front of him.

Seeing mama laugh as Tasha talked to her while they shared a seafood boil, Jerome went still. The two women were so caught up in whatever they were talking about that they didn't seem to notice anyone else around them. Jerome watched mama sign something to Tasha, who snorted, causing them to burst out laughing. He was too far away to hear what they were saying, but whatever Tasha said to mama next caused her face to soften. She then put more food on Tasha's plate, who beamed up at her.

*She's still beautiful.*

He didn't try to fight the memories of being with Tasha years ago as they rose to the front of his mind. The night they met, when she was working inside a food truck outside of Bottom's Up and threatened to call the law on him and several dudes from the bachelor party he'd attended. Jerome thought that was the last time he would be in her presence, but it was only the beginning.

Days later at Christ Corner, he found out that Senior, his daddy, had hired her to tutor the kids that went to their church. And after weeks of her standoffish behavior toward him, they became friends. To see her be so patient and passionate about tutoring her students, pouring encouragement into them, and having that extend to him at a time when everything and everyone seemed to be working against him, it didn't take long for his feelings to deepen. The two of them soon danced on the line of friends and something more, before he finally had to tell her how he felt.

Those months of being with Tasha were bliss. Not just kissing and holding her as often as he could, but the way she loved him then. Jerome never met anyone as fiercely loyal and protective as Tasha. With everything that she had to face, from being judged by everyone in town for her mama's sins to even Senior firing her after the congregation demanded it to save face - she still loved him completely. The day she allowed herself to lean on him and let him in fully... It shocked him to the core and left Jerome pleading with her to spend forever with him. Thoughts of their last night together, at the bed and breakfast out on Bejon Beach made him shiver with a need he'd almost forgotten he could have for another.

A strong gust of wind blasted Jerome out of his thoughts as more people entered the restaurant, and he took that as his cue to exit.

Not making eye contact with the small group that walked in, Jerome quickly marched to his SUV. Once inside and seated, he took a few deep breaths before starting the engine and gripping the steering wheel. His lungs burned for a drink, but Jerome couldn't put off going home much longer. Sofie had sent him several messages, and he knew what she was like when left waiting for too long.

Besides, his little man would be there, and Jerome promised himself that he would not drink around Ro. *I can do this. For him, I will bear all of this.*

Waiting for the red light to change, Tasha's face flashed before him as the light changed. The drive home was short and made him miss his old place across town something fierce.

As he was stepping out of his kicks, Jerome heard Sofie stomp toward him from behind. He hadn't turned around to face her before she demanded, "What the hell took you so long?"

"Hey Sofie." Jerome replied as cheerfully as he could.

"You ain't gonna answer my question?"

"Met new producers at the studio."

Sighing deeply, Jerome followed the sounds of his son in the den. His namesake was happily playing with a few scattered coloring blocks. Not wanting to argue with Sofie, Jerome sat down next to Ro and joined him in trying to stack the blocks on top of each other. Just as he placed the last one on the already wobbly tower, they all came crashing down. Ro's amused giggles erupted throughout their home. His wife's laughter followed as she walked over to them and for a brief moment Jerome locked eyes with Sofie. *When did things get like this between us?*

The two had first met backstage at his first concert after signing with the label. He thought that she looked as sad as he felt. So Jerome sat next to her after performing and asked her what she thought about his performance. Her reply surprised him.

"Why? If you think it was good then what I think shouldn't matter."

Curious, Jerome nodded, "Yeah, but I want to know."

Sofie then looked up at him and laughed. "Your lyrics are different but the beats sound just like everyone else's here. I say change that before whoever you trying to reach stop trying to hear you."

He then asked for her number and the two started dating soon after. It wasn't long before folks saw them out on dates around town whenever he was in between tours. Months went by and Jerome eventually began attending church with her.

Their wedding was quick and held at Christ Corner, just as Sofie had asked. No one suspected what his mama had asked the two directly. Jerome could still remember seeing the proud smile on Senior's face as he pronounced them husband and wife.

Jerome Earl Grant the third, arrived while Jerome was at a worship festival, two months earlier than expected. When he got the news, he dropped everything and took the next flight home to be by his wife's side. Him and Sofie lived at the hospital as they prayed for Ro to become healthy enough to come home.

They were a team then, inseparable.

Though once Ro's first birthday came and went, things changed. The hospital bills still needed to be paid and Ro was spending more and more time at his mother-in-law's house than with Sofie. Things were being said about his wife that Jerome didn't want to hear, so he welcomed touring again.

They hadn't slept in the same room or so much as held hands in well over a year, but Jerome didn't care. *As long as my namesake is taken care of, I'll continue to provide.*

# Chapter Six

## Closer

### Tasha

She couldn't catch a break.

Ximena's call was the first one Tasha got the next morning, and after her friend gave her the update about scoring tickets to the gala, she'd found herself wanting to go back to bed.

"Ximena, are you sure?" Tasha asked.

"Yes, I received the information directly from Paolo's assistant." Her stomach churned as Ximena confirmed the news, "All invitations have been sent out, and the one person on the list that we both know with additional tickets is Sebastian Gonzales."

Although they were somewhat friends from attending the same internship with Rebel Shots, Tasha hesitated to make contact with him for several reasons. Sebastian Gonzalez had become pretty popular, mostly for lingerie ads and boudoir shoots. So much so that he was highly sought after in Spain by many well-known agencies. But between his borderline creepy flirting and constant need to find a way to have others indebted to him, Tasha found herself not wanting to risk being caught in his sights, "It's not that I don't believe you, it's just, well, I was hoping it wasn't true."

"I know." Ximena agreed, "Remember, I've worked with him too in the past. And the whole time he was in pursuit of bedding me."

Tasha rolled her eyes, "And let me guess, when he realized he didn't have a chance in hell, he moved on to whichever model was still on set."

"Yes." Ximena confirmed before adding. "I spoke with him a moment ago."

"What did he say?" Tasha asked.

"He is going, but has not selected his entourage yet. Then he asked why I was calling him about it, and I explained that you would like to attend for networking purposes. Sebastian asked about you, and had me promise to tell you and I quote, 'My plus ones are either models or assistants.'"

"That snake ain't changed one dang bit!" Tasha spat out. "So, Sebastian will give us the tickets. As long as I agree to assist him with a shoot?"

"Exactly. He also said to tell you that he's looking forward to hearing from you soon."

"Oh, I bet Murica's finest sleaze is just lounging by the phone!"

Ximena's laughter rang through the line and Tasha joined her briefly before Ximena spoke again, "So you will call him? I know you would rather not, but he truly is our best chance."

Tasha sighed. "Yeah, I'll call him. Thanks Ximena."

Ending their call, she glanced out at the window and decided some fresh air was needed. Going to the front door, Tasha put on her shoes and grabbed the keys off the kitchenette counter.

In typical Southern fashion, the temperature continued to change, even as the sun shined outside. She had no plans for the day, after picking up the rental equipment she needed for the Woods Edge fundraiser, so Tasha decided to spend the day wandering around town. She almost passed by the bridal shop completely, but remembered that she would be meeting Alexa and Rachel there next week. Peering through the sales window, Tasha saw an associate putting a fully dressed mannequin on display when the one behind her caught her eye. Curious, she walked inside to get a look and fell in love with the dress on site.

Over the years, Tasha had assisted on several bridal and wedding shoots, but she had never paid much attention to the dresses, since most were never in her size. This floor length plus size dress, however, left her in a trance. With its simple yet sheer ivory flowy bottom, all her attention went to the three fourth sleeve arms. The weaving pattern displayed on the arms went down to the sides, allowing the rest of the fabric to flow freely. For a moment, Tasha wondered if there was a bodice inside the dress. Somehow, the garment looked soft, yet powerful, with the rest of the fabric being a shade lighter than the weaved sections around the waist. Tasha brought her eyes back up to the top of the dress as she reached out to touch the teasing material that was draped just slightly off the shoulders.

"Would you like to try it on?" Completely distracted with the dress, Tasha didn't notice as an associate came over to her.

Shaking her head, Tasha found herself asking out loud, "Who made these?"

"It's part of a collective by a new, local designer."

Hearing this, Tasha turned to the associate, "I'd like to buy it."

The clerk's eyes went from Tasha to the dress again before they asked, "Are you sure you do not want to try it on first?"

"Yes, I'm sure." Unable to take her eyes off of the dress, Tasha added, "Are there more dresses from the designer here?"

"Yes. If you will follow me, I would be happy to show them to you." The associate led Tasha further into the shop. "This is the rest of the collection."

"Thank you." Tasha almost whispered as she looked at the line of other full figured dresses now in front of her.

It was a small collection, but to Tasha, that felt intentional. As if they wanted the dresses to be part of something intimate. She was enthralled with the designer's work. Two more pieces piqued her interest, both varied in shades of off white and jade.

Though the one that took her breath away was the latter. Tasha had never seen such smooth satin before and that made her reach out to touch the fabric.

An image became clear in her mind, and before Tasha could tell herself no, she took out her phone and dialed Sebastian's number.

"Ah, gordita. You must have heard my thoughts." He smoothly crooned over the line.

Getting straight to the point, Tasha explained. "I'll be your assistant for one assignment."

"Three." Sebastian quickly countered, causing Tasha's left eye to twitch.

"Fine, two."

Sebastian laughed, "That is agreeable. And may I inquire why you wish to attend the gala this year, my sweet?"

Tasha rolled her eyes. "Ximena has kept me up to date on Pablo Coslado's works for years now and I want to meet him in person. Attending this gala is my chance to do that."

"Why on earth do you want to meet him?"

Tasha thought back to the last spread she saw of Pablo's activist work and answered. "I want to ask about collaborating with him for a future shoot."

"Tasha, Pablo works alone. And he is reckless in his pursuit during those shoots."

"I know. Those are just a few of the reasons why I want to meet him in person."

The associate returned and Tasha spoke to them again, "I would like these two dresses as well."

"Who are you talking to, gordita?" She heard Sebastian say as the clerk's eyes widened.

"Ma'am, these are not on sale."

She stared at the clerk. "I'll take them, along with the one I requested earlier."

The clerk nodded as they went to take the dresses to the front counter. "Tasha, where are you?" Sebastian asked.

"Shopping. And I've found three suitable dresses for the gala." She answered. "I have to go Sebastian. Thank you."

"Goodbye my gordita. I will see you in my dreams."

Tasha snorted. "Goodbye Sebastian"

Ending their call, Tasha went to the front counter and took out her business credit card. As she signed the receipt, the clerk asked cheerfully, "How would you like the dresses prepared for transport? "

In her awe of the garments, Tasha hadn't thought about how she was going to get them back to her suite. Thinking quickly, and remembering Alexa and Rachel's appointment with the shop being a few days away, Tasha asked, "Is it okay to come back later to collect them?"

The associate nodded as another clerk took the dresses to the back of the store.

THE REST OF THE WEEK went by so fast that before long Saturday arrived and she was out at the fairgrounds setting up her photo booth. Looking around at the Woods Edge fundraiser the following afternoon, Tasha found herself surprised at growing crowd.

There were more small businesses than she expected, each one setting up a booth for the outdoor event. A feeling of nostalgia from attending her first Christ Corner jamboree came over her, and Tasha ignored it as she picked up the tip box for the photo booth. Each person in charge of a booth had been given a box after signing in for the day, and told that an event volunteer would collect the boxes when each business signed out at the end of the day.

Tasha made sure to toss a few singles inside before she taking out the photo props booth with the boys. As she placed the last dollar in the box, Tasha felt eyes on her. *Guess it's time to put on a happy face.*

Turning around with a fixed smile in place, she wanted to leave at the sight of Jerome staring at her from across the field. At first she thought it was her mind playing tricks on her, but when he tilted his head and sent that still too familiar grin her way, she knew it was real. And his real presence, even from a distance, wreaked havoc on her entire body. Reminding herself to breathe, Tasha quickly looked away and tightly shut her eyes. *Come on! The boys will be back soon - get yourself together.*

She tried to think of something - anything else but the first man she let herself love. But after years of denying herself even a sneak peek of him online, her mind refused to listen to her request. Soon Tasha's body was facing his direction again, and seeing him hold a small boy in his arms, her chest grew tighter.

With her mouth now dry and a stinging sensation behind her eyes, Tasha's memories came to the surface in full force and without mercy. A series of their firsts whirled around in her mind, kisses, long embraces, days at the beach, his proposal... When flashes of the night she offered her body to him, along with a ring she had engraved promising her heart seared her mind, Tasha felt her eyes fill up with tears.

*Why did I come here? I should have known there was a chance he'd be here.*

From the distance, Jerome's smile faded and that was when she noticed the woman standing to his side. *Wasn't she the woman that was watching me at Devin's school last Friday?*

The shorter woman's back was to her as she kissed the little boy in Jerome's arms and Tasha's heart plunged to the bottom of her stomach. Before the woman turned around, Tasha finally found the strength to look away.

"Titi! We back!"

Hearing Darnell's voice, Tasha quickly wiped at her face and plastered the biggest smile as she could before looking at him and Devin. Trisha and Lloyd weren't too far behind, holding hands as they took in the growing crowd.

"Good!" Her voice felt raw as she went on, "There's a lot of folks here today, so I hope y'all are ready to be the best assistants ever!."

Devin hopped in front of her and shouted, "We are!"

"Alright, let's get started."

As she instructed the boys on where to place things, Lloyd took out his phone and snapped a few photos. "You ain't the only one that know how to use a camera!"

Seeing her sister glowing as she beamed over at her husband, Tasha felt a genuine smile spread across her face. Thankful for the distraction after seeing the last person she expected, she watched as Lloyd kissed Trisha's cheek.

*If he can make her happy, I guess I can give him a chance.*

Once the boys had placed the spare props box under the table and the blue markers where she asked, Tasha reached into her jeans and took out two ten-dollar bills. "Here's for helping me set up."

Devin and Darnell grinned as both of them reached out to take the money. "Thanks Titi!" they said in unison while Trisha inched closer.

"I'll hold on to this for y'all." Trisha said, reaching out for the bills.

Seeing Devin and Darnell's faces fall as Trisha collected their newfound wealth, Tasha shook her head at Trisha. "Why you do my babies like that Trish?"

"Girl! They don't need that money! You just like spoiling them." Trisha said.

As her sister wobbled away to sit and rest in one of the chairs for their booth, Tasha took out a twenty-dollar bill and whispered, "Y'all go and get something to eat before we start shooting, okay?"

From the corner of her eye, she noticed Lloyd narrowing his eyes on her, while the boys grinned.

"I can buy them something to eat." Lloyd said, as he looked directly at Tasha.

She tilted her head. "I didn't say you couldn't."

Tasha held his stare, until Darnell took his step daddy's hand, "Can we get cotton candy? Please?"

Lloyd smiled down at him. "Alright, but just one. Don't want ya teeth to fall out."

He turned his back to Tasha as he led the boys away from the booth. With the boys gone, Tasha joined her sister and took a seat and the two sat in comfortable silence, watching everyone else finish setting up. Though when Tasha glanced at Trisha, she couldn't help but notice how deep in thought her sister was. Trying not to worry, but wanting to check in, Tasha asked, "Everything okay?"

Trisha slowly turned to her. "If you thought you'd forgiven someone for something and moved on...what would you do if you found out they had more secrets?"

She thought over what Trisha had asked her, and Tasha's mind went to the odd remark Lloyd made about buying the boys' lunch. *Did he do some foul mess and Trish found out about it?*

"I'd move on because it's clear that they don't care about me, if all they keep doing is hurting me." Looking her baby sister in the eye, Tasha continued, "No matter what they've done since then, or how happy I was with them won't matter anymore either. Because when it's all said and done, they've shown me that no matter what that they can't be trusted."

Trisha nodded slowly before going to find the kids, leaving Tasha alone. Soon, some folks started to show up and she went to work. As the first group left, the boys returned, and Devin did not look like his normal cheerful self. Before another person showed up wanting their picture taken, Tasha asked him, "D, you okay?"

She was not prepared for the tears that appeared on his face. Worried, Tasha sat him down in the nearest chair and waited for his hiccups to cease. "Sydney said you don't love me!"

"Sydney? Who is Sydney, baby?" Tasha asked calmly.

"She from my class. She said you only being nice cause you gonna leave again. Because you don't really love me."

Sitting in the chair across from her nephew, Tasha turned to face him. "Devin, I love you more than every star in the sky, you know that."

"Then why you gotta leave?!"

Tasha's heart broke as she heard the pain in his voice. "I love my job too, Devin. It makes me happy. And even when I'm away, it don't mean that I don't love you. Do you know how much I love you?"

Devin looked up at her and sniffled. "I love you so much that I can see you, even when I'm far away from you."

Hearing this, he scoffed, "You can't see me if I'm far away, Titi."

As the younger boy rolled his eyes and huffed, Tasha explained, "What I mean is, wherever I go, I carry memories of you. Right here." Pointing to her chest, Tasha gently continued. "One time, when I was working, there was this really big waterfall not too far behind me. While I was shooting, I could have sworn that I heard you laugh."

Devin's eyes widened. "Really?"

Tasha nodded, "Yep. After the shoot ended, I went to that waterfall. You know what I saw?"

"What did you see, Titi?"

As she thought back on that memory, Tasha's eyes stung. Blinking quickly, she took Devin's hands in to hers. "I saw a group of little boys, about a year younger than you are now. They were laughing while taking turns pushing each other into the shallow end of the waterfall. Hearing their laughter that day reminded me of how you would laugh when we watched cartoons together on Saturday mornings."

That was during one of her first solo assignments, and Tasha remembered capturing a few shots of the kids playing in the waterfall that day. Making sure to play with the depth of field so none of the boys' faces were clear in the photos, Tasha shared her favorite ones on her website. 'Familiar Falls' was the title she chose for the collection.

"So even when you and I are apart, we are always connected D." she finished.

He seemed to think over what Tasha shared with him. "Okay. But Titi, I like you here."

"I like being here with you." Tasha said.

Seeing another group of people making their way toward the photo booth, Tasha stood.

"And the last time you left - you didn't tell us. Mama was really sad."

Tasha's eyes widened as Devin shared that information with her. "I'm really sorry Devin. I didn't mean to make everyone sad."

As he nodded, Tasha could see that he was not done, "Okay. You can leave again. But tell us when you do, okay?"

She saw the seriousness in Devin's eyes and nodded. "I won't leave without telling y'all. I promise."

Devin looked at Tasha before jumping out of his chair and giving her a hug.

# Chapter Seven

## Cheap Shots

### Jerome

The last thing Jerome wanted was to perform while being home, but here he was, getting ready to go out to some last minute fundraiser. All because Sofie called him while he was in a meeting with his producers at the label.

A week ago, the producers overheard his call and when asked if everything was okay, Jerome chose to tell them about the phone call instead of answering the question. "That was my wife. My son's school reached out to her to ask if I could perform for their fundraiser next weekend."

Jimmy was more excited than he normally was, and that should have been Jerome's first hint that he was about to be dragged into something he did not want. "That's a great idea! Gives you a chance to test out the new tracks in front of an audience."

As Jimmy reached out for his phone, Terrence asked Jerome, "Is this something you want to do?"

"What do you mean 'does he want to'?" Jimmy said before adding, "Why would he not?"

"Well, for one, we don't know what kind of audience he'll be in front of, and two, Jerome just got back from touring for a year. Maybe he wants to spend more time with his family before getting back on stage."

Jerome glanced over at Terrence and raised his head slightly in the younger man's direction.

"Good looking out Tech, but it's cool. I can do the show, if the label says it's alright," he said

"See? He wants to do it." Jimmy looked at Terrence once more before grinning at Jerome. "

The older man stuck his hand out toward Jerome and he took it, shaking it with his own.

"For now, just go home to the family and rest, okay?" Jimmy told him.

Jerome stood up to leave and as he reached the door to the office, Jimmy called out to him, "Oh, please shut the door when you leave. I want to talk to Terrence here privately."

They arrived at the outdoor event that Saturday as everything was kicking off and Sofie took his hand as they walked through the crowd. "See, ain't you glad I thought to ask you about performing?"

Even though he wasn't on board at first for this event, the more time he spent outside, the more he started to change his initial thoughts. It did feel good to be out, and as he looked down at little Ro in his arms, Jerome smiled. The sun was shining and for the first time since he'd been home, Jerome's stomach wasn't all tied up in knots about things out of his control. For the last year, all he did was think about how what the label seemed to want from him as an artist was entirely different from what he had envisioned for himself. Jerome wondered if this was truly the path that the Lord meant for him. He was going along with what was given to him, and the more Jerome thought about it, the more he knew that that had to change.

*I'll talk with Jimmy and the team next week.*

Sofie let go of his hand the minute she spotted some of her friends hanging out near a temporary tattoo booth, and he continued to stroll around the grounds. It didn't take long for him to begin thinking back to Christ Corner's jamboree. This event must have been inspired by it, because other than the small rides, everything else seemed to be set up almost the same way. His career then was nowhere near where it was now, but those times were simpler. Jerome would be lying if he said that he didn't miss those days. Though at this moment, he enjoyed being just a man out with his family. Jerome tried to soak up as much of the new feeling as he could before his performance.

Until he saw her again.

Tasha's hair was more muted than it was back in the day, with the exception of a few aqua blues and lilac purples that he saw peeking out from behind her large bun. Tasha stood in front of a booth, with a serene look on her face as she stared off into the crowd. Her deep brown skin shone, showing off her full face and cheeks, so much so that Jerome couldn't look away. And he was glad that he hadn't, because he would have missed her turning around and pausing when she spotted him. The look on her face changed several times, from shock to awe, before she whipped her head away. *Please turn back around. Please.*

God must have been in a giving mood, as Tasha slowly faced him again. With his heart elated just to make eye contact with her, after so much time had passed, Jerome didn't try to fight the smile that stretched across his face. Seeing a soft smile on Tasha's, Jerome willed himself to not walk over to her.

The moment ended when the sight of his wife caught his eye. Sofie placed a kiss on top of Ro's head and dark waves of shame thrashed around in his mind from the pull Tasha still had on heart. He knew Sofie was not the love of his life, but she was his wife. And he vowed to honor her, no matter what. Forcing his feelings down into the box he'd kept them in, Jerome cleared his throat. "What do you want to do first?"

"One of my girls said there's a photobooth here, so let's do that."

Panic raced like chilled iced water into his veins after hearing Sofie's suggestion. The last thing he wanted was for his wife to meet Tasha. But more than that, the last place he knew he should be was anywhere near Tasha.

He didn't even have a chance to try and get her to change her mind, as Sofie had already removed Ro from his arms and made a beeline for the photo area. He had to jog to keep up with her, almost falling as she came to a sudden stop. Jerome was about to ask her what was wrong until he saw Tasha talking to a few kids with props in their hands. He and Sofie never talked about his dating history, but from the look on Sofie's face, it was evident that she was well aware of his and Tasha's past.

"We could just take a few selfies. It'd be better than waiting in that line." Jerome tried to suggest, but it didn't look like she was listening.

Sofie dragged Jerome into the line and he spent their time waiting making funny faces with Ro, who giggled. Every so often, he would look up to see Tasha and observe her as she took photos and interacted with each group of people in front of them. He also noticed two little boys at her station again and wondered if they were the nephews she used to tell him about before Sofie tugged on his shirt, distracting him from his thoughts.

"We're next." She said.

**SOFIE**

Once she and Jerome made it to the front of the line, Sofie gripped his shoulder tightly and waited for Tasha to say something. When the woman finally noticed them, she paused for a moment before speaking, "Hi! Three for the shoot?"

Seeing the woman wearing a pair of sneakers and still being taller than her, Sofie found herself wishing that she'd worn heels to this function. Sizing up her husband's ex, Sofie took note of the short yet baggy yellow t-shirt over a white tank top with what looked like a camera lens drawn on it in black ink. Tasha also wore a pair of jeans that hugged her fuller figure. Sofie's eyes zoomed in on the sight of the round print from her stomach that was on display. Her attention then went to the little boy from Woods Edge as he walked over toward Tasha and said, "Titi, they too big for props."

She watched as Tasha looked at the boy and smiled. "No one is too old to have a little fun, D. Please bring me the bin."

"Good to see you Tasha."

*Oh? So he ain't gonna pretend not to know her?*

Sofie refused to glance up at her husband, wanting to see Tasha's reaction to him instead.

"Y-you too Jerome." Tasha finally said.

Finally, Sofie's curiosity won out and she took a peek behind her shoulder to see him and Ro staring at Tasha. She kept her sights on Jerome while waiting for the woman in front of her to say more. Instead, Tasha's attention went to Sofie as she spoke. "I'm Tasha. Nice to meet you."

Sofie let go of Jerome's arm and stepped away from Tasha to peer into the bin that the boy had brought over. Reaching out with her left hand, she grabbed a crown and tiara, flashing them in front of Jerome. "Baby, let's wear these for the shoot. That's how this works, right?"

Tasha's smile didn't reach her eyes and Sofie wanted to cackle as she heard the woman's high pitched voice over the crowd and music around them, "Exactly! You pick the props, we take the shots."

Another little boy, sitting next to the table and TV screen of the booth laughed, "Titi said it again D!"

Not seeing what was so funny, Sofie asked out loud, "What's wrong with that one?"

"Nothing wrong with my brother!" The boy next to Tasha said.

Jerome leaned down to whisper into Sofie's ear, "That's the name of their booth."

Turning to face him, Sofie almost said more until her eyes looked over his head. There was a sign that read, Props and Shots: T.D.D Photography.

"Oh. Well, I ain't know that." Sofie said.

Seeing Tasha smile widely at her, Sofie felt her face get hot as she narrowed her eyes at the woman.

"Let's get started. Please follow my assistant to your markers and I'll take your photos."

The boy next to Tasha walked in front of them and stopped a few feet in front of the light blue curtain. Sofie was about to tell him to fix his face, as he continued to frown while waiting for her to walk over, but Ro started to get fussy in Jerome's arms. "Give me my baby."

She reached out and took her son from Jerome's arms. Tasha spoke again, this time from behind a tripod. "Here comes the test shot!"

A bright flash left Sofie seeing spots and the boy near the monitor laughed.

"What the hell?" Sofie said.

She was more than a little agitated, and it must have shown as Jerome then placed his hand around her waist, pulling her in closer. Normally she would have told him to move around, but seeing Tasha's smug face drop from behind the camera, Sofie grinned instead.

"It's just a practice shot, so she can get the aperture and lighting right for the next photos."

The little boy tilted his head up to Jerome and asked, "How you know that?"

Sofie turned to look at Jerome, putting the crown onto his head, "Yeah, baby, how do you know that?"

Neither of them got an answer to their question as Tasha called out, "Okay! In 3...2...1!"

This time Sofie was ready for the flash from the big white domes that surrounded them. Or so she thought. Ro chose then to tug on her crown, dragging it slightly over her face as the lights flashed. No one spoke as Tasha moved from around the tripod. "You can view your pictures on the screen in just a few minutes."

*She ain't serious!*

"We have to do it again. Those shots ain't gonna come out good." Sofie blurted out.

The little boy looked up at her and pointed to the sign across from the curtain.

**Each group is allowed three shots, including the test shot.**

**Additional shots can be arranged by scheduling a private session at a later date.**

"We ain't know all that!" Sofie said, "And besides, ain't the customer always right?"

"No!"

Sofie's eyes flared as she looked down at the little boy.

"Devin, find your manners." Tasha said sternly.

Sofie looked between the two as the young boy scowled and pointed at her, "This lady started it!"

"And if you keep getting in grown folks' business, I'mma finish it too little boy!"

As Sofie went to hover over Devin, she didn't notice Tasha making her way toward them. Tasha's eyes leveled onto Sofie's while she ushered the boy to stand behind her. Sofie then felt Jerome's hand on her shoulders as they stood face to face. Tasha's voice was low, but even, "As the adult, you should lead by example and show the child how to resolve conflict. Not threaten them."

"Ohhhh! Titi's mad!"

Sofie's jaw dropped as she watched Tasha soften her face before turning to look at the younger boy with a grin. With her hand on the other child's shoulders, Tasha led him away and to the table. "Titi's not mad Darnell, just talking to the pretty lady, that's all."

*She thinks I'm pretty?*

Jerome interrupted her thoughts as he took Ro from out of her arms. "Let's see how the photos turned out, okay?"

Letting him lead her toward the monitor, Sofie tapped her foot as she waited for the photos to appear on the screen. When their images showed up, she wanted to knock over the entire setup. The test shot photo was easily the best one, as in the second photo Ro's hands covered her face and in the third picture, she wasn't even looking at the camera. Instead, all she saw was Jerome smiling directly ahead and her baby gripping the tiara with a smile on his face.

Sofie's eyes narrowed as she turned to look at Tasha. "We ain't paying for those!"

Tasha sighed as she met Sofie's glare. "I'm here as a volunteer. Any tips received go to Woods Edge Elementary to help them meet their funding goal for the next school year."

Jerome then reached into his pocket to take out his wallet, and Sofie's eyes were as big as saucers when she saw him place fifty dollars into the tip box. "Why are you giving them that much money?!"

"It's not for them, it's for the school." Jerome said.

Sofie understood what he was saying, but she couldn't help but add, "You're donating by performing later at this little event. You don't have to give them no money!"

"It's for a good cause. And every bit helps." Jerome told Sofie.

"Mister, you really a performer?" the little boy asked.

Jerome kneeled in front of him and smiled. "Yeah, I'm JPK."

They watched as the boy looked up at Jerome and asked blankly. "Who?"

A snort could be heard off in the distance, and Sofie knew it came from Tasha. Grabbing Jerome's hand, she dragged him away from the photo booth.

Still fuming over what happened back at the photo booth, Sofie loudly complained. "Can you believe how that little boy talked to me?" Thinking back to seeing Tasha's glare as she stepped in between them earlier, Sofie rolled her eyes. "I shouldn't be surprised, since your *friend* is known for her attitude."

When he didn't respond, Sofie's glare zeroed on him buying cotton candy from the nearby vendor. Jerome tore a smaller piece off and gave it to Ro before turning to face her. "You ain't hear a word I just said!"

"Sofie, please calm down. If you really want to take some family photos, I can get us a photographer and schedule a session. Okay?" He suggested. Once they walked away from the cotton candy stand, they found a small empty bench to sit at while Ro reached his tiny hands out for more of the treat.

"Did you know she would be here?" Sofie asked hotly.

Jerome looked at her and his shoulders dropped. "No, I didn't know."

She squinted her eyes at him and sighed. One more question was on repeat in her mind, so Sofie asked Jerome, "Well, did you know your little *friend* was back in town in the first place?"

"Yeah, I did." he answered.

*Why he couldn't lie like other dudes?*

Fuming, she hissed, "And you ain't think to tell me?"

Jerome looked around before explaining. "I haven't seen Tasha in years, Sofie. The only reason why I know she's in town is because mama had lunch with her last week. That's it."

Hearing him mention Evelyn set her teeth on edge. Unlike Senior, Evelyn never warmed up to her and Sofie always felt like she was on trial anytime she was in the same room as the older woman.

"Of course she's having lunch with ya mama! That woman don't like me no way." Sofie scoffed. "Bet they just out here talking about me like a bunch of -"

Jerome cut his eyes at her before she could say another word. "Mama ain't like that, and you know it. Don't sit there and act like she been mean to you, when all mama has done is try to spend time getting to know you and Ro."

Rolling her eyes, Sofie decided to keep quiet, for now. After Jerome ate the rest of the cotton candy, they took turns making silly faces and laughing as Ro tried to mimic them. When his phone beeped, Jerome stood. "I gotta go."

She watched as Jerome headed backstage. Now alone, Sofie held her son a little tighter. *He's with you, not her. You the one wearing the ring Senior gave Evelyn - not her ass.*

"Hey girl!"

Looking up, Sofie saw Regine, with Buckem walking toward her. 'Hey sis! What are y'all doing here?"

"Hey Sofie. You looking real good." Buckem drawled out.

Sofie wished she'd worn a longer dress as she felt Buckem eyeing her figure.

"Oh, a few artists from the label are performing and we wanted to show some love, right baby?" Regine said, wrapping her arms around Buckem's bicep.

"Yeah, yeah." was all he said as glanced at Sofie one last time before sitting down on the opposite side of the bench.

Sofie turned around to face the main stage, praying that Jerome would hurry up and do his set so she could leave. A hype man came out and spoke into the mic, "Y'all feeling alright?"

As the crowd cheered, he continued, "Good! Make sure to share the love at them tip boxes, located at each booth, so we can get new school supplies for the kids at Woods Edge Elementary. Can't leave nan child behind, ya heard?"

A few folks in the crowd cheered before the hype man spoke again, "Coming up to perform some tracks for y'all is another local fave. Now, he ain't as fly as me, but y'all show him some love anyway. Give it up for JPK!"

After he announced Jerome, more people started sprinting toward the main stage.

"Damn, they really feeling this dude like that? He ain't even start yet." Buckem mumbled.

"That's cause they ain't heard your new tracks baby." Regine purred, leaning into Buckem and planting a kiss on his lips.

Sofie wished she hadn't looked back at the two of them, as it took all she had to not gag.

*She stay doing the most!*

Jerome walked onto the stage, mic in hand. "How y'all doing?"

More shouts could be heard as he continued. "Before we start, let me lead us all into prayer right quick, alright?"

As the crowd grew silent, Sofie saw Buckem from the corner of her eye looking around in disbelief. "What kind of rapper does this shit?"

"Heavenly Father, we come here today to sing your praise and share your word. Please look over everyone here today, as well as those that could not be. Thank you for your many blessings and for guiding us to do your will. Amen."

Buckem laughed as the bass line to the first song blared through the large speakers near the stage. Sofie said nothing as more people made their way to the stage for Jerome's performance. The first song was a fan fave, as the crowd rapped along with Jerome. She found herself smiling as her husband sprinted around the stage, jumping up and down with his fans. When the song ended, Jerome continued to talk to the crowd. "Y'all still with me?"

The shouts and clapping that came from the folks in the crowd grabbed Ro's attention, as he started clapping.

"Aww! You like seeing your daddy onstage?" Sofie cooed, as Jerome began another track.

The crowd continued clapping as Jerome rapped over the beat. Some started to walk away, but most of them nodded along. She didn't know much about music, but Sofie could feel the vibe change as the next track began. The intro was slow, with a solid beat that had an old school choir sound blended over it. The crowd seemed to like it as well. Sofie watched the fans closest to the stage start to stomp their feet and clap even harder. But before Jerome could get a word out, Buckem shot up from the bench, startling her and Ro. "Aye! That's my beat!"

Both Sofie and Regine turned to look at him. "Baby, what you mean?" Regine asked.

"Bitch - you know I been working on my album in the studio! I just did a track with this same damn sound!"

Regine went silent, glancing over at Sofie as Buckem left the bench and took out his phone. They watched as he started recording the rest of Jerome's performance, shouting and cursing over the music.

"Move muthaf-" Before Buckem could get closer to the stage, security flanked him and one of them snatched his phone out of his hand.

"You can let us escort you off the grounds, or we'll radio in the city dogs." The beefier of the guards told Buckem.

Buckem spat out, "I'm good! I don't need no damn escort."

They all watched as the security guard handed Buckem back his phone and he turned around to leave.

"Thank y'all so much! God bless!"

Buckem stopped walking when he heard Jerome's voice again. He sneered up toward the stage before lowering his head and spitting on the ground, just as Regine rushed to his side.

Holding her breath until she could no longer see them in her sight, Sofie picked up her son and sprinted to the backstage area to wait for Jerome.

**Jerome**

His body still hummed with excitement from being out in front of the crowd as Jerome walked backstage. Though with everything that went down before he took the stage, it was hard to tell why he felt like a live wire. Pushing thoughts of Tasha's face from his mind, Jerome chose to focus on the response from the crowd after his set. A backstage assistant handed him a towel and a bottle of water, both he accepted.

*Maybe these new verses ain't all that bad. Thank you Lord!*

Wiping his face, Jerome continued walking from the stage as he guzzled down water from the plastic bottle. Once he made his way from behind the stage, he found Sofie waiting with Ro in her arms and taking deep breaths. He almost jokingly asked her if she'd been on stage with him until he saw the panic in her eyes. "What's wrong?" he asked.

"Nothing. Just ready to go."

He wanted to do as she asked, but something in her eyes gave him pause. "Sofie, what is it? Did something happen?"

The way her eyes shifted around at everyone except him told Jerome more than her words could. And after looking over toward Ro and seeing that he wasn't hurt, he leaned in close to Sofie before whispering, "Tell me what is wrong. Now Sofie, before Ro picks up your vibes."

She looked up at him and parted her lips before closing them and looking around again. Just as he was about to say more, Sofie hissed, "Buckem. He showed up, talking crazy about your last song. Security made him leave."

Jerome fought not to roll his eyes while tilting his head to the clouds. *This is exactly why I don't want to go to that album release party!*

With everything going on at the label, Jerome knew it'd be better to keep his distance until absolutely necessary. Pulling Sofie close, he tried to reassure her. "I'll handle it. Don't worry."

Folks were snapping pictures on their phones, but security kept anyone from getting too close. He watched as Sofie smiled while shielding Ro from most of the commotion and they quickly exited the outdoor event. To everyone watching, she looked fine, but Jerome noticed how she swept the space in their immediate sight. The whole time security followed close, Jerome kept his hand to the small of her back, ushering them to their SUV. Once security cleared their vehicle, Jerome watched Sofie put Ro in his car seat before opening her passenger side door and waiting for her to put on the seatbelt. He had only been on the road for a few minutes when his phone began to chime back to back again, but with his son in the car and Sofie now on mute, Jerome ignored the messages coming through.

They made it home and Jerome remained in the driver's seat as he watched as Sofie stepped out of the car and headed to the backseat to take Ro out of his car seat. As she carried Ro to the front door without him, Sofie stopped. "You ain't coming?"

"I'll be back. Go inside."

He watched as the two went inside the house before driving away. Checking his phone, Jerome saw that the messages were alerts from his social media accounts. Folks were tagging him about a new artist who accused him of using their beats during today's performance. Jerome felt a headache coming on, so he deleted the apps from his phone and made a reminder for himself to start looking for an assistant. Sofie had been on him to get one since last year, but with him being on tour, he didn't see the need for one. Though the constant pinging of his phone told him otherwise.

Just the thought of asking the label to help him find someone to work as his assistant, even for a short period of time, made Jerome roll his eyes. And with the way his current album was going, he didn't want someone else on staff that could report his every move to the higher ups at Trap Sons. Gripping the steering wheel, he kept his eyes on the road. *Who else do I know that could help me find someone?*

Immediately, Jerome's mind went to Tech, the kid he met at the label. Thankful to have gotten his number earlier that month while recording in the booth, Jerome put his phone on speaker while rolling up the windows before calling Tech. After a few rings, he answered.

"What's up? This Terrence."

"Terrence? Tech, it's JPK." Jerome said as he continued, "I wanted to reach out about a favor. But if it's too short notice, I understand."

"Oh, word? So you ain't mad at me for saying your new sound needs work?"

Thinking back to their last chat, Jerome chuckled, "You weren't wrong, so nah, I ain't mad. Like I said, I know you still busy, working with the label and all but-"

Terrence interrupted his explanation. "Nah, I ain't. Not anymore."

"What you mean?"

He listened as Terrence scoffed over the line, "Well, after your run in with ole Jimmy boy, he had a talk with me. Told me to pack my stuff and leave, since I 'challenged his authority' in front of you."

"What? I ain't know I was putting you in a spot, my bad."

*Just how did Jimmy come to that thought?*

From what he could remember, nothing about the conversation they had together didn't come close to the reason Jimmy gave Terrence for letting him go. Jerome let out a frustrated sigh.

"It's all good. I can get another job."

Jerome quickly continued. "That's actually what I was calling you about. I'm looking for an assistant. Think you could help me out?"

# Chapter Eight

## Messy Folks

### Sofie

She heard Jerome come home hours later and sighed. Buckem didn't cut up as much as Sofie knew he could, but she saw how Buckem looked at Jerome while he was on stage. Part of her wished that she never brought up performing at the fundraiser in the first place. Thoughts of receiving a call in the middle of the night from the law or the hospital saying that Jerome had been hurt left her unable to sleep.

It had been years since Sofie had those kinds of thoughts, not since Ro was born. Being in the hospital and watching her son fight for his next breath, Sofie felt as if her baby was paying for all of her sins. While waiting for word from Jerome, she begged the staff to let her stay with him. Hours went by as she stared down at her tiny child. It was seeing all the monitors around him flashing and beeping that brought Sofie to her knees.

"Lord, I know you and I don't get down like that, but please, if you save my baby, I promise to be everything he needs as a mama."

Sofie felt strong hands on her shoulders. Looking up into Jerome's eyes, she finally let out all the fear and pain that held her captive for the last few days as she threw herself into his arms, sobbing. With Jerome by her side Sofie saw a new side to him, one she saw as a sign that the Lord was answering her prayer. He took care of Sofie when she was discharged and they both prayed for Ro until he finally was released from the hospital. She thought things would get better, that was until the local news reported their story in the paper. Soon after, the streets began talking about things Sofie thought she had left behind her.

She knew Jerome heard what was being said, but he never questioned her about any of it, and Sofie thanked the Lord for that. In hopes of keeping the promise that she made in the hospital, she stayed home and focused on caring for her son. Though after Ro's first birthday, Sofie's past found her once again, as she came to miss the touch of a man that she knew would never be hers. With Jerome always on the road, seeing Patrick whenever she wanted was easy. And it felt good to have somebody make her toes curl on the regular. Until she would wake up after having him spend the night to find that he'd already left.

Sofie did like Jerome, but as the months turned into years, telling him the truth just didn't seem right. *He ain't never shared stuff from his past, so why should I?*

Though it was only a matter of time before folks from Christ Corner started talking. And once they started whispering about her, they never stopped. Which made not going to service all that much easier. Especially after her last time in attendance.

She thought back to being in the restroom after attending service for the first time, how she heard two older women mention her as they washed their hands. Sofie was just about to leave her stall until one of the ladies loudly whispered, "It's a shame what happened to her sister though! I can't imagine having to commit my baby for trying to take their own life - Lawd!"

Her hand trembled on the stall's door as the two women tsked and continued their conversation.

"Well, when you live the way she did, it was only a matter of time 'fore the devil calls you home."

"Hush yo mouth!" the other woman said.

"You know I speak the truth! And my grandbabies say that this Sofie ended up with the man who drove her sister crazy before she got with Junior."

Sofie's heart started pounding so hard in her chest that she thought it would crack open.

"Say what y'all will about that Daye girl, but at least she wasn't that fast - or foolish."

Once they dried off their hands and left the restroom, Sofie slowly opened her stall. Bloodshot eyes glared back at her from the mirror but she refused to let a tear fall. Snatching a paper towel from the wire basket in between the two sinks, Sofie gently patted under her eyes, taking care to not smear her makeup. Shallow, hot breaths came from her nose as she placed her hands on the cool countertop.

*These folks ain't no different! I should have known better...*

When her heartbeat finally slowed down, Sofie walked out of the restroom and plastered the biggest smile on her face. Now that she knew what they really thought about her, Sofie knew what game to play and she played it well. As soon as she reached Evelyn's side, Sofie took Ro from her arms and made up a lie about having to get home to prepare for Jerome's return. She felt all the women stare at her as they nodded. While walking out of the church, each step felt shaky. It wasn't until she put Ro into his carseat did she feel the wetness on her face.

*Damn gossip folks worse than folks in these streets!*

Shaking away the memory, Sofie finally drifted off to sleep.

**Jerome**

Deciding to spend some time with his son, Jerome made his way to Ro's room, only to find Sofie already there. She was wearing a long sleeved maroon dress that went well with her deep brown skin. "Morning. You look nice."

"Thank you." Sofie replied quietly.

He looked on as Sofie tended to their son and for a moment Jerome thought that maybe this was the change they needed to become closer. As her husband, he was ready to provide no matter what, but over these last few weeks Jerome found himself ready to take a break from touring, at least until the next album was complete.

*Is it too soon to think about us giving Ro some siblings?*

Jerome longed to have a big family, one that was full of love and joy. He smiled as he thought of the possibility of finally working toward making that come true.As Sofie finished putting on Ro's slacks, Jerome noticed the bow tie that she had clipped to his button white tee matched her dress and he smiled as he left to get dressed. After having a quick breakfast, Jerome drove them to Christ Corner.

Mama made sure to save them a seat and as they walked to the first pew, Jerome could have sworn he saw mama look at Sofie and frowned. But by the time he looked between the two of them to see why that would be the case, his mama was smiling, as Ro reached out for her. Sofie said nothing as their son waddled to mama and Jerome was thankful.

"Well, if it ain't my favorite daughter-in-law!"

Hearing Senior's booming voice, Jerome turned to face his daddy.

"It's good to see you too!" Sofie said as she accepted a hug from Senior.

A few members close by paused to watch the interaction, and Jerome decided to join mama in the first pew. When Sofie finally sat down, music began to play, signaling the start of service.

TWO DAYS LATER, HE received a call from Raven, Trap Sons' Public Relations director, requesting he stop by. *How could they already know I hired Terrence?*

He'd hoped to keep that news under the radar, mainly because he didn't feel the need to explain his decision. But as he put on his jeans and made his way downstairs to lace up his kicks, that's exactly what he thought he'd be doing.

Once Jerome arrived at Trap Sons thirty minutes later, he scanned the main conference room and tried to keep his surprise in check when he saw the empty chairs at the long table.

"Morning Jerome." Turning to the sound of Raven's voice, he forced a small smile on his face before walking toward the woman. "Thank you for being on time, I promise not to keep you long."

"Thank you."

"Please, follow me." she instructed, leading Jerome toward the smaller meeting room across from the main conference area. *Maybe they have something to talk with me about?*

When Raven sat next to the husky man wearing red-rimmed glasses, Jerome did the same, choosing a seat across from them at the small table.

"Let's get to it, shall we?" Raven said evenly before continuing, "First things first, congrats on your recent fundraiser performance. Now, onto your label mate Buckem's reaction and its aftermath."

Jerome listened on as the Public Relations director filled him in on what Buckem did during and after his performance last weekend. "So far your fanbase has not wavered, and we would like to keep it that way."

He gave Raven his full attention as he asked, "What do you need me to do?"

She turned to look at her assistant as they used a controller to turn on the screen. Jerome stared at the photos that Tasha took of them from the fundraiser, as well as several other photos, ranging from what looked like shots straight out of a science fantasy movie to more normal photos of people in different parts of the world.

"We've done some digging into the woman who ran the booth last weekend and would like to hire her to shoot your next magazine spread." Raven said. "We think it would be a good collaboration, seeing that she is also another local that went on to pursue their dreams and is now doing well in the photography field."

Jerome continued looking at the photos in front of him and felt a small smile grow across his lips. *Did Tasha really take all those pictures?*

"Were you and Ms. Tasha Daye ever close?"

Hearing the question brought him back to the present, and Jerome kept his eyes on the screen as he answered, "We were friends up until she left."

Raven nodded. "Great! Do you think she'll be willing to work with us for the shoot?"

With his heart hopping around in his chest, Jerome chose his next words carefully. "I haven't seen Tasha in years, so I don't know if she would help."

Raven pressed her lips together as she looked over the notes on the table in front of her. "I was hoping my intel got that part wrong." She then leveled her eyes at Jerome, "We have been able to get in touch with one of her contacts overseas, and they more or less said what you just shared."

The more Raven looked at Jerome, the more he fought the urge to leave. "Could you at least ask her? Perhaps she would consider the shoot, for an old friend?"

Feeling every bit exposed under Raven's gaze, Jerome spoke again, "I don't have her number. And as far as I know, Tasha don't work with rappers."

Raven's assistant quickly said, "Didn't she shoot the photos for your first album?"

Jerome blinked a few times, until his memories of that day were shoved back into the deep pockets of his mind. "Y-yeah, she did."

As Raven glanced at Jerome again, she took out a pen and quickly wrote onto a small sheet of paper. "The contact we were able to find gave us her cell phone number. Please consider reaching out to Ms. Daye to see if she would be willing to work with us."

She slid the slip of paper across the table to him. Looking down at the paper, Jerome quietly folded it in half before putting it in his front pocket.

"Okay."

On his way home, Jerome thought back to his meeting with Raven and how eager they were for him to get Tasha on board for this magazine shoot. Jerome knew the odds were stacked against him, but a part of him wanted to reach out to Tasha, if for nothing else than to hear her voice again after all these years. Cutting the engine as he parked the car, Jerome reached into his pocket and pulled out the slip of paper with Tasha's number on it as he went inside. Hearing the first ring, Jerome almost ended the call.

"Hi."

Reminding himself to breath, Jerome quickly spoke, "Hey Tasha."

Silence fell over the line before she asked, "Jerome? Is this you?"

"Um, yeah. My people at Trap Sons asked me to reach out to you." When she said nothing, he kept talking, "They set up a shoot for me with a magazine and wanted me to ask if you could do it."

"Oh. Well, um, I really don't know much about shooting for the music industry."

Thinking back to his album cover, he said, "I'm in entertainment, and you did my album cover."

Silence filled the line again and Jerome thought he overstepped until he heard Tasha's voice again. "You were the first and the last, Jerome."

It was short, but Jerome could have sworn that the atmosphere changed a little as her sentence lingered. Clearing his throat, Jerome said, "That's what I thought too, so I'll let the label know." Pressing his lips together, Jerome added, "Before I let you go, I also want to say sorry about what happened last weekend."

"Don't worry about it, Jerome. I doubt I'd be all that cool about my husbands' ex taking our family pictures either."

Not missing a beat, Jerome jokingly asked, "So, are you saying that we did date? Cause I was there and I don't even know if we did or not."

"I see you learned how to tell a joke over the years! Good for you."

A grin spread across his face as Jerome heard Tasha laugh. It was a sound he thought that he would never hear again, and Jerome welcomed it. Though soon Sofie's scowl flashed across his mind, and he knew it was time to end the call. But he had to ask Tasha just one last time about the shoot, "I learned all kinds of things over the years. Maybe you can learn something new too and work with me for this photoshoot?"

He listened to her sigh. "Thank you again for reaching out, but I gotta pass."

Deciding that it was time to let her go, Jerome spoke one last time. "Okay. It was good to talk with you Tasha."

"You too Jerome, Take care."

**Tasha**

Taking her therapist's advice from their last session, Tasha took a mental health day. No internet, no phone, complete silence from all technology. And she hated it.

Especially since the last person she spoke with the day before was none other than Jerome Grant. With Rachel and Alexa at work and Trisha at a doctor's appointment, Tasha was all alone. She thought about calling Evelyn, but didn't want to after talking with Jerome. Tasha knew that his mama would ask her what she'd been up to and Tasha still couldn't tell a good lie.

*I should've stopped by Rachel's work yesterday and got that key.*

At least she would've been able to keep herself busy moving into the house. Since the two would be leaving immediately after their reception for their destination honeymoon, Tasha volunteered to house and dogsit for the couple. But she had been so preoccupied with work and then talking to Jerome that Tasha forgot to pick up the spare key. Looking around her hotel room, Tasha sat up in the bed and started checking in with her body. Slowly rotating her neck from one side to the other, she listened to the familiar cracking as she then extended her arms to the ceiling.Next, Tasha wiggled her toes, lifting them up off of the floor. Being mindful of her breath, she closed her eyes as she put her feet back on the ground and got out of the bed.

Taking out her journal. Tasha picked up a pen from the hotel nightstand and spreaded out onto the floor to write down everything she had done since coming back home weeks ago and who she'd been in touch with. Her conversation with Devin at the fundraiser tugged the hardest on her heart, so she poured out her thoughts about what he told her that day. Only when a tear dropped onto the page did she take a break from writing.

She allowed herself a moment of honesty. As much as she loved her home away from home, it was just that - a far away place. Realistically Tasha knew she could work anywhere, that was one of the things she had come to love about being a photographer. But the idea of returning home, permanently, left her feeling unsure as hell. All Tasha knew was once Alexa and Rachel's honeymoon was over, she needed to make a decision. Grabbing her pen and journal again, she flipped to a new page and drew a line down the paper. Rolling her eyes at the ridiculousness of what she was about to do, Tasha wrote 'why' on one side of the paper and 'why not' on the other.

Tasha realized as she wrote on the 'why' side that she could go on and on. This surprised her, since as far back as she could remember, there was not much to living in her hometown. As she looked at her 'why' list, Tasha's eyes twinkled while she said the top reasons out loud.

"Family. Stability. Possibility of having my own space. Growth." she whispered.

So many things called to her since being back home, from her talks with Rachel about her job, presenting at Devin's school, and the one that started to consume her thoughts lately - the abandoned building near the plaza. Tasha was humming with the potential of what she saw in that space. Though in the sake of fairness, she turned her attention to the 'why not' section and almost rolled her eyes again, this time from not being able to think beyond one thing. "Him."

There was a reason she didn't say goodbye to Jerome in person four years ago, and Tasha had to be honest - at least with herself - about that. She'd spent so much time trying to leave this town, to only meet someone that almost got her to give that up. Leaving was scary, exciting, but the more Tasha thought back to her first months away and in Spain, she couldn't deny how being away from Jerome shaped her experiences. From her first day of orientation to her first official photoshoot, the thought of him was never far from her mind. And being back, seeing him with his family, talking to him...

Tasha felt like her heart was being swayed to test what kind of relationship they could now have, if any at all. *Because if I decide to take on these why's, I will have to face the why not's too.*

She closed the journal and stood to start her daily salutations.

Later that afternoon, she tried her luck by calling back the number Jerome called her from earlier. She wasn't surprised when Jerome sent her to voicemail, in fact, it was what she had hoped for. Keeping her message short, she said into the recording, "Hey Jerome. I thought about your label's offer and if the offer still stands, I can do the shoot. Call me back when you get this."

She ended the call and looked out at the night sky from her hotel room for a moment before going to bed.

A few hours later, her phone ranged. Thinking that it was Ximena or Trisha, Tasha rolled over and reached out on the nightstand to pick it up without looking at the caller ID. "Hey. Everything okay?"

When she heard a male voice clear their throat, Tasha squinted at the phone and her eyes flew open.

"I'm good." Jerome answered. " Sounds like you were sleeping. Did I wake you?"

*Why Lawd! Why you do me like this?*

Tasha rubbed the sleep from her eyes as she sat up in bed. "Yeah, sorry. You got my message?" she managed to get out.

"Yeah. But I have to ask, what made you change your mind?"

She would rather eat unseasoned chitlins than tell him the full truth to that question, so Tasha thought quickly. "Well, I don't have any other work lined up, and I'm looking to test out a theory."

"What theory?"

"Are all you entertainers really as over the top as you seem once you get famous?"

Jerome's laughter ranged out over the line, and settled into Tasha's bones.

"I can't speak for all rappers, but I promise you Tasha, I ain't changed all that much."

Hearing that brought a smile to Tasha's face. "That's good to know."

She remembered what their call was about and cleared her throat. "So, um, yeah, if y'all still looking for a photographer for your shoot, I can have my partner send your label my info and a contract." Thinking back on the thought she had earlier that afternoon, Tasha added, " On two conditions."

"Okay. I don't know what the label has planned for the shoot, but I can give them the message." Jerome told her.

"One, I get to choose the shoot location, and two, I would like your wife to be present."

Silence fell over the line and Tasha closed her eyes as she reminded herself to breathe.

"Sofie's never been with me for anything work related."

"Well, those are my conditions. Let your people know." Tasha reminded Jerome.

A few seconds passed before Jerome spoke again. "Okay. I'll tell Sofie about the shoot and give the label your message."

"Thank you."

As he ended the call, Tasha turned on the light by the nightstand and pulled back the covers, getting out of bed. When she walked over to the desk, she picked up her messenger bag and dug out the business card that Jay Jay gave her. Making a note to call him first thing in the morning to talk about the building, Tasha went back to sleep.

# Chapter Nine

## Lost and Found

### Sofie

*I can't believe I agreed to this bullshit!*

She had heard about the extravagant photoshoots that most artists had for their magazine covers, and Sofie was not impressed at all with this one. They were on location in an abandoned building, where it looked like someone covered the room in large black curtains. The room still smelled of paint and the fumes were working on Sofie's last nerves. She could see white paint buckets were set to the side and guessed that that's why the windows were open. When Jerome asked her to come with him to this photoshoot, she was excited. He'd never wanted her to come to a photoshoot before, and Sofie thought it might be fun. But when they arrived and she saw that damn motorcycle out front next to a pickup truck, Sofie almost demanded that Jerome take her home.

"Hi! Thanks for being on time, as we only have this space for half the day." Tasha told them brightly once they stepped inside.

"No problem. I see my assistant Tech beat us here and is already at work." Jerome said, as a lanky kid with locs down to his shoulder came toward them.

Surprised by the news of Jerome having an assistant, Sofie asked, "When did you hire an assistant?"

"Days ago." With the young man stood next to Jerome, the two dabbed each other up before he introduced them. "Terrence, this is Sofie,my wife. Sofie, this is Terrence."

Terrence looked around before leaning to whisper into Jerome's ear and Sofie's curiosity went up a notch as her husband's eyebrows bunched up on his face.

"You sure?" Jerome asked the kid, who nodded.

"I listened to it as soon as I heard about it. You haven't heard from the label yet?"

Jerome said nothing, but the look on his face told her that whatever this dude told him, something big happened. The two were quiet until Jerome took out his phone and spoke, "Good looking out Tech."

He turned around and the kid brought his attention to her.

"Morning. Sofie, is it?" he stated, looking directly at her.

"It's Grant, *Mrs*. Grant."

She looked over and saw that Tasha was talking to another guy, who was fine as hell. He sported a small goatee and had warm brown skin, like he spent all his free time outdoors working out. Sofie stared at him as he finished talking with Tasha and left the room. "Who is that?" she whispered to Terrence.

"He's the realtor for this building. Tasha's friend."

Sofie snorted. *They definitely more than friends.*

Tasha turned to face them as the man next to her looked in their direction. Her stride was quick as she walked over to them, stopping a few feet in front of Terrence. " Hi everyone. Thanks for being on time."

Glancing behind her, Tasha stretched out a hand in the direction of two large dark fabrics that were suspended in the air. "As you can see, the setup is simple. This is done to highlight you, JPK, the artist. Once I feel we've got enough variety of shots for the magazine, I'll let you pick the ones you like and send them to you directly, in case the label wants to go in another direction for the spread." Tasha told Jerome, who nodded.

"After that, if we have time, I can get a few shots of you and your wife."

Hearing this, Sofie whipped her head toward them."Wait, you're going to take photos of me? Of us?" she asked.

Tasha turned to look at her, "If that's okay with you, yeah. That's my plan for this shoot."

*I don't want to take no pictures in this dump!*

Sofie looked around at the room they were in again, and her lips turned downward. "Does it have to be here though?" She then looked down at her outfit, a simple cream maxi dress and gold heels. Normally this everyday fit made Sofie feel confident no matter who was in the spot, but even as she glanced over at Tasha in her all black attire and flats, she did not feel like her normal baddie self. "I'm not even wearing anything cute!"

Tasha stared between Jerome and her before explaining, "My shoots are always in unlikely places. We have this space for five hours, max, so if you wish to go home and change, that's cool."

"Sofie, you look fine." Jerome started as Tasha continued.

"To your left you'll see a divider for privacy if you need to change. In the meantime, you can call someone to come here with clothes and makeup, to save time, but either way, I start shooting in 20 minutes."

*This bitch!*

She didn't bother with hiding her frown as Tasha turned to leave, going to the opposite of the room to pick up a laptop and connecting it to an orange cord.

"Is she always that, um, upfront?" Terrence finally asked.

"Yep."

They turned to find the man that Tasha was speaking to earlier a few feet away. All his attention was on Tasha as she looked over the three bright lights in the room.

"She hasn't changed." the man said as he brought his eyes from Tasha to the three of them.

"And how do you know Tasha?" Jerome asked.

Sofie's eyes narrowed at Jerome's tone, as the younger man extended his hand out to Jerome. "I'm James, friends call me Jay Jay."

She watched as Jerome's eyes took in James and a smile showed up on his face. "Oh! Little Jay Jay! I remember you from church. How you doing?"

"I'm alright. Glad you remembered me, Tasha didn't and it hurt my feelings."

The two laughed as Sofie watched them both look at Tasha and continued their conversation.

"She came back into town for her mama's funeral a month ago, from what I heard." Jay Jay told them.

*So that's what brought her back here? She ain't acting like someone that just lost their mama.*

"Two days ago, she called me asking if she could borrow this space, as a prospective buyer. And after talking with my boss, they said it'd be okay." Jay Jay explained before adding, "Tasha even promised me some headshots today, for the trouble."

Jay Jay's eyes roamed over Tasha's frame as she continued to tinker with the lighting around them,

*I bet he wants more than a few headshots from her. Probably looking to get some backshots in too.*

"JPK, you ready?" Tasha called out.

Sofie watched as Jerome walked over to Tasha and she pointed down at the ground. Her eyes narrowed as the two of them started signing to one another. She knew Jerome had an older sister who was deaf, but since she never met her, Sofie saw no reason to learn. The two were at least a meter apart when Tasha began pressing a button in her hand. When she did, the lights around them flashed quickly, all while she kept talking to Jerome with her hands.

"Mrs. Grant, do you want me to drive you home to change? Jay Jay says he'll keep Tasha busy with his headshots until we get back."

Without taking her eyes off Jerome and Tasha, Sofie nodded. Finally looking away, she walked ahead of Terrence back to the entrance. "The sooner I go home and put on something decent, the sooner Jerome and I can leave."

### Jerome

Thirty minutes into the shoot, Tasha asked him if there were any poses he wanted to try again in sign language, and Jerome almost couldn't answer her back. To say that he was rusty in signing was an understatement, as he hadn't talked to Eva in months. "When did you get so good at talking with your hands?"

He heard her snort before she answered in sign language, "Years of practice. And a good list of online resources."

She then held her hand out and twirled her finger around in a circle. Memories of them together at Bejon Beach immediately came to mind, causing Jerome to blink several times, just in time to see Tasha sign, "Remind me to thank Evelyn Mae."

Jerome blinked before he signed back, "Thank her for what?"

Now it was Tasha's turn to look stumped before speaking out loud. "You know she and Eva have a Black Sign Language website, right?" Tasha continued, "The Blackest CODA Around? I've subscribed and have been taking their online classes."

He honestly had no idea, and the realization of how out of touch he had been with his family started to slowly close in on Jerome. Several rapid flashes could be seen around him. Looking up, Jerome saw Tasha staring at him.

"I-I think we got enough shots." she said softly. "You can view them on either the monitor or my laptop."

He turned to look at the monitor and saw miniature versions of himself on the large screen. Jerome walked off to the side as Jay Jay went up to Tasha. "You ready for me?" he asked with a grin.

Though it was Tasha's grin as it matched Jay Jay's that shocked Jerome when she said, "The real question is, are *you* ready for *me*?"

Hearing the two laugh, he watched as Tasha pulled on one of the black fabrics and it fell to the ground, revealing two smaller backdrops. "Pick one, and let's create a little magic."

As Jay Jay stood in front of the white backdrop, more flashes began to go off as Tasha talked Jay Jay through his shoot. He went back to looking at the photos that Tasha took of him and when he made it to the last shoots, Jerome couldn't help feeling exposed.

The black background with the gray and white splatters of paint made his deep skin look warmer somehow. As he stared at his downcast eyes in the photos, Jerome felt more lost than he did the last time he laid eyes on Tasha. For a second, he wished that he hadn't called her to do this shoot at all. Jerome heard small yet quick click clack steps coming closer to him.

"I brought something better for you to wear for our shoot."

Looking at his wife, Jerome took the suit from her and walked away to go change in the makeshift changing room.

# Chapter Ten

## Connections

**Tasha**

With the shoot behind her, Tasha greeted the new day with a smile. She had another day of nothing to do, so Tasha thought about taking her bike out on the highway to clear her head. While she was sliding on her favorite pair of jeans, her phone chimed.

**Hey. You busy?**

**-Jerome**

She stared at the message for a minute before sending her own.

**Hey! I'm not busy? What's up?**

**-Tasha**

Her phone began ringing seconds after she hit send and Tasha froze. By the time the third ring ended, she had mustered up enough courage to answer. "Hey Jerome. Everything okay?"

"Yeah, the label called and said that everything went well with the photos. So I wanted to say thank you again."

"Did you have any doubts, Jerome?" she teasingly asked.

When he laughed, she joined him. "No, not really. But with these folks, you never know."

"Trust me, I get it. My first few shoots, some of those companies drove me crazy with the stuff they would ask me to edit or change at the last minute."

"I hear ya. For my second album, one of the sound guys asked me to not rhyme so fast over a track they sent me. Said that it 'threw the count off' in his head." Jerome told her.

Tasha snorted, "Was this sound guy of the no rhythm nation?"

They both cackled as Jerome answered, "Yes, yes he was - you already know Tash."

Realizing what he said, Jerome added, "I'm sorry..."

She laughed softly. "Why? Tash is what my friends call me."

"Are we friends?"

The question hung in the air and Tasha closed her eyes as she answered, "I would like for us to be. That never changed."

"I want that too."

After spending time with him at the shoot, she worried that seeing him again would be too much. Especially during the shots with his wife. Thinking back to that day a week ago, seeing Sofie's hand securely all over Jerome's chest left Tasha's own chest tight.

While culling the photos between them, every snide remark from the women at Christ Corner came screeching back, rattling around in her head. All the ladies made sure to let her know when every forced interaction that they didn't like seeing her with him. How Jerome shouldn't even be seen with the likes of her, much less call her his girl. Blinking the memories away, Tasha made herself focus back on the pictures. *They do make a cute couple.*

That was days ago, but now, hearing Jerome say that he would like to be friends again someday, a new seed of hope filled Tasha's chest. *We'd never be as close as we once were, but at least we could maybe be friends...acquaintances again. Right?*

"What you doing today then? Wanna meet up for lunch?" Jerome asked her.

She grinned. "Where you wanna meet?"

It'd been a minute since Tasha had visited Caloo Bridge, and when Jerome suggested it, she found herself excited to hangout there.

Parking her bike under the old bridge, she looked around the familiar spot, pleasantly surprised that not much had changed. Just a few meters away were the boating docks and Tasha watched as small boats sailed under the bridge.

"Tash! Over here!"

She turned to the sound of Jerome's voice and saw that he'd sat at one of the benches with two brown bags and drinks. Walking over to him, Tasha looked down and inhaled the scent of fried catfish and fries. "Thanks for getting lunch. I got you next time."

"Bet." Jerome told her as he took out the containers and plastic silverware.

Tasha sat down and waited for Jerome to finish blessing the food before digging in. She almost bit her lip, "I'mma about to live over at the Seafood Shack - this fish is too good!"

Jerome grinned. "You been here for weeks and only had the seafood boil?"

"How did you know that I'd been there recently?" she asked.

Slowly putting down his drink, Jerome explained, "Well, mama told me, but I knew before that."

Taken aback, Tasha found herself asking, "But how though? It was just a random lunch."

"I, umm, saw you two inside."

Her eyes widened as he continued. "I saw mama's car parked in the restaurant's parking lot, so I thought I'd roll up and surprise her. But when I went inside, I saw y'all at a table together."

Seeing him now avoid her gaze, Tasha wanted to ask more but chose to keep their conversation light. "You could have joined us big head, but whatever! So, what's it like being on the road?"

"Tiring. But good, most days."

Tasha nodded. "I understand. When I started getting more assignments, I was happy flying back and forth to different locations.

But after three months, all I wanted was a hot bath and a 10 hour nap."

Jerome smiled up at her and Tasha grabbed her drink.

"Oh, so that's how you roll? Bet you got all kinds of frequent flyer miles." he said.

"I do! You ever wanna fly in style, come see me."

"I just might take you up on that Tash."

That was the second time he'd called her that, and Tasha forgot how much she'd missed hearing his rich voice say her nickname. Needing to change the subject, Tasha asked him about the photos. "So, which photos were your favorite from the shoot?"

She went to shoveling more fries into her mouth as Jerome answered, "They all were good, but the last ones really spoke to me."

His eyes drifted away from hers for a second as he continued, "Those were my favorite."

Tasha met his stare, "Yeah, those were good."

It got quiet and Tasha tried to keep her latest thoughts to herself, but she and Jerome must've been on the same wavelength because he then asked, "What were you thinking then? When you took those last photos?"

Tasha felt a lump growing in her throat. "I just focused on the, um, dissonance between you and the environment around us."

That was part of it, yeah, but Tasha couldn't tell him how the sadness in his eyes called out to her. How it all but shouted to be seen and be felt as he stood in front of her that day.

Clearing her throat, Tasha carefully asked, "When was the last time you talked to your mama, Jerome? Or Eva?"

She had a feeling that she knew what he would say, but Tasha hoped that she was wrong.

"It's been a minute. Well, more than that, with being on tour as much as I have been."

Hearing him confirm her suspicions, Tasha slowly shook her head, "Why?"

"I don't know," he whispered.

Seeing Jerome lower his head left her in need of comforting him. But images of how she did that for the last time burned in her mind. Flashes of his lips on hers left Tasha forgetting how to breathe.

*I have to leave - now.*

As she got up, Jerome asked "What's wrong?"

"This. This was a mistake."

Tasha turned to look at Jerome and waited for him to look her in the eye. "I don't know what is going on in your life, but Jerome, please get back to making time for those that matter."

His eyes narrowed onto hers, "What you mean?"

*I shouldn't have come here today.*

Turning to walk away, Jerome hopped up from the bench and quickly blocked her path. Tasha rolled her neck as she asked him a question of her own, "Your mama asked me to look into where you've been. She said that folks at Christ Corner have been talking about you."

Jerome looked at her and scoffed. "I ain't think you'd be one to gossip, Tasha."

Hearing him switch back to using her full name, she volleyed back, "And I never thought you'd be spending your time at Bottom's Up - drinking and buying lap dances."

The two stared at one another before Jerome stepped to the side, letting Tasha walk away.

**Jerome**

*Please get back to making time for those that matter...*

Tasha's words from this afternoon would not leave Jerome's head, even after he finished working out in his home gym and showered. Knowing that mama was so worried about him that she'd ask Tasha - of all people - to look into what he's been up to. As much as he wanted to, Jerome couldn't shake that off. The look in Tasha's eyes when she turned to walk away made his head hurt.

Later, as he was putting Ro to bed, Jerome's phone vibrated in his pocket. When he got to his room down the hall, Jerome looked at the caller ID and closed his bedroom door. Seconds after hitting the green button he heard Tasha speak, "I'm sorry for what I said to you before. "

"It's cool, you were just being honest."

He listened as she continued, "I was, but that don't make it right. I just - after talking with your mama, I promised I would find out what I could about you. And when I did, I couldn't bring myself to tell her everything."

Jerome let out a sigh of relief. "Thank you."

"Don't thank me Jerome. I mostly didn't tell her because I don't want to be the one to give her that kind of news."

Walking over to sit on his bed, Jerome spoke again. " Tasha, it's been so long since I've been home. I know that when I do call or visit that she's gonna be upset."

"Rome, if you don't want her to be upset, then go see her."

The line went silent. "You called me Rome." He hadn't heard the name in a minute and hearing Tasha say it, even now, made Jerome smile. "I guess you meant what you said before, about us being friends?"

He listened as she let out a sigh before laughing softly. "Yeah, I did. We were friends before everything else, right? And I don't know about you, but I miss having you as a friend. "

"Good. Cause I missed having you as a friend too Tash." Jerome closed his eyes as he said her name.

"O-okay then. Good night Jerome."

"Rome," he corrected gently over the line.

"Whatever! Good night Rome."

Jerome found himself laughing as she ended their call.

**Hey big head!**
**What you up to?**
**-Tasha**

Jerome's grin was wide as he woke up to Tasha's text message. He stretched and went to check on Ro, only to find his bed empty. Walking to Sofie's room, he saw that she was gone too. With no one in the house, he sent Tasha a reply.

**I ain't got no plans today.**
**Wanna meet up?**
**-Jerome**

They decided to meet at the Caloo Bridge again, and Tasha picked up lunch from the plaza. He tried not to stare too hard at Tasha as she looked his way, smiling with two bags in each hand. "I forgot to ask what you wanted, so I just picked up a few sandwiches and salads to go with our drinks. Hope that's cool?"

"That's fine."

He reached out to take the first bag from her, a slight static shock traveled through his hand. As he jerked his hand back, Tasha laughed. "You okay, big head?"

Rolling his eyes, Jerome reached out to take the bag again. "You gonna call me that every time we hang out?"

"Just making sure fame hasn't changed you, that's all."

The sun was sizzling hot as they walked under the pavilion .He took out the salads, popped open the chickpea one and reached for a fork.

"Oh, that one's for me."

Jerome looked at the caesar salad and tried not to frown.

Tasha laughed. "It's cool, we can share it."

"You sure?" Jerome asked.

"Yeah. Like I said, I didn't know what you wanted, so if you don't mind we can share."

Reaching into the bag, Tasha took out two forks and two sandwiches. "I thought you might like one of these."

Jerome grinned and grabbed the egg sandwich. Once he'd blessed the food, the two happily talked while eating their sandwiches and sharing the salad. "So, my nephews know who you are now." Tasha said.

"That's good. They really humbled me the other day, not gonna lie."

When their eyes met again, she couldn't hold in her laughter. She picked up her bottle of water and took a hearty sip, staring out at the scene around them.

"By the way, how old is your son?" Tasha asked.

"He's almost two now."

Reaching into his pocket, Jerome took out his wallet and pulled out a few pictures to show off his namesake. "Jerome Earl Grant, the third is his name, but we call him Ro for short."

The light conversation died down and Jerome took the last bite of his sandwich before washing it down with water "How much of the town have you seen since being back? I'm free all day if you want someone to show you around?"

"Thanks, but Jay Jay already gave me a tour." she told him.

"Jay Jay? You mean James, right?" Jerome knew he had no reason to feel any type of way about Tasha referring to the dude from last week's shoot affectionately, but he did. "Wasn't he one of the students you used to tutor at Christ Corner back in the day?" He remembered seeing the long glances James sent her way the day of the shoot and Jerome's smile diminished. "So, you two went out?"

"Yeah! I ran into him the day after I got back in town." Tasha explained."He's the one that helped me secure the spot we shot at last week. And after the shoot, he helped me clean up so I treated him to dinner. By the way, when did every place get fancy?"

Jerome blinked. "What you mean?"

"That new resort out near Bejon Beach? When we got there, I thought they wouldn't let me in, it was so formal looking."

He stared at her. "I wouldn't know. Ain't been to Bejon in a minute."

The truth was that Jerome hadn't been there in years. Partly because he was constantly on the road, but mainly because of the memories he had of walking along the beach with her. From the way her nose would scrunch up at him when he made her laugh to the night they spent at the tiny bed and breakfast before she left. Jerome spent several sleepless nights remembering their last trip to Bejon Beach and as he watched her now, a part of him wished that she hadn't been able to go there either. *Can't she see that James wanna be more than friends?*

Clearing his throat, Jerome stood and collected their empty containers. "I'll throw these away."

"Okay." Thankful to have something to do, instead of taking another trip down memory lane by himself, he walked over to the trash can. Jerome noticed someone familiar jogging toward him. His assistant wore a pair of bright lime green khaki shorts with a white shirt and had his thick locs pulled back in a low braid. "Hey Terrence."

"Hey boss! I was on my way to the label to meet with Raven and saw your ride up front. Is your phone on silent? I tried calling you but it just goes to voicemail."

Before Jerome could make up an excuse, Terrence continued, "The issue of Hit Breakers just released and I wanted to say congrats."

*I forgot that was due to drop today.*

"Hi! Terrence, right?"

Hearing the high pitch octave that Tasha used as she spoke to Terrence did not sit well with Jerome. He recognized the sound from when she first met his father, Jerome Senior, at Christ Corner, and it made him want to send Terrence on his way. Turning around to look at her, Tasha avoided his gaze. He watched Tasha walk toward his assistant, extending a hand. "Thank you for helping with the shoot."

Terrence's smile was way too big in Jerome's opinion while he shook Tasha's hand.

"Glad to do it. So, is Jerome trying to get you to come on to Trap Son's as the in-house photographer?"

Before he could say otherwise, Tasha spoke. "Yeah, I guess he was. But that shoot was a one-time thing."

"That's too bad, your work is dope." Terrence said.

"Well, it was good to see you Terrence. Take care Jerome." Tasha said.

Catching Jerome off guard, Tasha briskly walked away. He squinted at the back of her head. Not bothering to say anything to Terrence, Jerome sprinted to catch up to Tasha. "What just happened?"

She took two steps away from him. "What do you mean Jerome?"

Hearing Tasha say his name sent an icy shiver down his back, even with the sun beaming on them now in the absence of the pavilion. "Why you sound different? And this wasn't no get together for the label, so why'd you say it was?"

His eyes followed her gaze as Terrence waved in the distance. Tasha waved back and once he started to walk away, she looked hard at Jerome. "What was I suppose to do?" Jerome didn't get a chance to answer as she continued. "Just say that we were catching up, as old friends?"

"Yeah, that would have been cool. You ain't have to switch it up Tash." Jerome told her.

When she laughed, it sounded nothing like when she did it earlier. This time he felt like she was laughing at him, not with him and Jerome didn't like it. "Did I miss something?"

"You really think that telling folks that you, a married man, were out having lunch with an 'old friend' is a good idea?" Tasha asked.

"Why not?"

Tasha stared at him, rolling her eyes, "Fame hasn't changed you, though right now I almost wish it did."

"What you mean? We can't tell folks that we are out together, catching up?"

Tightly shutting her eyes, Tasha opened them and looked directly at Jerome, "Question, do the folks that you work with know our history?"

When he said nothing, Tasha nodded. "And does your wife know? About us?"

"Yeah, she does, but-"

"Can you honestly tell me that she would be okay with knowing that we met today? For something non-work related?"

Jerome held her stare as her words began to make sense, and he didn't like it. Tasha had just said the other day that they could be friends and now because one person saw them together she was ready to change her mind?

Her phone beeped and she busied herself with pulling it out and checking the message. "I have to go. And I'm sorry, but I don't think we should meet again like this."

"Tash, you said that we could be friends again. What changed?"

"I-I'm sorry. I thought I could do this, you know, be out with you and not feel like I did back then."

"What are you saying? Feel like what?"

He watched as her eyes scanned the space around them before landing on his. Seeing her brown irises flirt with the bright rays from the sun, so warm and full of depth, Jerome wanted to find out just how deep her thoughts were in that moment. So he waited for what felt like a lifetime before Tasha spoke, her voice ragged and raw with emotion.

"The feeling that no matter how I justify us being out together, or all my accomplishments since leaving, all folks in this town would see were my mama's mistakes when they looked at me. How they'll always hear my last name and judge me for all the bad stuff they heard – without getting to know me." Tasha turned her head and he caught the rise and fall of her chest as she turned back to him. "How no matter how much time passes, I'll always be the child of a crackhead ho."

It was the first time Jerome ever heard her say anything similar to what he'd heard members of Christ Corner whisper about when he attended. Hearing the words from her lips and seeing the crestfallen look on Tasha's face, Jerome couldn't get away from the feeling of shame that now surrounded them. With the growing air thick, on top of being outside in the heat, Jerome had to take in several short breaths. *Is this what pastors mean when they say, 'trial under fire'?*

Whatever it was, Jerome wasn't going to let Tasha go through it alone.

Taking a small step forward, he tried to prepare himself for her to retreat. But she didn't. Which is why he wasn't prepared at all for the well of tears that he saw build within her eyes. His hands itched desperately to wipe them away before they fell. All he wanted to do was take her pain away as he whispered softly, "Tash, do you really think that that's what people see when they look at you?"

"I didn't say that's what they see, Jerome. I said that's how I feel."

Blowing out a harsh breath of air, he looked on as Tasha sighed and spared him a final look. "We can be friends, Jerome, from a distance. I really wish you every happiness and all the success, but unless it's work related, I don't think we should see each other."

This time Jerome didn't try to stop her when Tasha walked away.

**Tasha**

Sending Alexa a quick text, Tasha marched to her ride. With her helmet secure on top of her head, Tasha straddled the motorbike and put the key in the ignition, reviving it to life. The sound of the engine's roar left her body humming, though after spending time with Jerome it didn't feel nearly as thrilling. Even after she had told him how the stares from strangers in town made her feel. The need to check in with Doctor Richardson to see about moving up her next session was strong after admitting all of that to him. So much so that Tasha found herself fighting like hell to not bawl her eyes out and scream.

*Girl! Get your mind right and move on.*

She forgot how easy it was to simply be in his company, chatting about nothing. If Terrence hadn't showed up when he did, Tasha knew she would have spent the whole day with Jerome.

And until that day, Jerome's eyes never held so much pity in them while looking at her. She expected him to turn away as she confirmed all the rumors about her mama to him, but he didn't. Instead, Jerome closed the distance between them and tried to comfort her. *Just like the good Doctor said people would - if I stuck around and chose to let them in.*

Remembering the sound of his voice and how she almost reached out for him at the park, Tasha just barely managed to get another word out before she took off. Being around Jerome was dangerous. The way they fell in step with one another, sharing food and teasing one another... Tasha didn't know much about being a musician, but she did recognize the song that now played on loop in the center of her chest. It was the way Jerome stole glances at her while they ate lunch, in the short touch of his hand as he took the bag from her earlier, and how he locked eyes with Tasha when she told him that they couldn't meet anymore. The baseline of her heart wanted no other accompaniment, just him. But Jerome Earl Grant Junior was not hers to have, not anymore.

The engines and music thumping from the cars around her couldn't drown out the sound of his laughter and Tasha gripped the handles tightly, almost willing the traffic light to turn green. When it did, she weaved passed several RVs until getting on the backroads to Alexa and Rachel's place. Since their wedding was just two weeks away and they were having a destination honeymoon, Tasha volunteered to take care of their place while they were gone. Luckly, when she made it there, they still weren't home, so Tasha let herself in using the spare key Rachel gave her. Tyrone dashed toward her, sniffing her feet while his tail wagged rapidly.

"Guess I better take you out, uh boy?" Tasha said.

Reaching over to the key hook, Tasha grabbed Tyrone's leash and bent down to latch it onto his collar. She opened the door and let him lead the way for their walk. Taking in the quiet that now surrounded her, Tasha watched as Tyrone strutted down the road, stopping occasionally to do his business or to sniff around a nearby tree. Over the last week, these walks helped clear her head, but today as she looked at the trees in the clearing, all Tasha saw was Jerome's face. Her longing to come back home had more to do with missing her family, Tasha could admit that much - at least to herself.

Soon Tyrone was circling around her heels, letting out sharp barks as he stared up at her. That was her que to take him back home. With the sun starting to set, Tasha brought her attention down to the tiny dog and sighed. "You don't know how lucky you are." Stepping over him, she headed back to the house. "To have a home with people you love - some of us ain't so fortunate."

Once they were back inside the house, Tasha removed her shoes and refilled his water and food bowls before making her way to the guest room. Taking out an old oversize shirt, she called Ximena and waited for her to answer. Hearing the hustle of cars mingling with waves from the shore, Tasha smiled as she wished to be at a beach too with her friend. "Ximena, any new news about the gala?"

She listened as Ximena giggled before answering her. "No, nothing yet."

"Okay. Just wanted to check in to be sure. I called Sebastian, and you should be hearing from him soon."

"When did you talk with him? I contacted his assistant and she said that he has left the country."

Tasha paused on her way to the bathroom. "I called him a few days ago." Narrowing her eyes, she focused on keeping her voice neutral before speaking again, "Maybe he went home to visit his mama?"

She knew that Sebastian's family resided in Puerto Rico, even though he now called Murica home. His father passed away last year and his brother returned home with his family to look after their mama. Every few months, his socials showed him there as well, so instead of assuming the worst, Tasha chose to think that that was where he may be.

"I do not know. His assistant said that he gave her a check for the entire month and told her not to expect him back for some time."

*If he gets caught up in some mess and can't go to this gala...*

"Thanks for letting me know Ximena. I'll call again soon." Smiling as she heard a male voice more clearly in the background, Tasha added, "Go back to enjoying your day."

She heard Ximena laugh before ending their call. Now beyond ready to wash the day away, Tasha went into the bathroom and took a warm shower. After putting on some lotion and her night shirt, she stepped out of the bathroom and saw her phone vibrating on the bed and Tasha went to pick it up. Seeing Jerome's name on the screen, all the feelings she thought she'd got rid of today came back. Deciding to put herself out of her misery before going to bed, she hit the green call button.

"Hello. Tasha Daye speaking." she said flatly.

When his voice reached her ears, Tasha knew she made the right call in telling him that they couldn't meet anymore. Just the sound of his deep rumble left her tingling all over.

"Tasha, it's Jerome. You ain't save my number?"

She did, but Tasha wasn't going to own up to that now.

"Hey, Jerome. Is this work related?"

He laughed, and all that did was send Tasha sailing onto the bed, completely frustrated with how the OG was testing her.

"Okay, okay, I heard what you said earlier. And even though I don't agree, I understand."

She waited for him to finish his thought. "But Tasha, we ain't doing nothing wrong, and I - I could use a friend right now."

Tasha heard him, loud and clear. From the few times that they were together recently, she suspected that he might be in a bad way. Though as she listened to him say as much out loud, Tasha couldn't help but think of the silent war that she captured in his eyes at the shoot.

"And besides, you ain't say that I couldn't call or text you."

The corners of her lips turned up as Tasha tried not to laugh. "You right, I didn't say nothing about that." She let out a small snort and soon heard Jerome laugh over the line. "Just don't get carried away with it, big head."

"Okay. I'll talk to you later?"

Hearing Jerome ask her that after calling to tell her that she didn't say he couldn't do exactly that made Tasha laugh even harder. "Yeah, but texting would be nicer."

"I see you still don't like talking to folks over the phone." Jerome teased.

"Nope - don't judge me."

His voice was soft as he told her, "I would never judge you."

Tasha listened as he cleared his throat, "Besides, as it says in the good book, " Do not judge, and you will not be judged."

Propping up onto her shoulders, Tasha recited the rest of the scripture, "Do not condemn, and you will not be condemned. Forgive, and you will be forgiven. Luke 6:37."

Silence fell over the line before Jerome asked, the awe evident in his tone, "How did you know that?"

Eyes closed, Tasha let out a yawn before answering, "Murica, Spain has some beautiful churches. I managed to attend a service or two when I wasn't working."

"That's what's up. I need to do the same, now that I'm back home."

"Your mama would like that." she told him.

A few seconds passed between them before Jerome spoke again, "I know. Thanks for answering the phone, Tash."

"You're welcome."

"I'll let you gone to sleep then, good night."

"Night, Rome." Tasha said softly before hanging up the phone.

The last thing she heard before drifting to sleep was Tyrone pouncing into the bed and curling up next to her for the night.

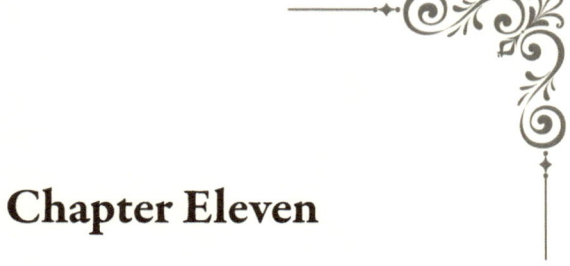

# Chapter Eleven

## Let Go

### Rachel

She watched as Tasha took notes and Alexa went for another bite of the 'Chocolate City' cupcake. Rachel couldn't blame her, as the triple chocolate cake with milk chocolate frosting was good. A few of the shaved mint chocolate pieces were stuck on the corner of Alexa's lips, and Rachel didn't bother using a napkin to wipe them away. She wiped the chocolate away with her thumb, finding herself unable to look away from the woman who Rachel couldn't wait to spend forever with. Alexa locked eyes with her and the two stared at one another before Alexa kissed her cheek.

"You like this one?" Alexa said.

Rachel blinked back tears as she whispered, "I love you, you know that?"

They stared at one another for a bit longer until they heard Tasha's voice. "The manager says that they can deliver up to a five tier cake to the venue. So, do y'all want a more traditional cake, like marble or vanilla bean? Or something else?"

"We'd like these mint chocolate cupcakes for the rehearsal dinner and a white raspberry cake for the wedding." Rachel said.

Tasha jotted down the request and immediately asked, "How many tiers? I was thinking with the added guests, four would be good."

Alexa snuck in another kiss before turning to face Tasha. "Yeah, four tiers is good."

"Okay, we're all set here. Next up is lunch, so—"

Rachel watched as Tasha took out her phone and looked at them apologetically. "I'm sorry y'all, I gotta take this."

Feeling Alexa entwined their hands together, Rachel closed her eyes and sighed. "We really doing this?"

"Yeah." Alexa said, going in for another kiss.

"Sebastian! Please tell me you're joking right now?!"

Hearing Tasha's voice over the neo-soul music that played inside the bakery, Rachel and Alexa looked over at their friend who paced in tight circles at the front entrance of the shop.

"I'm out with my girls, so you outta luck. I don't..."

Tasha paused mid step as her sentence faltered. She looked at her phone as if it grew three legs before quickly pinching the bridge of her nose with her index finger and thumb. Rachel knew that look well enough to know that whoever was on the end of the line was well on their way to getting cussed out. *I just hope whatever's going on doesn't mess up the rest of our day...*

"I know what I agreed to, what I do not understand is why you are in the States at all!"

They watched as Tasha briefly glanced over to their table and released an exasperated sigh. "Fine, I will be there as soon as possible."

Ending the call, Tasha walked back over to Rachel and Alexa.

"Umm, is it okay if we push lunch back a little?" Tasha asked.

Rachel and Alexa both spoke at the same time.

"Is everything okay?"

"Who was that?"

Tasha shut her eyes as she started to answer them. "That was, um, a business contact of mine from Spain. Apparently, he accepted a job offer here for Trap Son's and needs to be picked up from the airport. Now."

"Wait? What?" Rachel said.

"You talking about Trap Sons? As in the record label?" Alexa confirmed before continuing, "Why would they not hire someone locally?"

Tasha let out a shaky chuckle, "Long story short, they tried to and I declined."

As Tasha looked everywhere but at them, Rachel asked directly, "They tried to hire you on after working with Jerome for his magazine spread?"

Closing her eyes again, Tasha nodded.

Alexa asked. "And you said no? Why?"

Rachel looked at her fiancee and tightly squeezed their entwined hands.

"I'll give you three guesses." Tasha didn't wait for Alexa to speak as she added, "But before you go in on me, can we please go to the airport and pick Sebastian up first?"

"Yeah, let's wrap things up here and head out." Rachel told her, cutting Alexa off.

Seeing Tasha send a grateful smile her way, Rachel returned it.

"Though, I gotta tell y'all about Sebastian right quick. He's a flirt - in the worst way." Tasha said as she picked up her messenger bag and the car keys.

"That's fine, we about to jump the broom anyway, so he ain't gonna get far with us. That's all you playa." Alexa jokingly told Tasha.

They watched as Tasha shook her head and let out a frustrated sigh. "No, and no. Sebastian loves women, no matter their orientation, race, shape, or status. Y'all being engaged ain't gonna stop him from trying to get a whiff of your panties."

"Ewwww! Just what kind of folks you been working with Tash?" Rachel asked, turning to look at her friend, who led the way to the front door.

"He's mostly harmless, just wanna give y'all a heads up." Tasha said.

Her friend then opened the entrance door to the bakery and let her and Alexa walk out before following behind.

Once they arrived at the airport, Tasha drove through the pick up area. After going around the no parking area twice they found her friend, Sebastian. If Rachel had to guess, he was the same height as Tasha, with a fair olive complexion and light brown eyes. His wavy hair was in a small bun, bringing her attention to a long, jagged scar along the right side of his jaw. It was the one imperfection she could see on him.

"Ah, my sweet gordita! You are a sight for sore eyes!"

"Did he just call you fat?" Alexa's eyes narrowed onto the man in front of them.

Tasha laughed before explaining, "It's a term of endearment."

"It's something alright." Alexa murmured.

Bringing the car to a stop, Tasha parked and stepped out. Rachel looked on as her friend kissed Sebastian on each of his cheeks and tried to help him with his luggage. "This is nothing, my lovely Daye."

Rachel smirked as Tasha turned to open the trunk of the SUV to let Sebastain place his large case and carry on inside before closing it. When the two climbed into the car, Tasha made the introductions while starting the engine.

"Sebastian Gonanlez, these are my best friends, Alexa Shaw and Rachel Banks."

"It is certainly a pleasure to meet you both."

She watched the man eye Alexa from the rear view mirror and smirked as her fiancee mean mugged him. He then turned his attention to her and extended his hand. Curious, Rachel offered it and she almost laughed out loud when he gingerly took it and kissed her knuckles softly.

"Please forgive me for intruding on your day. However I can make it up to you, do not hesitate to let me know."

"Tasha described you well." Rachel said.

Upon hearing this, Sebastian glanced over at Tasha before letting go of Rachel's hand. "I promise, no matter what you have heard of me, I only aim to please."

Alexa snorted as Tasha pulled into the car rental shop. "Let's get you a rental and check in at the Cove."

### Jerome

With Ro in pre-school now, Jerome and Sofie were alone together at home during the weekday. They took turns taking their son to school, and today was Jerome's turn to drop Ro off at Wood's Edge Elementary. Once he parked and turned off the engine, Jerome found himself trying to think of the last time they'd actually gone out together without their son and when Jerome couldn't remember, he let out a sigh. *When did we get like this?*

They were friends before getting married and as he let himself inside the house, Jerome started to think of how he could get them back to that part of their relationship. In the past, he would leave her notes, asking about her day or if she needed anything, but Sofie never replied. Once, when he was touring, she asked him to text her when he added money to her account, but that was it. He went to the kitchen to make himself breakfast. While opening the fridge, Jerome thought back the last time Sofie asked him why he didn't make her anything as well and he grinned. *Maybe we can have breakfast together before I go to the studio.*

Remembering that she was trying to make healthier eating choices, Jerome started to make her an omelet. As he was cutting up the tomatoes and spinach, he heard Sofie make her way into the kitchen.

"Morning? You hungry?" he asked hopefully.

Jerome noticed that she was already dressed for the day and had a gym bag strapped across her shoulder but said nothing as he waited for her to answer.

"Hey. Going to go workout with Regine."

He turned to face the stove. "Okay." Quickly, he offered, "You want to have a quick breakfast before you head out?"

"Nah, I'm good."

Turning down the heat on the stovetop, Jerome watched as his wife left the house. He quietly finished preparing the omelet and cleaned up the countertop before sitting down at the dining room table to eat. Though halfway through his meal, Jerome's head felt heavy. As thoughts of his relationship with Sofie and the whispers throughout town swirled around his head he closed his eyes. *Lord, please guide me.*

Jerome stood up and made his way to his bedroom. Picking up the bible that lay on his dresser, Jerome tried to find words that would help him process what he was feeling, but he couldn't focus as flashes of his life before came into view. The days of him leading bible study, spending time with the younger members at Christ Corner and teaching them the word. Just as fast, Jerome saw images of him on stage, performing in front of his first crowd. Then he remembered the last year, him being out with the other artists from his label, one club after the other, one smoked filled room after the next. His chest heaved as he thought back to how he chose to deal with being on the road and away from his family and the church - drinking to dull himself from it.

A sick realization came to him, and part of Jerome didn't want to give it more space in his head, but as he looked down at the bible in his hand and read the first scripture he saw, Jerome had to.

*Cast your burden on the Lord, and he will sustain you; he will never permit the righteous to be moved. - Psalms 55:22*

He was afraid.

Afraid he had made the wrong choice, he was too afraid to speak up to the label. The fear of having to face Senior and mama if they knew the life he was living now. Most of all, he was afraid of Sofie leaving and taking Ro with her. Jerome let the feelings flow through him, and when it reached his shaking hands, he curled them into fists.

Looking at the Psalms once more, Jerome put the bible back on the dresser and went to his knees. Bowing his head, Jerome began to pray.

THE NEXT DAY JEROME drove to Trap Son's to meet with Raven and a few of the others. He wasn't sure what or why they wanted to meet with him, but since there was also a scheduled studio time for him afterwards, Jerome didn't mind. With new notes and bars that he was ready to try out and feeling calmer than he had in some time, Jerome strode into the meeting room.

"Ah, hell nah! You ain't say this fool would be here!"

Buckem leaped out of his seat and mean mugged Jerome. Standing still, Jerome brought his attention to Raven. "What is this meeting about Raven? I thought I would have more time to rest and be with my family before touring again."

"You do, no worries Jerome. This is more of a social strategy meeting. To resolve the issue between you and Buckem." she answered.

Before he could take a seat next to Raven, Buckem strode up to Jerome. Looking him up and down, Buckem snarled out. "You gonna act like you don't see me?" Buckem titled his head to stare Jerome in the eye and added, "Man up and admit to jacking my shit!"

When Raven tried to intervene, Jerome held out a hand toward her. "I put bars to a track given to me by the producers I work with.

Same as you. Make peace with that, as I have with whatever beef you have with me."

"Bentley, we have already discussed this. Please have a seat." Raven said.

Jerome matched Buckem's glare and continued standing until Buckem sat back down.

Raven spoke again. "We were going to talk to you privately about what transpired after your recent performance, but it seems that you are up to date on that news. Is there anything you would like to add at this time?"

He looked over at Buckem, "I'd like to move forward with working on my album."

"Try not to jack no one else's sound this time." Buckem mumbled, causing Raven to close her eyes before addressing him.

"As we already told you, the producer behind the issue has been dealt with. What Jerome said is true." Turning to face Jerome, she asked, "Is there anything that we may have overlooked? Or something else we are unaware of between you too that needs resolving? If so, please inform me now so we can get to the main point of today's meeting."

He looked over at Buckem. "There's nothing to resolve. Can we move on please?"

As Buckem sucked his teeth, Raven spoke again. "I understand and thank you for being level headed about this. The label feels that letting the fans see that there are no ill feelings between the two of you would be best. Which is why we have brought in a team to help us show that."

Before he could ask what she meant, Jerome saw two figures walking toward the conference room, one of which had been on his mind more than he cared to admit lately. A man with thick curly hair entered the room and Tasha followed. As she did, Jerome brought us eyes to hers and she didn't look away. Instead a tiny smile greeted him, along with a quick eye roll, causing him to hold back a laugh. *She seems as on board for whatever is going down as me.*

"Hello again Ms. Daye. Sebastian Gonanzles, is it?" Raven asked, standing up to greet the man that walked toward her.

"Hello. Thank you for extending such an attractive offer my way, Ms. Shawn."

Raven glanced around the room, taking Sebastian's hand. Jerome looked on as her cheeks reached her eyes and a giggle escaped her lips. "Well, you did come highly recommended. Thank you again for coming on such short notice." Clearing her throat, Raven gestured to the empty chairs and once Tasha and Sebastian sat down she took a seat and addressed the room.

"Sebastian, these are the two artists that you will be working with for the shoot. We would like to have Tasha come on board as your assistant, since the concept of the shoot stems from a previous shot she did with Jerome."

Up until he heard his name, Jerome had been staring at the glass window of the conference room. The view of Tasha in a simple lavender button down blouse and dark denim jeans was a welcomed sight. Not that he had expected her to dress more over the top, like he had gotten used to seeing with other photographers in the industry. Jerome took comfort in seeing her subtle but somehow confident look. Three small gold chains rested across her neck, one just over her collarbone.

She also had a pair of matching gold stud earrings in each ear. They were almost not noticeable behind her twists. Thoughts of reaching out and tucking the tresses behind her ears flashed through his mind when Jerome brought his attention to Raven.

"With the five year anniversary of his first album coming up, we wanted to revisit the site of that shoot. Since Tasha was the photographer, we thought it would be great to have her on board as well."

Jerome watched as the man turned to Tasha and whispered low in what he thought was Spanish. When Tasha picked up a pen and paper from the table and wrote on it, she handed it to Sebastian.

"I see. So, Tasha declined the offer of working with the label and you somehow were able to find me? Is that correct?" Sebastian directed to Raven.

"Yes. I hope you are not offended." Raven told Sebastian.

Jerome was surprised that Buckem hadn't said anything so far. He glanced over at Buckem and found him eyeing Raven. From the half sleepy look in his eyes, Jerome knew whatever was now on Buckem's mind was not fit for their situation at the moment. Bringing his attention back to the conversation, he listened as Sebastian spoke, "I am not offended at all, in fact, I would like to thank you again for providing me with another chance to work with Ms. Daye."

Seeing the man across from him wink at Tasha, Jerome set his jaw.

"And where will the shoot be taking place?" Sebastian asked.

When Raven spoke again, Jerome felt someone watching him. Turning his head slightly, he was met with a stare from Sebastian, who didn't bother looking away. The man sent a smirk his way and Jerome quickly refocused on the two women.

"There is a resort called Sandy Shores, on Bejon Beach. That is where the shoot will take place."

Tasha blinked at Raven before scribbling fast onto the memo pad in her hand. When she showed it to Sebastian, he looked over at Jerome again before asking, "Is there another location that we can choose for this shoot?" Sebastian smiled widely at Raven and added, "As I am new to the area, I would like an opportunity to scout other possible locations."

Raven brought her attention to Tasha. "With the timing of the shoot, we thought Sandy Shores would be the best option. Ms. Daye, you grew up here - is there another location you feel would be best?"

With everyone now watching her, Tasha glanced briefly at Sebastian before answering. "Well, lots have changed since I've been away. And the photoshoot you would like to recreate was taken at Bejon Beach..." As her voice flattered, Tasha paused and took a quick breath before speaking again. "No, I don't know of any other locations."

"Good! Then the original location it is. My assistant will give you the necessary paperwork on your way out."

Raven stood and waved over her assistant. When they entered the room, the assistant handed Sebastian a manila folder. As she started to leave, Sebastian spoke, "Since I was not the original photographer for the intended shoot, I would like to assign myself to the position of second photographer. At least for the principal shots."

Jerome noticed the gold chains on Tasha's neck moved a bit as she cut her eyes to Sebastian, but she remained quiet. Sebastian looked at the photos and paperwork within the folder before bringing his eyes to meet Jerome's. "Since this was Tasha's first, um.." He let the words hang in the air and Tasha crossed her arms as Sebastian finished. "...shoot with Jerome, the Preacher's Kid - is that correct?"

Tasha scoffed. "It was not a photoshoot and I had no idea photos were submitted for his album."

It was Sebastian's turn to stare at Tasha, and she chuckled dryly. "If I did know, I would have drawn up an invoice and sent a proper model release contract."

"That's my sweet yet shrewd Tasha, always thinking of the bottom line."

Sebastian turned to look at Raven, "With all things considered, I wish to take second on this assignment."

Raven glanced between the two and nodded, "This will change the pay structure for you, but otherwise won't be a problem."

"Of course. And again, thank you for contacting me." Sebastian stood and strolled over to Raven, taking her hand into both of his. "It was a pleasure to meet you, Ms. Shawn."

"Aye man! Cut all that out and get back to business."

Turning to the sound of Buckem's agitated voice, Jerome saw him openly frowning at Raven and Sebastian. The two smiled at one another and Raven's hand slipped away from Sebastian's.

"Thank you. Have a good day."

With that, Raven exited the conference room.

"I want a bunch of hoes in the background for my part of the shoot." Buckem announced.

Jerome found himself fighting a grin at the sound of Tasha's snort. Looking over at her, he saw Tasha gather her twists into a high bun and wrap them around one another until they were securely in place. Bringing his bottom lip inward, Jerome stared at her full lips.

"Just how do you see that request tying into the original concept of this shoot?"

Buckem stared at Tasha, and when he realized that she was waiting for an answer, he sucked his teeth and rolled his eyes. "My fans know my sound and my style. How I'm gonna look on a beach without some hot hunnies behind me?"

Tasha spoke under her breath in Spanish, and Sebastian snickered.

"What Tasha is trying to say is -" Sebastian was interrupted by Buckem, who now looked hard at Tasha.

"I don't care whatcha gotta do Romeo - make it happen." When Buckem stood, so did Tasha. She rolled her neck and Jerome readied himself to stop Buckem from so much as walking in her direction.

"Your vision for this shoot is not my concern." she said flatly and added, "If you are unhappy about that, call your handler back in here and work it out with her."

"I'm telling y'all what I want and you saying it don't matter?!" Buckem leaned over the table, getting Sebastian's attention.

"Tasha, sweet, it could not hurt to hear him out, no?"

Buckem tilted his head at Sebastian, slowly nodding. "See, ya man gets it. So you gonna listen to me or what?"

Jerome knew the answer before Tasha started to leave the room. Seeing Buckem's jaw slightly open, Jerome felt a smile spread across his face. *She still as stubborn as a hot mule.*

"I suppose we can look into something that would work for both artists." Sebastian said smoothly.

Tasha whirled around to face Sebastian, and Jerome saw her eyes narrowing in on him. For a moment, he almost felt sorry for Sebastian, but then Jerome thought of all the time this man must have spent in Tasha's company during her time away and dismissed that feeling.

"Gala or not Gonazales, if you and this - *artist* - push for a summertime skin flick shoot, I will walk."

Jerome's curiosity piqued once more when Sebastian simply smirked. "Are you looking to recreate *everything* from the original shoot, my gordita?

"No!" Tasha's eyes wavered as she quickly looked from him to Sebastian.

"Then why are the details so important to you, my sweet?"

Looking briefly at Jerome again, Tasha answered. "They aren't, but my reputation is." Tasha rolled her eyes as she stared at Buckem again. "This is exactly why I don't work with entertainment."

"Aye! Someone needs to check this bit-" Jerome was out of his seat before Buckem could finish his sentence.

"Watch how you speak to her, or any other women while in my presence."

Buckem stared at Jerome and scoffed. "You trying to tell ME what to do?"

When Jerome said nothing, Buckem laughed. "And if I don't - whatcha gonna do, PK?"

He remembered what Tasha said to Sebastian moments ago and chose to follow her lead. "I won't do the shoot."

Tasha and Sebastian looked on as Jerome continued. "Since the concept is based on my first album cover, guess what folks gonna say if you do it without me?"

Buckem stared at Jerome before cutting his eyes over to Tasha. He then pushed past Jerome, hitting his shoulder as he left the room.

"See? Everything will be fine. No need to worry." Sebastian's smile was wide as he glanced at Tasha.

When her eyes fell on his, Jerome sent a nod her way. He felt Sebastian watching their exchange, but as Tasha sent a small smile his way, Jerome didn't care. The two shared another glance before he left the conference room.

**Tasha**

The next day, Tasha and Sebastian drove to Sandy Shores bright and early for the shoot. Once they arrived, the two split up, leaving Tasha to start setting up before Jerome and Buckem arrived while Sebastian checked them in.

**I'm here.**
**Where we meeting?**
**-Jerome**

Fighting the urge to call Jerome just to hear his voice, Tasha bit her bottom lip. All night she tried not to think about the way Jerome looked at her during the meeting yesterday. But it was all she thought about, and she knew Sebastian was aware of her prior relationship with Jerome. His album cover was the exact photo on display during her introduction with the directors at Rebel Shots during their internship orientation. Now Tasha had two hard truths to contend with - one, at some point during this shoot, Sebastian was likely to ask her more about her past relationship with Jerome. *He's probably waiting for just the right time to spring it on me.* Tasha thought sarcastically.

And two, there was no way she could be in the same town as Jerome. Tasha was already counting down the hours until she could book a business class flight far away from him. Yesterday she got a front row seat to the people Jerome has been working with, and she knew it was only a matter of time before she had to go off on that Buckem dude. Raven wasn't bad, but she for sure could not help Jerome if push came to shove. Though Tasha was surprised to see that Jerome could hold his own. It excited her to see him handle Buckem and warmed her heart that he had her back when it came to what she thought about the photoshoot.

When Jerome stepped in and spoke up about the concept of their photoshoot, she wanted to rush into his arms. Too scared to text Jerome back while her mind wondered about how welcoming his embrace would be, Tasha instead texted Sebastian her location and told him to send the information to the others. Done with the set up, she cast a longing glance out to the beach before closing her eyes. Tasha's eyes burned as Jerome's blinding smile from the day of that impromptu photoshoot shot into her mind. Taking a deep breath, she slowly released it, taking her time to open her eyes. *OG, I know it's been a minute, but I could use some help out here.*

All she had to do was get through the shoot, and Tasha was gone. It was going to be tough leaving this time, especially after talking with Devin, but she would figure it out. *Maybe it's time to get him and the fam passports too?*

"Aye! We outchea!"

Her thoughts of what it would be like to fly with Devin and Darnell to parts unknown were put on hold by the sound of Buckem's voice. Tasha didn't turn around, instead she used the precious time left to try to prepare for seeing Jerome.

"Yo! You don't hear me talking to you?" Buckem shouted.

*Everyone at the resort can hear you.*

Tightening her hold onto her gear bag, Tasha looked out at the shore one last time as the two men made their way to her. "Let's get to work."

Two hours passed and the shoot was going surprisingly well, until a petite woman showed up with her hair in a sleek ponytail, wearing a flowing fuchsia dress. Tasha had to admit that the dress suited her and the location well. The woman also wore a pair of matching strappy heels. For a moment Tasha wondered how she got to this far on the beach wearing them.

"I'm not late, right?" the woman asked, while she walked over to Buckem.

Tasha caught a glimpse of Sebastian squinting at the woman before he lowered his digital camera. Placing a cap over the lens, Sebastian looked at the woman and said with a trained smile, "Excuse us, but this is a private shoot. I am afraid that I have to ask you to leave."

"Ain't no need for that. This my main piece, Regine." Buckem said, eyeing the woman in front of him.

Regine grinned up at Buckem and Tasha was left wondering why any woman would let someone refer to them like they were talking about something from a menu. Though with Jerome standing nearby, Tasha remembered that she was not in the business of judging anyone, especially with her present thoughts of the married man in her sights. She offered no assistance to Sebastian, choosing to see what would happen between the people in front of her.

They all watched as the woman went in to hug Buckem, who proceeded to palm her ass as he kissed her. Looking away did nothing to stop the slurping sounds from reaching her ears, and Tasha wished for a third time that day that she was anywhere else but there.

"Damn Regine, you lookin' gooder than a mug! Why you here so early?" Buckem asked Regine.

Looking up and finding Jerome staring at her, Tasha whipped her head toward the couple.

"Whatcha mean why I'm early? I barely had to get ready at the hotel before y'all left."

Sebastian and Tasha shared a look as Regine further explained. "I ain't want my picture taken in just any ole dress."

When Regine placed her hands out to smooth the imaginary wrinkles on the dress and winked at Sebastian, Tasha was thankful that he was the one shooting at that moment. "We are only here for the two artists. There will be no other company in these shots." Sebastian said.

He was firm in his approach, but it was clear from the blank expression on Regine's face that what he was saying made no sense. Deciding to help her friend, Tasha stepped forward. "You look stunning, but for this shoot, the label only wants us to take photos of the rappers. Sorry."

Regine brought her eyes to Tasha, "Whatcha mean?" Darting her eyes over to Jerome, Tasha watched the woman as she pointed at him. "He had his wife in a magazine - why can't I be in these pictures too?"

Tasha was not in the mood to list all the reasons why Regine would not be photographed, but she didn't have to tell the woman any of them, as Buckem grabbed Regine's arm with a scowl on his face. "Ain't no body got time for this! Go sit your ass down somewhere til we done, or find a ride back home."

Tasha saw the woman's face falter as Buckem went back over to Sebastian, who waved her over. "Please get me the second lens."

Carefully, Tasha took out the lens that he asked for and placed the other back in its compartment inside the lens bag. The tension in the shoot could be cut with a butterknife as she glanced around at everyone, bringing Tasha to say, "I think a quick break would be good for now, don't you?"

Seeing another tight smile grace Sebastiain's face, Tasha spoke again. "Everyone, take 30 please, and change outfits for the last shot."

No one complained as they all walked off, except Tasha, who began checking her gear for the sunset shoot. When the three guys came back, everyone had changed as she asked, even Regine, who donned a long bodycon dress with her strappy heels from before. With Sebastian controlling the light, Tasha wasted no time directing Jerome and Buckem for their group shots. Feeling the sun inching further and further toward the ocean, Tasha worked quickly to get the individual shots. She let Buckem do what he felt would work for his last shots before shooting Jerome's solo sunset shots. Instead of using her hands to talk with him, Tasha acted out the poses she was looking to get from him and asked him to mimic her.

"That's it - we're done." She announced before adding, " Great job everyone."

Tasha looked over at Sebastian and almost laughed out loud as he licked his lips while staring over at the half dressed women sitting inside the open bar area.

"That's it? We done?" Buckem asked Sebastiain, not once looking Tasha's way.

Sebastian said smoothly, "Yes, you and your...du jour can go frolick now."

She had worked with Sebastian long enough to know how to read between those lines, and seeing him wave the two off, Tasha knew Sebastian would be glad to never see either of them again.

"Thank you Sebastian. I'll take the equipment back to the hotel." Tasha offered.

She watched as Sebastian put away the rest of the lighting equipment before disappearing without a word, leaving Tasha and Jerome to finish packing up.

"You really love doing this?"

"Fo sho! Every time I get to pick up a camera and shoot, it's incredible."

"I see."

The two looked at one another for a moment before Tasha spoke again, "What about you? What's it like taking the stage in front of hundreds-"

"Thousands," Jerome said with a grin.

Laughing, Tasha corrected herself. "My bad, what's it like to perform in front of thousands of folks?"

She looked on as Jerome tried not to grin and found herself admiring the shadow of the full beard he was sporting.

"It feels good, real good." The smile started to leave Jerome's lips as he added, "But everything that happens before then just seems to get harder and harder."

Tasha knew what he meant, hell, she was here for this shoot because she wanted a ticket to an event so she could meet another photographer. "Yeah, it does seem to be that way, uh?"

"Tash?" Jerome called out softly.

She looked up at him and almost dropped her gear bag. With the last of the sun meeting the lazy waves of water, Jerome's eyes shimmered when he looked out at the sky, And once his gaze found hers, Tasha would have given just about anything to go back to the day when she took those first photos of him. His deep umber complexion was on display in the white t-shirt that he wore, and as Jerome stepped closer to her, the scent of the sea mingled with his slight woodsy and clover one.

"I know you said we shouldn't meet up again, but before you leave...."

Jerome reached out to rub the back of his head, causing his bicep to flex. She let her eyes travel slowly from his biceps to his shoulders. Soon, Tasha found herself admiring the curve of his neck as the veins pulsated before getting a full view of his strong and sharp jawline.

"What? What is it?" Tasha asked.

She could hear the softness in her voice as the words left her lips, but Tasha didn't care. Her eyes were now fixated on his lush lips and when he pulled them inward, Tasha found herself holding her breath.

"It's cool. Just - do you need help getting everything to your room?" Jerome asked.

Right now, the last thing she needed was to have Jerome see her to any room - especially one she wanted to be alone with him in.

"Tash? You good?"

Realizing that she hadn't answered him, Tasha took a deep breath and let out a shaky laugh. "I'm good. I'll see you around then?"

"Okay. Goodnight." he said.

Neither of them moved. Instead, Jerome's eyes looked her over again and Tasha re-adjusted one of the equipment bags over her shoulder before finally walking back to the resort.

ALL TASHA WANTED NOW that the day was done was to be alone. Being out in the sun all day shooting left her body begging for rest, but she still had work to do. When she arrived at the front desk, Tasha gave the clerk her ID.

"I'm here to pick up my room key. It should be listed under Trap Son's Records."

She waited while the clerk entered the information. When they handed her back her ID, the clerk said, "Yes, I see the three rooms were confirmed this morning."

"Three rooms?" Tasha said out loud. Confused, Tasha spoke again, "There should be four rooms, please check again."

The clerk typed on the computer and looked up at Tasha. "Ma'am, I am sorry, but the system is showing that a Sebastian Gonzales checked in three suites this morning, not four."

*Just what in the fresh hell is going on?!*

Not in the mood for any more foolishness, Tasha picked up a notepad and pen from the counter and scribbled on it, handing it to the clerk. "Could you please page this person to the front desk?"

The clerk looked at the name and then to Tasha who smiled sweetly. "Mr. Whorelazes to the front desk. Please report to the front desk, Mr. Whorelazes."

A few minutes later Tasha watched Sebastian jog to the front desk. Not giving him a moment to catch his breath, she asked. "Why are there only three rooms available for this shoot?"

Sebastian blinked several times before stumbling out," I, uh, I did not find it necessary to have the extra room..."

*I know I ain't hear him right!* Tasha's eyes shot up to the ceiling, "There are FOUR adults on this shoot Sebastian - - four rooms is VERY necessary!" He tried to speak, but Tasha was not done. "This ain't our first assignment together, so you know how I prefer to work - alone. Especially when it comes to editing."

"Yet you wish to have an audience with Pablo Coslado..." Sebastian said under his breath.

"The sooner these photos are culled and edited, the sooner I can leave!"

Sebastian stared at her as Tasha brows knitted together. Feeling her face growing warm, Tasha hissed at him in Spanish,"You have been known to do sly shit, but this is low - even for you. If I had not promised Ximena a ticket to this Winter gala, I would toss these SD cards in the trash!"

Tasha turned to the front desk clerk again, as Sebastian reached out to grab her arm. "I'm sorry, my sweet gordita - I did not think -"

"Finally something we agree on!"

Sebastian tried again. "Please, just spend the night in my room. There we can talk..."

His words began to fade into the background as Tasha snatched her hand away and glared at him. Her left eye twitched when she asked, "Please tell me you did not book three rooms with the hope of me spending the night with you?"

When he said nothing, Tasha reached into her messenger bag and took out her business credit card from her wallet. "I'd like whatever room you have available please."

"Gordita, please..."

"Sebastian Luis Gonzales, do NOT say another damn word to me."

The clerk cleared their throat, getting Tasha's attention. "We only have an oceanside honeymoon suite available, ma'am. "

Tasha tightly shut her eyes as she handed the clerk her card. "I'll take it."

Surveying her room for the night, Tasha couldn't help but appreciate the expansive space, with its paradisiacal yet quaint view. An inviting cream sofa sat adjacent to the queen size bed, allowing Tasha to fully appreciate the floor length three paneled windows that showcased the beach. Once her gear was tucked away at the office desk, Tasha kicked off her shoes and went rummaging through her duffle bag for a change of clothes to finally wash the day away.

After a hot shower and a quick meal thanks to room service, Tasha began working on the photos from the day. Before long, her neck ached and as she stretched from one side to the other, Tasha saw the clock in the room read midnight. Finishing up the last of the edits, Tasha sent the batch to Sebastian and copied the record label in the email. Still wired and not able to tune out the calming waves that traveled up to the window of her room, Tasha decided to throw on a fresh pair of denim jeans, a white top, and a pair of kicks. Making her way to the door to leave, she grabbed her blue hoodie, flip flops, and her phone.

The resort bar was still packed, given the hour. She didn't want to see anyone this late or have some drunk try to talk her into spending the night in their room, but it was the quickest entrance to the beach. Tasha cautiously walked inside the bar. Halfway to the beach, she paused. Hearing about Jerome drinking was much different than seeing it in person. She almost didn't recognize him, dressed in all black, until he raised a hand and the bartender walked over to him and poured more brown liquid into a fresh glass for him, taking the previous glass away.

She knew that if she kept walking, Jerome would see her. The last thing she wanted after their day together was any more awkwardness between them, so Tasha turned left and walked toward him. His signature woodsy scent teased her nose as Jerome faced her. "What are you doing up so late?" Tasha managed to ask.

He peered at her over his glass and Tasha had to focus on the contents in it to stop the slow heat from rising in the pit of her stomach at his gaze. "Couldn't sleep." Was all he offered.

Tasha pulled out a chair near him and the bartender started to walk over to them. She held out her hand. "Nothing for me, thank you." The bartender nodded and Tasha turned to find Jerome's eyes still on her.

"Well, since you're here, wanna be the first to see the photos from today?"

He waved over the bartender back over. " Close my tab." After he paid for his drinks, the two sat at the end of the bar and began talking about the photos.

"These are good Tash."

Pushing the feeling of hearing him say her nickname to the side, Tasha grinned at him. "I know." They shared a laugh before Jerome showed her the photo on his phone of him and Buckem just as the sun started to set. They were standing diagonally with their backs facing one another.

"I think the label will like this one." Jerome said.

Thinking back to her interactions with the other rapper, Tasha rolled her eyes. "Let's hope Buckem does too. Cause if he comes for my craft - I'mma catch a case."

Jerome laughed again while swiping at the rest of the photos. "How do you bring all that out in a picture? Jerome asked.

Looking up at him, Tasha waited for him to show her the photo. It was one of his solo sunset shots. From a distance, the composition was simple, but Tasha was glad she had been able to use the last good natural light for the shot. She wasn't sure if the exhaustion in his eyes was from shooting all day or from life weighing on him, all Tasha knew was she had to get the shot. Thinking about that moment and feeling his stare, Tasha chose honesty.

"I can see something has you stressed, and it ain't all work related. As your friend, I wanna help, but I don't know how." She hooked her heels together as Jerome continued to listen. "Whatever it is, you have folks in your corner. And you got my number, so use it."

Jerome picked up his drink and finished it in one gulp. Tasha stared at him as he closed his eyes and exhaled. "I thought I was doing okay, keeping everything together. You would be the one to tell me that I ain't."

Reaching out to take his hand into hers, Tasha stopped herself. When she started to drop it back to her side, Jerome grabbed it. Her eyes locked on their hands, now clasped tight together. "You right, a lot has been on my mind. But I'm handling it."

"You sure? Cause I meant what I said, I don't know if I can help, but I'll always listen." Tasha told Jerome.

Silence fell over them, with only the sounds of the music from the bar in the background. "Thank you Tasha. I can't tell you how much that means to me."

Trying to lighten the mood, Tasha nudged Jerome before looking down at his phone." Now, back to my skills." Seeing him grin, she continued, "For one, it helps to have a little bit of practice. And you were the model for the first shoot, so of course I had to step up and show out."

He laughed as he looked over at her. "Thank you."

"Why are you thanking me?"

"For doing the shoot. I know you didn't want to be here, but I gotta say, it's been good seeing you."

"You're welcome. It was good seeing you too, Rome." Tasha watched Jerome close his eyes and would've sworn he was taking the moment in. Before she joined him, Tasha stood to leave.

"You going for a walk on the beach?"

"Yeah, how'd you know that?" Tasha asked.

Jerome tilted his head at the flip flops in her hand, causing Tasha to chuckle.

"Can I come with you?"

**Jerome**

The beach was quiet, aside from the gentle laps the small waves made when meeting the shore. And once Tasha swapped her sneakers for the flip flops in her hand, they walked in silence for a few minutes before Jerome asked. "So, what's next for you?"

"What you mean?"

"Your next move, out in the world. Where is it?"

Tasha looked over at him and Jerome got lost in the way the lights from the resort lit up her features. Her doe-like eyes watched him and her bright smile drew him further in. He knew how wrong it was, but Jerome was falling for Tasha all over again. If he was honest, Jerome couldn't remember ever being over her to begin with.

He listened as she laughed softly, "Oh, well, back home. And then to my home away from home, Murcia."

*Did she say she was staying in town?*

Needing to confirm what he just heard, Jerome asked, "What, or who waiting on you back home?"

When she arched an eyebrow his way, he explained, "I'm just asking. Thought you already had plans to be halfway around the world by now."

"I do, but first I'll be the maid of honor in Alexa and Rachel's wedding. Then there's a gala that I gotta go to for work."

He nodded. "How Alexa and Rachel doing?"

Tasha sent a quick side eye his way. "You sure you wanna know?" When he nodded again, Tasha continued, "Well, Rachel is doing good. She got promoted to the director over at Creative Chords. But..." Looking at Jerome, Tasha seemed to be choosing her words carefully. "I don't think she likes you all that much these days."

Taken aback, Jerome asked. "What you mean?"

"I don't know, but whenever your name comes up, Rachel gets ornery as hell. I'm just saying."

Jerome tried to think of why Rachel would not be feeling him, but as he hadn't seen her in years, nothing came to mind. "Thanks for the heads up. Maybe I should buy her a nice wedding present?"

"Or, oh, I don't know, try to reach out to her in person?" Tasha suggested. "Ask why when she hears your name she looks like she wanna fight."

His eyes widened. "Dang, she mad mad, uh?"

When Tasha nodded, he decided to change the subject. "So this work thing, is that how you met ya boy?"

"You know his name, and yes, that's where we met. We were roommates."

"Wait, what? Y'all - "

Tasha rolled her eyes, "It was a co-ed internship, and we shared a room during our time together. That's it."

"Oh, okay. I was just surprised to hear that, is all."

As she bumped his shoulder, Tasha added with a scoff, "Besides, ain't like you can say nothing about it no way."

He looked at her, before coming to a stop. Hearing her say what he was thinking out loud left Jerome feeling a hurt he thought he was already over. Before he could stop himself, Jerome turned to face Tasha and leaned in close to her face, "There was a time when I could have plenty to say. When I could tell you how I feel about your little friend and be well within my rights to do so."

She stopped walking and looked away. "Now you don't. You have a whole wife, a son."

"Tash -"

"I wasn't finished." Tasha met his stare and Jerome watched her take a deep breath before she went on. "You have everything you wanted, so for the sake of us being friends again, I'm asking you not to bring up the past."

Her bottom lip trembled and his hands tingled as he imagined reaching out and cupping her chin. With the sound of the waves rushing to the shore, his gaze intensified while he pictured her soft lips meeting his.

Tasha took a step back. "And whatever you're thinking about right now, don't."

His cheeks grew hot and Jerome swallowed hard. "I ain't mean to make you uncomfortable. Just...Tash..." He closed the space between them. "I wanna be friends again, but we never really talked about things before you left."

"We did, Rome." Tasha quickly shook her head, "That night at Bejon, we talked about why I was leaving."

"Now you're back. And I gotta get some things off my chest." Holding her stare, Jerome explained, "I don't know how long you're gonna be in town, but with your track record, it won't be long."

Tasha scoffed again and asked flippantly, "Was that you throwing shade?"

"No, but you know it's true. You're a runner Tash."

"What do you mean? I'm not running anywhere."

"Really? So when conversations get hard you don't just up and walk away?" Her eyes scanned the beach and Jerome let out a deep sigh as she positioned her body in the opposite direction. "You're doing it right now - looking for an exit. I let you do it once and almost didn't recover."

Jerome quickly reached out and grabbed her hand. He looked at Tasha as her eyes went wide. Jerome knew the smart decision was to drop this conversation, but he couldn't. "Stay."

He barely heard her speak, as he brought their joined hands closer to his chest.

"Jerome, let me go." she whispered.

When he did as she asked, the memory of her saying the same thing to him years ago entered his mind. Tasha stared at him and Jerome brought a hand out to touch her cheek. Her eyes fluttered closed when the palm of his hand rested on her cheek, his other one followed. With the sound of the waves behind him, Jerome couldn't stop thinking about the last time they were this close together at Bejon Beach as he let his hands fall from her face. Though more memories thrashed around in his mind, from the first year of her being gone. It was those images that gave him the courage to ask, "You say you wanna be friends again, right?"

"I-I did, but..."

"Well, as your friend, I gotta say it's pretty messed up how you always leave when things get difficult." Before Tasha could speak,

Jerome continued, "We had a past, Tasha. And if we're really gonna be friends, I think we should talk about that."

Tasha narrowed her eyes at him, "Really Jerome? Because the last time I saw you years ago - you had your tongue down my throat, and just a minute ago you were looking at my lips like you wanted to do it again!"

He sighed, unable to deny anything she was saying. "I didn't say it'd be an easy talk, but we at least have to try." Jerome's eyes drifted down to her lips and he immediately brought them back up to meet her stare. "If that's too much, can we talk about why you dip when conversations get difficult?"

She let out a deep sigh before a dark chuckle followed. "You know what, fine, okay. Let's do it."

"Okay? So you ready to try?" he confirmed.

"After the week I've had, I doubt it can get any worse. So let's talk." Tasha pressed her lips together before dropping her shoes to the ground. Jerome watched as she sat on the sand, keeping her bag close to her chest while facing the beach.

"Maybe we should get a towel from the hotel?" he suggested.

When Tasha didn't answer him, Jerome joined her on the ground, ignoring the feel of the grains of sand making contact with his clothes.

"My granny was the only one I could talk to about anything. She listened to me talk about my favorite cartoons and boy bands without making me feel silly." A soft chuckle escaped her lips as she went on. "But I wasn't the only one my granny talked to." Tasha kept her eyes on the shore as she spoke. "When she died, I think a part of Kitty did too. That was when she started leaving us alone at home. At first it was for just a few hours, then it was for a day or two. When she came home late one night after leaving us alone for a whole week with no food in the house, I cried and yelled at her for not being there for us like before granny went away. It was the first time she hit me.``

Jerome turned to face Tasha, who whispered, "And it wasn't the last. From the eighth grade until my freshman year of high school, anytime she would get upset about something, I felt it. Until I learned ways to avoid her."

"Tash, I would never..."

"I never thought she would either, but after granny died she did."

The two quietly sat in the sand and listened to the ocean and gentle waves before Tasha spoke again, "I'm sorry."

Tasha finally turned to look at him, incredulous. "Why are you sorry?"

"I thought you was always leaving when things got too difficult to put into words. If I had known that...that you did it because of what happened to you, I wouldn't have pushed it."

"Maybe I needed to be pushed to talk about it, so you'd understand." Tasha's smile didn't reach her eyes as she faced the beach again, "But that's not the only reason I run when it comes to you."

"It isn't?" Jerome tilted his head, "What's the other reason then?"

"Jerome..."

"Tell me Tasha. Why you trying to keep me at a distance?"

He looked on as Tasha took several deep breaths while holding his stare. "The way you was looking at me earlier was not how friends look at each other. And I didn't mind it."

That wasn't what he expected her to say, leaving him at a loss of words. "Oh."

"Yeah." Tasha sighed, "Now you know."

Jerome turned his focus to the beach, trying to give the waves his full attention. But with everything Tasha shared with him running a marathon in his mind, that was easier said than done. Neither of them moved for felt like hours, until laughter rang out from behind them. When Tasha stood, he followed.

"I meant what I said before. If you're really in need of a friend, I want to help."

"Thank you Tasha."

Locking eyes with her in the dim light, his hands itched to take her face in his. Jerome allowed himself one last slow glance at her full and inviting lips and lush frame before turning toward the direction of the hotel.

# Chapter Twelve

## Be Real

### Tasha

The next day, Tasha met Rachel and Alexa at the bridal shop for their final fittings. It'd been far too long since she'd gotten to use her camera since being back home, so she was thrilled when the couple allowed her to take a few pictures after they'd gotten settled in and served a flute glass of apple cider by the bubbly assistant. *So glad I brought my old Canon! Maybe I can go for a more retro take on the more detailed pieces to their dresses and suits...*

While getting the close ups she wanted as the love birds tried on each other their outfits, Tasha didn't waste time, and before long was in her zone - taking one picture after another and directing her friends into the poses she thought would best capture their hands and silhouettes.

"Tasha, please put your camera away!" Rachel finally demanded, waving a hand as Alexa laughed.

"You said I could get a few pictures for my website." She grumbled while fidgeting with the straps to her digital camera.

"We invited you as our friend, not so you can treat us like models." Alexa reminded Tasha.

Rachel looked between the two as Alexa's face broke out into a grin. "Though I can't be mad at ya Tash - my baby do look stunning. Come here right quick, I wanna tell you something..."

Rachel beamed as Alexa leaned in to kiss her longingly on the cheek.

Too busy taking in more of Alexa's kisses, Rachel ignored the camera snapping from behind them. When Alexa released her, Rachel saw Tasha put the camera back inside her dark denim messenger bag before sitting down on the loveseat inside the bridal shop.

"Y'all still that much in love?" Tasha blurted out before rushing out. "I mean, I know y'all love one another, but y'all are, like *in* love, you know? How is that possible after all the years y'all been together?"

The two looked at her and grinned as Alexa wrapped her arms around Rachel's waist. "There's no one else I wanna be with then this chick here." Alexa said with a sigh.

She could see that something was weighing on Tasha's mind, but before Rachel could ask what it was, Tasha offered them a small smile. "Must be nice..."

The two looked at one another as Rachel pulled away from Alexa and joined Tasha on the loveseat.

*Maybe she'll tell me what's up without Alexa around.*

"Babe, did you see the new suits that were up front?" Rachel asked loudly.

Alexa couldn't give her an answer as Rachel continued. "You should go check them out - now."

As Alexa looked between them, Rachel craned her neck toward the three piece suit section of the store and watched as her finance sulked away, Tasha sent her friend a soft smile. "You ain't have to do all that. Besides, you two tell each other everything anyway, so whatever you want to say to me Alexa will hear it later."

Rachel shrugged. "I was trying to be polite before getting in your business."

They shared a laugh before Rachel made good on what she just said. "You know we love having you back home, but I gotta ask - is there a reason why you haven't talked about when you're gonna leave?"

Seeing Tasha's mouth hang up just slightly, Rachel gave Tasha a few beats to think about the question.

"Well, I have a work event to attend. So, in another two weeks or so I'll be on a plane."

"Are you sure?" Rachel prodded gently.

This time Tasha's left eye raised as she nodded. "Yeah, I know it's going to be hard to say goodbye to them again, but this time I will be sure to do it right."

*Why she won't be honest?* Rachel thought as she watched Tasha avoid her stare. *She really think that we don't know she falling for Jerome again?*

Ready to get to the heart of the matter before Alexa returned, Rachel decided to ask Tasha as politely as she could, "Who are you planning to say goodbye to this time?"

Tasha squinted. "To my sister and the boys, Rachel. Who else would I need to say goodbye too?"

*Welp. No one can't say I ain't try to be polite.*

Alexa appeared with two suits in her hands and plopped down in the empty chair next to Tasha. "We know you've been spending time with more than your family these days Tash. So stop beating around the bush and tell us what's up."

Rachel and Alexa watched as Tasha realized what they were saying, and she almost laughed at how quickly Tasha bolted up from her seat.

"Now see what you did!" Rachel half jokingly scolded Alexa.

"Your way was taking too long, babe." Alexa shrugged while looking over the suits.

Tasha was still not making eye contact with them as she spoke slowly. "Y'all thought that I was talking about Rome?"

*If this girl don't stop playing in our faces!*

Hearing Alexa cough, Rachel had to fight a smirk as she watched Tasha sit back down and quickly corrected herself.

"Jerome."

They shared a look at Tasha and Rachel leaned back, curious to see what was going to come out of her mouth next.

Tasha rolled her eyes and let out a deep sigh."Look, it has been nice having a friend..."

Hearing her use the word 'friend' when it came to Jerome caused Rachel to let out a snort. Alexa gently nudged her and they listened to the rest of Tasha's explanation, "To have a friend, besides y'all, to hang out with while back home, but I owe Jerome nothing."

"Really Tasha?" Alexa questioned. " Did he get divorced last month and we ain't know?"

Their boutique associate arrived to check on them and Rachel could see that Tasha was glad to have a few minutes to think.

" Ms. Daye, your dresses will be at the front for you to pick up when you're ready.."

Tasha nodded as the associate faced Alexa. "I'll place these suits in the dressing room for you to try on Ms. Banks-Shaw."

"Thanks." Alexa said before looking over at her fiancee. "I'll be back. Babe, talk some sense into her."

Tasha rolled her eyes as Alexa left.

"When you left the country for the first time, you and Jerome looked to both be broken up about it sis. And now..."

Tasha interrupted her. "He is married. With a family." Rachel nodded as Tasha continued. "Clearly he has moved on, so why would I need to bother telling him when I'll be leaving?"

Rachel took one of her hands into Tasha's and took a deep breath. "I didn't want to have to go there, but you ain't leaving me no choice. We know where y'all went before you left, okay? A yearly thank you card from the bed and breakfast came in the mail."

*I hate to open old wounds, but I don't want to see her broken up again over him.*

Rachel tightened her hold onto Tasha as she tried to remove her hand.

"You keep everything to yourself Tash, but we know that it hurt you bad to leave him back then."

As she watched Tasha's chest rise and fall, she knew that her friend wanted to be anywhere else but in this boutique having this conversation. But Rachel was her friend and she remembered how Tasha used to look at Jerome when they were together. Tasha had that same look in her eyes now. Both her and Alexa noticed and Rachel didn't want another three years to go by before she saw her girl again because she got hurt falling for Jerome one more time.

"I'm good Rachel. Really. I do keep things to myself, but I'm seeing someone about that."

*That's new intel.*

"Wait, you mean like a therapist? You in therapy Tash?!" Alexa shouted as she strolled back to the sitting area, wearing a hunter green three piece suit that was just a little too snug.

Tasha's eyes widened and Rachel thought she was going to give herself whiplash from swinging her head back and forth so fast.

"Well, are you?" Rachel asked.

"Not how I wanted to bring it up, but, yeah, I have a therapist. For the last year." Tasha confirmed.

Rachel was happy to hear that her friend had someone she could talk to when she was ready. "That's good Tash."

Alexa, not bothering to lower her voice, added, "Yeah, I was hoping you would finally go see someone, but don't forget you our A-1, alright? And we can listen if you ever wanna chat, okay?"

Rachel looked on as Tasha tried to fight her lips from turning upward and gave up, letting out a small chuckle, "How could I forget when your loud ass won't let me?" she asked, causing Rachel to laugh too.

*She's gonna be okay. She just needs time.*

"What my baby is trying to say is that you know you can talk to us too, right? Don't keep sitting on your feelings until it's too late, Tash." Rachel told her.

"I'm learning not to do that anymore, but thanks for reminding me." Tasha squinted at Alexa, scanning the outfit she had on. "How you still breathing in that suit? Ain't it a little tight?"

When Alexa simply rolled her eyes at Tasha, Rachel shook her head and giggled.

## SOFIE

*Why did I agree to this shit - again?!*

She looked in the full length mirror one last time before leaving her bedroom. Last week after his trip with Buckem and that photographer, Jerome told them that they all were going to church on Sunday. Sofie wanted to tell him that she already had plans, but Jerome didn't stick around to hear her say anything. She remembered watching him drag his weekend bag behind him after he spoke, heading to his room.

Sofie thought he was acting strange all week, so she called her girl to find out what exactly happened on Bejon Beach.

"Oh girl! Buckem had me up all night! After dropping a few hundred at that fancy restaurant, we went back to his room and-"

Feeling a headache coming on, Sofie stopped pacing in the kitchen long enough to interrupt her friend. "You can tell me all about Buckem later. I wanna know what went down at their shoot."

"Damn, that was rude!"

Sofie sat at the dining room table and waited for Regine to fill her in. She listened as Regine mumbled out, "When I got there, they had already been taking pics. That big girl had them out in the sun all day, from what Buckem said. And then the hispanic dude wouldn't even take no pictures of me!"

*If she don't get to the damn point - I swear!*

"And? That's it?" Sofie pressed.

"Well, yeah. I wasn't there at the beginning, so what else I'm suppose to know?"

She heard Regine suck her teeth and decided to lay her cards on the table. "So Buckem ain't say nothing else? Y'all ain't see Jerome with ole girl afterwards?"

Regine cackled, "Oh, okay! I see what's got you all stressed - you calling to see if ya man's creepin?"

Sofie rolled her eyes as Regine laughed. "Well, if PK is creepin, he was smart not to do it with us there. After they ended the shoot, we ain't see him again until we was going back to our room."

"Where?" Sofie demanded before adding, "Was he alone?"

"Girl, you trippin! Ya man was at the bar - alone. Looking all sad and shit.".

Imagines of Jerome and Tasha talking with more than their hands started to disappear from her mind. It had been so long since the two of them had sex, she honestly couldn't remember when it happened. *Regine's right, I'm tripping.*

Pressing her lips together, Sofie's mind went back to earlier that month when she saw Jerome shirtless before going to bed. *Should I give him some when he gets home tonight? Just to keep him in line - and away from that Daye bitch.*

Sofie took two deep breaths and released them slowly. "Oh, okay. I was just wondering, is all."

"Nah, you really thought ya man was out here doing you dirty! Girl...you may have a lame one, but Jerome ain't the cheatin type. Trust me - I know."

Squinting her eyes while thinking over what Regine said, Sofie chose to brush it off before asking, "So, what you and Buckem get up to in y'alls room that night girl?"

WHEN THE THREE OF THEM arrived at Christ Corner the next day, Sofie's mean mug was in full force. All the older ladies and their big bright hats passed by them, openly frowning at her above the knee dress. She ignored them while walking behind Jerome as she carried Ro inside the double doors to the church. He would stop every so often to say hello to someone and all Sofie wanted him to do was get to the pew so she could put Ro down and go to the restroom.

"Baby!" she heard Evelyn say.

The older woman almost knocked over several people in front of them to get to Jerome, and Sofie felt a little bad for not wanting to be there. She looked on as Jerome hugged his mama.

"Hey mama." Jerome said while still in her arms.

Evelyn let him go and looked over to Sofie. For the first time, she felt that the woman's smile toward her was genuine. "You brought the whole family with you?" Evelyn said.

"Hi Evelyn." Sofie offered.

Ro reached out to the older woman and Evelyn looked at Sofie before asking, "Hi Sofie! Is it alright if I hold him, baby?"

Sofie nodded as Evelyn took Ro from her arms. "I'mma go to the restroom."

Quickly walking through the growing crowd of church goers, she turned the corner and pushed open the door to the ladies restrooms. Once there, Sofie locked herself inside the stall to do her business. When she stood up and flushed the toilet, Sofie heard a group of women enter. Not wanting to pretend to be friendly, she decided to wait for them to wash their hands before going out.

One of them sighed before sucking their teeth. "We got to be the only church still wearing these tired ole choir gowns!"

When the others laughed and nodded in agreement, another woman said, "Y'all see who made an appearance today?"

Another one answered to no one in particular, "Yes sis! JPK and his little family. That baby sure is cute."

Sofie smiled as she thought about getting Ro dressed for the day in his slacks and suspenders. A third voice joined the conversation. "But that wife of his knew that dress was too dang short! Where she think she going in that?"

"Probably to that sinner's water hole - BU."

Someone snickered before the woman from earlier spoke again, "Y'all ain't right, talking like that about someone in the Lord's house."

"This my mouth and the Lord knows I'm right!" the woman loudly exclaimed.

The third one added, "At least when Jerome was with the Daye girl - he made it to church on time."

At the mention of Tasha's name, Sofie unlocked the stall and swung the door open. "Y'all should consider it a blessing that me and mine even step foot in this spot!"

She glared at the three women, who stared at her with their jaws open. The smaller of the group backed away, only turning to open the door to leave. The two that remained shared a glance at one another as they took their time putting back on their choir robes. While they were avoiding her stare, Sofie marched toward the exit door and refused to move an inch, even as the girls cautiously brushed past her to leave. Sofie's hand shook as rage blurred her sight. *Every time I come to this place - these chickenheads got something to say!*

Soon she heard the piano ring out as the welcome song began. Feeling anything but, Sofie stomped out of the restroom and to the first pew to sit with Jerome and Evelyn. When the choir began, she narrowed her eyes as she spotted the three women from earlier in the first and second row, signing.

Mid way through the service, one of the two girls from the restroom stood up to sing. With the rest of the choir behind her, Sofie listened as the girl began her solo. Rolling her eyes, Sofie sighed and prayed that the service would be over soon. Until the woman singing hit a note that clearly was not practiced - it sounded like a frog jumped out of throat and Sofie snorted.

"You good?" Jerome whispered.

Sofie flashed him a grin, "I am now."

When the woman tried to sing out the note again, the same sound tumbled from her mouth, and Sofie loudly laughed. The choir now had their eyes on Sofie, who leaned into Jerome's shoulder before draping her arm around his neck. She looked up at him and caught his disapproving glance, which only added fuel to her ire.

The final chords played out on the piano, and Senior directed the choir to have a seat. As they did, all the women in the second row began whispering to one another. One of them even stuck out a finger in Sofie's direction, making the others in the row hide their giggles behind their church fans. *I know these bitches ain't talking about me?!*

"Now, if any of you feel the need to be closer to our God, please come to the altar."

Sofie was up in seconds. She made her way to the choir instead of to God's table and loudly addressed the women. "I know you heifers ain't up here laughing at me!"

The soloist stood as well and shouted. "Ain't nobody scared of you - thotpocket!"

"Who you calling a thotpocket, you big boned bitch!"

Before she could lunge at the woman over the panel, Sofie felt Jerome's hand grab hers. With him leading them out of the church hall, Sofie's vision blurred as hot tears fell down her cheeks. The whole congregation seemed to be talking at once, but as they made their way down the aisle she overheard an older woman loudly whisper, "What's a thotpocket, Gladys?"

They hadn't made it past the church's waiting area before Jerome stared at her and demanded, "What's wrong with you? Calling a sister in Christ's house out her name!"

"Them hoes stay talking about me in this building! And I'm tired of it!"

Looking him in the eye, Sofie wiped away the tears on her cheek. "Don't act like you don't know they be talking about me in here! Since day one, no one's had a kind word for me in this bitch!"

"Sofie, please. No one's -"

She put her hands against his chest and pushed him away. "They is! Every time I come here, they whispering about me. Today, them hoes was up in the bathroom comparing me to your little friend from back in the day."

Seeing him hang his head, Sofie breathed heavily and watched him level his eyes to hers. "I'm sorry. I wish you had come and told me."

"What was you gonna do? Tell your Daddy?!" she shouted. "They suppose to be Christians, but when they think no one hears they ass be talking the most shit!"

"Please stop cursing."

"This my mouth PK!" Turning away from him, Sofie took another deep breath and spoke through clenched teeth. "Get my baby."

"Sofie, please..."

"I said go get my son!" Facing him again she saw Jerome staring blankly at her and threatened, "You go get Ro or I'mma go back in there and snatch him up myself."

She looked on as he sighed. When the entrance doors closed behind Jerome, Sofie covered her mouth as more sobs threatened to break free.

*I swear on my Mama - I ain't never coming back to this place!*

**JEROME**

"Aye aye! Ain't that JPK?"

"He really rolling through in here after that diss track Buckem dropped?!"

In a last ditch effort to smooth things over with Sofie after what happened at Christ Corner that morning, Jerome told Sofie that they'd be making an appearance to Buckem's album release party. Ignoring the not so quiet whispers as he and Sofie stepped inside Bottom's Up, hand in hand. Jerome started to make his way to VIP. He made sure to dress the part, wearing denim jeans and a basic black t-shirt. His latest kicks were a bright red, that under the lights seemed to match Sofie's mid length dress. He saw a few dudes eyeing Sofie and Jerome set his jaw while looking them in the eye. One of them grinned, and Jerome narrowed his eyes.

"You good?"

Turning to face Sofie, Jerome nodded. "Yeah, I'm straight."

"Okay. You just look...nevermind."

Before he could lean in to ask her what was she going to say, Regine strolled over toward them.

"Dang! Y'all really came."

Sofie walked up to her friend and gave her a hug. "I told you we would earlier girl, why you surprised?"

Jerome glanced around and didn't see Tasha, Jerome was ready to go. *Be seen and then leave.* He reminded himself.

Watching as Regine led Sofie to the VIP area, Jerome followed. When they were cleared by security, Jerome saw Buckem with a champagne bottle in each hand. He was surrounded by a few other rappers as they all moved to the track being played in the club. Wordlessly, Jerome surveyed the scene and decided that he and Sofie would leave once four songs were played. A hostess, much taller than him, made her way to Jerome, licking her lips and grinning before purring, "Whatcha drinkin' JPK?"

He looked out into the crowd again. "My usual." Reaching into his pocket, Jerome peeled two hundred dollar bills off his clip and gave it to the hostess. "This should cover that and whatever my wife and her friend get too."

The woman winked at him before sashaying over to Sofie and Regine. As the second song started, Jerome found himself nodding along to the beat. Taking out his phone, he went to the notes app and jotted down a few lines, until he heard the last person he wanted to talk to shout out his name.

"Is that you Jerome?! At MY party?!"

Jerome turned his head to see Buckem stagger over toward him. He knocked back a champagne bottle and shouted, "Aye! Bring me another bottle bitch!" As the guys around him laughed, Jerome frowned.

"Oh did I upsat the PK?" Buckem asked sarcastically. "I forgot you don't like me *disrespectin'* the females."

The second song ended, and before Jerome could say anything to Buckem, 'The Weakest Prophet' blared throughout the club. Feeling all eyes on him, Jerome kept his sights on Buckem. "There ain't no need to be calling women out their names."

"Says the GOLDEN PK!" Buckem slurred out loudly before pushing the empty bottle against Jerome's chest. "That might work where you roll, but you at my shit now!"

When the hostess returned and handed Jerome his drink. Staring down at the brown liquid, he tilted the glass slightly. With the dark contents reflecting his mood, he raised the glass higher to take a drink. But just as he was about to take a sip, Sofie and Regine's giggles stopped him. Turning to glance over at them, Jerome froze at the sight of Tasha sitting in VIP, staring his way.. Blinking rapidly and no longer seeing Tasha, he realized that she wasn't there. At least not physically.

*I don't want to be here either, Lord, this ain't for me.*

More giggles pulled him back to where he stood, and he let out a deep sigh as Buckem leaned in close to another hostess and grabbed her ass.

Tasha wasn't there in person, but her words ranged throughout his mind

Putting down the glass, Jerome looked over to Buckem just as the track ended.

"Congratulations on your album," he calmly said, "Stay blessed."

Turning around, Jerome only had put one foot in front of the other before Buckem's voice boomed out over the music, "Y'all hear this shit?" With his entourage looking on, Buckem swayed as he mockingly slurred, "Stay blessed."

As the crowd laughed, Buckem rushed to Jerome and leaned in close to his face. Jerome gritted his teeth but otherwise didn't move, meeting Buckem's glare. "You really think you special, uh, Preacher's Kid?"

"I don't think I'm anything, but this..." Jerome paused, taking in the vivid pink and purple lights. More than the faint smell of smoke reached his nose, and while staring out at the crowd of people watching his every move, he let out a dark chuckle and sighed. "... ain't for me."

Buckem scoffed and stared down at Jerome before he spoke again. "So, if I call you...a FAKE ASS prophet - you don't care?"

Stepping back, Jerome eyed Buckem's crew and then the man in front of him. "Call me whatever you want, I know who I am." The second the words left his mouth, visions of being on tour, playing with Ro in their home, with his joyful laugh ringing out, and the last Christ Corner Jamboree he attended flashed in his mind. Tasha's smile, even in his thoughts, was bright enough to dim the last lingering moment of doubt he had. "And whatever you and your crew say ain't gonna change that. My purpose is to remind folks how good the God I serve is."

The two men locked eyes again, and this time it was Buckem that backed up. Taking a swig from the champagne bottle, he smirked as Jerome finally stepped around him. Walking over to where Sofie and Regine were sitting, Jerome steadied his breathing before commanding evenly. "Let's go."

Sofie looked at him like he'd lost his mind, "What? We just got here!"

Jerome reached out for Sofie's hand. "I made my appearance, now it's time to go."

He looked on as Sofie pouted while Regine grinned.

"Girl, you heard ya man. Better get on home." Regine said with a glint in her eye.

Jerome's head was starting to spin as the DJ replayed 'The Weakest Prophet' and he stared hard at Sofie. When his wife leaned back into her seat, Jerome grinded his teeth.

"You can go. I wanna stay."

He blinked at Sofie before slightly tilting his head. "Sofie, I ain't leaving you here alone."

"I ain't alone - Regine's here."

Jerome closed his eyes before he looked around the club full of men and then back at his wife. "It's late and -"

"Why you trippin? Ya mama got Ro for the weekend, and I ain't been out in months. I'm staying!" Sofie shouted.

His throat burned for a drink and Jerome knew that if he didn't leave soon, he would be getting his usual. "Fine. Call me when you wanna be picked up."

Sofie's jaw dropped before she pressed her lips together. "Nah, I'll just call a rideshare."

The two stared hard at one another before Jerome nodded. He marched out of VIP, ignoring the chuckles behind him as he exited Bottom's Up.

**Tasha**

Spending the night at Bottom's Up was not Tasha's idea of a good time, but it was good for business. And since she was still considering her options when Raven sent her the invite, Tasha accepted. Looking around at the crowd of dudes pretending to like the lyrics blasting over the baseline to the track playing, Tasha wished she'd stayed on the couch with Tyrone for the night. Deciding that one turn around the venue would do, Tasha went to the bar and ordered a bottle of water.

Smiling at several girls, Tasha approached them first. While chatting with them, she made sure to hand each of them a business card.

"JPK just left."

Tasha looked behind her to find Velvet smirking at her.

"What happened to you being on the first thing smoking when you delivered your message?"

Tasha rolled her eyes. "Business. Besides, I'll be on a flight soon." Looking Velvet over, Tasha admired her white crochet bodycon dress. With the black lights on, she looked like a modern hippie work of art. "You look fly, Velvet. Still got my business card?"

"I know. And yeah."

Tasha nodded and went on her way. Walking around the mini stages, a flash of yellow light in the otherwise dark club caught her eye. Seeing a woman in a modest red dress, in comparison to all the other scantily clad ones, Tasha squinted. Another hand, much larger than the woman's, came into view, she backed up and rolled her eyes for a second time that night.

*Yep, it's time for me to go.*

She hadn't laid eyes on Patrick since being in town, and Tasha was not trying to see his grimy ass now. Though when the woman with him turned her face toward the light, Tasha's eyes widened. She looked on as Sofie and Patrick locked lips in the small space. A crowd of guys started to stampede to the stage, leaving Tasha with no clear exit.

They pushed her out of the way as several women walked out of the dressing room to strut across the mini stages. Not wanting to be the center of unwanted attention by walking behind the girls to the other side of the club, Tasha quickly stepped into the dressing room.

Tasha saw that the two were still in the room and quietly hid behind a large divider. Once the music started, she felt like she was getting a show of her own, courtesy of Patrick and Sofie. Through a small space in the changing divider, she watched as Patrick lifted up Sofie's dress and spun her around, bending her over one of the makeup stations. The moans and grunts that followed made Tasha feel sick. *How could she do this to Jerome?!*

When they finished, Patrick slapped Sofie's ass before adjusting herself.

"Yeah, you still ain't giving it to the Preacher's Kid. That puddin' thick as hell." Patrick drawled out.

Tasha's eyes narrowed as Sofie leaned into Patrick's chest.

"Ugh! Can you not talk about him? You know he tried to make me leave earlier?" Sofie complained.

Patrick took out a cigarette and lit it before laughing. "Wish I had been here to see that."

"That ain't funny! And this the last time we gonna do this Patrick - I'm serious!"

Patrick faced Sofie, wrapping his hands around her throat. "Who you think you raisin' your voice to? I ain't PK!"

He let go of her throat and pushed Sofie against the table before starting to leave.

"I know you ain't him, but you is Ro's daddy."

Hot, angry ears filled Tasha's eyes as Sofie's words replayed in her head. Blinking her eyes and trying to control her harsh breaths, Tasha continued to watch the scene in front of her as Patrick glared at Sofie before a dark smirk appeared on his face. "How I know that baby mine? Ain't you a married woman?"

"You know damn well Jerome ain't my baby daddy!" Sofie choked out before whispering, "I told you I was pregnant before I even slept with him."

Patrick took another drag of his cigarette. "And who gonna believe you, *trick*?"

Sofie wiped her eyes as Patrick turned his back on her and left the room. Tasha's entire body shook as she watched Sofie grab a tissue from the makeup station and fix her face before walking out of the dressing area.

*You know damn well Jerome ain't my baby's daddy!*

Tasha tried to shake the words from last night out of her mind, but she couldn't. With Alexa and Rachel away on their honeymoon and Ximena on a new assignment, she had no one to talk her through this. Her last therapy session was days before the photoshoot, and she didn't want to schedule an emergency session with Dr. Robinson.

*It's not my business anyway.* She thought.

After taking Tyrone out for his morning walk, Tasha managed to answer a few emails and see what Pablo's team had shared online about the gala. Everything was going well, yet here she was worrying about Jerome. To clear her head, Tasha texted Trisha and asked if she could swing by.

**Hey! The boys would love to see you.**
**Come through :)**
**-Trish**

"Titi!"

Darnell barrelled into her arms seconds after Tasha put down the kickstand on her motorbike. "Hey!"

"Why you ain't been here to see us?" Devin asked.

Tasha looked down at him and noticed he held the camera keychain in his hands. Kneeling to pick him up too, Devin looked away as he wrapped his arms around her neck. "I've been working, D."

When he said nothing, Tasha took wide steps with both boys on each hip. "I ain't forget my promise Devin."

She saw his head whipped around to look at her before he turned it away again. "Okay."

Tasha smiled and gave each boy a kiss on a cheek, causing them to break out into giggles.

"Girl! I know you crazy!" Trisha said, wobbling over to them. "You betta put them down 'fore you need a doctor."

Grunting as she bent her knees slightly, Tasha let go of Darnell and Devin and watched as they hopped out of her arms. "They ain't that heavy."

Trisha grinned as she shook her head. "So, you back from your gig?"

"Yeah, until Alexa and Rachel get back from their honeymoon. Then I'm heading out."

Seeing Trisha nod, Tasha looked around the house. Pictures of the boys hung on the main wall in the living room, along with a huge picture of the family. She looked at Trisha's smiling face, hand in hand with Lloyd in a white dress. The boys were in the photo as well, looking up and grinning at their mama. Tasha's heart warmed at the sight.

"I know it ain't fancy like the ones you take, but I like it." Trisha said, getting Tasha to look her way.

She saw her sister holding a brownish orange looking cushion as she went to sit on the couch. When Trisha placed the round cushion on the seat before sitting on it, Tasha broke out in a fit of giggles. "What is that?!"

"You laugh, just wait til you start having your own babies - this here is heaven sent!"

Trisha's words brought her back to what she overheard from Sofie last night and her eyes narrowed.

"I'm sorry, you know I'm just playing." she heard Trisha say.

Tilting her head, it took Tasha a minute to make sense of what Trisha was saying before she spoke, "Nah, I know you joking. I was just thinking about something."

"It must be deep to get you to mean mug me like that." Trisha said. "Wanna talk about it?"

Tasha looked at her sister and joined her on the couch. "If you heard a private conversation and learned something that could hurt someone you know, in a real bad way, would you tell them?"

Trisha thought the question over before asking one of her own. "Is this news going to change anything? Like, if you did share it with this person, would they make a different decision then the one they already made?"

She hadn't thought about that and it must've shown as Trisha then added, "If this news wouldn't change the person's decision, then

I wouldn't say nothing. It ain't your business, so don't go getting in it."

"Dang! When did you get so smart?" Tasha jokingly asked.

Trisha swatted at her shoulder, laughing. "I'm just saying. No need to give someone bad news if you ain't gotta. Let them hear it from someone else."

*She right. I should stay out of it.*

After spending the day with Trisha and the boys, Tasha put on her helmet and headed back home. While cutting through traffic, her mind was conflicted once again with Trisha's and Sofie's words on repeat. Pulling over to a gas station, she took out her phone and stared at the screen. Scrolling through her recent calls, Tasha found Jerome's number and pressed.

"Hello?" Jerome said.

Tasha bit her lip before getting to the point. "You home?"

"Well, yeah, I- "

She cut him off before she lost her nerve. "Can I stop by? I really need to talk with you."

A few seconds passed until Jerome answered, "Okay. Let me text you the address."

"Thank you."

When she ended the call, Tasha waited for the phone to vibrate. Seeing the text, she clicked on the message and brought her bike back to life.

TASHA BROUGHT HER BIKE to a crawl as she pulled into Jerome's driveway. She was surprised that he hadn't moved to a more secluded part of town, but Tasha was glad she didn't have to deal with any security or gated service to get to Jerome's place. Wiping her hands over her jeans, Tasha glanced around at her expansive surroundings before walking up to the front door. Knocking softly, she waited for Jerome to come to the front door. When the door opened and Sofie stared at her instead, Tasha took two steps back.

"What you doing here?" Sofie demanded, narrowing her eyes Tasha's way.

*You can't leave now, just go in and talk to him.*

Finding her manners, Tasha offered Sofie a tight smile and wasn't offended when it wasn't returned. "Hi. I, um, was hoping to talk with Jerome."

"My *husband*, Jerome?" Sofie confirmed.

"If this is a bad time, I could come back..." Tasha found herself saying, fighting the urge to sprint back to her bike and speed to Alexa and Rachel's house. She watched as Sofie's head turned slightly and saw Jerome make his way toward them.

"Hey. Please, come in." Seeing Sofie frown, Tasha tried again to make an exit.

"Really, I should have called earlier, but got caught up seeing my nephews and sister. We can talk later."

"Nah, you came all this way - come in and talk to *my* husband." Sofie told her.

Her tone suggested that the last thing Sofie wanted was Tasha in her home, but as she stepped out of the doorframe, Tasha found herself inside the house. With her heartbeat picking up with each step, she did a quick sweep of the space. High vaulted ceilings with cool beige paint on the walls. Besides the basic setup, the house appeared empty. No pictures adorn the end tables or walls, and if she hadn't spotted a couple building blocks next to the couch, Tasha would have found it hard to believe that a toddler even lived in this house." Y'all have a nice home."

"Thanks. So, what was it that you wanted to talk about?" Jerome said.

She looked up at him and for a second didn't recognize Jerome's face. Tasha wondered if he'd been sleeping, as the bags under his eyes said no. Feeling Sofie's eyes on her, Tasha regretted not taking Trisha's advice. "I, um, didn't see you at the album release party, so I wanted to ask in person if you'd be willing to sit down with me and review the B side photos from Bejon Beach."

Jerome squinted, "I told you what I thought about the photos before Tash."

He did, but Tasha had nothing else to lead with, so she kept going. Making up the story as she went on, Tasha thought fast. "You did, thanks. But since I am thinking of setting up shop back home, I wanted to reach out and see if you'd be interested in helping me with promotions." Her eyes lit up as more of her lying weaved into something believable. "Being that you're a local celebrity, I'd like to get a good foot in with several businesses as I renovate the new space."

"You staying here? In town?"

Tasha heard Sofie's high pitched voice and immediately felt herself wanting to roll her eyes. Nodding at the woman, she added, "If that is okay with the both of you. For your endorsement, I would be willing to give y'all a steep discount on any future photoshoots."

She watched as Sofie narrowed her eyes at her and Jerome. Strolling over to Jerome, Sofie gripped his shoulders and Tasha watched him shut his eyes. "Ain't that generous of you, *Tash*. We may take you up on that. When we need our family portraits done."

"I can't do this." Tasha blurted out.

Shocking both her and Sofie, Jerome chuckled, "You never was a good liar, Tasha." Biting her lip, she stared at Jerome as he asked, "Why did you really come here?"

*I can't do this, I shouldn't have come here.*

Tasha's eyes drifted back to Sofie and she frowned as Sofie's hold on Jerome tightened. For his sake, she tried to approach the purpose of her visit gently. "I, um, wanted to talk about Buckem's party. And a conversation I overheard before leaving."

Directing her eyes at Sofie, Tasha sent a silent warning to the woman. Which went ignored. "I think you should know what was said, since it concerns you."

When she finished speaking, Sofie's eyes flickered before narrowing hard at Tasha.

"Whatever was said about me, I'm sure I done heard before Tash. I know most the artists there don't like me." Jerome said flatly.

"If this was something an artist said, I wouldn't have made the trip out here." Tasha told him before adding, "It's more than that, and it's something I don't think you know."

Sofie released her hold on Jerome and Tasha continued, "But you, of all people, should know. Because it's important, and you have the right to full disclosure."

Trisha's words from earlier were loud in her head, *No need to give someone bad news if you ain't gotta. Let them hear it from someone else.*

She didn't want to be the one to tell Jerome, but Tasha knew he would want to know. Even if it hurts. And from what she could see from his wife, Sofie wasn't going to ever tell Jerome. Seeing Jerome's eyes without any emotion in them scared Tasha more than the devil, but she was not about to let Sofie continue to play him like this.

Focusing her sights on the woman flanking Jerome, Tasha spoke calmly, "You and I do not know each other, so please know that I am not here to start any drama."

Scoffing before glancing at her, Sofie sneered, "You could've fooled me, *trick.*"

Tasha's jaw clenched, but she took a deep breath. Before she could do anything else, Sofie rounded onto Jerome.

"Is this really the girl everyone whispers about at Christ Corner? Did you not have standards back in the day?!"

*Welp. No one can't say I didn't try,*

Tasha marched up to Sofie with her fists ready, but Jerome side stepped in between them and Sofie cackled.

"Tasha, just say what you need to say and go."

Hearing him speak so flatly toward her still sounded foreign to Tasha. She had to look up at him afterward just to make sure the man she thought was there was really him.

Sighing, Tasha brought her attention back to Sofie. "Last night, while at Buckem's album release party, I overheard Sofie talking to someone in private."

Jerome stepped forward, gently pushing Sofie aside as she tried to get in Tasha's face.

"I don't know what this is about, but Tasha, please do not upset my wife. "

Feeling the sting from his words build up behind her eyes, Tasha quickly backed away. Remembering the information that she gathered about Sofie from the girls at BU after leaving the dressing room that night, Tasha got her thoughts together. "Again, that ain't my intent, Rome, I promise. But you need to hear this."

"Who is 'Rome'? His name is Jerome! Stop living in the past and move on!" Sofie snapped, gaining both of their attention.

Tasha took a deep breath and exhaled slowly. "Did you know that Rookie from the club was Sofie's big sister?"

Jerome answered, "Yes, I knew about that Tash."

Tasha's eyes widened.

"Don't look so shocked, everybody knows that already *Tash*."

"Friends call me Tash and it's clear that that's something we'll never be. Address me as Tasha."

Sofie sucked in her teeth and rolled her eyes, "How 'bout I not address your irrelevant ass at all?"

"That works too." Tasha said evenly. "Now that that's out in the open, what about your relationship with your sister's ex?"

Jerome looked between the two of the women and then back to Tasha.

Sofie flipped her microbraids behind her shoulder, "Which one?" As she laughed at her own joke, Sofie went ahead and added, "You got a name? 'Cause before she was committed, my sis made rounds."

Now Tasha was ready to stomp a mudhole in this girl's ass. Done with being polite, Tasha bluntly replied, "Patrick - you know, the snake you were clinging to at Bottom's Up last night. "

Sofie and Jerome's eyes narrowed on her and seeing the way Sofie's lips twitched slightly, Tasha continued, "I can get security camera footage to back it up. You got anything else to say?"

Jerome turned his head slightly to look at Sofie.

Looking between the two of them and giggling nervously, Sofie answered, "I only stayed at the party to hang out with my girl. Patrick just wanted to say hey, that's all."

Jerome stared at his wife as she brought her attention to Tasha.

"Happy?" she tautly said.

Shaking her head, Tasha kept her tone low. "I know what I saw. And what I heard."

Sofie tried to link her hand with Jerome, but he stepped to the side, letting hers hang midair before she balled it into a fist.

Before Tasha could take a step, Sofie leaped in front of her, sneering as she called out to Jerome. "Look, just send your old little friend on her way and let's go to bed."

Tasha stared at Sofie. "Tell him, or I swear I will."

"Tell me what!" Jerome shouted.

His voice crackled in the air and despite the situation, Tasha found herself drawn to its sound. She turned to face him and it felt like she was seeing a new version of him for the first time.

A small set of crow's feet were beginning to etch around the corners of his right eye, which was now twitching in time to the faint veins noticeable on the right side of his neck. His eyes were in her direction, but Jerome seemed to be looking further away.

*You were supposed to find happiness, Rome.*

Tasha wasn't so full of herself that she thought that he couldn't be happy without her, but when she left, Tasha really thought it was because she couldn't give him the life he deserved. And after being back around him over these last few weeks, spending time getting to know this new Jerome, she finally realized that she was right. The younger versions of Tasha and Jerome would've made each other miserable trying to make their way in this world as a couple. Their time apart gave them room to grow, to live and see the world without each other.

Though now all she wanted was another chance to be by Jerome's side. To weather whatever came from being the woman in his life. Knowing that that chance was gone, Tasha would learn to deal with that - eventually. Leaving him would be the biggest regret of her life, but right now, she could not leave until he knew everything from last night.

"Ro is not your son."

Watching Sofie blink her eyes quickly as she pressed her lips together, Tasha knew that this conversation was far from over.

"What did you say? All cause I was hugged up some dude, you over here saying this shit?"

Tasha gave Jerome her full attention. "Biologically, Ro ain't yours."

Kicking off her shoes and pulling her braids into a ponytail, Sofie made her presence known again as she shouted, "You fat ass bitch! The minute I saw you, I knew you weren't shit!"

Tasha didn't bother with turning to face Sofie as Jerome used himself as a barrier between them again. She only brought herself to step aside slightly to keep Sofie's feet from hitting her as she wildly kicked in the air.

"Where's your proof? For any of this shit, uh? Show me the proof that Ro ain't his!"

With sad eyes, Tasha sighed. "At the party last night, I ended up in the dressing room and heard Sofie and Patrick talking. I hid behind one of the changing stations and heard her tell him that Ro wasn't yours."

She looked on as Jerome's eyes widened. His hands trembled slightly, and Tasha decided to keep the rest of what she overheard between them to herself. Tasha watched Sofie closely as Jerome let her go.

"I wish I didn't have to tell you any of this. But I know what I heard."

Jerome looked at Sofie, who still said nothing.

"I sat on this all last night, told myself it wasn't my business and to say nothing. But I couldn't."

Tasha glanced at Sofie, who now looked ready to bury her in the backyard as she continued, "And not just because Patrick ain't nothing but a fuckboy."

She met Jerome's stare and felt her heart grow heavy before looking at Sofie." Seeing you use the only man that...the one man I ever cared for in this sick game of y'alls, I couldn't. "

Jerome walked up to Tasha, shaking off Sofie's attempts to keep him away.

"Why are you saying anything now?" He asked softly.

Now that she was fully able to see past the old Jerome, Tasha met his stare. "Years ago, I left without looking you in the eye to say goodbye. That has been a regret of mine ever since, and I wanted no more regrets where you were concerned."

Sofie pushed her way past Jerome and soon she was face to face with Tasha. "You think you can talk to him like that? In front of me, bitch?!"

Tasha stared at Sofie and let out a sigh as the woman continued to scream in her face. *I would choose the same too, if it came down to it.*

Though just because Tasha understood why Sofie would give her kid with Patrick Jerome's last name, that didn't mean she liked it. Backing away slowly, Tasha waited until she had a few good feet between her and Sofie before turning to leave their house. But once she reached the front door, her heart ached, and demanded that she look at Jerome one last time. When she did, that same heart almost shattered into pieces from the sight of his face, wet with tears.

# Chapter Thirteen

## Who Is He To You?

**Jerome**

With Tasha gone, Sofie whirled around to find him wiping away his tears.

"I know you a PK, but damn!"

He watched as she made tight circles around him in their living room.. "How could she come into MY house and say that shit! Being with you has made me weak as hell because I know I should've whooped her ass!"

Jerome walked past Sofie and sat on the recliner chair in front of her.

"What? You ain't got nothing to say now that ya girls gone?" She taunted.

"I knew." Jerome whispered.

Sofie stopped pacing. Jerome didn't bother to wait for her to look at him as explained, "When I took Ro for his first annual checkup, I saw his blood type on the doctor's chart and it wasn't the same as mine. With all the whispers about your past going on then, I had a DNA test done. I know he ain't mine."

"What?" Sofie said with a shaky breath.

He went on as if he hadn't heard her. "I didn't want it to be true, so I went on tour and decided to act like it wasn't."

He saw Sofie's hands begin to shake and as he stood up from the chair, she backed away quickly while darting her eyes around the room. "Is Patrick his daddy?" Jerome whispered again.

Sofie wouldn't look at him or speak.

"Please don't make me ask again."

She straightened her stance and rolled her head before letting out a heavy sigh. "I don't know! Are you happy now?"

A fresh wave of tears began as Jerome looked at Sofie.

"But there is a chance? That he could be Ro's real daddy, right?"

The silence was suffocating him to the point where Jerome wanted to scream. "Why? WHY?!" Jerome shouted. "I know you never loved me, but what sin did I commit toward you to deserve this Sofie?"

Seeing her roll her eyes at him once more made Jerome feel sick. He made his way to the stairs and marched up to his room. Hearing more shouting he knew Sofie was on his heels. Quickly, he grabbed his gym bag and started pulling clothes out of the dresser.

"Where are you going? Back to you little girlfriend *Tash*?" Sofie spat out.

Ignoring her, Jerome snatched open the first dresser drawer completely and flipped it over. He ripped the taped envelope from the back and tossed a thick envelope onto the bed.

"I'm going away for a few days. Read the paperwork in that envelope while I'm gone."

Sofie squinted at him and then gingerly picked up the envelope. He watched as she tore it open and pulled out the adoption papers.

"When I come back, if I see these papers signed... We will never talk about what happened here tonight again."

Sofie's eyes widened as she looked between Jerome and the papers in her hand. "Wait a minute. You still want to stay with me?" She asked.

"No."

Sofie frowned. "Why agree to do this then?"

Jerome thought back to what Tasha said before she left. "If there is a chance that Patrick is the father, I want to make sure he has no rights to my son."

**Sofie**

Exposed and frustrated at everything that happened, Sofie drove to the one place she knew Patrick would be. When she got to Bottom's Up and started to go to his VIP section, one of the guards stopped her. "Hos or bros only," he told her.

Turning around, Sofie went to the bar and ordered a drink while eyeing the VIP entrance. Almost two hours passed and she had several drinks at the bar before seeing Patrick walk out. She rushed to him, screaming, "You ruin everything you touch!"

The guard from earlier started to walk toward them but Patrick waved him away. "What you talking about, trick?"

"PK is talking about taking my kid away cause of your ass!" Leaning in closer she hissed, "*Our* kid."

Patrick grabbed her by the wrist and dragged her outside. "You ever say that shit to me again and you and your sister will be sharing a room at the crazy house!"

A chill ran through Sofie as she thought about Sunset OutReach Center, where her sister was being held. "Then help me! He gave me some papers to sign after that bitch opened her fat mouth!"

Laughing, Patrick lit a cigarette, "You talking about Tasha Daye?"

"This ain't funny! What do we do now?"

Patrick side eyed Sofie while taking a drag from his cigarette. "Whatcha mean we? I told you to get rid of it the first time you came crying to me about that shit!"

His words now were just as cold as they were that day, and Sofie recoiled from the memory.``She was right about you, though. Everything she said was true.``

Flicking the butt of his cigarette into the grass behind him, Patrick's tone changed as he asked, "What Tasha say about me?"

Sofie watched as he waited for her to answer. "That you were and will always be a useless fuckboy."

She scurried back several feet as Patrick raised his hand toward her. Looking around he slowly brought his hand down. "You lucky I got a few more dances lined up, or I'd make you pay for saying that shit to me."

Patrick turned to go back inside and Sofie grabbed his wrist. "Help me! You said I was your best girl."

As he quickly turned and jerked his hand away, Sofie stumbled and fell to the ground just as more people were exiting the club. Hearing them laugh, Patrick crouched down toward her, making Sofie feel lower than dirt. "Yeah, you *was* the best girl. Now I'm done with your ass. Run back to PK and make him happy with what I taught you."

She watched as Patrick went back inside and slowly got back up on her feet.

Going to her car, Sofie looked back at BU and started to cry. *Why did I think he would help me? No one can help me.*

Starting the engine, Sofie made her way back home. Wiping away her tears and thinking about what both Jerome and Patrick said to her tonight made the drive longer than normal. She knew Jerome was a good dude and after seeing Patrick, Sofie knew what she needed to do. Reaching across the passenger seat to take her phone out of her bag, Sofie didn't see the bright lights flashing in front her. The truck's horn blared out into the night, causing her to whip her head toward the sound. The last thing Sofie saw was a blinding light as a shrilling scream left her body.

### Jerome

He drove for some time, trying to find a place to clear his head. Everything in him was telling him to not go see Tasha at Alexa and

Rachel's place, but her words were on loop in his head. *I just need to know what she meant. Is it what I think it is?*

Dismissing the thought, Jerome decided to drive by the studio in a last ditch effort to avoid going to see her this late. *Yeah, I just need to write out what's on my mind in a booth.* But as he turned down the street, Jerome could see at least six rides out front. Two had chicks perched on the hoods, dressed to kill any man with heart problems, as their entourages shared a blunt. With a heavy sigh Jerome turned the steering wheel and left and quietly made his way to Alexa and Rachel's.

Half an hour later Jerome spotted her bike in the driveway, as he stood in front of her friends' house.

*What do I say after knocking on the door?*

Before he could answer his own question, the door in front of him opened and Tasha's eyes widened. She had changed into a pair of deep orange yoga pants with a loose matching top.

"How did you know where I was?" she asked.

Jerome looked pointedly at her. "You can know where I live, but I can't know about your spot?" Not giving her a chance to answer he went on, "Even though Rachel ain't speaking to me, she still follows my socials. I scrolled through her feed and found this place."

"That's hella stalker-ish of you, PK."

Her frown didn't phase Jerome, but he wasn't interested in talking to her from outside. "You gonna invite me in Tash?" Jerome finally asked.

"We've said all that we needed to say to one another. Just go back home."

"No." Jerome told her flatly

She narrowed her eyes at him but Jerome brushed off her stare as he walked into the house. "You think you're the only one that can crash someone's spot?" Jerome asked, turning to face Tasha.

She looked ready to brawl or bolt and part of him wanted to laugh, as he thought back to telling her about her flighty behavior at Bejon Beach earlier that month. Tasha loudly shut the front door, pulling his thoughts back to the present.

"Okay, fine. I was wrong to show up at your house. Really I'm sorry."

"I ain't come here for an apology."

Sighing, Tasha asked. "Then what do you want?"

"Answers."

Jerome took his time walking toward her. "What did you mean by having regrets? You said before you left that you have regrets about how you left. What is it that you regret?"

She stared at him for almost a full minute before pinching the roof of her nose. "I'll explain what I meant, but I can't right now. Are you free tomorrow?"

Seeing where she was going in evading the questions he asked, Jerome shook his head. "Nah, tell me now."

A phone chimed on the end table and Jerome's eyes followed Tasha as she marched past him and picked it up. But before answering it, she glanced over to him and sighed. "I can't do this right now Rome, really. Let's talk tomorrow, okay?"

As Tasha's eyes shifted from him back to her phone, Jerome made himself comfortable on the couch.

"Jerome, please - just go home."

"I will. When you answer my questions."

"Look, I am sorry about dropping by your place and saying what I said. It wasn't my place and it for sure ain't none of my business. I have deadlines and to be honest I can't have you here right now."

The ringing of her phone stopped and Jerome watched as she narrowed her eyes his way.

Another phone, on top of her laptop, started to ring. Not even glancing at him, Tasha picked up the phone and went back out to the foyer area.

"Hi. I know Ximena, I was going to confirm my flight arrival with you tomorrow. What changed? Why?"

Jerome listened as Tasha let out a deep sigh. "Sorry I didn't answer earlier. When?"

From the corner of his eye, Jerome saw Tasha look his way before quickly looking away. "I don't know. Indefinitely? I promise, you'll be the first to know. Take care."

Ending her call, Tasha locked eyes with Jerome. " You really want to know what my regret was? Besides letting you in this house tonight?"

Despite the situation, he found himself grinning at her last remark.

"We were young Jerome, still trying to figure out who we were and what we wanted in this world. So my one regret about everything was how I ended things between us."

Jerome stared at Tasha and tried to stop those feelings from the day she left from taking over. It had been years and he remembered everything like it all went down yesterday. "Do you regret leaving?" He asked.

"No. Just how I left."

He tried not to feel hurt by what she said but Jerome couldn't help it. He was ready to be with her back then, and all she gave him was a phone call before getting on a plane. Now here she was, like a tornado, messing with the life he had now. He was done with keeping his feelings to himself. "Now that you're done getting everything off your chest, I guess you ready to bounce again, uh?"

She looked up at him and Jerome didn't care how she felt about his sarcasm in his tone as he continued. "It was easy for you then, so leaving now won't bother you at all. Just pack up and don't look back."

Tasha stared at Jerome and he waited for her to go off on him the way Sofie did earlier. Instead her voice was soft when she finally spoke again. "You can't honestly think leaving was easy for me?"

Her eyes leveled on his and Tasha didn't try to hide her tears. "You have no idea how much I came to want you in my life." Tasha said. Jerome looked up at her as she continued. "I never thought I would feel for you the way I did. And then that night at the bed and breakfast... I thought you'd be better off without me. So even though it hurt me to do it, I let you go."

Wiping her freshly fallen tears, Tasha stared at Jerome. He said nothing, as he let her words sink in. Now having the answers that he came over for, Jerome could leave. But his greed was not satisfied. "Why did you never call once you got situated?" He asked.

"Phones work both ways Jerome." Tasha volleyed back.

He stared her down, rolling his eyes. "I didn't think you wanted to talk to me, the ole country boy who only dreamed of sharing the word of God with a mic? I wasn't worldly enough to keep you around, so why try to keep in touch?"

She stared back at him and rolled her neck. "You seriously been out here in your feelings like this?" She stepped back a few feet before looking at Jerome again. "It wasn't like we dated all that long anyway, right?"

"And now here you are, showing up at my spot to speak on things that ain't none of your business." Jerome reminded her.

Tasha's hands went to her hips for a second before letting them fall to her sides. "Look, I know how important family is to you and I didn't want you to be in the dark about -"

Sighing, Jerome interrupted. "I already knew."

Her eyes grew almost twice their size.

"Yeah, but good looking out. I guess better late than never."

She frowned. "Why didn't you just tell me to leave when I showed up then, if you already knew?"

He took a step closer to her, only to move two steps back."I wanted to hear what you had to say."

Running her hand through her twists, Tasha shook her head. "I should really learn to mind my own business."

The two looked at one another before Jerome asked. "Why didn't you?"

He knew why, but Jerome wanted her to admit it. Now that he knew how she felt after leaving the first time, Jerome was more than confident that Tasha's feelings were the same as his.

She closed her eyes and shook her head. "I answered your questions, so please leave." He tried to speak again but Tasha cut him off, pointing a finger in his direction. "We are not doing this. You are *married*!"

As she turned her head away, Jerom leapt up from the couch. He was now inches away from Tasha's startled face when he demanded gently. "Answer me."

Reaching out his hand to cup the bottom of her chin, Jerome slowly brought her face close enough to feel her breath on his.

"This ain't right and you know it."

He did and Jerome didn't care. Soon she'll be gone and he'll go back to Sofie. But right now, Jerome had to know. "What I know is that since you've been back, I look forward to seeing you."

When Tasha tried to turn her head away again, Jerome followed, placing a hand on the side of her face. Itching to touch more of her, he let his hand caress her cheek before trailing down to her chin. "I wanna see you, and not 'cause we're friends, Tash. I miss you. I miss *us*."

Tasha's bottom lip started to tremble, and Jerome forced himself to remain still as he dropped his hand from her chin. Tasha quickly turned her back to him and stepped out of his reach.

"I wake up wanting to be in your space, even if it's only from across the room."

"Jerome, stop. Just - "

Hearing her voice crack chipped away more of his will. Jerome closed the distance between them as he walked around and stood in front of her. Tasha's gasp echoed in the space surrounding them and Jerome brought his face even closer. With their foreheads now touching, he breathed in her scent of frankincense and honey, wanting nothing more than to drown in it. "I miss you. Not because my marriage is only in name. Because my heart hurts when I'm away from you. I miss my friend. I miss what we had. I miss *you*, Tash."

He watched as Tasha closed her eyes and whispered. "I miss you too."

Jerome bit down on the inside of his cheek as he inched away from Tasha. Her eyes were still closed, and he was thankful for that because if he saw what he felt in her gaze, Jerome would not have any strength left. He stared hard at her one last time before he began to move away. Only when he reached the front door did he dare look back at her. Seeing Tasha watch his every move with the same longing in her eyes as his, Jerome let out a deep sigh and left.

AFTER LEAVING TASHA the other night, he checked into Cove's Creek and managed to get a few hours of restless sleep. Though that all came to end when his phone began ringing on the nightstand. Mama's high pitch voice rattled in his ear as she spoke fast, "Is everything okay? Lillie been calling me and I ain't heard from Sofie since she dropped off Ro! What is going on?"

"Mama, mama!" he said, cutting through her rambling. "I didn't stay at home last night. Let me call Sofie and I'll come pick up Ro, okay?"

Managing to calm mama down, Jerome ended the call and dialed Sofie's number. When she didn't answer after the third try, he got out of bed and grabbed his car keys to check out. His phone ranged again while he was driving, but he didn't answer.

Once he was back home and didn't see Sofie's car, Jerome started to panic. No matter how strained their relationship was, he knew Sofie would never leave Ro for this long with anyone. His phone started ringing again. Seeing his mama's number on the screen, Jerome answered. "I just got to the house -"

"Lillie just called me! She say that Sofie is at LM Hospital- she was in an accident!"

Jerome froze.

"It's bad, baby. They're saying that she may not make it out of surgery!" Mama told him through the phone.

After getting the rest of the details from his mama, Jerome ended the call and drove to the hospital.

"What took you so long to come here?!" Ms. Ward shouted as Jerome walked into the waiting room.

She was not alone, as three other women surrounded her. He listened as the older women spoke in hushed tones around Ms. Ward.

"How is she doing now?" he tried to ask gently.

Ms. Ward flayed her hands in the air and cried, "How would you be if a semi smashed into you while on the road?!"

Her friends tried to calm her down, but Ms. Ward's wails echoed down the hallway. "Lord! What did my babies do?! One locked away for hurting herself and one fighting for her life in this hospital - Jesus! WHY?"

A nurse approached them and Jerome waited for them to speak.

"Ma'am, I know this is a lot, but I must ask you to keep your voice down. Your daughter needs rest." she explained.

Jerome waited for the nurse to notice him before asking about Sofie.

"Her vitals are better than when she was brought in last night. We've stopped the internal bleeding and have stitched her up. Now we are waiting for her to wake up so we can assess for any more damage."

He nodded and thanked the nurse before she walked away. Turning to face the women, Jerome sighed. "Mama said she was struck head on by a semi truck? How? Sofie hates driving at night." Jerome said.

Ms. Ward sobbed into one of her friends' arms as the ladies led her back to the waiting room.

The one who stayed behind spoke, "We was hoping you can tell us why she was on the road so late at night."

Jerome thought back to what happened at their house last night and hung his head. " We got into an argument and I left, so I honestly don't know."

The older woman looked at him, but Jerome said nothing else. "Okay. When Lillie calms down some, I will tell her. Are you going to go inside and see her?"

Jerome nodded as the woman patted him gently on his shoulder. Waving toward the nurse from earlier, he waited for them to walk to him before speaking, "Can I go in and see her?"

"She's asleep right now, so please keep your time brief."

Nodding, Jerome let the nurse lead him into Sofie's room. The dim, warm light near her bed seemed to highlight the bandages and wires attached to her chest. He stepped closer inside the room as the nurse quietly left. A humming sound was all he heard as Jerome looked at Sofie in the hospital bed. Her normally warm beige skin was now waning and fragile in its current state. Jerome stood over her for another moment, watching the machines she was hooked up to help her breathe, before reaching out to take her left hand. It was cooler than he expected, but Jerome held it gingerly as he closed his eyes and prayed. When he finished, Jerome gently placed her hand back to her side, tucking it under the covers as he left the room.

Driving down the highway, Jerome never felt more lost. All he could do was blame himself for Sofie being hurt. *I should have stayed.* He berated himself again at another stoplight. *Why did I give her the paperwork like that?*

He remembered the shock on her face when he told her that he already knew Ro wasn't his biological child. But after Tasha left, his fear led him to act without thinking and he all but shove the adoption papers in Sofie's face. *Where was she going at that time of night?*

The only person he could imagine Sofie going to visit that late besides her mama was Regine, but according to the accident report, Sofie was nowhere near her friend's home. Now he had more questions than answers. Pulling over at a nearby gas station, he parked the car and cut the engine. Getting out of the car, he went inside and bought a cup of coffee. Adding a few packets of sugar to the liquid, he sipped the drink slowly as he got back inside. Though when he finished the drink, his nerves were still unsettled.

Taking slow deep breaths, Jerome recited, **"Cast thy burden upon the Lord, and he shall sustain thee: he shall never suffer the righteous to be moved."**

As he inhaled and exhaled one more time, Jerome looked around at the traffic and took out his phone. At first Jerome immediately dismissed the thought of calling Tasha. Putting his phone away, Jerome thought about all that took place yesterday, and as much as he wanted someone to blame, Jerome couldn't put Tasha at the top of the list. *This is on me. All of it.*

He ignored the whispers and stares for years. Never once asking Sofie about her past relationships, because he didn't want to talk about his own. Rushing into marriage after a few nights of seeking physical comfort in someone who he thought was hurting as much as he was back then. If he wanted someone to blame for setting all this in motion, Jerome had to start with himself. Starting the car up again, Jerome drove to Alexa and Rachel's house.

Jerome spent the entire drive trying to talk himself out of seeing Tasha, but the closer he got to her spot, the solid his resolve became. He could have texted her, or called, but Jerome wanted to see her face. The image of her walking out of his house that night haunted him, and Jerome needed to see her again to replace that look with something else. A look that didn't leave him feeling adrift.

When he reached the house, Jerome almost thought no one was there. He didn't see her motorbike outside and only a porchlight was lit in the distance. It wasn't until he almost passed the house did he notice light coming from one of the bedrooms. Backing up, Jerome drove back around toward the house and parked his ride. Knocking on the door, he heard soft music playing in the background. He made sure to knock harder the second time, and after Jerome did he heard the music pause.

"Who is it?" Jerome heard Tasha ask.

He looked at the door before clearing his voice. "Jerome."

As more seconds passed, he thought she hadn't heard him, but when he was about to say his name again, the door opened. Tasha stood in front of him, wearing a lavender pajama short set. Her hair was tied back in a big braid and despite his reason for stopping by, he couldn't fight his lips from turning upward at the sight of her.

"Why are you here?" Tasha asked, not moving to let him in.

Jerome sighed before speaking, "We need to talk. Please let me inside."

Stepping forward he watched as she peered around at the other scarce houses on the street before allowing him inside the house. As he walked in, Jerome heard her close and lock the door. He showed himself to the living room and turned to find Tasha on his heels.

"Are Alexa and Rachel in?" He asked quickly.

"No, they went to pick up Tyrone's new sister."

The confusion must have shown on his face as Tasha continued, "Tyrone's their French Bulldog. They bought another one to keep him company for when I leave after they get back from their honeymoon." She closed her eyes for a second and spoke again, "Jerome, it's late-"

"Sofie was in an accident last night." Tasha's eyes widened as he explained, "Her car was hit head on by a semi truck. I just saw her at LM."

"Oh my God!" Tasha rushed to his side but caught herself and stopped midway. "What about Ro? Where is he?" she then asked.

Sighing heavily, Jerome told her, "He's fine."

He watched as her chest fell and waited for Tasha to look his way.

"I'm sorry Jerome. If I had known..."

Shaking his head, Jerome cut her off. "This ain't on you. Yeah, you rolling through the way you did didn't help, but all of this was something I should have got out in the open years ago."

Tasha took a step forward before stopping herself again. He looked at her as she bit her lip and closed the distance between them. When her eyes met his, Jerome spoke, "I fought with myself about coming out here to see you." Shaking his head, Jerome whispered, "I know it ain't right, but Tash, this is where I want to be."

**Tasha**

She tried to look away, but Jerome caught her cheek with his hand.

"Please, go home Jerome." she whispered.

As he leaned in toward her, Tasha closed her eyes, inhaling his scent. Soon, both his hands were cradling her face. "I am home, Tash."

Her eyes shot open as she searched his.

"When I'm with you, that's exactly how I feel."

Finding the absolute truth in his warm irises, Tasha felt tears fill her eyes. Using the last of her strength, she tried to move backward and out of Jerome's reach. His left hand then dropped from her face as it slid down to her full waist, holding Tasha steady.

"Please let me stay."

He wiped away the first tear that fell from her eyes, and when Tasha went to speak, Jerome brought their foreheads together. More tears left a trail down her cheek, and he quietly wiped those away too. With a burning sensation in her throat, Tasha spoke. "Jerome... if you stay here tonight, I don't know if I'll be able to let you go."

Feeling him bring her closer, Tasha brought her hands around his neck as she rested her head on his chest. The steady beating of his heart, along with the warmth of his embrace was her undoing. Tasha was done fighting her feelings for Jerome, and as she felt him swoop her into his arms, Tasha sent out one silent prayer. *Please, Lord, forgive us for tonight.*

As Jerome carried her to her room, Tasha burrowed her nose deeper into where his neck and shoulders met, trying to commit to memory his scent. His breath hitched just before a pillow touched the back of her head, and Tasha's eyes fluttered open once more. She watched as Jerome lowered her onto the queen bed. Her hands were still securely around his neck and Tasha slowly brought her eyes up to meet Jerome's. She knew she should stop this, with one word Tasha could end this before they went any further. But she didn't want to.

After tonight, Tasha knew she could never see Jerome again. Being in his arms, hearing him say the words that lingered in her heart, there was no way Tasha could so much as be in the room as Jerome after tonight. So, instead of asking him to stop, she enjoyed the feel of his body close to hers.

*Just for tonight.*

His hands glided from Tasha's waist, slowly getting reacquainted with her curves. She shivered as his right hand grazed her breasts through the satin top she wore, and Jerome stilled his movements. Looking her in the eye, he whispered, "You good?"

Tasha nodded, hoping he would continue, but Jerome kept his gaze on her until she spoke. "I'm good."

Not sure what more he needed her to say, Tasha brought her hands from the back of his head, down to his shoulders. As her eyes took in his solid muscles, thoughts of what he would do next entered her mind, causing Tasha to bite her lip. Jerome's hands then made their way up to her collarbone, softly tracing lazy circles that left her taking shallow breaths. When his right hand went up to her neck, lifting her chin up to meet his stare, Tasha felt lightheaded. Her gasp could be heard in the quiet room as Jerome stared down at her.

Jerome said nothing as he began to stroke her neck, applying the slightest pressure before inching up closer to her nape. She felt what little tension she had leave her body as Jerome continued rubbing small circles at the back of her neck. He soon brought his hands further into her head, massaging Tasha's scalp. When Jerome started to use both of his hands to knead each side of her head, a moan escaped from Tasha's lips.

"Rome..." she managed to say.

His lips were on hers seconds later, and Tasha thought she was going to dissolve into the mattress. Each kiss was soft, leaving her wanting more. She could taste the sweet notes of something he had earlier on his tongue and found herself curious as to what else was waiting just behind his full lips. Brushing her tongue against his, Tasha allowed herself to enjoy being in his arms as she stroked his back. It wasn't until her lungs began to beg for air did Tasha pull away, and the way Jerome stared at her had Tasha ready to return right back to his waiting lips.

"We don't have to go any further."

It took a little longer for his words to reach her ears, but when they did, Tasha blinked.

"I don't want you to regret this," he added.

"I thought that was my line." Tasha tried to jokingly say, as Jerome reached out to touch her cheek.

"I meant what I said, being with you is enough for me, Tash."

She believed him, that wasn't the problem. It was the ache at her core that left Tasha conflicted. From the moment she let him inside the house, Tasha knew where they would end up and now she had to call on all the strength that she could find within to speak. Choosing her words carefully, she said, "I hear you. Thank you."

Jerome kept his eyes on her, but Tasha could see his lips twitch ever so slightly. "Thank you?" he asked.

Taking in shallow breaths, she answered, almost more cautiously than before. "For reminding me to not do something that we might regret. Because I had no intention of letting you go, at least not tonight."

She watched as his Adam's apple bobbed and wasn't surprised when Jerome released his hold on her. "I know. And I'm sorry for putting you in this situation Tash."

Before he could go on apologizing, she shook her head, "Rome, this is all on me. I didn't have to open the door when I saw it was you on the other side. I wanted to see you. I wanted to be with you too." Tasha bit her lip. "I want..."

Her mind went back to their last night together as a couple, at the bed and breakfast. Hearing him be sorry for things she felt responsible for in the first place left Tasha's stomach in knots. If she hadn't left the first time, Tasha would be able to have Jerome in every way. Of course he moved on and started a new life, found a wife, and now had the family that she wanted him to. All because she thought that she couldn't give that to him. Now, as Tasha looked into Jerome's eyes, she wanted to be his wife. She wanted to carry his children, she wanted nothing more than to try again with the man who never left her heart.

But she couldn't. He wasn't hers anymore.

The weight of that truth held her heart in a vice grip, taunting her. Tasha's eyes burned and she went to turn her head, praying that Jerome wouldn't notice while she turned off the lamp on the nightstand.

But she must have reached her limit on answered prayers for the night, as Jerome reached out and gently brought her face back to his, concern etched in his eyes showing from the glow of the moon in the bedroom window.

"Tell me what's on your mind, Tasha."

Hearing him speak so softly, she reached out to him. Tasha wrapped her arms around his neck, a fresh set of tears followed. "I shouldn't have let you go, Rome. All I want right now is for us to be together. And it's my fault that we can't be."

His grip on her tightened, and all the emotions Tasha had been keeping locked away was released. She cried into his chest as Jerome rubbed comforting circles on her back. "Tash, it's not just on you." He brought a hand out to gently stroke her cheek. "When you told me why you couldn't be my wife back then, I didn't want to admit it, but you were right."

Sniffling, Tasha looked up at Jerome as he continued, "Yeah, I was hurt, but back then we both were just starting out. You wanted to see the world, and I knew that before we got together."

"But then we-"

Jerome cut her off. "Let me finish, please." Despite the situation they were now in, Tasha rolled her eyes. "Then when all that stuff went down after New Years' Eve, I knew you were gonna leave. So I prayed that if it was meant to be, you'd stay and we would work it out."

She watched as Jerome closed his eyes and turned away. Clearing his throat, he went on. "When you said no, I was hurt and spent weeks praying that you would come back. But then I started spending more time in the studio and on the road. While on tour I couldn't help but think of what that would have been like for you."

Her forehead wrinkled. "What you mean? How what would have been?"

Jerome sighed as he answered her question, "Me always gone, while you would have been at home, with mama, Senior, the church - all of it."

She didn't need to answer as Jerome did for her. "You would've hated it."

"Well, not the being with Evelyn part."

He chuckled. "Okay, not that part, but all the other stuff? I was wrong for not considering that. Like you said, I hadn't thought about 'the after.'"

Tasha's eyes locked onto his, as she thought back to their conversation that night. "You remembered that?"

As he nodded, Tasha released her hold on him. "Thank you for telling me."

Jerome kissed her forehead and she let out a yawn, causing him to chuckle. "I guess we better get some sleep, uh?"

The last thing Tasha wanted to do was sleep. She knew the moment that she did that, morning would be here, and she would have to say goodbye to Jerome. And that left her heart feeling heavy as hell. Instead of telling him that, Tasha curled in as close as she could into his chest.

"Yeah. Goodnight Rome."

Tasha then focused on the sound of Jerome's heart, the sound of its steady beats luring her to sleep.

WAKING UP TO AN EMPTY bed and sharp barks from outside, Tasha sighed. Rachel was now at her parents place until the ceremony, and she'd almost wished it was her that she had to deal with this morning. *I know Alexa saw Jerome leave.*

Any other time, Tasha would be jumping out of bed to see her bestie. Though after spending the night with Jerome, she knew questions were waiting for her on the other side of that door that she didn't want to answer/ But with Alexa and Rachel's wedding hours away, she knew she had to do just that. Thanking the Lord that the guest room came with its own bathroom, she got out of bed and showered before stepping out into the foyer and toward the kitchen. With Alexa's back to her, Tasha slinked into the barstool and put on a happy face as she said chipperly, "Morning! You ready to make things official with my girl?"

Alexa turned to face her, a questioning glare fixed on her face as she eyed Tasha. "Oh, you ain't slick sis, coming in here with all that false cheer. I already filled my baby in on who I saw creeping out of your room at 6am."

Tasha grabbed the bottled water on top of the kitchenette counter and twisted open as she waited for Alexa to continue.

"You ain't even gonna deny it, uh?" Alexa asked, as Tasha avoided her stare. "What happened to you 'not having anything to say' to Jerome? Guess you had to use more than words to part ways with PK?"

Heat flared white hot in her cheeks, prompting Tasha to look up at Alexa. "It-it wasn't like what you think! We didn't sleep together." she mumbled out.

When Alexa scoffed, Tasha couldn't blame her. *If it wasn't me that it happened to, I wouldn't believe it either.*

"Oh, well, what did y'all do all night, Tash?" Alexa asked before adding, "I ain't trying to be all in your business, but Tash! What was you thinking?"

Finishing the bottled water, Tasha sat the empty bottle on the counter. "He was here, and shared some bad news with me - about his wife. By the time we realized what time it was...I didn't want him to go." she admitted. "So I let him stay." Tasha lowered her head and waited for Alexa to go off on her having a married man over the night before their wedding. *I deserve it. All of this is my own damn fault.*

A minute of silence went by before she found the courage to lift her head up. Seeing the concern in Alexa's eyes made her own fill with tears. "You not gonna go off on me? Tell me what a dumb ass, lame ass excuse that was?" Tasha asked.

Alexa walked over and sat across from her on the empty bar stool. Taking her hands into Tasha's she let out a sigh. "No need to do that, since you seem to already know. Besides, you can't lie worth a damn, so I believe you when you say y'all didn't sleep together." She scoffed as Alexa continued, "But Tasha, I hope for your sake that this is the end of it. I don't want you to get hurt behind whatever unresolved feelings you have for Jerome."

Thankful that Alexa chose not to go in on her, Tasha blinked back her tears and nodded. "I'm gonna be alright, I promise." Lifting their joined hands, she looked at Alexa and felt the corners of her lips turn upward. "Now, you ready to marry the love of your life today or nah?"

"Oh, hell yeah!" Alexa beamed at her. "I been ready to do that."

"Good! Let's get packed up and head out to the country club to get you married then."

THE TWO GOT DRESSED and made their way to the country club, meeting the rest of Alexa's entourage, her older brother Keith, and two of her college friends. Wanting to put thoughts of spending the night with Jerome just hours before behind her, Tasha threw herself into her maid of honor duties, checking in with Rachel's entourage, helping Alexa get into her suit, and keeping Keith from getting too tipsy before the ceremony. Before long, Tasha and the other guests were waiting for Rachel to make an entrance through the recently installed black grand archway. Smoothing down the sides of her off the shoulders floor length dress, Tasha heard Alexa nervously chuckle, "You nervous?"

"I should be asking you that." Tasha answered.

The look on Alexa's face was almost serene as she smiled at Tasha. "Nah, I ain't nervous. Been ready to make Rachel my ole lady for long enough."

Tasha couldn't bring herself to tease Alexa as she saw the seriousness on her best friend's face. Instead, she reached out and straightened the outside of Alexa's vest and stepped back to admire her friend, who stood tall before turning to face the entrance. As if on cue, the small orchestra softly transitioned from the light and flowy sonnet inspired sounds to the sweetest rendition of the classical wedding march Tasha had ever heard. Her breath got caught in her throat the moment she saw Rachel, accompanied by her parents on each side, begin walking down the golden aisle. From the corner of her eye, Tasha noticed Alexa's hands trembling and looking up she watched as Alexa blinked rapidly.

Quickly, she reached into her small clutch purse and pulled out the small pack of tissues she stored inside before leaving the house. *Didn't think I'd need them for Alexa though. Good thing I brought more than one pack.*

Sure enough, as she handed Alexa a tissue, Tasha looked down the aisle and caught sight of both of Rachel's parents sniffling. Her lips tilted upward when Rachel finally made it to the archway and extended her hand to Alexa. Seeing her closest friends in that moment, surrounded by their family and friends in the open space full of large white pillars, twinkling white tealights, and the ordained minister that proudly beamed down at the couple, Tasha felt her heart constrict in her chest.

"Everyone, welcome." the ordained minister announced to the crowd, "We all have the pleasure of bearing witness to the union of Alexa Shaw and Rachel Banks..."

Alexa and Rachel were all smiles during their reception, and Tasha found herself getting nervous as her turn to make a toast came near. One of Rachel's bridesmaids had finished delivering a speech about how she knew Alexa was it for Rachel that left everyone at the venue in tears. She had nothing prepared, as Rachel suggested that she speak from her heart.

A small clicking sound got her attention and Tasha's eyes narrowed as Keith, Alexa's older brother, stood next to her with a smirk on his face as he raised a glass. "The maid of honor would like to give her toast now."

"The hell I do Keith!" Tasha hissed as his grin got wider.

"Don't be shy now, Tash. You always got something to say, so here."

Thrusting the mic toward her, Tasha eyes blazed across at Alexa's brother one last time as she took the mic and faced the crowd. Clearing her throat, she looked at her best friends, clearly unaware of anything around them except each other and a small part of Tasha was envious. Shoving those thoughts down to the corners of her mind, she smiled. "I have been fortunate enough to know Alexa since high school, and can tell you all that I never thought she would find someone who'd want to go out with her more than once, much less marry her."

As the crowd laughed, Tasha continued. "That all changed when she went away to college and met Rachel. When Rachel came to visit during their first holiday break together, I saw a side of Alexa that I never saw before. To say that she was hopelessly in love, even back then was an understatement. When Alexa would normally walk away, or cuss someone out for talking to her crazy, I saw her try to meet them halfway and hear them out with patience - even when Rachel wasn't around."

Rachel kissed Alexa's cheek and smiled as they looked at Tasha. "For the first half of their relationship, I found myself wondering, "What happened to my friend? This new chick done showed up and she acting brand new. But that's not what it was at all."

Jerome's smile flashed across Tasha's mind, freezing her in that moment. Their time together over the last month played through her thoughts and she cleared her throat again. "When you meet someone that loves you, flaws and all, the way these two do, it brings out all the best in you, allowing you to grow and change for the better. That's what you do when you love someone, you see them as they are and love them. In time that love flows over into every part of their lives, and changes how they respond to everything - in the best of ways. So, thank you Alexa and Rachel, for showing me how love can change someone for the better. Tha—"

Tasha's eyes stung as more memories with Jerome flooded her mind. "Thank you for making me believe in love. I love y'all."

The glass in her hand shook slightly as Tasha reminded herself to look out into the crowd one last time. "To Rachel and Alexa - may you two know nothing but acceptance and happiness for the rest of your days together."

She closed her eyes and a memory of being enclosed in Jerome's embrace held her mind captive. His solid chest and deep brown skin, akin to thick aged trees, along with that familiar and faint spicy citrus scent, rooted Tasha to the spot. The cheers around her managed to bring her back to the now, and she felt hands reach out and take the microphone from her. Looking down and seeing her best friends fighting back tears, Tasha let a few fall.

Fighting the wave of emotions that continued to make their way to her chest, Tasha looked at her friends, her bonus sisters, as she spoke from her heart. "I love y'all so much."

"We love you more Tash, come here." Rachel said through tears. Tasha leaned forward, giving each of them a kiss on their cheek before Alexa and Rachel wrapped her into their arms.

# Chapter Fourteen

## Every Little Step We Make

### *One Week Later*

**Sofie**

"That's it baby, one step at a time."

Hearing her mama's voice as she worked with her physical therapist, Sofie moved her hands along the rails. Dragging her left foot to meet her right one at the end of the bar, she panted while avoiding mama and Evelyn's expecting eyes.

*Why they gotta be here every day?*

Her therapist smiled encouragingly. "I think we can stop here for today. Good job Sofie."

Catching her breath, Sofie looked at the woman and nodded. As she started to guide Sofie back to her wheelchair, they all saw Jerome enter the rehabilitation room. Sofie rolled her eyes once the therapist eased her into the seat. She watched as he walked over to mama and Evelyn, hugging them before coming over to her.

"How you feeling?" Jerome asked.

Squinting her eyes while looking up at him, Sofie answered, "Feeling tired of hearing that question every damn day."

Jerome returned her stare and set his jaw. "We just want to make sure you have everything you need, Sofie. That's all."

She thought back to their last night together and the paperwork Jerome wanted her to sign, giving him rights to Ro. Thinking about how close that almost became a reality, Sofie winced. Jerome kneeled down in front of her. "What's wrong? What hurts -"

"Everything! I'm in pain every damn day and y'all won't even let me see my son!"

Sofie didn't miss Jerome's flinch from her words, but seeing him close his eyes and reach out for her hand made her even angrier.

"Why won't you bring Ro to see me? Can't you do that much for me? Or are you hoping I just give up and die?!"

"Sofie! Why you speaking like that to your husband?"

Mama's voice ranged out and Sofie looked on as both Evelyn and her mama stood on each side of Jerome. With her being in the wheelchair, it felt like all three of them were looming over her, watching her every move. And Sofie wanted to put an end to it all.

"That's all he is - my lame ass husband! Can't even bring my son to see me while I'm in this awful place."

Evelyn stepped in front of Jerome. "Baby, he just don't want to scare Ro with all this. But I promise you, Ro is being taken care of."

Sofie eyes turned into daggers as she directed her attention to Evelyn, "You can't promise me a damn thing! Ro ain't even his son - he's mine and I want to see him!"

Silence fell over the group as Sofie's words echoed throughout the room.

An orderly quietly pushed their cart out of the room. Sofie saw the shocked expressions on mama and Evelyn's faces, but she didn't care as she shouted. "Just bring me my son and get me out of here!"

"That's enough Sofie!"

Her mama now stood in front of her and Sofie saw the disappointment in her eyes before she harshly whispered, "Just what you mean - Jerome ain't Ro's daddy?"

Sticking her neck out to get as close to her mama as possible, Sofie spat out, "I meant just that - PK ain't the daddy. Thank God!"

Lillie slapped Sofie hard enough to whip her head to the other side. "Have you lost your damn mind girl!" Glancing quickly between Jerome and Evelyn, Lillie pulled her closer and hissed, "You managed to get a good man and still can't keep ya legs closed to any other Tom, Dick, and Harry that come along?! Ain't you learn nothing from what happened to your sister?"

Grabbing her stinging check, Sofie turned away from her mama and demanded through clenched teeth, "Now, y'all gonna get my son or what?"

She looked on as Evelyn stared at Jerome. "And before y'all bother to ask, Jerome been knew he wasn't the daddy."

"Jerome, is this true?" Evelyn asked him softly.

He let out a deep sigh before looking at his mama and nodding his head.

"I'll go see what your doctor says about having you discharged early." Jerome told Sofie as he left the room.

Evelyn narrowed her eyes at Sofie before following him.

## TASHA

As soon as Tasha touched down days later from her return flight to Murcia, she welcomed the hustle and bustle of all the people around her, speaking in different dialects and going about their day. After getting her luggage from baggage claims, Tasha weaved through the crowds, taking out her cell to call for Maeto, her favorite taxi driver. Though before she could hit send on her phone, she heard Sebastian's voice. "My gordita! Are you not a sight for weary eyes, no?"

Rolling her eyes as she watched him stroll over toward her, Tasha asked, "Why are you here?"

He took two steps back, clutching his right hand over his chest. "I am wounded by you, my sweet." Not missing a beat he went on,

"Ximena told me you may be feisty after your flight. Perhaps you need to eat?"

Tasha started to protest, but her stomach growled instead, causing Sebastian to chuckle. "Ah, see, I know what my gordita needs. Allow me to feed you before you scowl at me some more."

"Sebastian, I can take care of myself. Please just drive me to my studio so I can get settled in."

Sending a grin her way, Sebastian spoke again, "I know you can take care of yourself, but I enjoy taking care of you. And I want to apologize for my behavior at the last photoshoot."

She listened to the sincerity in his voice and looked Sebastian directly in the eye. "Fine. But if you try anything..."

"I promise to be well behaved, my sweet."

He eyed her once more, starting from the bottom and slowly bringing his eyes back to her face. When she rolled her eyes at him, Sebastian only shrugged. "Well, I said that I would behave, not that I wouldn't appreciate the view."

Laughing, Tasha walked over to the passenger side of his car and opened the door to let herself inside.

A rain shower in Murica two days later created scatters of glistening lights that littered the streets. She watched more and more people begin to make their way inside the Colsada Museum, which was decorated to match the theme, along with the sculptures of famous Greek Gods on display. A buzz of flashing lights from the cameras outside could be seen and heard as Tasha looked on in awe. She was finally about to attend the most anticipated event of the season. Her body vibrated from the excitement growing in her chest.

Tasha took a deep breath, reaching out for her friend's hand. "Thanks for being here with me tonight."

Ximena grinned, "Thank you Tasha for inviting me. This event is amazing!"

Sebastian strolled up behind them and looked at the two of them appreciatively. "We have yet to go inside, sweet Ximena. How do you know it is amazing?"

Rolling her eyes, Tasha handed Sebastian her free hand. "Don't be raining on our parade. Unlike you, we've never had a seat to the grown folks' table."

"Yes! Allow us a moment to enjoy this experience, Sebastian." Ximena told him.

He casted his eyes downward and took his time bringing them back up, fully taking in the women in their formal dresses. When Tasha shook her head at him, Sebastian winked. "I am simply taking Ximena's advice and am enjoying the experience."

Tasha couldn't lie, she knew her and Ximena looked good. After modeling two of the dresses that she purchased from home for her friends, Ximena and Sebastian both agreed that the jade piece was the best for the gala. With a quick trip to a local seamstress as well as a specialty shoe boutique, Tasha could barely walk in her new heels and cinched waisted dress. To calm her nerves, Tasha softly recited one of her favorite scriptures, ***Rejoice in hope, be patient in tribulation, and be constant in prayer.***

She still found herself struggling with sticking to the last part of the scripture, but ever since she heard those words in a church service years ago, Tasha committed them to memory. Whenever she was about to take a leap of faith with a new project, she would think of those words and draw courage from them. Tonight was no exception. Though when Tasha walked forward, linking arms with her friends to take the first steps up to the museums' entrance, she looked up and went still as Jerome's face flashed across her mind.

"Gordita? Are you alright?"

Hearing Sebastian's voice, Tasha turned to him and nodded. "Let's go inside."

Once they were cleared by security, Tasha felt Ximena's grip on her hand tighten. They both looked around the room before turning to face each other. "Can you believe this right now, Tasha?"

Sebastian chuckled. "I have secured you both an entrance to the event, as promised. Now I request permission to find a new muse for the evening."

Grinning, Tasha looked at Sebastian. "Permission granted. Don't get yourself into trouble, okay?"

"It is so touching to see that you care, my sweet."

Now it was Tasha's turn to laugh, softly swatting at her friend's shoulder. "Gone ahead and flirt with someone else already."

When Sebastian took his leave, Tasha spotted the man of the hour, Pablo Coslado. She watched him politely pose for a photo before his assistant led him away from the growing crowd. *Okay, guess it's time to introduce myself.*

"Tasha...is that..." Ximena started before Tasha nodded.

The two walked in step toward the photographer and his assistant before stopping a few meters away. She had to hold Ximena back to stop her from getting closer. "He doesn't like too many people in his personal space." Tasha reminded Ximena.

She looked up quickly and could have sworn that his assistant was smiling at her. Dismissing the thought, Tasha opened her mouth to speak, but was interrupted. "Tasha Daye? It is good to finally meet. This is Pablo Coslado, as I am sure you know."

Blinking several times, Ximena nudged Tasha before she remembered to speak. "Uh, yes. This is my good friend and fellow photographer Ximena Ortega. It is a pleasure to meet you both."

Pablo's assistant beamed. "Thank you."

"If it is alright, I would like to speak to you sometime soon about a potential collaboration, Mr. Coslado."

Directing her attention to him, Tasha took in more of his strong features. He was a striking man, even as he looked up at Tasha while she was wearing three inch heels.

"I have time now, Ms. Daye." Tasha felt Ximena grip her hand again as Pablo continued, "Since you have come all this way, I would hate to miss the opportunity to hear your proposal."

Pablo then looked at his assistant, who stepped forward and extended a hand toward Ximena. "Would you please join me so that Ms. Daye has a more private audience with Mr. Coslado?"

"O-of course."

Ximena accepted his hand and was led away, leaving Tasha with Pablo. Clearing her throat, Tasha spoke. "I know that you're a busy man, so I won't take up too much of your time."

"Please. Take as much time as you need." Pablo said.

The longer he stared at her, Tasha could see that he meant every word. She blinked rapidly to avoid getting lost in his dark irises. "Thank you."

When he reached out his hand, Tasha accepted it, allowing hers to get acquainted with his slightly calloused ones. Pablo walked them to a nearby balcony. He remained quiet until they were outside again. Now in front of a view of the night sky that took Tasha's breath away, she almost forgot what she was supposed to be doing. "I know that you prefer to work alone, but I would like to work with you. As an apprentice."

Seeing him raise an eyebrow, Tasha explained, "For years I have followed your career, as many others here, and what I love most is how you don't let technique disrupt your storytelling. You go to places that others wouldn't dare, alone, and ... I wish to study you so I can learn how to do the same."

"Is that so?" Pablo asked before asking a question of his own. "Just how will you study me?"

Straightening her back, Tasha looked directly at Pablo. "I want to capture photos of you in your element. And learn from you how to tell better stories with my own work, while asking you questions in between assignments."

"From what I have seen, you are quite good at storytelling with your photos as well, Ms. Daye."

Tasha's eyes widened before she sputtered out, "Y-you've seen my work?"

"I have." Pablo stared at Tasha before adding, "Seeing my home through your eyes has given me a new perspective. That is no easy thing to do."

"Thank you." Tasha said, watching as Pablo flashed her a grin.

"When would you like to begin this apprenticeship? I can have my assistant send over my schedule to you first thing in the morning."

Her mind was going a mile a minute, and it took all of Tasha's good sense to not break out into a praise dance. *He really is agreeing to my proposal?* Though the main thought that Tasha couldn't let go of was, *PABLO COLSADO has seen AND LIKES my work?!*

Looking at him again, Tasha willed her heart to be still and thought quickly. She had no immediate work on her schedule, but for some reason felt herself not ready to leap into anything that time consuming. "Thank you. Is it okay if I get back to you after looking at my schedule?"

"Of course. May I ask why?"

This time, instead of seeing Jerome's face, Tasha saw Devin's. And then Darnell's. One after another, images of all her loved one's came into view, and Tasha was now blinking back tears as the memories she created with them recently wrapped themselves around her heart. "I, um, whew - was not expecting this, to be honest."

Pablo held Tasha's gaze as she explained, "I've been known to drop everything for what I felt was a once in a lifetime shoot, no questions asked. And if we were having this conversation months ago, I would've cleared my entire schedule without hesitation. But right now, I can't. "

"I thank you for your candor. It is very refreshing."

The two stared at one another again, as Pablo gently caressed Tasha's hand. "No matter what should happen in the next few months as far as you being my apprentice, I would love to formally invite you to next year's gala, Ms. Daye."

Looking at Pablo, Tasha closed her eyes and thought of how best to show her sincerest gratitude for the invite. "Thank you." she said in his native tongue as she slightly bowed her head.

Watching his gaze soften as she righted herself, Tasha continued in Spanish, "I would also like to mention my friend again from earlier, Ximena. She has been integral in my research on you. "

"I thought you came here as Sebastian Gonzales' guest? Why are you not discussing him, a more well known photographer?"

Tasha laughed at Pablo's questions in English. "Yes, I did manage to talk Sebastian into adding us as his guests, but when it comes to work ethic, vision, and tenacity, Ximena has him in spades - well known or not." Thinking fondly of her years of working with Ximena, Tasha felt the corners of her lips turn upward. "She now runs a successful expat second shooter business locally. Should you wish to expand your networking circle more internationally, I cannot think of anyone more deserving. "

Pablo looked up at Tasha and grinned. "From what my team has told me, you two are professional and persistent. I will speak with your friend shortly. It was a pleasure to meet you."

He then took Tasha's hand into his, bringing it to his lips.

"I must go attend to my other guests, but thank you again Ms. Daye, for your company."

"Thank you for your time Mr. Coslado."

As Pablo turned to leave, Tasha looked out into the dark night's sky. *What am I doing?! Why am I seriously not jumping to get this opportunity off the ground?*

Her answer came in the form of her nephew's laughter ringing in her ears. Following being able to attend her best friends' wedding. When the image of her time with Trisha entered her mind, Tasha reached out to grab the railing to steady herself. Finally, the image of seeing Jerome's eyes the night they went walking along Bejon Beach together spurred her into action. Removing her small clutch bag, Tasha took out her phone and scrolled down until she saw his number. Pressing the call button, she waited until the line went straight to voicemail.

"I know you're probably busy back in the States right now, but I...I just wanted to see how you are doing. And to thank you for being my friend."

Tears filled Tasha's eyes, and she wiped them away when she found herself whispering, her voice raw with emotion, "Reconnecting with you over the last few months has been a blessing. I know it didn't start that way, but now that I've had time to really think it all over, that's the best word I can come up with to describe it. And I hope that no matter what happens, wherever life takes us, that we will always be friends, Rome. Goodnight."

Ending the call, Tasha stared up at the sky again before going back inside.

# Chapter Fifteen

## Officially Missing You

**Jerome**

Two weeks had passed since Sofie's accident. He knew she was ready to be released, but with her injuries the doctor strongly advised against it. When Sofie tried to protest, Jerome reminded her, "The sooner you get better, the sooner you can get back to Ro."

He made sure to visit her daily, keeping his distance when she was with the physical therapist and showing her video and pictures of Ro. Jerome had asked mama not to say anything to Senior about what Sofie announced weeks ago, and she agreed. Even though his mama had respected his wishes, Jerome knew he couldn't pretend with Sofie anymore.

When Sofie was finally released from the hospital, Jerome brought her home. He made sure that Ms. Ward was there as well to watch Ro while he made the drive to the hospital.

"Hey Ro Ro!" Sofie cried out.

Jerome watched as his namesake wobbled as fast as he could into his mama's arms. While Sofie was re-uniting with Ro, Jerome removed the house key from his car keys and placed it on the counter next to the divorce papers that he had drawn up earlier that week. Watching Sofie play and fuss over Ro one last time, Jerome made his way to the front door. Though before he opened the door, Sofie called out to him.

"Where you going?"

Choosing not to answer her question, Jerome explained, "I made sure to buy groceries and had a cleaning crew stop by while you were gone, so you shouldn't need anything for a while."

The two stared at one another.

"Thank you." Sofie said.

The sincerity in her voice was not missed, but Jerome knew that he had made the right decision as he finally walked out of the house.

The drive to his new rental home was short, yet quiet. Jerome welcomed the silence, knowing that it wouldn't last for long. By the time he reached the small parking lot to the condo, he heard his phone ring. Cutting the engine and taking off his seatbelt, Jerome sighed as he took the phone out of his pocket and pressed the green button.

"Divorce papers?! Really?" Sofie shouted over the line.

"We tried, and it didn't work. Let's just end it now before Ro="

"Oh, that's right. You only proposed to me when I told you I was pregnant anyway. Now that your *Tash* is running around town, you wanna have an instant family with her, uh?" Jerome said nothing as he unlocked the door to his condo.

"What? Cat got your tongue? You didn't think I'd found out she was still in town?"

Kicking off his sneakers and sitting on the sofa, Jerome tried to end the call, "I haven't seen Tasha in weeks. And this ain't got nothing to do with her."

"Like hell it don't! The minute she came back here, you changed up. Started sneaking off to see her and shit."

Closing his eyes as he rubbed his temple, Jerome could feel his head starting to throb.

"Then she showed up with old news and you were quick to take her side – what about me? I'm still your wife! Not her wanna be high and mighty ass!"

Jerome didn't want to argue, he was too emotionally exhausted for a fight. And to be honest, he didn't care what Sofie thought.

"I'll be back to pick up the papers later this week. Sign them so we can move on."

Her high pitch voice left Jerome's ear buzzing. "Oh, so you ain't even gonna try to deny it now? Well, I hope you ain't got no plans to try and take my son. Good luck getting custody to a baby that ain't yours!"

The dial tone was all that Jerome heard before he could utter another word.

**TASHA**

While out getting groceries the week after arriving back from Murica, Tasha saw Evelyn again.

"Hi Ms. Evelyn." Tasha said as she walked over to the older woman in the produce aisle with her cart. "It's good to see you aga-"

Evelyn quickly closed the short distance between them and wrapped Tasha into her arms, hugging her tightly. "It is good to see you! Jerome told me you left weeks ago. What brought you back?"

Tasha looked away before she looked at Evelyn again. "My little sister just had her twins, a boy and a girl, Faith and Moses."

Evelyn beamed at her, "Oh! That is good news!" A beat passed before Evelyn spoke again, "So, how long you visiting?"

Tasha didn't want to keep the truth from Evelyn, but the hopeful gaze she saw in the woman's eyes gave her pause. *She's gonna find out eventually. This town is too small for her not to bump into you again.*

Picking at a stray hangnail, Tasha answered Evelyn. "Well, I was thinking of staying. Right now I'm looking at places to live and maybe work in between spending time with the family."

Evelyn grinned as she hugged Tasha again. "You sound busy, baby girl! Though it sho would be good to have you over for dinner sometime. How about this Sunday?"

Tasha pressed her lips together and before she could say no, Evelyn continued, "I know you and Jerome aren't together and all, but I thought that we was still friends. Was I wrong?"

Guilt immediately made itself at home in her chest, and Tasha reminded herself to breathe evenly. *One dinner couldn't hurt, and Senior might not be so bad to deal with if Jerome isn't there.*

"I would love to see you this Sunday, Mrs. Evelyn. What time should I stop by?"

Evelyn broke out into a grin as she reached out to touch Tasha's cheek. "Okay baby girl! Be to the house by 5 pm!"

Leaning in to hug Evelyn one more time, Tasha waved Evelyn off and made her way to the check out register.

Soon after making her way back to Alexa and Rachel's and putting away her groceries, Tasha received a text while out with the puppies for their evening walk. It was from Trisha, and something about the short message left her more than a little confused.

**I'm sorry.**
**Please forgive me Tasha.**
**-Trish**

*Forgive her for what?*

She didn't have to think long about the meaning behind Trisha's text, as her baby sister began to send more rapid fire short messages. By the fourth message Tasha had scooped up the puppies and began sprinting back to the house.

Hot tears and sweat gathered around Tasha's face as her sister poured her heart out with each line - which started with why she asked her about forgiving someone that hid something from her at the school fundraiser months ago, to Trish sharing the most heartbreaking story from their high school days that Tasha never knew. All the small glances from Trisha during their time together slowly began to make sense. *It wasn't something between her and Lloyd - it was her and Tina.*

**Tina agreed to help me.**
**But only if I kept how she got the money a secret.**
**Tash - Please forgive me.**
**-Trisha**

Just when Tasha didn't think it was possible to think any worse of her big sister, learning about what she put Trisha through - using Trisha's pain to her advantage, she suddenly felt dizzy. She was able to bring the puppies to their food and water bowls before squatting low and forcing heavy breaths out through her nose. Though even doing so while tightly shutting her eyes didn't keep the horrific images out of her head. And after a few minutes, Tasha knew what she had to do next. *I'll deal with Tina later. Right now, I need to see Trish.*

Twenty minutes later after weaving through traffic, Tasha hopped off of her motorbike and had barely cut off the engine before Devin swung open the front door to her sister's home. Darnell was right behind him as he turned his head and shouted. "Titi's here!"

When the boys gave her a hug, they each held her hand while walking into the house. She saw Lloyd march down the hallway and the way his eyes cut to her, she immediately tugged on the boys' hands. "D, go play with your brother outside please."

The front door hadn't fully closed before Lloyd stood in front of her and harshly whispered, "She's been crying all day." She didn't get to ask why as he added, "Now, I don't know why and I know you don't like me, but Trisha is my wife. And we appreciate all you've done for us while I been looking for more steady work, but not another day is gonna go by where I have to see her like this."

Taken aback by his words, Tasha nodded as she walked around him and headed to the babies' room. Just as Lloyd said, Trisha was wiping her face while rocking Faith to sleep. She remained quiet until Trisha turned to see her and more tears streamed down her face. "Trisha, please put Faith down."

Her sister rocked Faith a little longer before kissing her softly on the forehead and placing her into the crib. The two stepped out of the room and not seeing Lloyd in the living, she went to the couch and wanted for Trisha to join her. Meeting her sister's eyes, Tasha pushed down the burning knot in her throat and spoke as clearly as she could. "Trish, I don't know what to say. Why didn't you tell me sooner?"

"I-I really am sorry. I never could bring myself to talk about it 'cause..."

Tasha reached out to take her sister's hand. "It's okay. That was a dumb question to ask you. I just need you to know..." Tilting her head upward and blinking back tears, Tasha took two deep breaths and met Trisha's stare again. "Trish...what Tina did, and what happened to you back then...none of that is your fault. None of it."

The wail that left her little sister left Tasha in ruins. Grabbing Trisha and holding onto her as tightly as she could, Tasha choked back her tears as she whispered, voice shaky with emotion, "I'm sorry Trish, so sorry for what they did to you."

Even when Tasha heard the front door open, but she couldn't tear herself away from Trisha. It wasn't until Trisha finally stopped sobbing and she freed herself from Tasha's embrace did the two see Lloyd sitting on the small love seat next to them. Trisha gripped Tasha's hand before glancing over at her husband. "Baby, there is something I need to tell you."

Trisha looked at Tasha and then to Lloyd, and Tasha gripped her hand even tighter. "When I was a junior in high school, I started seeing this boy, Malcolm. He'd taken me to play miniature golf and to the water park a few times before asking me out to a house party. So caught up in being the girl of an upperclassman, I didn't hesitate to say yes."

A moment passed and Trisha paused, taking a deep, shaky breath. "Before we left that night, he'd given me my first real drink, a berry wine cooler."

"A wine cooler?" Lloyd questioned. "I thought you hated those drinks."

Tasha blinked back tears as she remembered that fact too, but remained silent as Trisha looked at her husband. "By the time we'd gotten to the house party, I'd had more wine coolers than I could remember, along with some vodka shots while dancing with him. When I started to feel sick, Malcolm pulled me aside and took me into a room in the back of the house. B-but when...when I laid down on the bed, he left an-and six other boys c-came in the room. I tried to get up when I saw them lock the door but I couldn't..."

Hearing Trisha tell Lloyd the full story was almost too much to bear, but Tasha held Trisha's hand the whole time. And when Trisha finished, Lloyd said nothing as tears spilled from his eyes. Removing her hand from Trisha's, Tasha stood up slowly.

"I'm going to go check on the twins." she whispered.

When she got far enough down the hallway to avoid being seen, she turned to see Lloyd wrapping Trisha in his arms.

**Jerome**

Sunday came faster than Jerome was ready for it, but he didn't want to hear mama yell at him. He already had one woman in his life doing that. So when she'd called him two days ago, requesting that he stop by for dinner, Jerome said yes right away.

Things with Sofie were starting to calm down. For all her bark, once Jerome gave Sofie time to look over the divorce papers, she did sign them. He gave her the house and was ready to pay for all of his namesake's expenses until he was of age. Jerome even offered her a monthly allowance. All he wanted in return was shared parenting with Ro.

With one issue behind him, Jerome drove to his parents' house to face another. Though when he got there, Senior was in his usual spot, the leather recliner chair in front of the living room TV. The two nodded at one another after Jerome let himself inside. When Senior continued to ignore his presence instead of demand to know when he was going to give up his 'sinning lifestyle' like he did the last time they spoke, Jerome went into the kitchen and greeted his mama. *Guess I was worried for nothing.*

"Hey mama, I'm here."

Kissing her on the cheek, Jerome surveyed all the dishes on the stove. "Mama, it's just me, you don't have to cook this much food."

She laughed, "Now I know you ain't got no food at your place, with everything going on with Sofie, so I'm making sure that you do after today."

Jerome sighed and reached for one of the spare aprons from the wall hook.

"Oh, no baby, I don't need your help in here today. Just gone ahead and take the cornbread out of the oven and set it on the table."

Doing as he was told, a knock was heard at the door. "Are y'all expecting someone?"

Neither one of his parents answered Jerome as another set of knocks were heard at the door. After he set down the cornbread, Jerome went to open the door and was rooted to the spot. Both he and Tasha's eyes widened as they saw each other for the first time since she left months ago.

"Right on time baby girl! Come on in!" Evelyn called out to Tasha.

Jerome watched as Tasha instead turned around to leave.

His heart dropped to the bottom of his stomach, until Evelyn was standing next to him. "Tasha Daye! Don't make me come outside and bring you in here!"

Tasha stopped walking and slowly turned back around to come inside the house.

"Y'all children today! Just working my nerves..." Evelyn said as she went back to the kitchen and stirred the pot of greens.

"Hi Ro-Jerome. Mr. Grant" Tasha said to them as she stepped further into the house.

"Ms. Daye." Senior replied, never taking his eyes off the TV.

Evelyn called Tasha into the kitchen and Jerome looked on as she wrapped Tasha into a hug. The two smiled at one another and Tasha grabbed an apron. "Check the rice baby girl and tend to them greens." Evelyn instructed while crushing up a few vanilla cookies for the banana pie in front of her.

Jerome ran to the bathroom to wash his hands before returning to the dining room table to sit down. Still not on speaking terms with Senior, Jerome chose to look into the kitchen as Evelyn and Tasha worked in tandem to finish up dinner. While they laughed and chatted with their hands. Jerome quietly took out his phone and snapped a picture of the two together. He found himself staring at the image before hearing Senior get out of his recliner and join him at the table.

"Y'all must be hungry today! Already at the table." Evelyn said as she brought out two plates of food. Setting each one in front of him and Senior, Tasha walked out with the other two plates and waited for Evelyn to sit before putting a plate down in front of her. Jerome watched as she then went back into the kitchen and returned to the table with four glasses. He quickly got up to help her, but almost tripped as Tasha returned with the pitcher of sweet tea.

"You okay?" Tasha asked as Jerome straightened himself out.

Hearing Evelyn snort behind him, Jerome's ears begin burning something fierce.

"Sit down boy so I can eat my food while it's still hot." Senior mumbled.

Doing as he was told, Jerome waited for Tasha to finish pouring the sweet tea. As she made her way over to Senior, Jerome's jaw tensed up when he saw a small smile on Seniors face as Tasha filled his glass.

"So Tasha, you were telling me the other day about your new job. Have you any photos to show me today?" Evelyn asked.

"I do." Tasha said before filling Jerome's glass and hers.

"Though my last client didn't like most of them, there were enough for us to use for their campaign this fall. I'll be sure to send you the magazine too when it's in stores."

Senior stared at the two of them and huffed, keeping his eyes on the plate in front of him. "Seems like you moving up in the world, Ms. Daye. From pictures of loose women to respectable companies overseas."

Jerome sighed as Tasha chose to continue talking to Evelyn. "I want to hear about your volunteer work at the hard of hearing center, Ms Ev- "

"Mrs." Senior tried to correct her when he finally looked up from his plate.

"Evelyn. I bet your signing is getting really good these days." Tasha finished.

Mama tightly smiled before bringing her right hand in front of her mouth and slowly down.

This was the first time that Jerome had seen Evelyn sign anything in front of Senior without Eva being in the house and he tried not to let his shock show. Senior cleared his throat before looking at Tasha.

"Ms. Daye, just how long will you be in town?" Senior asked.

Wanting to know the answer to this question too, Jerome ate slowly as he listened. Though instead of answering the question directly, Tasha asked one of her own. "Why do you ask Mr. Grant? Is Christ Corner looking for another tutor?"

The air around the table felt heavy as Tasha sent a tight smile to Senior. "My friend Rachel Banks-Shaw tells me that you have called them more than once looking for a tutor since firing me years ago."

Tasha reached out to pick up her glass of sweet tea. The table was still as she took a hearty sip and picked up her fork to cut a slice into the cornbread.

Senior stared hard at Tasha. "I see you still are in touch with Ms-"

"Mrs." Tasha reminded him gently.

Senior narrowed his eyes at her before Evelyn intervened by addressing Jerome. "Baby, how is Ro? Lillie said that he has been talking up a storm lately."

Blinking a few times, Jerome looked at his mama. "Yes ma'am. Ro's doing real good. He's learning his ABC's in school and now they're working on colors and numbers."

"It would have been nice to see my daughter-in-law today." Senior said, never taking his eyes off of Tasha. "Such a beautiful woman. Why did she and the baby not come with you today boy?" Senior questioned.

Jerome closed his eyes as he realized that he hadn't told anyone about the divorce. Sighing, he looked at Senior. "She is no longer my wife."

Both Tasha and Evelyn turned their heads in his direction.

"Once Sofie was released from the hospital, we signed the divorce papers. Now we are waiting for it to be final according to the courts."

Jerome saw Tasha's chest rise as she blinked at him. Picking up her fork again, she went back to eating quietly as Evelyn reached a hand out to take his. "You'll be okay, baby. God doesn't give us anymore than we can handle. You know that, right?"

"Yes ma'am."

Senior's fork clanked loudly against his plate when he dropped it and whipped his head toward Evelyn. "Stop coddling him, woman!"

Turning to face him, Senior scoffed. "You young folk think marriage is a game. That Sofie was a gift from God and you want to let her go? What is wrong with you boy?!"

Jerome looked at Tasha as he spoke, "She didn't love me and I never loved her. Not in the way a husband should love his wife." He noticed Tasha's breath hitch and continued, "Marriage between us was a matter of circumstance for Sofie, so I drew up the papers and wished her well."

Going back to his plate, Jerome felt Senior staring him down but otherwise said nothing. Dinner went by almost in complete silence, except the small talk that Tasha and Evelyn took part in with one another. Senior was the first to get up from the table and went back to his recliner as he turned on the television. When Evelyn stood up to take Senior's plate in the kitchen, Tasha placed a hand on her wrist.

"I'll clean up...Mama Evelyn." she said softly.

Seeing Evelyn smile widely at Tasha, Jerome finished the last of his sweet tea and began helping Tasha with clearing the table. Evelyn made sure to eye him as she stood and left the table. "You two gone ahead and cleaned up then. I'm going to call Eva and see if I can show little Lyn what I learned this week at the center."

"Yes ma'am." Jerome and Tasha call out together, making Evelyn chuckle while walking away.

Now alone with Tasha, the two cleaned up in silence. An no sooner had they finished, Tasha went outside and Jerome followed her out of the kitchen.

"Can we talk?" he asked tentatively.

When she nodded, Jerome walked with Tasha out the front door and led them to the porch swing. Memories of their first Christmas together as a couple came racing to his mind and Jerome steadied his breathing before holding the porch swing so she could sit down without it swaying.

"I didn't know you would be here today." he started before quickly adding, "But I am glad to see you."

"Me too."

He watched Tasha's mouth slightly drop open while she looked his way, "I-I meant that I didn't know you would be here today either. Seems like your mama's been up to her Southern tricks."

The two chuckle softly before Jerome spoke again. "I'm happy that she was."

He saw Tasha's shoulders rise and let out a sigh. "How long will you be in town?"

Tasha looked at him again before bringing her hands together in her lap. "Indefinitely?" She looked out toward the street and added, "Really leaning toward not leaving, at least not permanently."

Hearing her say what he had been praying for, Jerome couldn't stop himself from reaching out to tuck one of her loose twists behind her ear. Tasha's breath hitched as he took his time, gently bruising his thumb over the top of her ear lobe before dropping his hand back to his side.

"I'm sorry things didn't work out with you and Sofie." Tasha said.

He knew that she was trying to distance herself from him, but Jerome wasn't having it. Scooting closer to Tasha, he whispered. "It wasn't meant to be."

She bolted from the swing, sending it rocking back slightly. Not ready to see her leave, Jerome asked as he stood, "Please stay a little longer."

Right now, he was ready to spend the night on that porch swing, if it meant he could be there with her. Having Tasha back in his life was the blessing Jerome didn't dare have asked for, and now that she was here, he wanted to be beside her always. The two stared into each other's eyes for what felt like forever until Tasha gently spoke, "I'll begin an apprenticeship in Murica soon next year. We're still working out the dates, but this photographer is even more random with their schedule than I am."

Jerome didn't speak, choosing to admire the way a few stray twists along the nape of her neck lay against her dark brown skin.

"And between helping my sister with the kids, I figured I could set up shop here - once my apprenticeship ends." she explained. "I just didn't want to tell everyone yet, since I don't want to let y'all down again."

"You've never let anyone down, Tash." he whispered. "I knew what your plans were from the day we became friends."

"But then we became more." she said softly, "Even though I fought it, you found your way into my heart. And I keep breaking yours." he listened as her voice trembled "I'm sorry Jerome. Really, I am so sorry for hurting you."

Her words reached his ears, but Jerome chose to ignore them. When Tasha turned away, he grabbed her from behind, wrapping his arms around her waist. And as she melted into his arms, Jerome knew that no one would ever have a hold on him the way that Tasha Daye did.

"Please let me go."

He couldn't bring himself to do what she asked. Instead, he gravely whispered,"Now that I know you're back, with no plans on leaving...Tasha, I want you to stay."

Tasha cleared her throat, and Jerome listened when she spoke, "I know, but Jerome...it hurts when I see you. And I can't keep doing this to us. You may be getting divorced, but Sofie and Ro still need you. I'm sorry." She broke free from his embrace and didn't look back as she went inside the house.

Hearing the door close, Jerome stared out at the road in front of him. He could hear Tasha and Evelyn chatting and turned toward the door. A few minutes later, he saw the door open and watched Tasha as she walked back out with several plastic containers of food in her arms. She looked at him one last time before loading the containers into the back of her ride and putting on her helmet. Jerome stared at the road again until he could no longer see her before finally going back inside.

"That girl must have a death wish, riding around town on that demon bike." Senior said out loud. With Tasha gone, Jerome decided it was time to go too.

"Mama, I'mma head out."

"Okay baby. Take them leftovers with you." Evelyn told him.

Looking at the tupperware on the kitchen table, Jerome shook his head. "I don't want them." he mumbled..

"It's clear what you *do* want, hmm" Senior taunted before adding, "Now that Ms. Daye is back in town, you done quit on your marriage. Ready to finally lay –"

"Stop! Just stop!" Jerome marched over to Senior. "Tasha is the love of my life, and you talk about her like she is nothing more than trash off the street."

Senior looked up at his son, "Like mother, like daughter."

Evelyn gasped when Jerome snatched up Senior from out of the rocking chair. The older man reached for Jerome's hands while dangling mid-air, but Jerome's grip was iron-clad as he cried out, "You bitter, heartless man! How can you still preach with all that hate in your heart?!"

"Baby please! Please stop!" Evelyn shouted to Jerome.

Senior tried to speak, but Jerome kept his hands securely around his daddy's throat. "What is it about Tasha that makes you hate her? All she's guilty of is loving me..."

Dropping Senior like a sack of potatoes to the ground, Jerome didn't look back as his daddy caught his breath. Jerome walked out of the house as Senior could be heard shouting at him, "You never come back here, boy! You hear! Fall into sin with that woman, I don't care. But you are to never darken my doorstep again!"

Jerome looked back to see Evelyn trying to get past Senior. She finally broke through and rushed to his side.

"Mama, I am sorry."

Falling to his knees, Jerome felt Evelyn's arms embrace him before she gathered his face in her hands to look at him. "Baby, you ain't got to apologize to me. Just make sure to not let her go this time, you hear?"

He looked over and saw senior staring hard at them, "But Senior and-"

Evelyn grabbed his face. "You is grown Jerome! And if Tasha is the love of your life like you say she is, ain't nothing nobody nowhere can say to stop you from being with her."

Kissing him on his forehead, Evelyn continued, "Now, go find her, before it's too late."

Jerome got up from the ground and hugged Evelyn before getting into his car.

## RACHEL

Hearing Tasha pull up in the driveway, Rachel made her way to the door with Alexa hot on her heels. "I'mma be late getting back in tonight, so y'all don't have too much fun without me."

Rachel nodded as the two went outside. When they saw Tasha walking toward them with several containers, Rachel grabbed them. "How was dinner?"

Alexa looked between the two of them and shared a worried look with her wife, "Since y'all having a girls' night, why don't you park your bike in the garage Tash?"

"Okay."

They almost didn't hear Tasha speak when she turned away from them and started to push her motorbike to the garage entrance.

Alexa went to Rachel and kissed her. "Take care of our girl, alright?"

As Alexa stepped back, Rachel nodded. "Call when you're on your way home, no matter the time."

Giving Rachel another kiss, Alexa walked toward the garage and got into her car to leave. Hearing the garage door begin to close, Rachel went back inside and found Tasha in the kitchen, looking at her phone.

"Guess you ain't hungry, uh?' When Tasha didn't answer, Rachel tried again. "You want to watch some trashy reality TV? There's a new episode of- "

"I'mma just take a shower and go to bed. Is that okay?" Tasha asked.

"Yeah, of course." Rachel stepped aside so Tasha could go to her room. When Tasha closed the door, She saw Tasha's phone flashing on the kitchen counter. Picking it up, Rachel shook her head when she saw Jerome's name flash across the screen. *Ain't he done put her through enough?*

Soon she heard the shower running in Tasha's room and decided to sit on the couch. While surfing through the channels with Tyrone and Tia next to her, Rachel heard a car pull up in the driveway. Thinking that Alexa forgot something, she got up. Though when Rachel got to the door and saw Jerome getting out of his car, her eyes narrowed on him through the glass window. She watched as he stopped a few feet from the door and looked around. His chest rose and fell quickly before he started to walk to the door and knocked.

If the puppies hadn't started yelping, she wouldn't have answered it at all, but with their barks growing louder, Rachel didn't have a choice. When she partially opened the door, Rachel saw Jerome's wide eyes on her before he backed up a few feet.

"H-hey Rachel. How you doing?" he asked.

The hesitancy was evident in his voice as she shoo'd the pups away from the door. Wanting him to leave before Tasha got out of the shower, Rachel got right to it. "What do you want, Jerome?"

His blank stare told her that he wasn't expecting her cold response.

"I, um, want to see if Tasha was home?"

She saw the hopefulness in his eyes, and if this conversation was taking place years ago, Rachel would have welcomed him inside the house. But the way Tasha looked earlier still in her mind, Rachel wasn't about to have Jerome stressing her best friend out. Meeting his stare, Rachel flatly replied, "No."

"Oh, okay. Can you tell her that I came by?"

His half smile left her shaking her head. "Absolutely not."

Jerome's mouth parted open before he quickly closed it. When he didn't make a move to leave, Rachel heard the shower in Tasha's room turn off.

"We told you not to hurt our girl, and you did."

Taking a step forward, Jerome started to speak but Rachel cut her eyes at him and continued, "I know she was the one that left, but I don't wanna see my girl leave again and never come back because her heart got broken by a married man."

" I can't help how I feel." Jerome said, staring at the ground.

Curious, Rachel found herself asking, "Just how *do* you feel about her, JPK?"

Jerome looked up at her and Rachel saw him take a breath before giving her an answer. "I don't blame Tasha for leaving. But having her back in town these past few months has been incredible." When he turned his head and cleared his throat, Rachel was taken aback by the intensity in his stare. "And I'm not gonna let her walk away again."

She started to ask him what his wife thought about that until Jerome stepped closer. "If all we ever are is just friends, I will accept that. But until she tells me not to, I will keep hope that once my divorce is final that we can be together again."

*He's getting a divorce?! Then why did Tash come in here looking so tore up?*

"I'm sorry for bothering you. Please tell Tasha I want to talk to her when she gets in."

Jerome stepped back a few feet before turning around to leave. Suddenly he stopped and looked at Rachel again. "And whatever I did to make you doubt me, or my intentions, I am sorry. Just - when she left, I couldn't bring myself to keep in touch."

Rachel's eyes widened as she found herself asking, "Why?"

His laugh was low, but she heard the bitterness in Jerome's tone all the same. "Your best friend is the love of my life. And even though she left me, I knew that no matter what, Tasha would keep in touch with y'all. I-I... I was jealous."

*Damn. So that's why he wouldn't visit or work with me all those years ago.*

Rachel looked at him and nodded. "I'll tell her you stopped by."

When Jerome finally left, Rachel closed the front door and saw Tasha wiping her eyes with her nightshirt while sitting on the bed.

"How much did you hear?" she asked gently.

"Everything."

Rachel went to join Tasha. "Why didn't you tell us he was getting divorced? And why you ain't just come out when you heard us just now?"

Tasha lowered her head. "I couldn't Rachel."

She looked at Tasha, who looked like she was trying to will herself not to cry. "Tash, I love you, but I don't understand. Just go -"

A fresh stream of tears fell down Tasha's face. "You think I don't want to be with him again? All I wanna do is grab Jerome and never let him go, but..but..."

"But what Tash?" Rachel asked again.

Tasha started to speak and her voice cracked when she pushed the words out, "What if we still can't make it work?! Even after all this time? W-what if we try again and don't make it? I couldn't take it!"

Tasha was hiccupping as she rubbed small circles against the upper part of her chest. "I just...I need time to be sure. Before I see him again and tell him how I feel. I - I need time."

Trying to calm Tasha down, Rachel nodded as she wiped more tears from Tasha's face. "Okay."

When Tasha stood up, so did Rachel before she added, "It's a good thing Alexa told you to park your ride in the garage before she went to work, uh?"

Tasha threw herself into Rachel's arms. And as she listened to her friend cries lessen, Rachel sent a small prayer up to the heavens. *Lord, please help my girl get through this so that she can finally be with the person she loves.*

## JEROME

A whole month passed and Jerome hadn't heard from Tasha. He knew that she's still in town because Evelyn had been meeting her. To her credit, mama hadn't said anything. It was the new photographs that he saw when he visited her while Senior was at church. He knew that Tasha took the photos of her before mama could try to hide it.

"How is she?" Jerome asked, voice barely above a whisper.

Evelyn looked at him, her eyes taking in his downcast face before answering Jerome. "She's okay. Spending her time with all them babies and her sister." A small smile showed up on her face. "Yesterday she told me that she's working on opening up a place to take pictures that's all her own."

"That's good."

Before he could turn to leave, Evelyn wrapped him into her arms. "Oh baby..." she said soothingly as she slowly rubbed small circles across his back.

His phone vibrated in his pocket, so Jerome let her go and looked at the screen. He stared at the screen for so long that Evelyn soon looked down at it too. "Baby, is that Tasha?"

He slowly nodded and she shouted, "Thank you Lord!"

Pushing him toward the door, Evelyn called out to him, "Jerome, baby - go! Go and meet her now! I'm tired of see both of y'all looking so pitiful.``

He half smiled as he got into his car to read the text.

**Hey Rome.**
**You free early tomorrow morning?**
**I really would love to see you.**
**-Tash**

Jerome sent her a reply and drove to his condo to get some rest.

The next morning he arrived at the park across from Caloo Bridge, and saw Tasha already there, looking out into the pond surrounding the park. The sun was rising and Jerome sighed as he watched the light capture her features. She looked good. Tired, but good. Wearing a green halter dress with white kicks, Jerome saw her take a few deep breaths before hearing him approach from behind.

"Hey. You look good."

The two sat next to one another and stared off at the sun as it rose for the day.

"How's Sofie and Ro?" She asked.

Jerome can hear the sincerity in her voice and it warmed his heart. "They're good. Sofie's still going to her rehab."

He saw Tasha softly smile as she tried to steady her hands. Her gaze went from the sunrise to her shoes, as her feet bounced rapidly against the grass. To ease her nerves, Jerome reached out and placed his hand on top of hers. Tasha's eyes closed briefly before they landed on him. Trying to remain patient about why she asked to see him so early in the morning, he sent a small smile her way. "Do you remember the first night you showed up to see me? After I went to your place?"

Jerome nodded but sent up a silent prayer that she didn't call him out here to talk about that night.

"Well, I was doing more than editing photos from a previous project when you got there." Tasha inhaled slowly before speaking again. "That night, I had a therapy session scheduled too. I missed it because I didn't want to tell you about it."

Jerome looked up at her, his grip tightening on Tasha's hand.

"I'm fine now, but I wanted you to know."

"Why?"

She stared out at the view in front of them and sighed. "It was time. I'd been meaning to begin going, but didn't have the money or time to do it. If I'm being completely honest, a part of me was really scared to start. And, well...four years ago I left you because I thought I was too damaged to have you in my life. Now I'm working on getting better, not just for me but for everyone that I care about."

"Thanks for telling me all this, you didn't have to." He started, but Tasha shook her head.

"Yeah, I did. I need you to know. Because..."

He waited for her to continue.

"This time I'm not leaving."

Jerome stared hard at Tasha before asking, "What are you telling me right now Tash?"

Afraid to get his hopes up, but too in love with Tasha to not stop himself from doing so, Jerome watched as she met his stare. "My sister needs me. And I miss being around what little family I do have. I want to be a part of my niece and nephews lives."

He reminded himself to steady his breathing as she went on, "I don't want to be without you in my life Jerome."

Blinking away tears, he whispered, "I love you Tash."

Taking his face into her hands, Tasha brought them close. "I love you Rome."

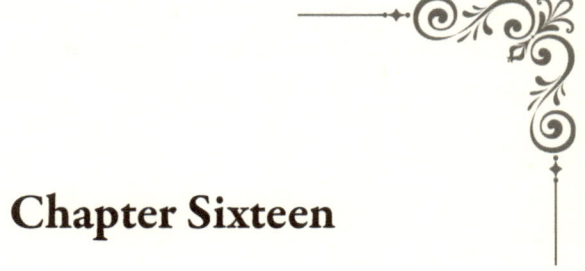

# Chapter Sixteen

## New Beginning

**Tasha**

> **I love you.**
> **- Rome**

Tasha bit her lip while looking down at her phone and sending Jerome another text.

> **You said that in your last message big head.**
> **What else you got?**
> **-Tash**

"Tash, did you hear me?"

Looking up to find Trisha, Alexa, and Rachel all sending her side eye glances, Tasha said the first thing she could think of to buy some time. "Uh?"

It had been a week since she and Jerome agreed to see each other again, and Tasha would be lying if she said that he wasn't more than a little distraction. But it was the sweetest, cheesiest distraction she could ever ask for, and Tasha loved every second of it.

She was supposed to be enjoying a child and puppy free afternoon out at Tastee's, the new coffee shop in town with her girls, but Tasha could see that her otherwise absence from the conversation was getting annoying.

"Alexa was asking you about that building you trying to buy? For your studio or whatever." Trisha asked her.

Remembering the old bookstore that she wanted to convert into a multi creative space and photography studio, Tasha nodded quickly, "Oh, yeah. I've been talking with Jay Jay and he's lined up a few contractors for me to interview once the deal is set."

Rachel was smirking at her so hard that Tasha had to ask, "What?"

"Don't you mean *James*? That tall glass of water that's sweet as hell on you?"

Tasha rolled her eyes at her friend. "Alexa, you and your wife need to leave them reality TV shows alone - her imagination starting to get out of control."

Trisha sent Tasha her signature stank eye. "Nah, Rachel ain't the one out of control - you is with that phone. Who you messaging anyway in the middle of the afternoon like that?"

"Trish, she ain't got no other friends. You know who she chatting with." Alexa said.

Feeling her phone vibrate in her hand, Tasha glanced down and tapped on the screen. A picture of Jerome, grinning while outside of SweeThangs showed up. But it was the message below that made Tasha snort.

**Just picked up a few of your faves.**
**You know I got your sweet ass!**
**- Rome**

*Stay cussing in his texts! But won't say that mess to my face.*

Hearing someone clear their throat, Tasha slowly looked up and saw her girls eyeing her.

"10 dollars say they sexting!" Rachel shouted.

Before Tasha could utter a word, Alexa lunged out and snatched her phone out of her hands.

"You heffa! Give me back my phone!"

"Nah, you wanna sit up here and half listen to us, then we gonna see what has your full attention!" Trisha told Tasha, playfully holding her back.

Tasha groaned as Rachel and Alexa huddled together and looked at the messages on her phone. When Alexa cackled, she knew they were looking at the last message that Jerome sent.

"Y'all some weirdos!" Alexa said.

Rachel grinned at Tasha, shaking her head. "That man busy as hell working on his album, and he still made time to drive an hour to SweeThangs for you?"

"I wanna see!" Trisha whined.

Tasha didn't even try to fight when Alexa handed Trisha her phone. "Lawd, I knew he was lame, but if you like it sis, I love it."

"I do! Now give me back my dang phone."

Trisha handed Tasha her phone, and she snuck one more peek at Jerome's message before putting it down on the table.

"Well, this was fun, but I gotta feed my baby before she goes back to work." Alexa announced, grabbing Rachel's hand and helping her up from her seat.

Trisha was next to stand. "Yeah, I gotta go too and make sure Lloyd ain't let them boys mess up the house."

They all laughed as Tasha waved them goodbye. Remembering that Trisha's first therapy session was tomorrow, Tasha called out to her.

"I'm glad you decided to talk to someone. You know, about everything." Tasha said as Trisha walked closer to her.

Seeing Trisha's eyes scan the almost empty coffee shop, Tasha waited for her to speak. "It's time. Not gonna lie though, I'm scared than a mutha."

"I was too, for my first session. Just - share what you feel comfortable with. And if you ain't feeling the therapist, don't be afraid to leave and find another one, okay?"

"Bet. Love you sis."

"Love you back."

Tasha watched as Trisha turned around and walked out of the coffee shop. With no other plans for the day, she took one last sip of her drink and collected the other cups to throw away on her way out. The sun beamed on her when she walked to her bike and took out her key. With Trisha stepping out of her comfort zone to start healing old wounds, Tasha revived the engine and headed to the source of hers.

THE DRIVE TO HER CHILDHOOD home wasn't a long one, and Tasha stared at the house for a minute before climbing off her bike. As she walked up to the front door, memories of growing up and growing pains followed. Some good, some painful, but by the time she had reached out to knock on the front door, all but one of them were now behind her.

"Who the hell is it?" Tina shouted.

Tasha said nothing as the eight year version of herself forced her to keep pounding on the door. Each time she did, flashes of things she prayed over the years to forget entered her mind.

When Tina cracked the door open and saw Tasha staring at her, she failed to notice the way Tasha's hands vibrated. Blinking away her tears, Tasha spoke, "You coming outside or you gonna let me in? Either way, you gonna hear me today."

"Who the hell you think you is?! Talking bout what I'm gonna do?" Tina demanded.

Tasha steadied her breathing as she zoomed in on Tina's face. "Did you use what happened to Trish to keep her from telling me what you and Kitty did?"

Tina stared back at her before scoffing. "She was always soft when it came to your self-righteous ass. I don't know why she saying anything now."

The need to knock Tina's head into the door frame and drag her into the yard for a long overdue beat down left Tasha's hands on fire. Shoving them into the pockets of her shorts, Tasha bit her trembling lip, "What the actual fuck is *wrong* with you?"

"We needed the money. You had it, so I took it. Let this -"

Tasha's hands went on autopilot, ejecting from her pockets and pushing Tina hard. Though seeing Tina stumble to the floor and sliding backwards until she crashed into the loveseat behind her didn't feel nearly as good as Tasha had hoped it would.

"You bitch!"

Realizing that the first person she admired, after Kitty, was too far gone to be forgiven left Tasha with an odd sense of peace. She watched Tina scramble to get up and stay near the sofa, eyes narrowed onto hers. Tasha sent a small prayer out into the universe for her big sister.

*Lord, please show mercy when you call her home.*

Tasha finally trusted her voice enough to not scream as she spoke. "I can forgive you for the money, but what you did to Trish...after what happened to her? I wouldn't wish that shit on my worst enemy. And I can never forgive you for that."

Tina inched closer to the door as Tasha continued, "Yeah, our childhood was snatched up from us by Kitty and her addiction, but you...what you did is on you! Own that shit Tina!"

As Tasha walked away, Tina shouted, "You bring your big wanna be bad ass back out here again and I'mma call them city dogs on ya!"

Tasha didn't even turn around to acknowledge Tina as she got on her bike and drove off.

———— ⌘ ————

JEROME WAS WAITING for her as she parked her bike into the driveway, but he seemed to be in no hurry for their date. The two were able to clear their schedules to head on out to the traveling fairgrounds for the afternoon. And after seeing Tina not that long ago, Tasha couldn't wait to spend the day with him. Removing her helmet, she gently shook her twist free while strolling over to Jerome, planting a quick kiss to his lips. Though when she went to pull away, he brought her closer and claimed her mouth again. "Jerome! Let me go freshen up." Tasha asked, wrapping her arms around his neck.

"Freshen up? You look good as you are Tash," Jerome said in between their kisses, "Smell just as sweet too."

That got a chuckle out of both of them before Tasha remembered the text he sent earlier. "Wait, how did you get here before me, anyway? Didn't you go to SweeThangs?"

"I did, and you're welcome," he answered, sending another peck to her lips. "Now, you gonna keep asking questions, or do you want your CBD?"

Her eyes lit up at the mention of the dark chocolate cupcake with its butter pecan filling and sea salt caramel drizzle over chocolate frosting, the CBD. Memories soon followed from the first time he brought her one of the delectable treats, as a surprise during their time working together at Christ Corner. Bringing her gaze to meet his knowing smirk, Tasha felt her lips turn upward. *What did I do right to have this man back in my life?*

"We can split the CBD inside." Tasha told Jerome before adding, "And since you're early, we have more time to greet each other properly."

Laughing as his eyes grew twice in size, she explained with a wink, "Just kisses, I promise." When he let out a shaky chuckle, Tasha untangled herself from his grasp and sprinted to the front door.

---

AN HOUR LATER THE TWO were walking hand in hand at the local fairgrounds. Until a giant display of stuffed animals next to row after row of small balloons caught Jerome's eye.

"Which one do you want me to win for you?" he asked Tasha, with an air of confidence that made the butterflies soar from her stomach to her ribcage.

The guy running the dart game grinned their way, and Tasha couldn't find it in her to refuse his request to win her a prize. Instead, she glanced at the stuffed animals and raised a finger toward the bright blue and gray-ish elephant, with its floppy ears and fuzzy looking appearance standing out among the neon printed others.

Jerome wasted no time marching over to the vendor and paying for two rounds of darts. But it was clear from his ginger handling of the darts that he was not equipped to play this game, much less win. His first two attempts at popping three balloons had those that passed by hiding their chuckles, but Jerome's determination was evident as he went back to the vendor and received three more darts.

Tasha tried not to, but couldn't help the giggle she let out as Jerome tried for a third time to win.

She watched as he threw the last of his darts all at once, a classic move by desperate players and all but one of them landed on the ground.

"Rome, really, you don't have to win me anything." She told him gently as the man running the booth smirked.

Jerome looked back at the board full of balloons and shook his head. "How did I have all those darts and only hit one balloon?" He asked, clearly exasperated.

Grabbing his hand, Tasha led him away from the booth and her nose picked up a heavenly scent of freshly fried funnel cake. "Come on. I think I just found something way sweeter."

Sure enough, a few stations down, Tasha saw one of the food trucks putting powdered sugar over the crunchy and warm treats.

"Have you ever had one of these?" Tasha asked Jerome as she got in line.

"Nope. But the look on your face makes me curious to try it."

As they got to the front of the line, Tasha ordered a classic funnel cake and Jerome paid the cashier as Tasha explained, "The few times I remember coming to a fair as a kid, this was one of the few things Kitty would splurge on us." Thinking back to her middle school days when the four of them would come to the fair, Tasha smiled. "Kitty would let us miss school, so we could all take the bus during the day to go. Money was tight so we'd only have enough to pay for the entrance and maybe two rides each. Just before we left, me and Trisha would ask Kitty for a funnel cake."

Jerome reached out and tore a piece off and popped it into his mouth. As he chewed, Tasha could see his lips curling up into a smile. "Tash, it's pure sugar. No wonder y'all wanted it so much."

She said nothing as he tore another piece of the cake and put it toward her lips. Tasha eyed him just before opening her mouth. The more she chewed, the more she found herself agreeing with him. Looking up at him, Tasha rolled her eyes. "Okay, so you're right. It really is fried dough piled high with sugar."

Jerome then took another piece for himself, "But it is *really* good fried dough piled high with sugar."

Laughing, Tasha took another bite and the two walked around, taking in all the bright neon lights and rides.

"Oh! Let's get in line for this one."

Turning to see what had him all hyped up, Tasha almost rolled her eyes again as she saw the line for the high ferris wheel. Tossing the rest of the funnel cake into the trash, they got in line and Tasha leaned against Jerome. He shuffled them forward as the people in front of them moved and soon they were being seated into a cart.

"Why do you like ferris wheels so much?" Tasha asked, out of genuine curiosity.

"I don't know, maybe because I couldn't ride them as a kid. Mama is terrified of them so when we did go to a fair, I never got to ride them. By the time I was in high school, everyone my age thought they weren't cool anymore." Tasha nodded as she listened as he continued with his story. "When I got to plan the jamboree, that was the first thing I made sure to have for the event, even though I didn't get to ride one either year."

She looked up at him and asked, "You were only in charge of the jamboree for two years? And never got to ride the ferris wheel once?"

As Jerome nodded, Tasha started filling in the blanks. "So this is your first time, ever? On a ferris wheel?"

Tasha stared up at Jerome as he grinned, bringing his hand out to rub across his jawline. He hadn't shaved in what looked like a few days and Tasha had to admit that seeing the stubble facial hair on his face was a good look.

"Well, how is it? Being high in the clouds after all this time?"

He looked down at Tasha before kissing the crown of her head. "I always feel like I'm in the clouds when I'm with you, Tash."

Hearing his voice drop an octave after saying that sent her heart soaring. "Rome, are you flirting with me?" Tasha teased.

When his eyes met hers, Tasha reached out to touch his cheek. "Is it working?" Jerome asked.

She wrapped her hand behind his head, bringing him closer. "Yeah."

Feeling his lips on hers as they reached the top of the ride, Tasha thought she was in heaven. Though just as Jerome's tongue swept across hers, a droplet of rain splashed onto her forehead. More rain followed and she heard people below scrambling to find shelter. And she took in the sight of more rain falling down on Jerome as he grinned at her.

Tasha was no fool, she knew what reuniting with Jerome meant when she called him weeks ago. Though in that moment, Tasha felt her resolve shift and ascend while staring into his warm eyes. The glow that mirrored back her way from him was indescribable as it settled within her heart. So much so that in those few seconds she knew no one would ever shake her to the core as profoundly as Jerome Grant Jr. did. All she could do to still her thoughts when she accepted this unspoken truth was send out a small prayer to the heavens. *Lord, when he asks me again, please do not let me hesitate in saying yes.*

Finally their cart was back down on the ground and the conductor released their rail. Jerome grabbed Tasha's hand and they sprinted toward the parking lot.

# Chapter Seventeen

## New Year, New Us

**Jerome**

With the season now behind them and a little help from a few patiently waiting family and friends, Jerome was ready.

This year, Alexa and Rachel were having a small New Year's Eve party at their home and that was where part one of his plan would begin. He knew that Tasha had spent the weekend at her friends' and was helping them decorate when he called to tell her that he was running late getting back in town.

"Is everything alright?"

He heard the disappointment in her voice and almost confessed before looking at the boxes in the back seat of his ride. "Everything's okay. Just a last minute meeting with Terrence, I promise." he explained into the earpiece as he drove to his new home.

"Okay. Well, I'm already at Alexa and Rachel's so you don't have to worry about picking me up. Just be careful on the roads getting here later, okay?"

"I will. Love you."

Ending the call, Jerome turned into the garage before texting Rachel.

**Part one of the plan - done.**

**-Jerome**

Seeing two thumbs up emojis from his partner in crime, Jerome went inside the house with the boxes and began setting everything up.

Evening came much quicker than he thought it would, so once the movers left, Jerome went and took a shower. As he was getting dressed, Jerome heard his phone beep. Going to look at the screen, he smirked.

**Our girl is putting on a good show, but she's been checking her phone every 30 minutes. You better be ready PK.**

**-Alexa**

He pressed the thumbs up icon and hit send. With just four hours left in the year, Jerome headed to the party. There were more people there than he was expecting, but it didn't take him long to find Tasha on the second floor of the house. He took her in before walking up to her, in a long, one sleeved champagne gown, Jerome saw her look down at her phone and smiled. Taking out his phone, he sent her a message.

**I'm here. Sorry for being late.**

**-Rome**

He watched her from the corner as Tasha's head jerked up after looking at the message. Seeing her twists gathered around her head and away from Tasha's face, and how the lights in the living room seem to light up her eyes, Jerome felt his chest tighten as he walked up behind her.

"Hey." he said softly.

Tasha quickly turned around to the sound of his voice and threw herself into his arms. Enjoying having her so close, Jerome was taken aback when Tasha let him go and swat at his shoulder.

"You were pushing it tonight Rome!" she said with a pout.

Reaching out to bring her face closer to his, Jerome pressed a sound kiss to her lips. Feeling her relax into his touch, he let her go and tried not to let his lips turn up into a smile.

"I know, I'm sorry," he told her.

Time seemed to freeze around them as Jerome committed her face to memory in that moment. He watched as her eyelashes fluttered before she leaned up to kiss him again. Just before their lips could touch, Rachel appeared behind Tasha.

"Look who made it babe!"

Alexa then appeared by his side, grinning up at him.

"Better late than never!" she shouted as Rachel pulled Tasha into a hug. The two sway from side to side as a new song filled the room and Tasha took Rachel's hands into hers, spinning them around. Listening to the two giggle, Jerome forgot that Alexa was standing beside him, until she elbowed him in the ribs.

Alexa stared at him before asking, "Is everything in place?"

He nodded and Alexa brought out a fist to pound against his. "Good! Now, go have fun!"

Jerome cut in between Rachel and Tasha, grabbing her hand and bringing her close.

As her hands roamed over his satin blazer, making their way to his button down shirt, he noticed how her eyes gaze over him before coming back up to meet his. Bringing him in even closer, Tasha teased, "I love seeing you in a suit. But can you keep up with me while wearing it?"

Grabbing one of her hands, Jerome stepped back and lifted their entwined hands in the air before spinning her in a circle and pressing her back close against his chest. He leaned down and whispered in her ear, "I know you do. And yeah, I can."

After dancing and mingling with a few guests, the two finally made their way outside for some air. Once they reached the sliding glass doors, Jerome slid it open. Tasha let go of his hand and kicked off her heels, whirling around him on the terrace. He took in the grin on her face, as the night sky shined on her face, and Jerome's heart felt full.

"We are really here! Together!" she said before grabbing his hand again. A slow R&B song began playing from inside and Jerome placed his other hand on the small of her back.

"There is no other place that I want to be, than right here with you, right now." Tasha whispered before placing her head onto his chest.

The house lights flashed and they turned to see Alexa and Rachel shout, "10! 9! 8!..."

He looked down and saw Tasha staring up at him. The twinkle in her eye told him what she was about to do, as Tasha brought her hands around his neck and planted her lips onto his. As soon as Jerome felt her tongue against his, he tightened his hold on Tasha and heard fireworks shoot and crackle loudly in the distance. She pulled away slightly before looking at the bright lights that sailed into the sky.

"Happy New Year Tash." Jerome whispered, kissing her check as they both looked forward.

WITH PART TWO OF THEIR plan completed, Jerome brought Tasha inside and went looking for Alexa and Rachel.

"Thank you for having us over tonight." he said as Rachel grinned at him.

Confused, Tasha looked between the two of them, "Wait, what do you mean?"

Jerome turned to face her. "I have to get back home, Tash, so I can go over the upcoming tour dates with Terrence and Raven."

At least that part was true.

Tasha looked at her friends and then back to him. "I was going to stay and help them clean up for the night."

Rachel jumped in and kissed Tasha on the cheek. "We love you for that, but we got it."

Before she could try to protest, Alexa walked her way and leaned over before kissing her other cheek. "Go. You've been waiting to be with PK all day. We got this."

Jerome pulled Tasha close and mouthed, 'Thank you' to the two of them as he led Tasha outside to the car.

The ride was mostly quiet, until Tasha started to notice that they were not taking the normal route to the condo. "Rome, where are we headed?"

His stomach started doing somersaults as he kept his eyes on the road. "I forgot my bag at this place I was visiting earlier. Just swinging by to pick it up."

Tasha made herself comfortable back into the passenger seat, and Jerome started breathing normally again. Soon they were in front of the house that he was at earlier and he heard Tasha whistle. "Whose place is this?" she asked, in awe.

Jerome cut off the engine and got out of the car, before walking over to the passenger side door. He waited for Tasha to put on her heels and stepped out of the vehicle, her eyes still on the house. He watched her stare up and down at the two story building. The sky blue painted home looked almost white at night, contrasting with the deep creme vaulted walls and wide black ceiling fan inside that could be seen from one of the large windows in the front. A large, thick wood panel fence stretched around the home, and several strings of tea lights could be seen from the back yard as they made their way to the front double doors.

"You like it?" he gently asked.

She turned to look at him and grinned. "Well, so far it looks inviting. I don't know who you know in the business that lives here, but I can't wait to meet them."

Hearing this, Jerome took her hand into his. Her eyes widened as he pulled out a key and unlocked the door. When Jerome opened the door Tasha's hands immediately covered her mouth. Inside, more dimly lit lights were on, and Jerome watched as she took a step forward. Closing the door behind him, Jerome looked over on the counter and picked up the home remote, allowing the Smooth R&B music to play softly throughout the house.

Not sure what she would like, Jerome only had his furniture from the condo brought over, along with the framed pictures that he had gotten from their first Christmas and New Years' Eve together, thanks to Alexa and Rachel. He watched as Tasha stared at the photos of them on Bejon Beach and blinked away her tears, while following the white rose petals to the sliding glass doors that led them outside.

As she opened the sliding doors, Jerome reached into his pocket and held on to the ring he'd placed there before leaving earlier.

"Rome...what is this? Where are we right now?" Tasha asked again, her voice hardly above a whisper.

As she finally stopped in front of the circle of long white stemmed roses, Jerome got down on one knee.

"This is our home."

Turning around to the sound of his voice, Tasha's sobs tugged at his heart as Jerome continued. "And where I want to start our forever, together. I want you by my side for the rest of my life, Tasha Daye. So, I am asking you now, in this New Year, will you marry me?"

Walking toward him, his eyes stung at the sight of unshed tears in hers. His grip on the ring box in his hand tightened while she looked down at him. And his heart took flight when a smile graced her face. "Yes, I will-"

He was up before she could finish giving her answer, and wrapped her into his arms.

"I will marry you, Jerome Grant!"

Hearing her finally say the words, he remembered the ring that he still had in his hand. And he gently released her, Jerome took her left hand and placed the simple gold infinite band, with a golden tan pearl in its center, onto her ring finger. Sighing as the ring slid onto her finger with ease, Jerome looked at Tasha again before pulling her in for a kiss.

## TASHA

Ringing in the New Year always filled Tasha with joy, but as she stared at the engagement ring on her left hand, Tasha couldn't imagine the last time she was this happy.

"You like it?" Jerome asked, hugging her as the two laid on one of the wide patio lounge chairs outside.

Tasha turned to face him, pushing the thick throw off of them and placing a soft kiss onto his lips, "I love it."

She watched as Jerome grinned. "Mama helped me pick it out after Thanksgiving."

Hearing that Evelyn not only gave her blessing to their union, but was there to help Jerome choose a ring brought more tears to Tasha's eyes.

To have everything that she wanted - a man who loved her unconditionally, a job that allowed her to express herself and pay the bills, and Trisha back in her life - Tasha couldn't fight the tears as they left her eyes. *Thank you Lord. Thank you.*

Jerome wiped away her tears as he kissed the crown of her head. "I love you, Tash."

She eased out of his embrace, and stared down at him. "I can't wait to call you my husband, Rome."

The unshed tears in his eyes as she spoked moved her heart. Jerome sat up and wrapped his arms around her, nuzzling into her neck. With the sun now making its appearance, Tasha was almost ready to greet the day. But first, she had a question, "How soon do you want to jump the broom, future husband of mine?"

He laughed and Tasha leaned in closer, enjoying the sound.

"You going somewhere? What's the rush?"

Tasha turned to look at him and rolled her eyes. "Do you have a date in mind? We could go to the courthouse tomorrow and sign all the paperwork, right?"

Jerome blinked several times before explaining, "There's more to it Tasha."

A bit confused, Tasha pressed further. "So...a week? A month? What timetable works for you?"

He looked deep in thought before answering her. "A year. That would give us more than enough time."

Tasha looked at Jerome like he'd lost his mind, "Wait a minute! You mean to tell me that you want a year long engagement?" Another question entered her thoughts and she quickly asked, "And where would I live during this time?"

"Here. In our home."

Now Tasha was sure that Jerome wasn't thinking straight."Rome, baby, I think a year would be too long."

"Some folks have longer engagements Tash, it'll be fine."

*Ain't no way I'mma wait that long!*

She was about to tell Jerome as much before he continued, "And I want you to have the wedding of your dreams, so there ain't no need to rush."

Tasha didn't want to argue, but she'd only been engaged to Jerome for a few hours and was already ready to consummate their union. But Tasha knew who she was marrying, and she knew Jerome wanted to wait before things went further with them physically. That meant she would have to wait until they said their vows and the ink dried on their marriage contract. Or so she thought. With the way Jerome's eyes were taking her in, Tasha found herself needing to confirm her suspicions.

"So... when can we begin living together as husband and wife then? Today?" she asked, bringing a hand around his neck. "We technically already slept together, since we chose to sleep under the stars last night."

She saw Jerome fighting a smile and Tasha became even more hopeful, as she brought her other arm to Jerome's neck and sent a quick kiss to his lips, "Because I got to be honest with you - I'm ready to be yours Rome. In every way."

All her previous thoughts were confirmed when Tasha felt him reach out to grab her hands and pull them from around his neck. The newfound hope she had dashed away when Jerome's lips formed a straight line.

"Tasha..." he started to say, but her need for him had Tasha making one last attempt at turning things back to her favor.

"The papers are just a formality, Rome. Why wait to have them when we already made the commitment in every way that matters?"

He looked at her and sighed, "It's more than just papers to me. I want to do this right, you deserve that much Tasha. And..." Tasha waited for Jerome to speak again. "The first time I did this, it was rushed. I don't want that for us."

This was the first time he ever brought up his actual wedding to Sofie and Tasha tried to keep her face neutral as she said gently, "It wouldn't be like that for us. I lo-"

"It's ain't just about love, Tasha. Sofie and I, umm, were together physically before I asked her to marry me. She was a few weeks pregnant when we got married."

With her jaw clenched, Jerome went on, "When she told me she was pregnant, I wanted to protect the child. So I asked her to marry me, and she took care of everything else. The ceremony, telling mama and Senior, all that."

Tasha nodded. She didn't like it, but hearing Jerome tell her about his situation with Sofie, she understood. Ready to resume their day on a good note, she decided to move the conversation down a lighter road. "I haven't thought much about what my wedding would look like, since I never thought I would ever get married."

He smiled at her, rendering her train of thought hazy. "Then let's talk about that. Years ago you said that you wouldn't want lots of folks on your big day. I'm cool with that."

Hearing that he remembered what she shared with him that day - the first day they kissed - made Tasha grin. A new burst of joy tingled throughout her hands as she placed them into his and nodded again, "Okay. What about location? You want us to say our vows in a church or somewhere else?"

"Somewhere else. I know a spot you'll like." Jerome said.

As she watched his eyes twinkle while looking at her, Tasha felt warm all over. "Got it. Anywhere works for me, as long as you are there."

The two continued sharing their ideas for the wedding, until their phones started ringing. Jerome reached for his first and touched the screen. "Folks are finally up and commenting on our posts."

Peering over his shoulder, Tasha saw all the likes and messages under their engagement post from his social feed. Her heart felt as if it would soar away at any second. "Good. Because I'm ready to be Mrs. Tasha Daye - Grant."

Jerome jerked his head back slightly, with his eyes on her. "Wait-what?"

Tasha laughed, "You heard me, Mrs. Tasha Daye - Grant."

He seemed to think it over, rubbing his chin. "Okay, Mrs. Daye - Grant."

Hearing their last names together, as one, Tasha found herself fighting back tears again and blinked them away. "So, in a few months' time, it'll be official? You'll be my husband?"

"And you will finally be my wife." he whispered, leaning in to kiss Tasha once more.

### Jerome

After their morning chat, Jerome and Tasha left the patio and took showers in separate rooms, before having breakfast. Ever thankful that he thought to do some grocery shopping in between having everything moved into the house, Jerome sat at their kitchen counter and watched as Tasha made them a light breakfast of eggs and toast.

He didn't want to say anything while they were outside, but he honestly didn't know if they should live together while engaged. But the thought of not being able to see Tasha first thing in the morning left a hollowness in Jerome's chest. That got him to thinking more about what he said about having a long engagement.

Last night was incredible, falling asleep with Tasha in his arms. It had only been hours since they went public with the engagement, and he was finding it harder and harder to keep his hands off of her. Even now, as she plated their meal and poured him a cup of coffee, Jerome found his eyes roaming her plush and inviting figure. Now wearing a pair of jeans and a light green blouse, Jerome envied the fabric as it draped itself around her soft skin.

"What month exactly works for you?" he asked suddenly.

Tasha looked at Jerome as she placed his coffee and the plate of food in front of him before sitting across from him. "I'm free anytime this week."

*She ain't making this easy.*

"Tash, be serious."

"I am!" she told him as she playfully picked up a piece of toast, spreaded it with butter and honey before taking a bite.

When she closed her eyes, Jerome got lost in his less than gentlemanly thoughts and cleared his throat. "Okay, how about sometime in the spring?"

Putting down the toast, Tasha took a sip of her hot tea and Jerome waited for her answer, but got another question instead. "What will we do with our time between now and then?"

Several vivid thoughts ran through his mind before he could stop them, causing Jerome to reach out for Tasha's hand. When he brought his eyes up to hers, she sent a knowing smirk his way. "Since you so adamant about us having some time to get everything in place, I want to make a suggestion." Jerome nodded as she continued, "I think we should go to therapy. Couples therapy."

His eyes widened. "Therapy? Um, I wasn't expecting that."

"I love you Jerome, and I want to start this chapter right too. I think going to therapy will help."

He brought his hand out to rub the back of his head. "I hear you, I just don't know if therapy is for me."

Tasha squeezed Jerome's hand, before brushing it against her lips. "I'm not looking for an answer now, but at least consider it. If couples' therapy is too much, at least think about seeing someone on your own, okay?"

The concern in her voice was unmistakable, and even though Jerome wasn't completely on board with the idea, he could at least think it over. "Okay. I'll think about it."

Jerome raised their joined hands and placed them over his heart. "So, you'll stay here?"

He thought Tasha was going to say no, when her eyes shifted from between their entwined hands to the ground. But then she looked at him again and grinned.

"There is nowhere else I want to be.

AFTER LEAVING THE HOUSE, Jerome made his way across town to join mama for lunch at Rock 'Em Sock 'Em Ribs.

"Baby! I am so happy for you!" Evelyn engulfed Jerome into a hug, rocking him back and forth. "Now, how long do I have to pick out a new dress?"

Jerome grinned, "Is early spring enough time?"

Hearing mama gasp, Jerome chuckled.

"A spring wedding! Oh baby, that's good. Gives folks plenty of time to get here and see y'all finally jump the broom!"

The two were soon seated at an indoor table, and Jerome sighed.

Evelyn asked, "What's on your mind?"

Not wanting to go into all the details, Jerome told her about Tasha's suggestion that they go to therapy. "I want to do things right this time, mama, but therapy? I don't know about all that."

"What's there to think about? Go to therapy!" Evelyn hissed. "Your fiancee is looking to build a strong foundation with you by talking things out with someone experienced in helping folks with their marriages. Why don't you want to go?"

Jerome understood what she was saying, and not wanting to lie, he decided to tell the truth. "Tasha has been seeing a therapist for awhile now, but I feel like they'll just make me feel lame for how I think about things."

"Baby, that ain't what therapy is. Tasha has her reasons for going to see someone. And do you really think your fiancee would let someone speak to you any kind of way in the first place?"

They both shared a knowing smile, as Evelyn continued, "You ain't ask me, but I'mma tell you anyway - give it a try."

Their server came by to take their order, and Evelyn finished her thought, "Go to therapy, or marital counseling - whatever you want to call it - go."

He thought over what she said and nodded.

**Sofie**

Madison, a petite blonde, grabbed her work bag before turning around to say goodbye to Sofie. "I'll see you again in two days, alright?"

"Okay. Thanks Madison."

Sofie watched as the woman showed herself out of the house after their latest round of rehabilitation exercises. She slowly walked around the room, picking up toys that Ro left out from the day before.

"You go sit and rest!" her mother called out, marching up to Sofie and taking the bucket of blocks out of her hands.

"Mama, I'm fine." Sofie told her. "I've been walking on my own for days now, I can handle a few toys."

She looked down as Lillie put the blocks into a plastic bin. Seeing her mama wipe her face before facing her again, Sofie's voice softened. "Mama, I'm okay."

"I know! I just don't want you doing too much too soon." she said.

Sofie reached out to pat her back and was brought in for a hug. The two stayed that way for a minute, until Sofie's phone chimed. As she pulled away from Lillie, she swiped the phone's screen to see the message.

**Girl! Did you see this?**

**-Regine**

Her eyes became slits as she stared at the picture. But it was the caption that followed the article's headline that almost made Sofie throw her phone across the room.

***Rapper JPK rang in the New Year with a proposal to his long time girlfriend!***

"Baby, what is it?" Lillie asked.

Putting her phone away, Sofie fixed her face before answering, "Nothing mama. Can you start breakfast before Ro gets up? I wanna take a shower."

Her mama nodded and walked to the kitchen, leaving Sofie standing in the middle of the living room. Trying her best to keep her composure, she went to Ro's room. He was up already, sitting upright in bed and rubbing his eyes.

"Morning Ro Ro!" Sofie sanged before joining him on the bed. "You hungry?"

"Um uh!"

"Okay, Granny's in the kitchen fixing breakfast. Let's wash your face and brush your teeth first."

Picking him up, Sofie carried her son to the bathroom and helped him wash up and brush his teeth before sending him to the kitchen. With him gone, Sofie sat on the edge of the bathtub as she took out her phone again. Touching the screen with her finger, she zoomed in on the ring that Tasha wore on her left hand.

*I would never want that tacky shit on my hand!*

Sending Regine a message, she pretended to have already heard the news. Regine didn't waste time responding.

**Some jewelers are talking about the ring.**
**Say it's a Melo Pearl or something from a limited line in China.**
**-Regine**

Never hearing that name before, Sofie looked up 'melo pearl' on her phone. Seeing the images, she clicked on one photo and dropped her phone.

*That ugly mess cost MORE than the rings he gave me?!*

She knew the estimated price of the rings Jerome gave her after having them appraised the week after they were married. According to this website, the engagement ring he got Tasha was almost five times the amount of both her rings combined.

Her face grew hot as angry tears blurred her sight. Jerome was never flashy when they were together, but clearly had no problem dropping dough on her. *And if what everyone has been saying is true, they never even had sex! How could he be so gone for Tasha if they never even did that?*

# Chapter Eighteen

## Name That Sin

**Jerome**

Later that afternoon, after seeing mama off at the Bingo hall, Jerome drove to his childhood home. Knowing how fast the news about him and Tasha would reach his daddy, he wanted to be the one to tell Senior about his engagement.

*Whether he likes it or not, my life is with Tasha now.*

The drive didn't take long, with it being just before rush hour time, and for that Jerome was thankful. He parked his ride behind Senior's old four door sedan and trudged to the front door, giving it two hard knocks. When his father swung the door open, Jerome reminded himself to stay still as the older man snarled his way before huffing out, "Ya mama ain't here."

"I know." Jerome said evenly. "I came to see you, sir."

Raising an eyebrow, Senior asked, "What for? To apologize? Or you finally coming back to the Lord's house and giving up this rapping foolishness?" When Jerome sighed, Senior continued, "Then ain't nothing for us to discuss."

"I asked Tasha to marry me, and she said yes."

Senior's brows slammed together and two deep creases appeared in his forehead. "You came all this way to tell me that? What you expect me to do - give my blessing?"

"You've said more than enough about how you feel about Tasha, and I don't need nor expect you to give us your blessing."

Senior spat out, "You right - I won't!"

"But I wanted you to hear about it from me, not no stranger." Jerome tilted his head higher, making sure to keep his eyes directly on Senior's. "I love her, and we will be married. I want you to at least come to respect that."

"Don't you tell me what I better do, boy! You just all set to keep on ruining your life - I can't stop you, but I- I-"

Senior's last sentence was cut short as he brought a hand to his chest. Jerome stepped back in shock as his daddy crumbled to the floor.

Panic filled his voice as he shouted, "Senior? Can you hear me? Senior!"

Jerome fought to keep the fear in his chest from rising forward, as he fumbled to take out his phone. Dialing 9-1-1, his voice loudly cracked as he spoke to the operator, "M-my father fell - and I-I - he's having trouble breathing. Please send an ambulance!"

## TASHA

When she got the call from Jerome about Senior, Tasha was out with Trisha and the boys. Bringing their playdate to an end, she drove to LM Hospital and found Jerome pacing the emergency room floor, wringing his hands together.

"Jerome?"

He turned to face her and she would have given anything to take away the pain she found in his eyes. Going to him, Jerome engulfed her into his embrace as he choked out, "H-he just fell...I-I-told mama I'd be there soon, but Tash..."

Her hands caressed the back of his head, before she brought one down to his back. She slowly rubbed small circles in the middle of his back and quietly stood beside him, watching as Jerome took several sharp breaths. When he pulled away, she met his stare while he wiped his eyes with the back of his hand.

"It's okay, he's gonna be okay."

"We don't know that, Tash. I'd just told him about us. Then he clutched his chest and-"

To stop Jerome from thinking the worst, Tasha brought both of her hands upward and held his face gently. "God's got him, Rome. And he will take care of him, okay?"

Jerome nodded quickly and Tasha kissed both of his cheeks and continued, "I'll stay here while you go to mama Evelyn." His eyes were on hers and she answered the unanswered question out loud, "It'll be fine, I promise to keep my distance and keep you updated. Baby, please go see mama Evelyn and get some rest."

He pressed his lips to her forehead and embraced her one last time before going to the nearest desk. She watched as he braced the counter and spoke to the people behind it, each glancing briefly in her direction. Walking back to her, Jerome took her hands into his, "Okay, the staff say you can sit with him in his room. I'll be back with mama soon."

"Take your time. I love you."

"I love you." Jerome whispered before kissing her cheek and leaving the hospital.

After being shown to Senior's room and getting as comfortable as possible, she managed to get some sleep. When the sun greeted her hours later, Tasha took out her phone to text Jerome when she heard the bed beside her groan. She took several short breaths to prepare herself for whatever Senior had to say about her being there instead of Evelyn or Jerome.

"What happened?" The older man slurred out. "Where am I?"

Tasha took her time turning in the chair to face him, taking note of his bulging eyes at the sight of her. "The doctor's said that you had a massive heart attack. You've been here in LM for twelve hours."

Standing and wanting to put some distance between Senior's glare, Tasha reached for the pitcher of water. When the plastic cup was half way full, she extended it to him and explained gently, "Jerome was here, but he went home to give Mrs. Evelyn an update and to get some rest."

He frowned at the cup and Tasha sighed when she sat the water on the small table next to him. Making her way back to the chair, she started to say more but Senior promptly rolled over as he mumbled under his breath. *I hope they'll be here soon.*

"Why are you here?" Senior groggily asked.

Tasha fought not to roll her eyes as she turned to find him trying to sit up in the bed on his own. She looked at him and shrugged. "Soon as Rome comes back, I'll leave."

"His name is Jerome. Jerome Grant Junior!" Senior shouted before scoffing. "Not that you know anything about good upbringing and lineage," he added with a huff.

Squinting at him, Tasha couldn't resist asking, "How did you create someone like him, while being the way you are?"

Senior didn't answer her question, instead he groaned as he lowered his head. Seeing him panting while gripping the bed railing, Tasha tried to make her voice neutral as she spoke, "Do you nee-"

"Just leave!" Senior yelled.

"I can't. My fiancé hasn't gotten here yet."

"Oh, that's right. The boy finally ruined his life and asked you to be his wife? I knew I failed him, just as my daddy almost failed me."

Tasha arched an eyebrow in Senior's direction. "So, that's your deal? Daddy issues?"

"Don't speak so flippantly to me! Just every bit like your mama!" Senior shouted.

Tasha stood up from her chair and inched closer to him. "What do you know of my mama, Senior?"

The old man sneered before answering her, "She was just as wild as you were. Always popular with the boys too."

Silence passed between them as Tasha stared at him.

"You even have her eyes. She was beautiful, I can at least say that much now."

"Y-you knew my mama?" Tasha whispered.

"Everyone knew your mama girl! Even though I'd graduated years 'fore her, me and my friends still went up to the school to watch her play basketball."

Tasha swayed slightly when Senior's eyes softened. "Tabitha 'TKO' Daye, the best defense player to ever come from our high school." She looked on as Senior stared off at the wall in front of him before letting out a soft sigh.. "She had a way of making me feel like a little boy. Probably why my daddy didn't approve."

Tasha's hands went to her mouth as Senior continued. "Oh yeah, before she became 'Kitty' to all y'all, she was 'Tabby' to me. My Tabby cat, always grinning up at me, with those big brown eyes... But daddy told me to end the relationship, so I did, the night after her senior prom.

Tasha slowly backed away from him. "You and my mama...y-y-you.."

"He told me she was unclean, came from a broken home and would only ruin me if I stayed with her. So he made me end things with her. After I enjoyed one last night-"

"You SON OF A BITCH!" Tasha shrieked.

As she rushed toward him, the door to his hospital room fully opened. Tasha whirled around to see Evelyn and Jerome's shocked faces coming toward her.

Jerome reached her first, gripping her shaking hands. Feeling Evelyn's arms circling around her waist, Tasha stammered out,"I-I always wondered what happened to Kitty...Never, never would have thought- You just up and left her?!"

She felt Evelyn's hold on her lessened and caught a glimpse of the older woman going to sit down in the chair across from Senior. Just when she thought she had an opening to unleash her rage onto Senior, Jerome took a step between her and the bed his father laid in. Tasha started to speak, but the steel glare Jerome leveled at his daddy stunned her into silence. For a brief second she seriously wondered what her fiancé would do to Senior if she and Evelyn weren't in the room at that moment.

"Well, I suppose all that was bound to come out sooner or later." Senior grumbled. She watched as he cleared his throat, taking his eyes off Jerome to glance at her again. "But I did leave her a note saying sorry. My daddy said-" he feebly attempted to explain before she cut him off.

"FUCK yo Daddy!"

Looking at Senior, Tasha's entire body warred between the need to run away and the need to put a hurting on him. Her inner child, who longed for someone to be held responsible for the mistreatment she suffered, screamed for her to beat the older man into a never ending sleep. Slowly pointing a shaking hand to Senior's face, she was surprised when Jerome didn't stop her from stepping closer. But that moment of surprise changed in a blink of an eye when Jerome leaned down and whispered into Tasha's ear. "I'm right here baby, please give me the hurt."

She longed to do as he asked, to put down every single pain she felt and leave it for him to take from her. The memories of abuse from Kitty flooded her mind, waves of torment now wrecked all her senses. Her knees buckled as Jerome slowly turned her to face him. Her eyes burned with unshed tears as she focused on the love of her life. Seeing Jerome stand in front of her, holding her in place, she knew he always would, no matter what. With that blinding truth washing over her, Tasha threw her arms around his neck and sobs broke through as she cried against his chest.

Her second of clarity was short lived when Senior's hospital bed creaked under his weight, snapping her away from Jerome's comforting embrace. Tasha jerked away from Jerome and whirled around to stare at Senior once more. "You and your daddy deemed her unfit, and after you...after you *enjoyed* Kitty one last time, you left her without so much as a why or a goodbye."

Jerome reached for her hand and she accepted it, but kept her glare fixed on Senior. With Jerome warmth pulsating through their joined hands, Tasha spoke through clenched teeth. "You and your Father played a part in creating the monster that became my mama. The first person that taught me how ugly and unfair this world was - I had to endure her for years!"

With a tremble in her voice, Tasha asked, "Did you care about her at all?"

Sitting up right in his bed, Senior shouted, "I did care for her! In my own way. But she-"

Tasha held out her other hand and Senior stopped speaking. "I *knew* there was a reason you ain't never liked me! I reminded you of what you could have had. You bum ass -"

Tasha felt Evelyn's eyes on her as she let the sentence falter in the air. This whole time, the woman she'd come to cherish as a mother said nothing, but the weariness and pain on display made Tasha pause.

Seeing that she wasn't Senior's only victim, she turned to look back at Jerome, who held her gaze. Tasha squeezed their joined hands and released his before focusing her attention back to Senior.

"Y'all played a role in breaking her, I have no doubt in mind about that. You left her alone in this world and she spent the rest of her life chasing the high she must've had when she had you by her side. From what you just admitted, sounds like Kitty gave you her heart and all you could be bother to give her in return was a fucking post-it note. All because your daddy said so."

More tears filled Tasha's eyes and she didn't concern herself with brushing them away. "And here I was, actually praying for your ass, hoping that you and Rome would have a chance to mend things between y'all before it was too late."

Tasha turned to the chair where Evelyn sat to collect her things and made her way to the door. But before she left, Tasha turned her head and looked at Senior one last time.

"I'm thankful that my Jerome turned out to be stronger than you. And I hope you and your daddy burn in hell."

**Jerome**

*I need to find her.*

That was the only thought that raced through Jerome's mind after mama told him to leave Senior's room, and he prayed that Tasha would be where he thought she'd go first. When he made it to their house, Jerome sighed in relief when he saw her motorbike in the driveway. The house was silent as he let himself in. He saw her out on the patio, staring out into the distance. He stared at Tasha, watching her as she was facing out into their backyard.

"I did the math, in case you were wondering." Tasha said softly, chuckling as she turned around to face him. "Tina is two years older than Eva, so at least we ain't related."

"Tash..."

"If you want, we could always take a paternity test, just to be sure." she added.

Jerome walked to her and brought a hand out to Tasha's check, searching her eyes before he spoke again. "I'm sorry. For everything you went through growing up and everything you are going through now."

As her shoulders slumped over, a sob broke from Tasha that left Jerome with a burning lump in his throat. Tasha's body shook as Jerome took her into his arms.

"Rome - I.." her voice cracked and Jerome gripped her tighter.

Wanting nothing more than to take away the pain she felt, his voice was strained and low as he whispered. "I got you, Tash. I promise - I got you."

Jerome lifted Tasha into his arms and carried her to the nearest lounge chair. He cradled her until her cries became whimpers. It wasn't until the sun began to set did Tasha whisper to him. "I know he's your daddy, but Rome - I-I don't think I can ever step foot inside that church again."

He listened as she continued. "Not after today, knowing that he could be part of why Kitty was so...so..."

"You don't have to explain. And I would never ask you to do something you don't want to do."

As Tasha pulled away from his embrace, Jerome took her hand and they walked back into the house. The two held one another close on the couch before falling asleep.

Jerome looked over at Tasha after waiting for her to step out of the car. She looked around at the people entering Everlasting Baptist Church. It appeared to be smaller than Christ Corner, but Jerome liked that. There was also a playground on the property and the thought of bringing Ro to service someday came to mind. When he closed the passenger side door, Jerome took Tasha's hand into his. Seeing her shoulders relax, Jerome smiled before kissing her cheek.

Several folks smiled warmly at them as they made their way inside, and Jerome looked at Tasha as she returned the greetings.

A group of little girls ran past them, one of them bumping into her side. He watched as the girl, with her hair braided down the back of her head and held in place with a bright yellow ribbon, looked up to them with bright eyes.

"Sorry ma'am." she mumbled.

Tasha let go of his hand to kneel down and look at the girl. "It's alright. You not hurt, are you?"

When the child shook her head, Tasha nodded. "Okay. See you later."

They watched the girl run to catch up with her friends. Standing back up, Tasha grinned at Jerome and took his hand as he led them to a seat in the pews.

Once the service ended, Jerome and Tasha went to greet the pastor, who hugged both of them, "Thank you for visiting Everlasting Baptist Church!"

Tasha smiled as she addressed the pastor, "Thank you for welcoming us, Pastor Johnson."

"Of course, we are all children of the most high. I hope to see you two again."

Jerome looked at Tasha and smiled, "Thank you Pastor Johnson. We are looking to start marital counseling, so we'll pray on it and let you know. "

As they made their way toward the church double wide doors to leave, an elderly woman with a cane stepped in front of them.

"You two must be new to Everlasting. Name's Eula Rae Clemons, but you can call me Sister Red."

"Nice to meet you Sister Red. I'm Tasha and this is my fiancé, Jerome."

Tasha extended a hand to the woman, but the older woman was quicker than she looked. Jerome watched as Tasha's eyes widened from how fast Sister Red snatched her left hand. Seeming to be judging instead of admiring the ring on her hand, Tasha cut her eyes to Jerome who finally spoke up.

"Yes ma'am. This is our first time visiting the parish."

Sister Red squinted, as she continued looking over Tasha's engagement ring, "I ain't never seen someone give that kind of a ring before...Where did you buy it?"

Jerome blinked at the woman as Tasha pulled her hand away.

"Please forgive my mama, she can be nosey sometimes."

An older man made his way to them. "Hello, I'm Brother Isaiah Clemons. It's nice to meet y'all."

"Nice to meet you too, Brother Isaiah." Jerome said, as he reached out to shake the man's hand.

"Hello." was all Tasha offered.

Jerome looked on as Tasha glanced between the older man and back to his mother.

"I ain't nosey! Just curious." Eula said sharply.

Tasha's left eye began to twitch and Jerome knew it was time for them to be on their way. Just as he placed his hand on the small of her back, several women walked over to join them.

"Welcome to Everlasting Baptist Church! I'm Sister Cynthia Harper, and these are my sisters, Bettie and Synclair."

Before Jerome could introduce them, the shorter one spoke, "No need to introduce yourself, we all know you Jerome Senior's boy."

"His name is Jerome Grant Junior, not boy." Tasha cut in between them. Hearing Eula Rae chuckle, the women shared wide eyed glances and Tasha continued, "You all enjoy your day."

Jerome led them away from the crowd and noticed Tasha's shoulders relaxed again once the group was behind them.

"I sho hope they come to service again! That young gal got bite!" Eula Rae could be heard saying as Jerome opened the car door and waited for Tasha to get inside before closing the door.

The car ride was silent until they were halfway home.

"What did you think of the service today?" Jerome asked hopefully.

He liked this church more than the one they went to last week. As a son of a pastor, he got used to folks' staring at him, but at least at Everlasting Baptist Church he didn't feel as though he was on display.

"It was nice." Tasha said flatly. "The service was relatable and no one asked for a CD."

At the last church, two women rushed up to them before the service started and asked for his latest album. Jerome almost forgot about the incident and found himself laughing at the memory. They soon were at home and as they made it to the front door, Jerome asked Tasha, "Would you like to visit Everlasting again next week?"

Tasha was silent as she took off her shoes, and Jerome took that as a good sign. Once he closed the door, he saw Tasha looking directly at him. "Yeah, I think we should go there again."

Jerome's smile spread across his face as he leaned closer to Tasha and gave her a quick peck on the lips. "I think so too."

THE NEXT WEEK, JEROME sat in Pastor Johnson's office, drinking his second cup of coffee. His nerves were all over the place as he stared around the tiny room. Only one photo was hung on the wall, a framed portrait of Jesus. In the photo, Jesus had skin that almost matched his and the eyes seemed to bore onto Jerome's every move. He knew it was silly, but Jerome couldn't help thinking that the picture was quietly judging him.

"She'll be here in a minute." he replied as Mr. Johnson looked at his watch.

Hearing the door open, Jerome stood and watched as Tasha finally entered the room. She sent a small smile his way before kissing him quickly on the lips and looked at the pastor. "Please forgive me for being late. A meeting with my contractor ran longer than expected."

"It's alright. Y'all are my last appointments for the day, so I have time."

Jerome took her hand and led them to the small couch. When Tasha leaned against his shoulder, he inhaled her familiar scent of frankincense and honey. His breathing slowed down afterward and he looked at the pastor again as he explained. "We're recently engaged and are looking to get married in the Spring."

The pastor looked between the two of them and beamed. "That is wonderful news! Congratulations."

Tasha squeezed his hand and Jerome looked over to see her eyes soften.

"So y'all want to begin marital counseling?" Pastor Johnson asked.

When the pastor began scribbling notes onto a notepad, Jerome felt his throat go dry.

"Yes, that's why we're here." Tasha confirmed.

Pastor Johnson stopped writing long enough to stare at them, and just like with the photo, Jerome felt like he was on trial. "Okay, well, I like to meet with couples at least once a week for at least 4 months before they say I do. Since y'all want to get married sooner, if you can commit to meeting me twice a week for two months, I would be happy to begin our sessions."

The sound of the clicking clock on Pastor Johnson's desk got louder and louder as Jerome processed the words coming from his mouth. Feeling Tasha's hand squeeze his again, he looked over to see her brows knitted together. She turned to face Mr. Johnson and said, "I can do that. How about you Jerome?"

"Y-yeah."

As Jerome felt Mr. Johnson and Tasha staring at him, he added, "I'll make sure to let my assistant know to block that time off on my schedule."

Jerome tightened his grip on Tasha's hand while he watched the pastor jot down more notes.

"And how long y'all been together?" Pastor Johnson asked.

Hearing Tasha sigh, Jerome glanced over to see her tilt her head. "Well, we, um.."

"I was married to someone else last year." he blurted out.

When the pastor went back to writing on his notepad, Tasha leaned in and whispered, "Rome, you good?"

He kept his eyes on the pastor before continuing, "Tasha and I, our past is complicated. But when my first marriage was officially over, I asked her to marry me."

"Oh, okay." Pastor Johnson nodded, taking more notes before asking, "And have y'all talked about or started to share your finances with one another?"

Jerome took a deep breath as Tasha answered. "No, not yet."

"To what? The talking or sharing of expenses?"

Tasha lips pressed together, leaving Jerome to explain, "Neither, but since I'll be the sole provider, there hasn't been a need for us to discuss that."

"Jerome - " Tasha started as the pastor spoke.

"I see." Pastor Johnson said.

Tasha's head whipped between Jerome and Pastor Johnson and he saw her eyes narrow at the older man. "May I ask what it is you see?"

Jerome gently caressed the top of Tasha's hand as the pastor grinned.

"That's it for today." As Jerome looked at Tasha and she shrugged, pastor Johnson added, "When y'all ready to meet again, be sure to call and schedule an appointment."

"Yes sir, thank you." Jerome said.

Pastor Johnson stood from behind his desk and Jerome and Tasha joined him. Tasha was the first to walk out of the office and Jerome followed her.

"You sure you alright?" Tasha asked Jerome for the second time.

The two arrived at home minutes ago and Jerome wanted nothing more than to shower and hold Tasha in his arms for the night.

"I'm good."

Tasha dropped her purse on the counter and slipped off her kicks. He watched as she walked over toward him and planted a kiss on his lips. Jerome closed his eyes as he brought his arms around her and held Tasha tightly. Listening to her sigh into his chest, Jerome felt the pressure from earlier float away. He pressed his lips to the crown of her head and sighed. "Is each session gonna be like that?"

Tasha leaned back to look him in the eye. "You want to go again?"

Jerome looked at her shocked face and released her, going to sit on the couch. "I do."

Expecting Tasha to say more, Jerome watched her slip on her house shoes instead and grinned. "Okay, it was a little rocky at the end, but I'm glad that you want to try again."

The minute she joined him on the couch, Tasha curled up onto Jerome's chest. He sighed again and felt his heartbeat slow down. They sat in silence for a few minutes, as was becoming their normal routine, until Jerome thought back to last Sunday and laughed.

"What's so funny?" Tasha asked, looking up at him.

Jerome smirked at her and answered, "I'm just thinking about last Sunday and started to thank the Lord that you ain't hurt that sister for snatching your hand."

Tasha cut her eyes at him, but Jerome saw her lips fighting to not turn up. Tasha then looked down at her ring and said, "Her grip was strong!"

They both laugh as she went on, "I mean, she ain't wrong, it is different from most engagement rings. That makes me love it even more. And mama Evelyn helped you pick it out?"

"Yeah, the shop owner said that the pearl was made by snails, instead of oysters. That's when mama said it'd be perfect for you - given our situation."

Tasha looked at Jerome and smiled softly. "So what's it called?"

"What?"

"The type of pearl? What is it? "

Thinking about the price tag on her finger, Jerome immediately went to change the subject. "Tash, let's talk about it later. Right now I want to go shower and have something to eat."

Untangling himself from her embrace, Jerome heard Tasha speak again.

"I just want to learn more about the company. Can you tell me the name please?"

He was hoping they would be closer to their wedding date before this came up, but Jerome should've known that while he planned, God would have the last laugh. Sending a quick prayer up above, he met Tasha's stare. "It's a melo pearl."

"I never heard of them before."

Jerome's chest rose and fell quickly as he thought about that day at the jewelry shop. Mama had been so excited when she spotted the ring that once the clerk told him about its origins, Jerome knew that he wasn't walking out of there without it. While he signed the receipt, Jerome knew his mama saw the cost when she slumped down in the seat next to him, eyes as wide as saucers.

"You okay?" Tasha looked on as Jerome stared at her hand and then back to her face.

He reached out for her hand and tried to fight off the panic creeping into the center of his chest as he spoke, "I wanted you to have something special Tash. Because you are special to me."

"Rome, what are you trying to tell me?" He started to walk them to the couch but Tasha stopped, causing their hands to part. "Just tell me. Whatever it is can't be that bad, Rome."

He sighed. "It's a 10 carat melo pearl."

When Tasha stared at him, Jerome closed his eyes as he reached into his pocket for his phone. After typing on the screen, Jerome handed Tasha his phone and she looked at the screen. "Why are you _"

Her head snapped back up to Jerome's as she breathed out, "I know you didn't..." Before he could say a word, Tasha spoke again. "Jerome! You spent that kind of money on a ring?!"

"It's your engagement ring."

She handed him back the phone and Jerome watched as Tasha blinked several times before looking back at him. "Whew, um, I understand what you mean, but...Okay."

"Okay?" he questioned.

"Yeah, okay. It's a one time purchase, right? And I do love my ring...just..."

"What?" Jerome asked.

"We never really sat down and talked about our spending habits or finances before. Do you normally make impulsive buys like this?"

Jerome reached out for her hand. "Wasn't nothing impulsive about this."

"That wasn't my question."

He raised a brow at Tasha as she continued. "Like, do you spend your cash on crazy stuff all the time? What about Ro's wellbeing?"

He jerked his head back. "My son is set, don't worry about that."

Tasha looked at him, with her lips slightly turned down. "I kind of feel like I should..."

"What you mean Tasha? You really think I just blow all my funds on whatever?"

Seeing her gaze soften, Jerome listened to her reply. "Look, that's not what I - it's just now that we're doing this, I want to make sure we're good, not just in body and spirit, but our wallets too."

He nodded. "I want that too."

"Okay, so you have everything squared away for Ro, but what about the future kids you trying to have?"

"Tash, we good, I promise."

As he went in to bring her closer, Tasha stepped out of his reach. "Are we though? Can we really start a family in this house? "

Seeing the seriousness in her stare, Jerome sighed. "What do you really wanna ask Tash?"

"Well, with your old home ...and our new one, what does that cost you a month? And your alimony and other expenses..." seeing Tasha run her hands through her hair, he wanted nothing more than to end this conversation.

"Maybe we should go ahead and open a shared account? Something to cover our expenses as a couple. Starting with this house."

Jerome looked at Tasha, hard. "I got us. Wouldn't have never let you step foot into this house if I thought I couldn't provide for you in it. So keep your money."

"But Jerome, things happen, and it's just good sense to-"

"I said I got us!"

Tasha looked up at him and when she took a step back, Jerome's heart started to ache. "Tash - I can provide for you and the kids we're going to have. Don't worry - "

"If you tell me not to worry, that's all I'm gonna do! Let's be real, in life, things can change for the worst at any time, and I'm not trying to be out on my ass with kids!"

His chest rose at the sound of her voice.

"You can say you got us all day, but I know first hand that saying and doing are two different things!"

"Oh, so because I spent a little extra cash than most on the ring on your hand my actions don't match my words?"

Now pacing the living room, Jerome tried not to notice how close she was getting to the front door.

"You know that's not what I mean." Tasha quietly said.

"No, I don't know. Cause right now all I hear is you doubting that I can provide for mine, Tasha! I know you ain't had that before ..."

Seeing her widened expression, Jerome tried to speak again, but Tasha spat out, "You right - as a jit, I ain't have a stable home. And THAT'S what I'm trying to get you to understand. I want us to have a plan, because I know better than most what happens when there ain't one. You grew up in one home, with both parents and never seen the kind of struggles I did."

"Just cause I had both folks and grew up in a nice house, don't mean I don't know nothing about struggling, Tasha."

He tried to keep his voice low, but Tasha was now even closer to the door. "You really trying to play the struggle olympics with me right now? I asked you a direct question about your finances, so WE as a couple can make sure that WE were on the same page and YOU turned into something else."

Wanting her to come back to him and away from the front door, Jerome walked toward the sliding glass doors that lead outside.

He looked at the glass and thought he saw her coming closer. Turning around, Jerome's smile disappeared when he saw Tasha pick up her purse. His heart pressed hard against his ribcage when she started to put on her shoes. "Tash - what are you doing? "

She didn't look at him as she answered, "Leaving."

"Wh-what? Tasha, you ain't gotta go."

"Yeah, I do."

Making his way to her, Jerome spoke fast, "Tash, just wait! We can -" after the front door closed behind her, Jerome stood in the middle of the living room, alone. Snatching his phone from out of his pocket, Jerome pressed one and was immediately sent to voicemail.

He tried two more times and each time the call went to messenger, Jerome gritted his teeth. With his heartbeat echoing in his head, Jerome stared at the front door before going back to the sliding glass door and closing it. Finally, he marched to his bedroom, slamming the door shut behind him.

He was up hours before his alarm the next morning, not able to sleep. After tossing and turning for half the night, Jerome gave up on sleeping and instead went for a run outside. Thoughts of his last talk with Tasha played throughout his mind while on his run, and he wanted to see her. So many things came to mind, but the one thought that took up the most space was seeing Tasha leave their home without looking at him. He picked up the speed as he sprinted around the corner and back to the house. Once he was exhausted enough, Jerome cooled down and walked inside. Seeing her house slippers in the same spot as yesterday, he looked away and shut his eyes.

*She really just up and left.*

Jerome brought a hand out and pressed the side of his temple before walking into their bedroom to take a shower. When he stepped out of the bathroom, he left the drying towel on the rack as he picked up his phone to call Tasha.

"Morning Jerome." Tasha answered flatly.

Jerome squinted his eyes as he briefly held his phone away from his ear and looked at it. He was glad to hear her voice, but Jerome wanted her back home in the worst way. Trying to remember to stay calm, Jerome cleared his throat. "Where are you?"

"Out."

Feeling his face get warm, he tried again. "Tasha, can you tell me where you are? I just want to know that you're okay."

"I'm okay." she told him.

The distant tone of her voice was getting on his last nerves, but Jerome managed to ask one last question, "When are you coming home?"

"Do I still have one to come to?"

Gripping the phone in his hand, Jerome all but barked onto the line, "Tasha, please don't make me come looking for you!" Hearing silence, Jerome took two deep breaths and spoke again, "Just - can we finish our conversation? Please?"

"I don't need to see you to do that. Let's finish it now."

He titled his head to the ceiling. *She's really not coming back?!*

Jerome rolled his neck from side to side. "Tasha, just, tell me where you are." Hearing her sigh, he waited for her to speak.

"I got a room at Cove's Creek."

Now that he knew where she was, Jerome felt a little of the tension in his shoulders disappear. "I will call Pastor Johnson and set up another meeting with him today. Will you meet me there?"

"Okay. I will meet you there."

He breathed a sigh of relief. Before he could say another word, Tasha spoke. "I love you Jerome."

Closing his eyes, Jerome let her words soothe him as he whispered, "I love you Tasha."

"SO, Y'ALL HAD YOUR first fight,uh? Good."

The two stared at him, wide eyed and Pastor Johnson laughed. "I've been doing this a long time, and a blind man could see that you two ain't never so much as raised your voices at one another."

As Pastor Johnson looked between them again, he reached into a drawer and took out two small notebooks. "Now, each week we meet, I want you two to write down how you felt before our session and after inside these here books." When Jerome reached out to accept the notebooks, the pastor continued, "There are also questions on some of those pages and I want y'all to answer them before our next meeting - separately."

The two of them nodded.

"Alright, now tell me what brought on the disagreement."

They both stared at one another and Jerome listened as Tasha answered, "I started talking about our finances and let my fear turn into anger."

Pastor Johnson began writing on his notepad again. "How so?"

"Well, something he said in our first session, about being the sole provider, was already bugging me. And when I started asking questions and making suggestions about how we could go about securing our future...I felt like he was dismissing everything I said. So I got mad."

Watching Tasha study her breathing, Jerome's eyes soften when she said calmly, "**A soft word turns away wrath, but a harsh word stirs up anger.**"

"Ah, I see. And you know The Book of Proverbs. That's good, real good."

Smiling softly, Tasha explained. "I'm learning."

The pastor then looked over at him, "We all know every story has more than one side to it, so Jerome, go ahead and share yours please."

Taking a deep breath, Jerome did as he was asked. "I was raised to be the man of the house. And hearing her say all those things made me feel like she didn't trust me enough to provide like I was taught to. So, maybe I was trying to change the subject in my need to reassure her that I was a provider and protector where she and our family is concerned."

This time, when the pastor scribbled into their notebook, he looked up and nodded slowly at them both. "Now, love may be what brought y'all here, but in a marriage, that is just one step on this journey. And one key thing that is gonna help y'all on this journey is honesty." Clasping his hands together, pastor Johnson instructed. "I want you two to face one another and think back to that argument. Then tell each other what you don't want to bring into your marriage from that incident."

Tasha glanced down while she rubbed her hands on the front of her denim jeans. Meeting his stare, her voice was soft as she began, "I know you will protect and provide for me, but Jerome, I don't want just that from you in this marriage. I want a partner. I want us to share the responsibility of protecting and providing for each other."

When she quickly tilted her head upward and brought it back down, he saw the unshed tears in her eyes as she continued. "Life is hard enough, and as much as you want to provide for me and our future kids, I want to do the same for you. So please hear me when I make suggestions on how to do that in the future." She wiped at her eyes with the back of her hand, "And I grew up in a house where yelling was an everyday thing. I don't want to bring that into our home."

"I hear you, and will do my best to remember that we are partners - equals in our marriage. I promise." Jerome whispered as he looked at Tasha and he took her hand into his. "But you can't just run out every time we disagree, Tash. When you do that...I feel... like you just gonna up and leave me again."

Closing his eyes as he felt Tasha rub small circles across his knuckles, Jerome's feelings from yesterday came back and started to pull him into a place he didn't feel ready for. He bit his lip as he turned his head further away.

"I know it's hard, son, but communication is the strongest foundation for a marriage." Pastor Johnson said. "Look at your future wife and tell her what's on your mind."

Doing as the pastor instructed, Jerome tightened his hold onto Tasha's hand. When she enclosed it with her other hand, he cleared his throat. "When you first left all those years ago, it just - made me feel... It made me feel like I wasn't enough."

With his hoarse voice, Jerome continued. "Growing up, with Senior always telling me that if I don't take his place that I was worthless and wasting my life away - I started to think that he was right. And that's why people always leave me."

"Jerome, you are *not* your daddy. He's wrong - you are *more* than enough and more valuable to me than anything I have." Tasha whispered.

"I know how wrong he is now, but seeing you walk out of our home last night brought all those feelings back. It reminded me that no matter how much I love people and give them, they won't always stay in my life. No matter how much I want them to."

Looking up at the ceiling, Jerome closed his eyes and took a deep breath before releasing it. "I love my sister, and she left. And then you. Just thinkin' about it now makes my chest tight, Tash."

"I'm sorry." Bringing her forehead to touch his, Tasha spoke again, "No matter what, I am never leaving you again."

Tasha's hands slowly caressed his cheeks and she brushed away the tears that fell down from his eyes. As he let her words seep into his skin, Jerome pressed his lips to hers and pulled her close, wrapping his arms around her waist.

Pastor Johnson cleared his throat, but Jerome refused to let Tasha go. They both turned to face him as he spoke again. "I think we can end here today. And I look forward to seeing you both again next week."

Jerome nodded. "Thank you Pastor."

He kissed Tasha's forehead before finally releasing her and standing. Tasha reached for his hand as she did the same, nodding at Pastor Johnson while he led them out of the room.

## Tasha

THE NEXT WEEK, AFTER spending days curled up with Jerome at home in between mapping out her work itinerary with Pablo and Ximena, along with his work schedule at Trap Son's and spending time with Ro, Tasha finally made plans to have a movie night at the theater with her besties.

"Y'all had all day to be boo'd up!" Tasha called out to Alexa and Rachel, who couldn't seem to keep their hands off of each other as the three of them moved up the line to get their movie tickets.

They were too content to ignore her as Tasha could see in the pixie glass window Rachel covering Alexa's neck in quick light pecks.

"I swear! Being around y'all is like being with a couple of love sick teenagers sometimes..." Trying not to let them see her grin, Tasha took out her card and stepped up to the box office cashier.

"Three for 'Surrender' please."

After getting their tickets Tasha didn't bother calling either of her home girls as she strutted towards the movie theater's entrance. Feeling hands tug on her elbows, Tasha stopped walking to give Alexa and Rachel her signature side eye.

"We sorry Tash." Rachel cooed gently, pulling her close. "Right babe?" Rachel said to Alexa who immediately squinted at the two of them.

"Hell nah I ain't sorry!"

Reaching across Tasha to swat her wife's shoulder, Rachel brought her eyes back to face Tasha. "She ain't mean it Tash."

Looking between the two of them, Tasha handed them their movie tickets and tugged them along. "I've known Alexa long enough to know she ain't never sorry for wanting to kiss all up on you. It's cool."

A yelp squeaked out of Tasha's mouth as Alexa pressed her lips close to hers. Rachel laughed as Tasha's mouth dropped open.

"That's why you my girl Tash!" Alexa told her.

Laughing, the trio were about to swing the glass door open until someone behind them spoke.

"Damn, you into women and threeways too?"

Tasha looked into the glass window at the group of women behind them. Before she could decide to ignore it, Alexa was already turning them around to face Sofie and her crew.

"What y'all say?" Alexa asked, letting go of Tasha's wrist. Rachel, in ride or die fashion, followed Alexa's lead. Tasha didn't want to get into it with Jerome's ex, so she reached out to grab Rachel's wrist, but the more level headed one of her friends wouldn't budge.

"Come on y'all. Let's just go and see the movie." Tasha's suggestion fell on deaf ears as her girls stared down at Sofie and her friends.

"Nah, Tash. These heffas had something to say." Rachel stepped closer to Sofie before glaring at the other three women. "We wanna know what's on they minds, is all."

Alexa's smirk was in full effect as she beamed over at the love of her life, and Tasha knew that this confrontation was going down whether she wanted it to or not.

The shorter woman with Sofie, rolled her eyes as she squared up to meet Rachel's five foot four frame."My girl said what she said."

Tasha saw Alexa eyes narrow in on the woman flanked to Sofie's left and followed her sight. As the woman reached into her bag, Tasha quickly did the same as she went to stand in front of Alexa and Rachel.

"Hey Derrik."

Tasha removed her hand from the side panel of her messenger bag but kept an eye on the girl now in front of her who started to back up to take a phone call.

"Tasha." Sofie finally said.

"Sofie. Good to see you."

She could feel her girls watching her every move, so Tasha offered Sofie a small smile and went to turn away.

"I can't believe he left you for *that*."

The shorter friend scoffed as Tasha froze. In one last attempt to separate Rachel and Alexa from the women in front of her, Tasha asked them gently, "Can y'all go ahead and pick our seats please?"

She wasn't surprised at all when Alexa rolled her eyes and Rachel brushed past her to stand next to Alexa instead.

Closing her eyes briefly, Tasha sighed before looking at Sofie's unofficial mouthpiece. "What's your name again?"

The woman looked up at Tasha as she sucked her teeth. "Does it matter what my name is? Homewrecker!"

Alexa was now making her way to the shorter woman, but Tasha pressed a hand on her shoulder.

"You know what? You right - your name ain't important."

Tasha then leveled her eyes to Sofie. "But I want to make one thing clear - there was no need for me to wreck a home that was built on shaky foundation."

Rachel's snicker must have been all Sofie needed to jump into Tasha's face.

"What you say trick?!" We was happy until you brought your loud ass around!"

Tasha stepped back and Sofie ran her manicured nails through her wavy bob before narrowing her eyes at Tasha. "It don't matter no way. Enjoy my sloppy seconds."

As Sofie and her friends started to walk away, Tasha spoke again."Thank you."

Sofie whirled around to face Tasha again. "What did you say to me?"

Tasha didn't break eye contact as she walked toward Sofie. Standing in front of the former Mrs. Grant, Tasha held her stare as she laid her feelings bare. "Thank you. I mean that with my whole heart."

The women behind Sofie broke out into laughter, but Tasha wasn't done. "If you had tried even once, to at least be Jerome's partner, I would not have had a chance in hell. He would still be married to you. Because he took vows, for better or worse, and you gave him a son."

Tasha could see Sofie's friends' laughter come to a halt and as she thought about the last several months, Tasha couldn't keep the tears from blurring her vision.

"I was too afraid to let myself think that Rome and I could even be friends when I came back home. Did all I could to avoid seeing him, for weeks I kept my distance. But God, my God!"

Alexa reached out to take her hand when her voice cracked and Tasha accepted it before speaking again. "I think about where I was then, and how blessed I am now... And now..."

Images of spending the day at the park with her niece and nephews, playing dominoes with Trish, Lloyd, Rachel and Alexa, and watching the sunrise in the home that she now shared with Jerome, Tasha let the tears fall freely. "I can never say anything ill toward you Sofie. Because of you, I have everything the Lord ever meant for me. So, thank you."

"Damn..." Alexa whispered to Rachel, who was using her long sleeved shirt to wipe away her tears.

"Come on Sofie, you don't need to be giving this ho no more of your time." the taller friend said, as she led Sofie away from Tasha. The two women share one last glance at one another before Sofie friends' open the theater doors and they all walk inside.

Wiping away her tears, Tasha reached into her pocket and took out her phone to check the time. Seeing her screensaver picture of her and Jerome at Bejon Beach, Tasha broke out into a grin.

"Just what kind of hold does PK have on you?" Alexa asked, causing Rachel to swat her wife's arm.

Looking at the ring on her finger, Tasha rolled her eyes before looking at her girls. "One
that will take more than a few haters to break."

Rachel grinned as she dragged her wife along to the theater's entrance.

# Chapter Nineteen

## Abundance of Love

**Tasha**

Two weeks before her wedding, Tasha drove with Evelyn to the bridal shop, as the older woman sat in the passenger seat. Evelyn insisted on bringing a small, medium size box with her for the trip, but Tasha didn't mind. *She'll share what's inside soon enough.*

"I don't know why I couldn't drive. This is *my* car Tasha."

Tasha grinned. "Since you ain't want me to hold whatever it is in your hands, it's only right that I drive."

"Well, you did get us here in one piece, so I guess that's alright." Evelyn said while unlocking the door and stepping out of the vehicle.

The two entered the shop and Tasha spotted Alexa and Rachel standing in the waiting area. They both brought Tasha in for a quick hug. "You sure about this, Tash?" Alexa said teasingly before looking over at Evelyn and adding, "I know Jerome is your son and all, but I have to ask."

"I see I'mma have to keep my eye on you young lady!" Evelyn teased back, causing everyone to laugh.

A clerk came out to greet them. "Hello! Who here is the future Mrs. Daye-Grant?"

Without hesitation, Tasha stepped forward as she answered breathlessly, "I am."

"Your dress is ready. Give me a moment, and I'll walk you to the dressing room to help you with putting it on to show your party."

"Okay."

Tasha looked on at Evelyn as she sat with Alexa and Rachel on the couch. It was Rachel who leaned over to Evelyn and asked in the lowest whisper she'd ever heard, "Mrs. Evelyn, have you seen the dress already?"

Keeping the dress a secret from everyone, especially the more than curious Rachel, had been harder than Tasha thought. She pretended to check her phone, while watching out of the corner of her eye in one of the small antique mirrors at the counter as Evelyn answered her friend with the shake of her head. Rachel leaned in closer and whispered, "All we know is that she bought it months ago - before her and Jerome even got back together."

"Babe, I think it's time we take a break from watching them reality TV shows."

"Why'd you'd say that?"

"Cause! Since we started watching them - you stay looking for drama where there ain't none!"

"No I don't! I'm just stating facts." Rachel said with a pout to her wife.

As Evelyn broke out into laughter at Tasha's close friend's antics, the assistant waved her over and led Tasha down the hall. Once she was inside the dressing room, she closed the door and eyed the gold framed full length mirror. Seeing her chiffon ivory colored dress hanging on the golden rack inside, Tasha felt her heart thud louder with each second that passed, as she reached out and removed it from the delicate hanger. It wasn't until she slipped the fabric over her skin and glanced down to inspect the three fourth sleeves did her heart begin to slow down a little. *I hope they like this dress as much as I do.*

A knock at the door interrupted her thoughts. "Is everything okay?"

"Y-yes. I'm coming out now." Tasha announced, her voice higher than normal.

As she stepped out in front of the smiling assistant, Tasha followed cautiously behind them in the flowy dress, making sure to gather the sides of it with both hands as they returned to the waiting area. Pausing just before turning the corner, she looked on as the assistant greeted the trio.

"Ladies, are you all ready to see the bride?"

"Yes!" they shouted in unison.

"I would like to present the future Mrs. Tasha Daye-Grant."

As Tasha turned the corner, holding the ends of her dress, Evelyn gasped.

Letting go of the sides of the dress, Tasha stepped forward, stopping before she could see herself in front of the three way mirror. No one said a word as she looked at her reflection. Looking over at her best friends and future mother-in-law, Tasha noticed the tears that threatened to fall in Evelyn's eyes and her heart slowly started to sink.

"Why aren't y'all saying anything?" Tasha asked. *They don't like my dress? Is it too much?*

Rachel stood up, "Have you seen yourself in this dress? It's - girl look in the mirror!"

Doing as her friend demanded, Tasha took another two steps forward and quickly brought a hand over her mouth. The dress felt fine, but seeing herself wearing it for the first time since purchasing it was an experience that gripped her heartstrings. *I feel...I feel soft, and strong, and so much more all at once. How is that even possible?*

The intricate gold stitch patterns that were woven into the dress went from the boned bodice to its flowy bottom, gleaming ever so slightly under the fluorescent lights. So caught up in admiring herself in the full length mirror, Tasha didn't notice Evelyn as she now stood behind her until she spoke. "Baby girl, you look beautiful."

Turning to face her, Tasha watched as Evelyn opened the box she brought to the shop with care. "I had planned on giving this to Eva for her wedding, but when that didn't happen, I held onto it. Guess I was just getting sentimental in my old age."

Tasha glanced over at Evelyn as she spoke again. "I know how you feel about him, but the day I married Jerome's daddy was such a special day for me. It was the day my mama gave me this." Revealing the white linen veil from within, Evelyn slowly extended it to her with both hands. "I was hoping that you would try it on. Just for the fitting."

Her eyes landed on Evelyn's and seeing the sparkle behind the older woman's eyes made her answer easy. Nodding, Tasha felt her throat tightened as she managed to say, "Okay."

Tasha stooped low a little so that Evelyn could place the veil over her hair. She straightened her pose and looked at Evelyn again, who stepped back to adjust the veil around Tasha's shoulders before whispering, "Thank you."

Hearing the sniffles from behind them, Tasha blinked back her tears. Soon Evelyn went to remove the veil, but Tasha took hold of Evelyn's hands as she asked softly, "Can I see it first please?"

When Evelyn nodded and stepped back, Tasha turned back to the mirror. *It's...pretty. And unexpected.* Reaching out to fan the veil over her shoulders, Tasha cleared her throat when she faced Evelyn again. "May I wear it for the wedding? I know you might want to save it for Evelyn Mae someday, but-"

Closing the space between them, Evelyn wrapped Tasha into her arms. Swaying them from side to side, she answered, her voice thick with emotion, "I would love that, baby."

TWO NIGHTS BEFORE THE wedding, Evelyn had turned their kitchen into hers with ease as she cooked a feast. Tasha's cheeks hurt from beaming at Evelyn, even as she voluntold her and everyone what to do around the house before Jerome got home from Trap Son's. Just seeing her mother-in-law float around and playfully putting Eva, Marcus, and Evelyn Mae to work made Tasha's heart happy. She'd been tasked with setting the table and took in the mouth-watering spread of dishes that were being placed on it.

"Oh, Granny! This all looks so good!" Evelyn Mae mused, reaching out to take a piece of fried chicken.

Slapping the young woman's hand away, Evelyn reminded her, "Aht! When Jerome gets here, then we can eat."

Tasha caught Evelyn Mae pouting out of the corner of her eye and laughed as she quickly signed, "I sorry."

Hoping to cheer her up, Tasha gave her an update, "He did text me ten minutes ago, saying that he'd be here soon. So you won't have to wait much longer."

Evelyn Mae's smile was wide, showing off her pearly whites as she shouted, "Thank Goodness! Cause I'm ready to eat."

Just as they turned to leave the kitchen, the sound of keys at the front door got their attention. Evelyn and Tasha both waved to Eve, who now sat comfortably in her husband's lap. The thought of being able to do the same with Jerome soon rushed to Tasha's mind, along with all the other ways they'd finally be close. Feeling her face grow hot, Tasha hung back and waited for Jerome to say hello to everyone.

When he finally walked through the door and saw them, the way Jerome's eyes lit up made her fall for him all over again. He went to Evelyn and hugged her tight. "You ain't have to do all this mama." he said.

"I know, but I wanted to."

Once he washed up, Jerome stood beside Tasha and Evelyn listened as he said grace.

After dinner, Tasha and Evelyn found themselves out on the patio. She had been trying for weeks to have Evelyn move in with them. But no matter what suggestions or tempting ideas Tasha sent Evelyn's way - from redecorating parts of the house to yearly trips together to New York, Evelyn always refused. She looked at the older woman and even knowing the answer, Tasha tried a more direct approach.

"Please stay." Tasha asked gently as the two watched the others get comfortable on the couches and loveseat inside. "There's a room made up for you upstairs, that way you don't have to leave until after the wedding. Or never, if you want."

Evelyn took Tasha's hand into hers. "Baby, you know I can't stay."

They hadn't talked about what happened that day in hospital, but Tasha knew from the soft yet firm tone in Evelyn's voice that that was about to change. Evelyn looked at her while gently stroking the top of her hand. "I know hearing about Senior and your mama was hard." Tasha looked away as Evelyn continued. "But he is my husband and I took vows. I know what you think I should do, and I hope you don't think less of me for my choice. But baby girl, I can't leave him."

Tasha brought her eyes to Evelyn's and watched as her gaze softened "Thank you for not letting the past get in the way of your future with my son."

"I let Jerome go too many times already." She told Evelyn. Gripping the older woman's hand as she thought back to what she put her soon-to-be husband through, Tasha's voice was thick with emotion as she vowed, "And I will never make that mistake again."

The two stared through the clear sliding glass door at their family before Evelyn spoke once more. "Being here with all of y'all these past few weeks has been such a blessing. Seeing my babies surrounded by so much love...my heart is at peace. And I get to finally call you my daughter."

Hearing the joy in Evelyn's voice as she called her daughter, Tasha lowered her head. It didn't stop the tears from spilling down to her cheeks. And as she let go of Evelyn's hand to wipe them away, the older woman's gaze landed on her face. Unable to stop herself from telling Evelyn what she'd longed for, almost as much as she longed to call her mama, Tasha sniffled. "I wish you would stay."

One touch of Evelyn's hand to her cheek was all it took before Tasha broke out into a sob. "Oh, baby, It's alright." Evelyn said as she brought Tasha into her arms. "Everything is gonna be just fine."

SITTING WITH HER GIRLS the night before her wedding to the man that held her heart, Tasha felt peace like never before. Lloyd was home with the little ones and Tasha could see that her baby sister had plans to enjoy herself. Walking over to sit next to Trisha, she giggled as her sister stretched out even more on the loveseat before grabbing a dark chocolate covered orange from the nearby tray.

"I see you enjoying the spiked fruit that Rachel provided."

"Yes ma'am I am!" Trisha told her cheerfully. "With my baby girl and boys away for the night, I'mma live it up!"

Tasha grinned as she reached over her sister to try some of the fruit left out. Closing her eyes, Tasha moaned as the mixture of bitter, tart, and semi sweet notes covered her tongue.

"Save all that there for tomorrow night!" Trisha shouted, causing the other ladies to laugh.

Her sister didn't know about her and Jerome's decision to hold off on sex until they were husband and wife, but something must have shown on her face because Trisha stopped smiling.

"I did it again, uh?" Trisha whispered.

Tasha looked at her sister in genuine confusion. "What you mean? You ain't do nothing."

Bringing her watery eyes to meet Tasha, Trisha rushed her words out. "You always said I was too much and that's why we never got along. And I had to go be loud just now when everything was good between us. I -"

Starting to understand what her sister was saying, Tasha took one of her hands into Trisha's. "You ain't never too much. We just didn't know how to talk to each other, Trish, that's all."

Feeling her sister grip her hand tighter, Tasha beamed. "Besides, you ain't said nothing but a word!" Tasha shouted before standing up and bringing Trisha with her. "Tomorrow I finally get to marry my Rome!"

Rachel and Alex laughed as Tasha bumped Trisha gently with her left hip.

"And there will be moaning and then some when we leave our reception!"

Seeing Trisha double over in laughter set all of them off, causing Eva to walk over and tap Tasha on the shoulder.

Signing slowly, Tasha filled Eva in on her last outburst and the older woman grinned something wicked before bumping her hip against Tasha's. As the group's laughter died down, Tasha looked at each of the women in the room and tears filled her eyes. Eva looked at her and offered a small smile as she brought a hand up to rub comforting circles onto her back.

Signing while looking at her sister-in-law, Tasha spoke from her full heart. "I just...feel more than I thought I could right now. Thank y'all. Thank y'all for being happy for us."

The women engulfed her in a group hug. They all silently rocked her for a while before each one of them kissed Tasha's cheeks and forehead. When they released her, Tasha let out a shaky breath. "I love y'all so much. "

### Jerome

The garden area at the Sandy Shores resort provided just enough sun and shade that no tents were needed to cover the two dozen guests in attendance. Jerome was buzzing with excitement to see what Tasha had done with the banquet area that the resort allowed them to use, once he rented out an entire floor for their guests.

When the orchestra quartet began playing 'Here on Paradise', Jerome's attention went straight to the aisle. He saw Tasha enter the space, solo, and for a moment imagined Senior holding her hand. Slowly letting the thought fade into the background, he looked into the crowd and saw Trisha with her family watching as Tasha came closer into view. Devin, her oldest nephew, wasn't watching Tasha, but was instead giving Jerome his full attention. Nodding solemnly, he sent the boy a soft smile before looking down the aisle again.

A veil was draped over her head and softly framed Tasha's face as it fell to the middle of her back. Jerome looked out into the small crowd and saw Evelyn Mae hold mama's hand as she wiped away her tears, and his heart swelled.

Tasha's hair was in several big fluffy twists, and swept gently around her head. With a few stray twists on each side, Jerome felt his throat burn as he glanced down the aisle at her. Seeing Tasha walking toward him, after all those years, to symbolize their love and commitment to one another for the rest of our lives together - he took a deep breath and let it out slowly.

His tears fell freely from the sight of Tasha walking to stand next to him. They were finally going to vow to be each other's partner, confidant, husband and wife, in front of their family and friends.

As he continued watching her, Jerome's vision blurred. Eva nudged Jerome and he looked over his shoulder to see her smiling wide while holding out a handkerchief. Accepting it and quickly wiping his face, Jerome looked up and saw that Tasha was now directly in front of him. Not waiting to be told, he lifted the veil from Tasha's face. When his hands dropped, she held out her hand and grabbed Jerome's as though it were a lifeline, bringing her closer to him. Feeling her warmth, Jerome needed more. So he pressed his lips to Tasha's forehead as she brought her other hand out to touch his cheek. When Jerome looked at Tasha again, he saw the tears in her eyes as she smiled.

"This is really happening." Tasha whispered.

Jerome nodded before leaning down and kissing her cheek.

Someone in the crowd shouted, "Let the man marry y'all already! It's hot out here!"

Everyone laughed, except Jerome. He could hardly believe that he was about to say vows to the woman he had prayed for years ago. Seeing Tasha's glowing face turn to Pastor Johnson's, Jerome followed.

"Dearly beloved, we are all gathered here today to witness the union of Jerome Earl Grant Junior and Tasha Dielle Daye. If there is anyone here who wishes to object, may they speak now or forever hold their peace."

Jerome couldn't hear a word as Tasha gripped his hand.

"These two have written their own vows and will share them with us." the pastor said.

He stared at Tasha and brought her hand up to his lips, kissing it softly.

"You came into my life and I prayed that you would stay. That didn't exactly happen."

Thinking about the last few years without her, Jerome felt his heart sped up as he continued. "Everything that you said I would have, I got. But in the end, none of it mattered, because I was without you. And now that we're here, with our family and friends, I want to thank God for returning the most heavenly gift that he bestowed upon a sinner like me. I love you Tasha."

Jerome held Tasha's trembling hands as he slipped the ring onto her finger. He looked into her eyes to see more tears fall down Tasha's face. He smiled before brushing them away with his free hand, and before he could drop his hand, Tasha grabbed it again with both of hers, turning it slightly to kiss the inside of his palm.

Rachel quickly stepped close to Tasha and took the bouquet from her while Alexa appeared with the ring box. Tasha took it and as Jerome watched her take a deep breath, his heart smiled. His eyes refused to leave hers as Tasha opened the box.

For a second Jerome thought he'd have to reach out to catch her when he noticed Tasha's knees start to sway.

There was nothing wrong with the ring she had picked out for him, but Jerome knew the only ring he wanted to accept that day from her was the first one she had given him years ago. He didn't go into details about their first night at Bejon Beach, just enough that when he told Alexa what he wanted to do, she agreed to switch the rings out without telling Tasha. Seeing the look on Tasha's face told Jerome that they made the right choice.

She turned to look back at Alexa before focusing on him. As he smiled down at her, Tasha leaned forward and kissed Jerome on the lips, causing everyone to cheer. She slowly separated from him and entwined their hands again as she spoke.

"Before I met you, all I wanted was to leave this town. I never even allowed myself to imagine finding the love and safely I feel when I'm with you. To be honest, it scared me. Back then, you were an unexpected surprise. Though it wasn't until I thought it was too late did I realize what you really were - a blessing in disguise."

After she removed the ring from the box, Tasha briefly closed her eyes. Looking on as she slowly looked up at him, Jerome gave Tasha his hand. He watched her as she finally slipped the ring onto his left finger.

"You are my blessing Jerome, one I will never take for granted again. I love you."

Overcome with emotions, he bought her hands together and brushed his lips along her knuckles before placing another kiss to her forehead. And in unison, the two recited the vows they wrote together weeks ago.

"I vow to be consistent in my care of you. Respectful of your wishes and christlike during all trials and tribulations that we may face together as husband and wife. You are my light, my sword, my most beautiful gift. One I will always choose and cherish, all the days of our lives."

THE TWO MADE THEIR way to the entrance of the resort. Though before they walked out to see their family and friends one last time, Jerome pulled Tasha in for a kiss. Having her in his arms, as his wife, felt better than he dared imagined. When he released her, Tasha's eyes were still closed.

"You ready, Mrs. Daye - Grant?"

That got her attention, as Tasha's eyes were now on his. She leaned against him, pressing her lips to his right ear. "Yes, Mr. Grant."

A shiver ran down his spine as he heard her alluring voice whisper into his ear.

Entwining their hands together, Jerome led the way as they strolled outside from the banquet hall. A shower of white rose petals greeted them, along with more cheering from their loved ones, as Tasha and Jerome headed to their car. Once inside, Tasha turned to face Jerome and the two shared another lingering kiss.

"Let's go home, husband."

# Epilogue

***Five Years Later***

He could hear the afternoon waves crash as they came rolling to the sandy shores of Bejon Beach. Holding Tasha's hand, Jerome glanced behind him to see Ro take his little sister's hand.

"Careful Ro." He called out as the two rushed toward the water.

His namesake turned to face him, grinning as his daughter, Grace started to tug on his hand. "I will Daddy!"

It had been a decade since little Ro came into his life, and Jerome still loved hearing him call him that. He watched his two children as Grace let go of Ro's hand and signed 'go' before taking off to be closer to the water.

"Grace - wait up!" Ro called to her as he followed behind.

Little Grace was only three years old, but she had Ro wrapped around her finger. As the water came up to her feet, Grace started to jump up and down, causing Ro to get wet. He didn't seem to mind at all, getting closer to his sister before picking her up. The two spun around and both Jerome and Tasha looked on as their daughter's laughter ranged out into the sky.

"Seems like it ain't Ro you gotta tell to be careful."

Jerome glanced over at his wife. Nearing the end of her second trimester, Tasha never looked more beautiful. Her afro blew gently in the breeze, along with the blue sundress that she wore. When Tasha suddenly stopped and closed her eyes, Jerome went still.

"Tash? What is it?" Jerome asked, trying to keep the worry out of his voice.

She brought her eyes to him and sighed. "It's fine. Just your son in here cutting up."

He watched as Tasha took a few short breaths and chuckled. Bringing their joined hands to her belly, Tasha spoke again, "Wait for it."

With her hand over his, Jerome did as she asked and seconds later felt a tiny poke. Another came after and he closed his eyes, trying to capture the memory to store forever in his mind. The feel of the ocean breeze against his skin, the warmth of Tasha's hand in his, the sounds of their children playing together - all of it. Each thought brought more tears to his eyes and as he opened them to stare at his wife, a few fell down to his check.

Tasha's hand reached up to wipe them away.

"Rome, it's okay. I'm okay." she said reassuringly.

"I know." He whispered before adding, "I just...wanted to pause and take a moment to thank the most high."

The two stood silently in place, until Jerome lowered his head to touch Tasha's forehead. As he sent a prayer of gratitude to God for the many blessings bestowed upon him, Jerome brought his lips to Tasha's temple. She locked eyes with him once more and whispered, "I love you."

"I love you." Jerome said softly.

"Mama! Daddy!" Grace called out to them.

The two looked out at their children and saw them sprinting toward them. Their smiles filled Jerome's heart even more and he waited as Grace made her way to his side. Ro walked over to Tasha and the two smiled softly at one another before everyone walked forward.

Jerome knew this was the life he'd prayed for, but he still sometimes couldn't believe how the Lord continued to bless him. It wasn't always easy. There were times where he felt tested and tired. Though today was not one of those days and Jerome chose to rejoice in that. As he listened to the waves once more, along with his children chatting up their mama, Jerome immediately sent out another prayer of thanks.

*Thank you Lord for blessing a sinner like me with such heavenly gifts. Thank you.*

## Author's Note

THIS SEQUEL WAS A LONG time coming, and at one point, I thought it'd be best not to release it.

To know that this world, these characters, came to be from a seven word a day challenge still blows my mind. And with everything that has transpired over the last three years, from my return to the States to deciding where I want to be (physically and mentally) for the next chapters of my life - I knew I had to see that Tasha and Jerome's story got an ending that would feel resolved.

It might not be ideal to say, but when it comes to writing and publishing stories, I am my first audience. The stories that I pen are the ones that speak to me. I publish them with the hope of maybe someday helping others who need an escape from their world for a few hours. And if along the way, that reader is able to resonate and find comfort in my work, well, that is more than I dared hope for.

Thank you for taking a chance on an indie author like me. Take care and stay blessed.

## Thank You

*FROM THE BOTTOM OF my heart, thank you for purchasing a copy of **Dove Cry Too**!*

*It is my sincerest hope that you have enjoyed reading this book.*

*If you have, please make sure to leave a review on all your favorite social media platforms, so that other readers will find and read **Doves Cry Too** as well.*

*Stay blessed!*

*K. McCoy*

**About the Author**

K. MCCOY IS THE AUTHOR of the novel, *A Dove's Cry.*

Through indie author webinars, she helps authors write drama filled, heart gripping, and authentic stories. In her many years of publishing, she has traveled around the world, crafting stories based on real-world experiences, combined with hopeful possibilities. As a serial hobbyist, you can find her studying other languages, tinkering with her camera, or trying out a new Yoga pose when she's not writing or working on another bittersweet story.

Find out more about her latest journey by visiting her website, authorkmccoy.com.

**Author's Other Works**

VISIT K. MCCOY'S WEBSITE to get your copy of these amazing reads today!

ANLHOLOGIES
*The Heart of the Season: An ATA Anthology*
*March for Justice: An ATA Anthology*
*Darkest of Dreams: A Cryptid Horror Anthology*
*Cupid's Kiss: A Penning Valley Valentine's Day Anthology*
*Holiday Bliss: A Penning Valley Christmas Anthology*

COLLECTIONS
*A Season to Love*

NOVELS
*A Dove's Cry*

## The New E.R.A.

*AND FOR ALL OF YOU ravenous avid readers - I have an extra sweet treat for you to sink your teeth into.*

*Allow me to present you **The New E.R.A.**, my first-ever action packed, supernatural novella!*

The United States government lied - again.

They convinced desperate citizens, looking to escape the never ending epidemic, to sign up for a nation-wide airborne booster shot. If successful, it would have made the participants' immune systems virtually invincible to further viruses.

Out of the half a million Americans believed to have taken the drug, only thousands survived.

But those that survived were, in fact, reborn.

With a thirst for vengeance and blood.

# Chapter One

*Ripped Roots (excerpt)*

Panic started to take over when he dragged me toward the back of the SUV and I could feel my skin growing hotter. When he turned me around, I saw the plastic tarp on the ground and a roll of dark duck tape. The gleam from the moonlight made the knife next to a box of condoms that much easier to recognize.

"Let me go!" I shouted.

My vision got blurry before everything around me appeared crystal clear. Even my hearing felt like it was surround sound as I heard birds flapping away from a tree branch. I tried to kick him to get free, but with a good few inches on me, he gripped my arm even tighter. Finally, I released a scream and the dude's hand came hard across my face. The taste of my own blood didn't scare me. It was the need for more that did.

With my free hand, I dug my fingernails into his face.

"Ahh! You bitch!"

A trickle of blood began to drip from his face and surprising myself, I licked my lips. When he reached out to hit me again, I was ready. Crouching low like the instructor at the Y taught us, I shielded my face with my forearm. I kicked him as hard as I could in the shin and blinked several times as I heard a bone break.

His face twisted in pain as I tried again to get away, but a new panic rippled throughout my body. A dull ache invaded the space where a heartbeat - my heartbeat - should have been. While realizing that I couldn't hear my heart beating, he lunged forward and grabbed my shoulder, sending us stumbling to the ground. With me sprawled on top of him, my mouth just above his neck. I could hear his breathing and zeroed in on the echoing of his pulsing veins. The surging desire to strip him of his life force won out over the small voice of protest as I speedily pressed a hand on his face and shoulder, pinning him down.

He squirmed beneath me, but that only urged me on further. His panic, fear, guilt, and pain - I could smell all of it emitting from his pores. It was so intoxicating, no matter how much I tried to ignore the allure, my body screamed to taste it. Every nanosecond I denied myself to the rapid pulse underneath his skin my head throbbed. It felt like molten lava was being doused onto my skull, causing me to throw my head back.

A cry ripped through me before my head finally dove downward to the thick vein that called out to me. Warm blood filled my mouth, and no matter how much I tried to tell myself not to, I kept gulping in more. He screeched and withered underneath me, which goaded me into sucking harder.

"What the fuck?"

My lips parted from his neck as my head snapped to the sound from behind. I growled while the guy beneath me stretched out a shaking hand. With my eyes still on the second guy from the SUV, I thought back to what they had planned to do to me. Rage took over as the thought flashed through my mind. I barely felt his neck snap under my hands before he went still. I heard his final heartbeat just before his head smacked the concrete.

Two more guys jumped out of the SUV, each had a gun in their hands. My eyes widened when I heard two small churns, followed by short clicks. Gripping the shirt and waistband of his baggy jeans, I sent their boy flying toward them.

"Oh hell nah!"

Hard stomps pounded against the concrete as one of the guys took off in the opposite direction. Bullets popped loudly and buzzed above my head, but none landed on me. When I had another thought to reach for one of their necks, I was in their face in seconds. The feel of their racing pulse around my hand felt so good, I found myself biting back a moan as I licked the corners of my lips. A small whimper reached my ears, and I squinted my eyes toward the other guy. His terror filled eyes were on me and I turned my nose up in disgust at the smell of urine and watched as a wet patch formed at the front of his jeans.

Keeping my grip on the guy's throat, I took a quick look at their ride. A black Tahoe with spinners was considered corny in my neighborhood, but I needed to get home. I stretched open my mouth and felt the sharp edges as my teeth scraped the insides of my cheeks.

"Where are the keys?"

"Wh-what?

"Give me the keys to the Tahoe."

"Fu—"

I cut off more of his air supply as his friend reached into the pocket of their jeans. He tossed the keys at me and in a flash they were in my other hand. The hunger wasn't as bad as it was before, but I still wanted more. Shaking my head, I thought back to what I did seconds ago.

"Please don't kill me! I'm somebody's son!" the guy in front of me pleaded.

"Ain't I somebody? Somebody's daughter? Sister? Mama?" I choked out, thoughts of my baby girl hammering through my mind.

My head cocked over to the guy that I held up midair. He was wheezing and turning blue, but I refused to let him go. *How many others did they do this shit to?*

"I-I sorry! Please! Don't kill me sister!"

"Oh, now I'm ya sister? Ain't that a bitch?"

I let the guy in my grasp go and stared down as he tumbled backwards, taking in sharp and shaky breaths. My body ached with each step as I lumber over to the driver's side of the Tahoe and climbed into the seat. The engine rumbled as I turned the ignition and drove away.

ARE YOU READY TO DISCOVER more of *The New E.R.A.*?

Then make sure to become an OG "Fanga" and follow K. McCoy at buymeabeer today!